Cold Revenge

Book Three of the Sidney Becker Mysteries

LINDA BERRY

Copyright © 2020 by Linda Berry

Cold Revenge is a work of fiction. Names, characters, places, and incidents either are products of the author's imagination or are used fictitiously. This work is protected in full by all applicable copyright laws, as well as by misappropriation, trade secret, unfair competition, and other applicable laws. No part of this book may be reproduced or transmitted in any manner without written permission from Linda Berry, except in the case of brief quotations embodied in critical articles or reviews. All rights reserved.

ISBN: 978-0-9998538-9-4

Published in the United States of America

www.lindaberry.net

Five Star Reviews from Amazon Readers

— Cold Revenge, featuring brilliant homicide investigator and small town Police Chief Sydney Becker, should be at the top of the reading list for every fan of murder mysteries. Linda Berry delivers the goods with a devious plot that would make even Alfred Hitchcock envious." – Dave Edlund, USA Today bestselling author of Lethal Savage

— I truly enjoy the way Linda Berry paints pictures with words, engaging all the human senses. Her hero, Sidney Becker, is a strong woman, yet with vulnerable soft spots. This is a story of resilience. This is the story of women globally. Please keep telling it! – Dr. Ann LaFrance, Clinical Psychologist

— Berry's characters and plot development create a great visual for readers to become immersed and feel as though they are physically involved in the story. I strongly recommend this book! – Kathleen A Whattam

— Sidney is one of my all-time favorite protagonists. Berry's done it once more, giving readers a thrilling, edge of your seat, mystery. Absolutely worth it! – Omar Syed

— I absolutely love this series and this book is just as mysterious as the previous two. Please let there be a 4th book!! – Sarah Webb

— I inhaled this book! From beginning to end, I was hooked. Linda Berry has a knack for complex characters, descriptive scenes, and plenty of good old-fashioned suspense. – Jaen Martine

—Another excellent book in this series. Engaging characters and well plotted mysteries are two of the hallmarks of this author and she did not disappoint. – Anne Glass Kasaba

To Our Heroic Men and Women in Uniform
Who Provide the Thin Blue Line
That Protects Civilized Societies from Anarchy
And Who Rush Toward Danger
While Everyone Else Runs Away

Books by Linda Berry

Hidden Part 1

Hidden Part 2

Pretty Corpse

The Killing Woods

The Dead Chill

Cold Revenge

To learn of new releases and discounts, add your name to Linda's mailing list:

www.lindaberry.net

ACKNOWLEDGMENTS

I OWE A DEBT of gratitude to the extraordinary editors who helped craft Cold Revenge into a suspenseful and entertaining work of fiction.

A heartfelt thank you goes to Rob Hall, who invested countless hours identifying the stress fractures in the construction of this story. Every bit of Rob's twenty years of experience in uniform—as a deputy sheriff, patrol cop, homicide investigator, and police chief—was drawn upon to ensure that the law enforcement underpinnings of Cold Revenge were authentic and accurate. In the process of collaborating on my last two books, Rob has become a trusted advisor and a very dear friend.

A warm thank you goes to Jeanine Pollak, editor extraordinaire. Her innate sense of story, and her remarkable eye for detail, applied the final gloss and sparkle to the story.

A special thanks goes to my good friends and associates LaLoni Kirkland, Denice Hughes, and Cynthia Gould. And to Dr. Ann LaFrance, for her observations and guidance on the behavior of some of my characters.

And finally, great appreciation goes to Mark Fasnacht, whose skill as editor and project manager ensured this novel rose to the highest professional standard.

CHAPTER ONE

WITH DREAD GNAWING at her gut, Police Chief Sidney Becker drove down Main Street as fast as she dared, her flashing lights reflected in the closed storefront windows. Slowly and soundlessly, the morning sun crept over the brick and stone buildings of historic downtown. The tree-lined streets of Garnerville had the drowsy purr of a Saturday morning as the community gently shook itself awake. The mild foot traffic of Lava Java Coffee shop was the only establishment showing signs of life. Sidney could almost smell the roasted coffee and fresh pastries. Too rushed to eat, she had gulped down a cup of strong coffee and ignored the hungry rumbling of her stomach.

She gunned the engine as she reached the highway heading north. The road tunneled through a lush forest of pine, maple, and alder. Broken clouds scudded overhead and the mist-shrouded water of Lake Kalapuya winked through the trees. The quiet beauty of the Oregon Cascade foothills belied the grisly task that lay ahead.

Sidney had been roused from sleep twenty minutes earlier by her dispatcher. The body of a woman had been found by a farmer in a field adjacent to his property, about fifteen miles from downtown. This was the second body discovered in a remote area in the last three weeks. The other body belonged to a middle-aged male. Due to animal predation, the cause of death could not be determined. The implications of two bodies found in remote areas in a short period of time troubled her. As a former homicide detective in a big city in California, Sidney instinctively viewed every death as a potential murder, but until proven otherwise, the death of the man would remain classified as unsuspicious.

The radio crackled and the scratchy voice of Officer Amanda Cruz burst into the cab. "Morning, Chief."

"Morning, Amanda. What's up?"

"I just got to the scene. The coroner hasn't arrived yet. Want me to get started processing?"

"Yeah. Go ahead. I'm about ten minutes out. See you shortly."

Garnerville was a small town with a tight operating budget, which made it necessary to hire officers with broad skill sets. Amanda Cruz, a Latina in her late twenties with six years under her belt as a patrol cop, was also a crime scene specialist. Sidney hired Officer Darnell Woods, a young African American, straight out of the Academy two years ago. He was diligent, a fast learner, and an ace with computers. The two covered the day shift and had already been on duty since eight. Sidney and Officer Granger Wyatt covered the evening shift. Resolving a brawl at a beer joint last night and rushing a drunk with a broken jaw to the ER had racked up three hours of overtime. She had barely gotten four hours of shut eye before being called to this scene. If her instincts were correct, this would be a homicide investigation, which required every officer on board.

The two-lane county road left the forest behind and snaked through rolling foothills into open country. Here the land had been wrestled into ranches and farmland generations ago. An occasional house and weathered barn flashed by with sheep, goats, and sturdy cattle scattered across grassy pastures. It was the end of April, and wildflowers turned the meadows into kaleidoscopes of color.

Sidney turned onto the narrow dirt road that led to the Rawlings farm. The deep tread of the Yukon's tires clawed up pebbles and rattled them against the undercarriage. On the left, brown-and-white cattle grazed. On the right, the season's first crop of tender green shoots sprouted across the hay fields.

Set back from the road, the two-story white farmhouse appeared, standing apart from the immense barn to the south and the tree-shaded stables to the north. Up ahead, three Garnerville police trucks were parked on the shoulder. The words SEARCH & RESCUE and K-9 Unit were blazed on the side of a white truck from the sheriff's department. Sidney spotted Amanda in the middle of a field squatting over something on the ground. The two K-9 deputies and their bloodhound were off in the distance in foot high grass, scouring the field. Sidney's other two uniformed officers, Granger and Darnell, waited by the vehicles with a man dressed in overalls who stood poised in tense expectation.

The nagging dread in her gut intensified as she pulled over and parked. She hoped the body was in good enough condition to tell its story of demise. Unlike the man found at Steelhead Lake, a recreational area, there was no good reason for a woman to be out here in the middle of this field in farm country. Sidney stepped out into the hard, clear morning light. A hint of manure seasoned the air.

"Morning," she said as she approached her officers.

"Morning, Chief," they responded, expressions somber.

Granger introduced Ned Rawlings, a weather-beaten, middle-aged man with deeply seamed skin and bits of straw clinging to his overalls. Looking a little in shock, he stuck out a dry, calloused hand with knobby fingers. "Morning, Chief," he echoed.

Everyone turned to the sound of another vehicle as the coroner's white van parked behind her Yukon. She nodded a greeting to Dr. Linthrope who was driving, and his forensic assistant, Stewart Wong, then turned back to the farmer. "You find the body, Mr. Rawlings?" she asked gently.

He scowled. "Yep, I did."

"Sorry. I know it must have been a terrible shock. Want to tell me what happened?"

He sucked in a deep breath and puffed out his cheeks as he exhaled. "I was taking the dairy cows to the barn to milk and saw them crows flapping around out there in the field. Pecking at something. Something dead. Wanted to make sure it wasn't one of my goats, gone astray. Went out to look." He ran a hand over his face. "Whew. Not something I ever want to see again. A woman. Birds been at her. I know she wasn't there yesterday."

"Did you hear anything unusual during the night?"

He shook his head. "Nope. I sleep solid. Work hard. Sleep hard. Wife didn't hear nothing either." His eyes widened and he jerked his head to the north. "Wait, I did hear something, now that I think about it. My nearest neighbor is just up the road. I heard his two dogs barking like crazy. It went on for several minutes."

"That unusual?"

"For that long, yeah. I didn't think much of it. Figured it was a coyote, or a fox passing through."

Movement on her periphery caught Sidney's attention. She saw that Amanda was guiding the doctor and Stewart single file through the grass, both dressed in field clothes. Stewart was in the rear, pushing a gurney. "What time was that, Mr. Rawlings?"

The farmer scratched his grizzled chin. "Hmmm. I'm gonna say somewhere around midnight. I lay there awake for a while and looked at the clock. It was quarter past twelve."

"Anything else you recall?"

He shook his head. "Nope."

"Thank you, Mr. Rawlings. That was helpful. If you see anything around here that looks out of place over the next few days, please give us a call." She handed him her card.

"I surely will. I need to get back to work. Cows don't milk themselves." Ned stuck the card into a pocket and headed up the drive toward the barn.

Sidney turned to her officers. "Either of you see the body?"

Granger nodded, his blue eyes bright in the morning sun. "I arrived first. Ned was waiting and he took me out there. Not much to see." He cleared his throat. "Unfortunately, he covered her with his jacket."

Sidney felt her jaw harden. "Damn. That may have contaminated the crime scene. Fiber, hair, or his own DNA could have been transferred to the body. A defense attorney's dream."

Granger sighed. "Yeah, well, at least it kept the crows off. They don't see well at night and they typically roost. Maybe they didn't have time to do a lot of damage."

"Let's hope."

"Then the K-9 unit arrived," Granger continued. "Amanda showed up right behind them. We all went out with the bloodhound, using one path in and out. Tried not to disturb anything. The hound got a good whiff of the body, and now they're out there searching the field, looking for the access point."

"Good work." Though Granger had only been on the job for a year, he grew up on a local cattle ranch and had a country boy's down-to-earth sensibility. He was also a former Marine with combat and leadership experience, and he'd proven to be cool headed in emergency situations. He had taken charge in her absence this morning and gotten everyone doing their jobs.

"See any tire tracks pulled over to the side of the road? Any parked vehicles?" she asked.

"No." Granger hooked his thumbs on his duty belt. "I drove north up this dirt road a couple miles. It's a back road to Aspen Lake, but after passing Ned's neighbor, it quickly got overgrown. Doesn't look like it's been used lately. I also drove south all the way to the paved road. A bunch of tire tracks run over each other, but none were pulled over to the side of the road."

"I got here just a few minutes before you did, Chief," Darnell said. "Haven't had time to take a look."

"Well, we'll see if the hound picks up anything," Sidney said, staring off into the field. Dr. Linthrope and Amanda were squatting on the ground and Stewart was leaning over them, his camera flash pulsing. "I better get out there. Judging from the farmer's reaction, it won't be pretty."

Granger's solemn gaze met hers and they shared an understanding. In

Afghanistan, he'd witnessed horrific combat injuries; bodies burned and torn apart by IEDs. Stored in Sidney's own mind was a seventeen-year stockpile of crime scene images—victims who had been subjected to every imaginable kind of violence.

"You two need to spread out and canvass the community," she said. "Hit every farm and ranch within a three-mile radius. It's quiet out here. Not a lot of traffic. See if anyone saw or heard anything."

"Got it, Chief."

"Copy."

The two men hustled toward their vehicles.

Sidney pulled a pair of nitrile gloves from her duty belt, snapped them on, then trekked through the meadow, which was carpeted with a variety of grasses and wildflowers. The clarity of the cool air enveloped her. The world went still. No wind. Not even a blade of grass moved. Everything was slow and hypnotic. Something inside her chest compressed tighter as she reached the three people working with their backs to her, blocking the view of the victim's head. The only sound was the whisper of their boots in the grass.

The dead woman had a slim build and lay on her stomach with her arms at her sides. Amanda was busy bagging her hands to preserve evidence. Sidney was relieved to see that the victim was fully dressed—hiking boots, jeans, a red down jacket. That kept the birds away. Then Linthrope moved out of the way and Sidney saw the side of her face that had been exposed. The beak of a crow is pronounced and sharp. When feeding on something dead they start with the soft eyeballs. She swallowed. Nasty.

Lean, mid-forties, of Chinese descent, Stewart lowered his camera and nodded a greeting. He was an extreme introvert who was somewhat lacking in social skills, but his compulsive attention to detail made him an excellent forensic specialist.

"Ah, Chief Becker," Dr. Linthrope said pleasantly. Light reflected off his glasses as he glanced up at her. His gaze followed hers to the corpse and his expression sobered. "Ah, yes. Unfortunate. This young woman's face took some damage."

"Mice and other scavengers could have helped themselves to a meal this morning, too," Wong said, pushing his wire-rimmed glasses higher on his nose. "We just had a few crows. Didn't eat much." He resumed shooting photos, talking all the while. "The body of a woman who fell off a cliff in the French Pyrenees was devoured by vultures in forty-five minutes. Gone, before rescue workers could even reach the body. There were only bones, clothes, and shoes left on the ground."

"Thanks for the heart-warming images," Amanda said dryly.

Dark humor was accepted at crime scenes. Truly awful and inappropriate comments sometimes helped alleviate the gruesomeness of the job. Sidney knew it was Stewart's way of making a social connection. "What do we have?" she asked. "Cause of death?"

"Not conclusive at this point," Linthrope said. "But she does have a gunshot wound." Sidney squatted next to him.

He moved strands of blood-matted hair aside and pointed to a wound at the base of her skull. "Small caliber. Probably a .22. Until we do the postmortem we won't know if this was the COD." He shrugged. "It could have been the coup de grace, or insurance, or a message."

"Time of death?"

"Again, hard to say. Rigor has fully developed and passed. That usually takes a minimum of eight hours. It was cold out here last night, which slows down the process. I'd put the window between nine p.m. and midnight. He glanced at Amanda, who stood at the foot of the victim. "Want to give us a hand, Officer Cruz? Let's turn her on her side."

Amanda stepped forward and maneuvered the woman's legs while the doctor and Sidney carefully turned her on her side. Above them, Stewart's camera flash pulsed light over the victim.

"Well, it's clear she wasn't killed here," the doctor said. "There's no blood beneath her. Okay, let's lay her on her back. Gently."

Once the body of the woman lay on her back, they saw no additional wounds or blood. Half of her face had been pressed into the grass and been spared by the crows, showing no marks or bruising. Her eye was half open, her lips slightly parted.

"No lividity," Sidney noted.

"Right," Doctor Linthrope said. "If she died lying face down, her blood would have settled into her face. All the blood from her back would head towards the ground. Lividity displays itself as a dark purple discoloration, yet her face is pale."

"So after she was shot, execution style, someone turned her on her back," Amanda said.

"The killer may have been vengeful, or sadistic, and wanted to watch her die," Stewart suggested.

Sidney closely studied the woman's face. "Or he wanted to put something in her mouth."

"Something's in there, all right," Linthrope said, squinting into her mouth. Wielding a pair of tweezers from his kit, he opened her mouth a little wider and teased out a ball of wadded paper. As the paper unfolded, inked squiggles became letters, and the letters became words. He read out loud:

Killing you was the purest love I've ever known.
The sweetest revenge.

The hair stood up on the back of Sidney's neck. They were all silent for a long moment, reflecting on the message left by the killer.

Linthrope dropped the paper into an evidence bag and labeled it. "The handwriting slants to the left. That could mean he's left-handed. Maybe we'll be able to pull a print or DNA off it."

"Creepy," Amanda said. "He enjoyed killing her."

"Definitely vengeful," Stewart said. "It certainly speaks to motive. The killer perceived some kind of injustice committed by this woman. He was exacting revenge."

"Maybe a scorned lover, or a business deal gone horribly wrong," Amanda added. "It's always about sex or money."

They looked to Sidney to get her take on it.

She appreciated their enthusiasm, but her policy was to base theories on facts. She'd been on the job too long to speculate without sufficient evidence. "Let's wait for lab results. Any defensive wounds on her hands?"

"None that meet the eye," Linthrope said. "But there could be skin or fiber under her nails."

"Let's see if she has any ID."

Amanda checked the pockets of the victim's jacket, then her jeans. She came up empty until she reached into a half pocket in the front. "Hmmm. What's this?" She pulled out something small and displayed it on her gloved palm.

They all gathered around and leaned in to look. It was round and flat with uneven edges and a raised image.

"It's a very old coin of some kind," Linthrope said. "Or a very good replica."

"Maybe planted by the killer," Amanda said. "Could be useful."

Sidney shrugged. "Or not. Some killers get their jollies screwing with cops. They leave oblique clues. Make us chase our tails trying to figure out what they mean. Get a photo of that coin, will you Stewart? Send it to me."

Amanda held out her gloved hand while Stewart took a few shots of each side, then she dropped it in a plastic evidence bag.

Sidney heard her phone ping as the photo transferred.

"Well, no ID," Linthrope said amiably. "Hopefully her fingerprints will be in the system. We'll see what else her body can tell us during the autopsy."

The doctor's calm demeanor belied the nature of his work. Death rarely fazed him. Now seventy, Linthrope reminded Sidney of Albert Einstein, with his cumulous of white hair, well-lived in face, and scalpel-sharp intellect. He and Wong had been processing bodies in the tri town area for two decades, and he had been an M.E. in Portland for twenty years before that. He had witnessed every kind of death imaginable, every state of decomp. His unruffled attitude and professional manner took the sharpest sting out of the grim proceedings.

They spread the body bag on the ground. To prevent further injury to the deceased, all four grabbed a limb and carefully moved the victim to the bag. The long zipper whispered, then each grabbed a corner, lifted, and strapped the black cocoon onto the gurney. Walking single file, the doctor led the procession out of the field with Sidney in the rear steering the gurney. Stewart stayed behind, now on his hands and knees, carefully combing through the crumpled grass where the body had lain, looking for any evidence.

After they deposited the gurney in the van, Sidney told Amanda to collect a DNA sample from Ned Rawlings. "If his DNA was deposited on the victim from his jacket, it'll have to be identified and eliminated."

"I'll get right on it."

Sidney turned to Linthrope. "When will you have something for me?"

"We'll run some lab tests, run her prints. The usual. Should be finished with the autopsy mid-afternoon."

They were interrupted by the sudden sharp barking of the bloodhound. The K-9 handlers stood three hundred yards up the road where it bordered the field. They waved to Sidney to join them.

"They found something," she said. "Catch you later, Doc."

Sidney had worked with both handlers. Deputies Kyle Mumford and Maria Sanchez were dressed in the brown uniforms of the sheriff's department. She also recognized Bruiser. The bloodhound had long floppy ears, diamond-shaped eyes, and a wrinkled, tawny coat. Specializing in search and rescue, Bruiser had tracked dozens of lost hikers, skiers, and missing seniors over the years, both dead and alive.

An athletic man in his forties with a bald dome and rugged features, Kyle pulled back on the leash and told the hound to sit, which he did, tail wagging.

Sidney exchanged a quick greeting. "It's definitely a homicide."

"No surprise there," Kyle said.

"What'cha got?" Sidney asked hopefully.

"We've mapped the killer's path in and out of the field, beginning and ending here, where his vehicle was parked," Maria said. She was in her thirties with short black hair, a solid build, and strong features. "We didn't find any footprints in the plant growth. Too thick. But there's a definite pathway of crushed grass and flowers. The killer was focused. Dumped the body and left. No side trips." Maria pointed to an area alongside the road. "See this sweeping texture here in the dirt? He wiped his prints and tire tracks off the side of the road. He tried hard to be the invisible man, but he wasn't careful enough. Look at this." Maria pointed into the grass where they had placed a couple of plastic markers by patches of bare earth. "Here we have a pretty good outline of the right heel of a boot. And over there, we have the whole print of the left boot."

"My guess, he's a size ten," Kyle said.

Sidney sat back on her heels and saw the clearly defined pattern of the boot. "Hallelujah. This should be easy to identify. You can even read part of the logo. V-i- something. We'll run it through the database. I'll have Stewart make some plaster casts." She straightened and smiled at the deputies. "Good work. The invisible man made a mistake. Let's hope he left more of his signature on the body."

"It's a relief to find something tangible, after finding zip with that dead guy at Steelhead Lake," Kyle said, looking dispirited.

"You did what you could. He'd been dead for weeks," Sidney said. "Exposed to the elements. A snowstorm."

"And a whole bunch of animals," Maria added. "We only found part of his skeleton. Didn't help that his skull was missing."

"It's probably buried under the snow somewhere," Kyle said.

"Could he be related to this case?" Maria asked Sidney.

"Hard to say." Sidney shrugged. "There's no evidence linking them. He could be a hiker who got lost and froze to death."

"The sheriff's department in Lane county has a K-9 unit with a cadaver dog," Kyle said. "I'll contact them and see if I can get back up there. Have another look."

"That'd be great." Sidney smiled her appreciation.

"Hope to hell we don't have some nut job running around killing people for kicks," Maria said.

The message found in the victim's mouth told Sidney otherwise. The woman was deliberately targeted—but she didn't share that information.

Stewart was walking out of the field gripping his forensic kit. Sidney waved him over and showed him the boot prints.

His eyes glimmered with interest. "Yowzah. Great impressions. Don't get anything this well-defined very often." He opened his kit. "I'll get some casts made."

"Send some of your crime photos to the station. We need to start a crime board."

He gave her a thumbs up.

Sidney's phone buzzed and she unclipped it from her belt. "Yeah, Granger."

"The son of a farmer saw a truck parked up at Aspen Lake last night around midnight. Sounds suspicious."

"Ask his parents if we can take him to the lake. Let's inspect that location."

"Hold on."

Sidney heard him talking to someone, then he got back on the phone. "His dad said it's okay. His name's Jason Hines. Seventeen. Senior at Garnerville High."

"Bring him over here and drop him off."

Sidney disconnected and turned to the K-9 handlers. "Can you go over to the lake with us? We may have something."

"Sure thing."

Fifteen minutes later, Amanda returned with the DNA swab. She joined Sidney as Granger's patrol truck bumped slowly up the road and pulled alongside them. The door opened and Jason Hines got out. He was red-haired, freckled, and unusually tall. Sidney was six feet, but he towered over her by half a foot. Lean and athletic, he wore jeans and a gray sweatshirt with the Garnerville High School logo on the back.

Sidney opened the back door of Amanda's Jeep Cherokee and motioned for the teen to hop into the cage. His brows lifted in surprise.

"Don't worry, you're not under arrest." She smiled, then sobered in a mock display of toughness. "At least, not today."

Jason gave her a little salute and climbed in. Sidney hopped up front and Amanda headed north up the dirt road with the K-9 unit following behind.

CHAPTER TWO

"TAKE A LONG, DEEP BREATH. Hold it. Slowly release. Repeat." Barefoot, Selena quietly wove her way between the bodies sitting in the Sukasana pose in her yoga studio. She lightly touched random students between the shoulder blades to remind them of their posture. All eyes were closed. Faces relaxed. Soothing music quieted their minds and Selena's organic candles brought the fragrance of a flower garden into the room. She returned to the front of the room and ended the class with her usual parting. "Open your eyes. Smile. Go out into the world and have a beautiful day. Be kind to all you meet. Namaste."

Twenty-five students got to their feet, some stretching, some rolling up their mats, some heading out the door. A few idled in the gift section that featured Selena's organic products—scented candles, potpourri, herb flavored honey and vinegar. Lalisa Preeda, a physical therapist of Thai origin with soft brown eyes and glossy black hair, sauntered over. The two had spent hundreds of hours hiking the mountain trails around Garnerville together.

"Been to the monastery lately?" Selena asked.

A Buddhist, Lalisa was well-acquainted with the monastery on Elderberry Ridge. Her nephew, visiting from Thailand, was in training there to become a monk.

"No. Been too busy with work. I'm going to visit Nopadon tomorrow. He's turning twelve." Her dark eyes sparkled. "And I want to watch the Bhutan archery team."

"Archery team? What's that all about?"

"The monastery is hosting a team of young archers from Bhutan. They're here to compete against archery teams in the Pacific Northwest."

"I didn't even know we had archery teams." Selena narrowed her eyes, thinking. "Where's Bhutan?"

Lalisa picked up a scented candle from the counter, sniffed it, and put it back down. "It's a tiny country located in the Himalayas between China and

India. A mystical kingdom. Trouble-free and blissful."

"Shangri-La, huh? Sounds pretty far-fetched."

"Not really. It's well-documented that they have one of the highest levels of contentment in the world. Archery is the national sport. Like we love baseball. Every boy grows up learning to master archery. They can shoot the stinger off a bee at 80 yards."

Selena laughed. "Funny."

Lalisa laughed, too, flashing white teeth. "In all seriousness, they can hit a two-foot target at a distance further than a football field."

"No way." Selena rolled her eyes.

"Don't believe me? Come see for yourself. Come meet the boys."

"Sounds really interesting. Sure, I'll go with you."

"Tomorrow morning? Meet you here at eight."

"It's a deal."

Lalisa left, and Selena was locking up when her phone buzzed. She answered brightly, "Samara Yoga Studio."

"This is Karli at Alpine Ridge Memory Care," a tense voice said. "Your mom got out of the building. A delivery man left the kitchen door open."

Selena felt a dull thud in her stomach. "How long ago?"

"Not sure. Another patient saw her walking toward downtown about an hour ago. We have two aid workers looking for her. Should I call your sister?"

Selena's sister, Police Chief Becker, was busy investigating a possible murder. "No, I'll take care of it. What was my mom wearing?"

"The patient said she was wearing white silk pajamas, but we can't really trust her memory. A patient named Ray left with her."

"I'm heading downtown right now. Call me if you find her first."

Selena's heart was racing. Her mother, Molly, suffered from early onset Alzheimer's disease. Her memory fluttered like a leaf in the wind, coming and going. During periods of lucidity, Molly turned into a clever escape artist. Once free from the memory center, she flitted around town acting out her wildest impulses. Previous escapades found her buying lingerie at The Pink Pussycat and washing down filet mignon with a pricey Cabernet at a high-priced restaurant. The business owners in town knew Molly Becker, but not many were aware of her declining abilities. They had no problem charging her expenditures to her daughter, Police Chief Becker, at least the first time around.

Increasingly, Molly was using poor judgement in her fashion choices. She made more than one appearance in the lobby of the center wearing Pink Pussycat lingerie fit for a stripper. She had been promptly escorted back to her apartment for a wardrobe redo.

Molly was slowly transitioning from the intelligent, reasonable mother who raised Selena and Sidney, to a woman with loosening standards of behavior. The filters that had always directed her conduct were fraying. As she steadily lost pieces of her identity, she was becoming increasingly frustrated and confused. For Selena and Sidney, it was challenging to navigate the emotional labyrinth of their mother's new normal. And it was frightening. They were getting glimpses of what might happen to them as they got older.

Selena's dread deepened. It appeared her mother was wearing silk pajamas when she made her escape today. Molly was so vulnerable. She could easily be taken advantage of by the wrong kind of man.

Selena broke into a jog, heading down the tree-lined street toward the historical center of town where most of the shops and restaurants were clustered. Several blocks in, her phone buzzed. It was Britney, the barista at Lava Java. Breaking her stride, Selena panted, "Please tell me my mom is there."

"Boy, is she ever. She's wearing quite the outfit. I seated her out on the back patio to avoid unwanted attention."

"I'll be right there." What the hell? What was her mom wearing? Selena paused to call Alpine Ridge and inform Karli of her mom's location. Then she broke into a faster sprint, dodging people milling on the sidewalk. Breathing hard, she slowed to a walk and entered the coffee house trying to appear unflustered. Past experience had warned her that looking alarmed did not go down well with Molly.

It was midmorning on a workday. The place was half filled with tourists and young people taking up table space with electronic gadgets. Britney was multitasking behind the counter, but she caught Selena's eye and nodded toward the back door.

Through the window, Selena spotted a couple sitting in the sun-dappled shade of the birch trees. Coffee cups and half eaten croissants sat on the small table in front of them. It took a moment for Selena to recognize her mother behind the Catwoman mask that hid the upper half of her face. Molly wore a form-fitting, full-body black leotard unzipped low enough to reveal her generous cleavage. A handsome gray-haired man, dressed in a golf shirt and khaki pants, sat next to her with his arm looped across her shoulders.

Selena took a moment to assess the situation. Why was her mother wearing a Catwoman outfit? Who was that man? What was she going to say? Selena put her hand on the doorknob. Then she froze.

The man leaned over and kissed Molly on the mouth. Her mother responded passionately, and the kiss lingered and deepened. Why was this stranger kissing her mom like that in public?

"They should get a room," a young man at a nearby table said, catching her eye. His two male friends laughed.

Selena glared.

Their smiles faded, and they tugged their gazes from the window.

Finally, the gray-haired man lifted his mouth from Molly's, and they stared into each other's eyes, faces flushed. Molly's head tilted back, lips parted, inviting another kiss.

Calm down, Selena told herself. Don't go barging out there half-cocked. Her mom tended to become volatile when Selena was ruffled, and it wasn't easy to calm her down. She stepped out on the patio before they engaged again.

CHAPTER THREE

A THICK CARPET of dead leaves left over from autumn hid the pits and ruts in the road, forcing Amanda to drive at a snail's pace. After a mile, the road became increasingly overgrown with tall spring grass. Sidney turned and glanced at Jason through the steel mesh barrier. Even sitting down, he was unusually tall, his hair brushing the roof. "So, Jason, what were you doing at the lake at midnight?"

"I come up here with my friends," he said. "Mostly in the summer. This was the first time this year. But it was a full moon and the girls thought it would be awesome. They were right. Everything was really bright and clear. The water was like a mirror, reflecting the moonlight. We built a big bonfire on the shore. Looked at the stars. Chilled. Hung out."

"Sounds beautiful," Sidney said. "How many of you were there?"

"Six. Scott and Matt are my best friends and teammates. Basketball. We were with our girlfriends."

"What time did you get there?"

"Around ten-thirty."

"And you saw a truck?"

"Yeah. Not at first. We went up the main road where there's a parking lot. That side of the lake has a beach and a boat ramp. It's where families come in the summer. The truck was parked on this side of the lake. It's all forested. You have to use this road, which isn't maintained."

"So only locals know about this road?"

"Yes, ma'am."

"And the lake would normally be deserted this time of year?"

"Yes, ma'am."

The passengers bounced and the car rattled and vibrated over a string of ruts. "So when did you notice the truck?"

"Not until the driver turned on the engine. I guess around 11:30. We could hear it idling. Then we saw it through the trees. It creeped us out that someone had been sitting there watching us. Then the driver slowly drove away without turning on the headlights. We would never have known it was a truck if not for the full moon."

"Did you see the driver, or the make of the truck?"

"Nah. Too far away and behind the trees. But it was a dark color. Maybe blue, maybe black. And it had a shell over the bed."

The teen was very observant.

The Jeep's right tire suddenly hit a pit, and everyone bounced in their seats. Jason's head hit the ceiling.

"You okay?" Sidney asked.

He grinned back at her, rubbing his crown. "That was nothing, ma'am. I get knocked around harder than that on the court every day of the week."

Sidney smiled back. He was a likable kid.

"What did this guy do, anyway? Is someone dead? Is this guy the killer?"

"I can't answer those questions. You'll find out soon enough in the newspaper." Sidney could see the sparkling blue water of the lake up ahead through the trees. "Better park, Amanda, before this road destroys your Jeep. We'll walk the rest of the way. Show us the way, Jason?"

"Sure thing, Chief Becker."

Amanda parked and grabbed her forensic case from the back.

Maria pulled up alongside them. Kyle opened the hatch, dropped the tailgate, and the bloodhound jumped down from the truck. Kyle attached a stout leather leash, and speaking in a firm voice, he opened a bag with clumps of grass collected from the crime scene. Bruiser sniffed, reacquainting himself with the scent of the killer and the victim.

The group set out, following Jason's long-legged stride through the damp carpet of caramel-colored leaves. Even though she was focused on her investigation, Sidney enjoyed being out in the woods. The job of police chief demanded long hours that required her to be on call twenty-four seven—not much time left over to commune with nature. Birds flittered overhead, and a gentle wind sighed through the branches, carrying the scent of the forest.

She and Jason left the group and hiked to the edge of the water. His gaze swept the opposite shoreline and then he pointed to a wide, sandy strip of beach to the east. "That's where we were last night."

Sidney made out a fire pit hemmed in by large rocks.

"The truck was directly across from us on this side of the lake."

"So maybe a couple hundred yards further down," Sidney said. "Let's head in that direction."

They rejoined the others and continued walking, surveying everything in their path and on both sides of the narrow road, hoping to spot a clue. A continuous set of depressions in the leafy mulch indicated that a heavy vehicle had recently passed through, but there were no distinct tire marks.

Bruiser ranged slightly ahead at the end of his long leash, ambling back and forth, pausing occasionally to sniff at a tree or patch of moss. After several minutes, they spotted a mammoth fallen trunk lying next to a small clearing about as wide and deep as two parking slots. The tire tracks turned into the clearing which had an almost unobstructed view of the lake and opposite shore. Sidney spotted the firepit used by Jason and his friends.

Bruiser's demeanor changed instantly. His ears and tail lifted, and though Kyle weighed about 200 pounds, the hound began pulling him as if he were a child. When they reached the clearing, the hound began trotting back and forth, and then, showing no hesitation, he zeroed in on a specific location on the fallen tree. He looked up at Kyle and whined once.

"Bruiser, sit," Kyle said. The hound obeyed, almost quivering with eagerness.

"Everyone, stay back," Kyle said. "He's caught a scent. We don't want to cross-contaminate the area." He crouched and examined the area the hound identified on the trunk. The deteriorating bark was mossy and crumbled into earthy sediment on the ground. Kyle straightened, and turned back to them. "From Bruiser's reaction, there's definitely something here. Possibly, our suspect urinated."

Sidney prayed that was the case. Getting a DNA sample from the killer was more than she had hoped for. With a cold feeling in her gut, she studied the clearing, picturing the truck with the camper shell parked here. The killer probably had the dead woman in the back while he bided his time. She reflected on his cold-blooded disregard for her humanity—shoving a wadded note in her mouth that expressed his enjoyment of killing her—then looking for a place to dump her body, as though she was garbage.

"I'll get some samples, Chief," Amanda said, opening her kit. There was nothing in her tone, but her jaw muscles were flexing, betraying her emotions. She too, was imagining the details of the murder. "Then I'll search this whole clearing,"

"This is so cool," Jason said, rolling back and forth on the balls of his feet, his hands shoved into his pockets. "Just like on CSI."

The young man's cavalier attitude snapped Sidney out of her intense concentration. Most folks who weren't intimately acquainted with death on a daily basis had a morbid fascination with murder. She thanked Jason for his help, then turned to Maria. "Would you mind taking Jason back to the vehicle, Maria? We need to keep the whole area clear."

"Sure thing," the deputy said. "Let's go, Jason."

Nothing on the ground on either side of the tire impressions looked disturbed but Bruiser was sniffing the air and facing the water, his body tense, his long ears lifting and falling.

"He wants to head down to the lake," Kyle said.

Sidney and Kyle followed Bruiser through the trees to the water's edge, where the scent ended at a trampled patch of grassy earth. Kyle crouched over a small portion that Bruiser was sniffing, then pulled him back, and looked up. "There's a tiny amount of dried blood here."

Sidney studied the shape of the matted area, that looked like the configuration of a body, then she squatted next to Kyle and saw the small stain. "The victim had a wound from a .22 at the base of her skull. She wasn't shot here, though. There'd be more blood. Looks like he killed her somewhere else and brought her to the lake. Then he laid her on her back, and some of the blood transferred to the grass. My guess, he was planning on leaving her here, but the teens showed up and made him nervous."

"Good thing, or we may not have found her for a while. We'll give this area a good going over," he said.

While Kyle and Bruiser continued their search, Sidney took photos with her cell phone. By the time they joined Amanda back at the clearing, she had collected a few bags of bark and sediment from the fallen tree. "I scoured this area, Chief, and found this. It was on the driver's side of the truck, as though he tossed it from the window." She held up a plastic evidence bag with a filtered cigarette butt inside. "Looks fresh."

"Good find. Hopefully, this will help us link the suspect to the murder. Now we just need to find him. Follow me. You need to get a sample of some blood down by the water's edge."

Fifteen minutes later, Bruiser had found nothing else and they retreated back to their vehicles. Kyle loaded Bruiser into his crate. "Looks like we made some progress today," he said.

"We did," Amanda said with a smile. "The force was with us."

Everyone piled into their vehicles and the K-9 team went their separate way.

Back at her Yukon, Sidney instructed Amanda to take Jason home, then she contacted her two male officers and asked how the interviews were going.

"Just finishing up, Chief," Granger said. "Between the two of us, we've hit about twenty households."

"Anything of interest?"

"Maybe," Granger said. Always wary of folks who might be eavesdropping on cop chatter using scanners, they never put details of an investigation on the air.

"Wrap it up. Head back to the station."

"Should I stop at Big Burger, Chief?" Darnell asked.

Sidney had a terrible habit of barreling through work without eating, and sometimes barely sleeping. Now the thought of a quarter pounder dripping with special sauce and melted cheese made her stomach growl. "Do it. Order enough for the whole office."

"You want your usual?"

"Copy that. See you at noon."

CHAPTER FOUR

MOLLY AND THE HANDSOME gray-haired stranger glanced her way as Selena stepped onto the patio. Peering through the Catwoman mask, her mother's celery green eyes blinked several times, as though she was surfacing from the depths of a lake into bright light. Recognition was sinking in.

"Hi, Mom."

"Hello, dear." Blushing, Molly stared up at her for a long awkward moment.

"Aren't you going to introduce me to your friend?" Selena asked.

"What's the matter with you?" her mother asked indignantly. "It's your father. Clarence."

"Actually, Molly," the man said softly, his brown eyes meeting hers. "I'm your friend from the center. We sit in the dining room together."

Molly's eyes narrowed, and she stared hard into the man's gaze. "Don't get mad at me, but I don't remember your name."

He patted her hand. "That's okay. You can call me Clarence."

The stranger was encouraging Molly to call him by her husband's name. Selena struggled to control her angry impulses, that were telling her to grab her mother by the arm and get her away from him. "What is your name?" Selena asked evenly.

The man stared back with a pensive expression, as though deep in thought and mining for a long-lost memory. "How soon do you need to know?"

Selena frowned. Was he trying to be funny?

"They call me Mr. Tibbs," he said abruptly, in a commanding voice.

What? That was a line by Sidney Poitier in the classic film *In The Heat Of The Night.*

He grinned, his eyes sparkling and crinkling at the edges. "I got you with that one, didn't I, luv?" he said with a really good Cockney accent. "I'm just playing with you. I'm actually Roger Daltrey."

"As in the rock group The Who?" she asked, lifting her brows.

"Yes, indeed. Or am I?" He looked confused for a moment, then his face took on another expression entirely. "I'm your mom's table mate back at Alcatraz." This time he used a wise guy accent, talking out of one side of his mouth. "Any minute now, the flatfoots will be showing up to drag us back to our cells." Then he laughed and his voice went back to normal. "All kidding aside, my handle is Ray. And you're one of Molly's lovely daughters."

Under other circumstances, Selena might have found him amusing. But not now. "Yes. I'm Selena."

He shook her hand, and his grip was surprisingly strong. Overall, he looked like he was in terrific shape.

"Sit down," he said. "Get off your jambs. Can I fetch you a cup of high octane?"

"No, thanks. I'm fine." She wasn't. She was trying to sort through her emotions, which flitted from anger to confusion, and back to anger. What kind of crazy was Ray? Why was he living at the center, and why had they disobeyed the rules and left without proper authorization? What kind of relationship was he having with Molly? Was he taking advantage of her, pretending to be her husband? Were they having sex? "Where did you get that outfit, Mom?"

Molly sipped her cappuccino and smiled. "I look pretty, don't I?"

"Yes, very pretty," Ray said, his eyes softly appraising her.

Even though her straight blond hair was streaked with gray, Molly was still a beautiful woman. She had a curvy figure, a gorgeous smile, and Scandinavian coloring that showed little sign of aging.

"We went shopping," Molly said happily.

"At the Pink Pussycat?" Selena asked. Her mother had a penchant for the kind of seductive attire the sex shop had to offer.

"Yes. And this." Molly reached into a shopping bag next to her seat. In one hand, she held a slinky, leopard-pattern nightgown. In the other was a bottle of strawberry scented massage oil. "Clarence bought these for me."

Ray paid? The Pink Pussycat was not cheap.

A pretty young woman dressed in the uniform of a care worker suddenly stepped out on the patio and approached them. She had a long blonde braid and a slender build. Her Alpine Ridge name tag identified her as Riley Schaffer. "Hi, Ray! Hi, Molly!" she said brightly. Her expression looked more amused than concerned, and she shot Selena a look that seemed to say, "Let me handle this."

"Well, look at you two," she said. "Just having a great time on the town. My, oh my, Molly. What an outfit you're wearing."

"See what else I got?" Molly beamed like a child on Christmas morning, holding up her other sex shop treasures.

"Gorgeous, Molly."

"Clarence bought them for me."

"Oh, that's very nice."

Though friendly, Selena noted the controlled professionalism in Riley's tone. As a caretaker at Alpine Ridge, she was trained to work with the unique challenges of patients suffering from memory impairment. Subject to sudden chemical impulses, their behavior was unpredictable, and sometimes even violent.

"Hey, I bet you two would love to go for a ride in the shuttle bus," Riley said, her tone enthusiastic. "It's parked right out front. We can drive through the park and look at the spring flowers."

"Tulips and daffodils. Crocuses!" Molly exclaimed. She had been a highly skilled gardener her entire life. In addition to gorgeous shrubs and flowers, Molly had grown most of the vegetables the Becker family ate. Her passion was shared by Selena. The two had worked in the yard together since Selena was knee-high, transforming their acre of property into a slice of Eden.

A tall, stocky male care worker appeared on the patio and beamed a smile at the escapees. "It's me, Tyler. Ready for your trip to the park?"

Molly and Ray waved back, and then got to their feet and joined him.

"You're Molly's daughter. I've seen you at the center," Riley said, with a friendly smile. Her eyes were an unusual shade of blue, almost violet.

Selena didn't recognize her, but there were many care workers at the center, and they rotated shifts. "Yes, I'm Selena."

"I'm Riley. It might be a good idea if you came back to the center."

"I'm planning on it. Management has some explaining to do." Strident measures needed to be taken to ensure Molly didn't escape again. "What's going on with Ray and my mom?"

"Nothing to worry about. They spend a lot of time together at the center. I think it's sweet. Your mom's been less anxious since Ray moved in."

"What's his trip?"

"Brain injury. His reality is like a bag full of fragments of his life, all jumbled together. We never know what he's going to pull out next. He relies on quotes from movies and TV shows quite a bit. They seem to stick in his mind."

"I noticed."

Her gaze was direct. "He's just a sweet old guy. He gets muddled, but never angry. He's harmless, Selena."

"Is he having sex with my mother?"

She shrugged. "I'm not entirely sure. We can't watch them every minute. We can't lock them in their rooms."

Of course Riley was right. Selena definitely needed guidance on this subject. Were there negative consequences for memory impaired people having sex? "How was Ray able to buy that stuff for my mom?"

"He has a credit card. They see the name on his card and his credit is golden. Last name's Abbott."

"As in James Abbott?"

"You got it," she said with obvious distaste. "The real estate mogul and former CEO of Netstorm Electronics."

Selena's throat tightened and she felt a cold feeling in her stomach. Memories of the serial killer who terrorized Garnerville last autumn loomed large in her mind. James Abbott had been having an affair with one of the victims, and briefly, he'd been a prime suspect in her murder. During the investigation, Sidney discovered a string of vile secrets that Abbott successfully kept under wraps. These days, he and his wife were mentioned in local newspapers almost daily, and were touted for their generous philanthropic activities.

Watching Selena, Riley's gaze sharpened. "You okay?"

"Yeah, I'm okay," she said, though her voice was tense. "I just don't appreciate that Abbott's buying up every lakeshore property he can get his hands on. Driving up prices. Average people like you and me will never be able to buy the luxury homes he's building."

"He's also trying to buy acreage up on Bear Creek Ridge." Vexation darkened Riley's violet-blue eyes. "He wants to build high density condos up there."

Selena's anger flared like the strike of a match. Some of her favorite hiking trails were in the hills above the lake. The woods were her cathedral. If a large swath of forest was destroyed, not only would the town's avid nature lovers suffer, but there would be a significant loss of habitat for birds and animals. She imagined the stunning view of the forested hills, as seen from downtown, marred by rows of condos. "That won't get approved," she said hotly.

"I hope you're right," Riley sighed.

"Let's get in the shuttle bus!" Molly's impatient voice cried out.

Waiting with Ray and Tyler in her skintight Catwoman outfit, Molly looked like she could be an extra in a Marvel movie—until she crossed her arms and stamped her foot like a six-year old. "I want to see the flowers!"

"We better get going," Riley said. She and Tyler escorted the couple around the side of the building and through the alley to Main Street.

Following behind, Selena felt a pain like a dull bruise inside her chest that never completely went away. Watching her mother's beautiful mind disappear in slivers was like losing a museum of priceless artifacts. Molly's wise and humorous anecdotes, her virtual pharmacy of natural remedies, her exquisite culinary skills and recipes that only existed in her head, were vanishing. Her father, Clarence Becker, who had been police chief for fifteen years, died from a heart attack four years earlier. With her mom in memory care, Selena felt the sting of losing both parents prematurely. She and Sidney, who were exceptionally close sisters, were now housemates in the home they once shared with their parents.

After being ushered into the bus, Molly and Ray sat staring out the window with excited expressions. Her mom removed the Catwoman mask and looked carefree with her hair blowing around her shoulders from the open window. Brushing a strand from her cheek, she waved at Selena, a big grin on her face.

It tugged at Selena's heart.

Looking completely competent, Riley sat in the driver's seat with her hands resting on the wheel, engine running.

"I'll meet you at the center, Riley," Selena said. "I need to run home and get out of my yoga clothes."

"No problem. Give us an hour. We're going to take them on an adventure." Riley gave her a thumb's up, shut the door, and pulled away from the curb.

Selena's phone buzzed as she parked in front of the police station. It was Granger Wyatt, one of her sister's junior officers, whom she'd been dating for six months. In addition to being extremely good looking, he had the mental toughness of a combat veteran and a cop, which was very appealing and reminded her of her father. Granger also had rock solid family values. He moved into the bunkhouse at the family ranch after his deployment to help care for his father who had Parkinson's disease. And he did most of the ranch chores, in addition to his full-time job as a cop. But from the start, Granger had come on strong, and he admitted to Selena after four months that he was in love with her. Selena had yet to reciprocate in kind. She kept him at bay, taking it slow and careful. She was newly divorced, after being emotionally abused by her ex-husband for years. She was in no hurry to lose herself in a relationship again.

"Hey," she answered. "How'd the investigation go?"

"Not good."

"Homicide?"

"Yep. That's why I'm calling."

"You're working late and calling off our dinner date."

"Yeah. Sorry."

"Hey, I'm a cop's daughter. I know the ropes."

"Want to give it a try tomorrow night?"

It had been a week since their last date, and she missed him, but she didn't want to "need" him. Selena loved the simplicity of their current relationship. After the chaos of her marriage to Randy, she needed structure, and she needed to feel like she was in control. Generally, she and Granger cooked dinner together, watched a movie, made love—then she gently coaxed him out the door. Admittedly, the whole evening sometimes felt rushed, like they had to get everything accomplished within a certain timeframe. But that's what she was able to commit to right now.

"You there?" he asked.

"Yeah, sorry. Let's talk tomorrow." She quickly hung up before her emotions kicked in and exposed her weakness. She really wanted to see him, but more importantly, she needed to stay in control of her life.

CHAPTER FIVE

SELENA ENTERED THE STATION, bypassed the administrator, and headed down the hall to her sister's office. Inside the cramped room that used to be their father's office, Sidney sat preoccupied, fingers tapping the keyboard of her computer. She could be unnervingly focused, just as their father had been. She ran the department as he had: tough on crime, fair with her staff, and relentless when investigating a case. Sitting in her crisp blue uniform, with her hair tightly knotted at the nape of her neck, Sidney exuded toughness and authority. Her strong features were softened by her beautiful full mouth and expressive hazel eyes.

"Got a few minutes?" Selena asked quietly.

Sidney lifted those hazel eyes and frowned slightly. "You look stressed. What's up?"

Selena seated herself across from her desk. "Mom escaped from Alpine Ridge this morning."

"Jesus. Is she okay?"

"Yeah, fortunately. She left the care center with a guy named Ray. I found them at Lava Java having coffee on the patio. Before that, they made a visit to The Pink Pussycat where he bought her presents. Including a sexy Catwoman outfit, which she was wearing."

"A Catwoman outfit?" Sidney looked astonished. "For real?"

"For real. Mask and all. I'm sure no one recognized her. I didn't."

"Thank God for that." Sidney shook her head. "What is Mom's fascination with that sex shop?"

Selena shrugged. "Living out fantasies she suppressed all her life, I guess."

"Who's this Ray guy?" Sidney asked.

"Mom's new tablemate at the care center. She calls him Clarence."

"She thinks he's dad?" Another note of surprise.

"Yeah. They were kissing like honeymooners."

"Mom was kissing some old coot?" Sidney's brows lifted in surprise.

"He's actually pretty good looking."

"And it was consensual?"

"Oh yeah. She was into it."

Sidney looked impressed.

"Why do you look like you're okay with it?"

"Because I am," Sidney said. "I'm glad Mom got herself a boyfriend. She's still young and pretty, and she's living with a bunch of withering old people. I'm glad she's spicing it up a little."

"They may be having sex."

Sidney studied her for a long moment. "So? It's not like she's going to get pregnant."

Selena crossed her arms, frustrated that her sister was taking a liberal attitude. Born and raised in Garnerville, Selena had led a sheltered life, and was far more conservative when it came to relationships than Sidney. She met her ex-husband in high school and stayed loyal to him to the bitter end. Granger was only the second man she'd ever slept with, and she was having all kinds of reservations about him. On the other hand, Sidney had lived a cosmopolitan lifestyle in the bay area of San Francisco. As a homicide detective, she'd had a job that commanded respect, worked with the best minds in law enforcement, and got killers off the street. Sophisticated and fearless, Sidney had dated all kinds of men, but she suffered a few failed relationships and was still single at thirty-five.

"As long as it's consensual," Sidney continued, "Mom can make her own decisions about her love life."

"She has Alzheimer's. She's confused. She thinks he's dad." Selena chewed on her bottom lip. "I don't like it."

"What are you going to do? Get her a chastity belt? Station a Doberman outside her apartment?"

Selena saw her point but that didn't mean she had to like it.

"How did Ray pay for the lingerie?" Sidney asked.

"His credit is golden in Garnerville. I forgot to mention that his last name is Abbott."

Sidney's face paled. Her eyes narrowed into slits. "You don't mean …."

"Yeah. I do." Selena exhaled her irritation. "His son is James Abbott."

Sidney scowled. "That puts Mom's situation in a whole different light. I don't want her anywhere near James Abbott, for any reason. He's dangerous."

"I agree. So what about Ray?"

"Hmmm. Wait a minute. I remember reading about Ray Abbott a couple years ago. He was in a serious car accident in Portland. He made headline news because he's filthy rich. He had a brain injury and was in a coma for a couple weeks."

"That's him. His memory seems to be shot full of holes. Overall though, he seems pretty harmless."

"Harmless or not, we need to keep him away from Mom. We don't want her in the same orbit as anyone in the Abbott family. She needs a new tablemate, effective immediately. Preferably a harmless old lady. And more importantly, Alpine Ridge needs to tighten their security."

"I'm hoping that's possible."

"They better make it possible." Sidney let out a forced sigh. "Mom's getting worse. We've dodged a bullet every time she's escaped. They're looking at a big lawsuit if anything happens to her."

"I'm heading over to Alpine Ridge right now to talk to management."

Sidney tossed her a stern look, her mouth set in a grim line. "Good. Don't go easy on them."

"Don't worry. I won't."

***

After Selena left, Sidney went back to her paperwork. Her officers returned one by one through the back door from the parking lot, walking past her office to the conference room. Arms full, Darnell paused in her doorway and held up bags from Big Burger, reminding her that she had skipped breakfast. Sidney wrapped up her report and followed the aroma of food down the hallway.

Sunlight fell through the blinds of a room that barely accommodated a rectangular table that seated eight. The conference room also served as the break room, with a refrigerator pressed against one wall. Winnie, the administrator, kept the sideboard buffet stocked with coffee, pastries, and chips. Historical town photos and portraits of former police chiefs hung on the walls, including Police Chief Clarence Becker in his dress blues.

Darnell, the man of the hour, was distributing drinks, burgers, napkins, and packets of ketchup. Creatures of habit, everyone took their usual seats. The four officers were joined by their dispatcher, Jesse, and Winnie, whose workstations dominated the front lobby.

Sidney unwrapped her cheeseburger and chomped out a big bite, suddenly feeling as hungry as a wolf. Ignoring the gruesome crime scene photos looming on the crime board, everyone ate with gusto. For a long minute no one spoke, just munched, sipped, shoved in fries, and used napkins liberally to catch the dripping sauce.

"Man, these burgers are good," Winnie said, holding a French fry in one hand, and a half-eaten chickenburger in the other. "Messy, though. My diet's going to hell, but I don't care. One day a week you have to live a little." Always dieting, Winnie managed to maintain a well-rounded figure which she highlighted to its best advantage with form-fitting outfits.

"Messy is right," Jesse said, wiping his chin with a napkin. "Next time, get bibs." Reed thin, Jesse could eat anything. His extravagant mop of gray hair was the fullest thing on his body. A retired science teacher, he was unflappable and highly organized; perfect traits for a dispatcher.

Granger won the eating contest, wolfing down his entire meal in minutes. Ranch labor burned every calorie, and like Sidney, he was a gym rat. "Thanks for remembering we need to eat, Darnell. I was about to chew my arm off."

"You're the man, bro," Amanda chimed in.

Darnell grinned. "I confess, I ate another burger while driving back to the station."

Amanda threw a fry at him. "I could easily have eaten two."

Darnell ate the fry.

Sidney washed down her last bite with soda. Shifting her attention to the crime board, she stood and jotted notes in the margins around the photos with a black marker. When she turned, everyone had finished eating and was facing her expectantly, laptops opened. Winnie and Jesse excused themselves and went back to their workstations.

"Okay, let's do a quick summary of what we learned today." Sidney pointed to a photo of the victim. "We discovered this woman's body in a field near the Rawlings farm. She was fully clothed, with a single gunshot wound at the base of her skull. COD is unconfirmed at this point. We know only a few facts about the suspect." Sidney tapped various photos as she spoke. "Boot prints, and possible DNA from his urine, a cigarette butt, and this note that was placed in the victim's mouth. The note alludes to revenge. This coin was also found on the victim."

Sidney paused to sip her drink, then proceeded. "The killer drives a dark truck with a shell over the bed. He smokes Marlboro filtered cigarettes. His boot size is about a ten."

She turned to face her team. "The killer knew of an obscure back road to Aspen Lake, which suggests he's a local. I believe he went to the lake to dispose of the body and was caught off guard when the teens showed up. Maybe he panicked, knowing they saw his truck, so he decided to dump the body in the field, and get the hell out of the area."

Next, Sidney pointed to the skeletal remains of John Doe. "Nothing substantial links our suspect to the death of John Doe, other than both bodies were left near a lake. Because his head was missing, we don't know if a note was placed in his mouth. The K-9 unit is going back with a cadaver dog. If they find the skull, we might be able to identify him. Until we have conclusive evidence indicating otherwise, John Doe is not classified as a murder. That sums it up, for now." She looked at her two male officers. "You two find out anything from the neighbors? Any suspects?"

"No suspects," Darnell said. "Got a lead to follow, though. While driving over the hill to school, a teenage girl saw a black truck with a camper shell parked off the road two days in a row. Condensation fogged the windows, suggesting someone had possibly slept in it. The second morning, she saw a guy getting out of the cab. She went by really fast and didn't see him well. He wore a hoodie, but she thinks he was average height and build."

"When did she see the truck?"

"Wednesday and Thursday mornings."

"And our victim was killed Friday night. That sounds promising." She turned to Granger. "You get anything?"

"No, now that I know the truck was a dark color. Different folks saw different trucks. None dark. Only one had a camper shell, but it was red."

Winnie waltzed into the room and handed a printout to Sidney, her manner practically humming with enthusiasm. "Stewart ran the prints on our Jane Doe. We have an ID." She passed out copies to the other officers.

An air of anticipation sparked the room. Everyone followed along as Sidney read the information out loud. "Her name is Olivia Paisley. Date of birth is 1985, which made her thirty-five years old. Current address is 244 Cedar Lane, just a few blocks from here." Sidney looked up, her adrenaline pumping. "Okay. Get to work. Let's see what you can pull off the internet about Olivia Paisley."

While the fingers of her officers clicked their keyboards, Sidney poured herself a mug of coffee and studied the crime board.

Amanda was the first to pipe up. "I ran her through DMV records, Chief, and got her photo. There's no mistake about it. She's definitely our Jane Doe."

"Print out her photo." Sidney wrote the name Olivia Paisley under the victim's photo on the crime board.

"Vehicle make?"

"Subaru. Two years old."

Sidney jotted notes in the margin.

"Olivia Paisley is mentioned in three articles in the Jackson Bulletin,"

Granger said. "She was a social worker here in town. This article says she'd won recognition for her work with kids."

"A social worker? Anyone recognize her?" Sidney asked. Linnly County, which incorporated the towns of Garnerville, Jackson, and Cedar Springs, was rural and sparsely populated. The folks who worked in Social Services were well known to local law enforcement, but Sidney had never worked with Olivia Paisley.

"Wait, this article is old," Granger said. "This newer article says she quit her job three and a half years ago."

"Before our time." All three of her officers were hired by Sidney since she'd been in office, just short of three years.

"Public records show she's been divorced for two years," Darnell said. "And she was the sole owner of the house she bought two years ago." His eyes scanned his screen and then he looked up with a startled expression. "Her ex-husband is Thomas Thornton."

"The ER doctor?" Sidney asked.

"Yeah."

They all knew Dr. Thornton. Each of them routinely transported injured victims to the ER. Dr. Thornton was on call three nights a week. Sidney knew him to be a calm, highly skilled professional. But as the ex-husband of the victim, he just moved to the top of the suspect list. As the only experienced detective in the department, questioning suspects was her responsibility. "Doctor Thornton needs to be questioned, but more pressing right now, is to do a security check on Olivia's house. If that's where she was murdered, there could be other victims. In the meantime, everything related to this investigation stays under wraps." Sidney exhaled slowly, taking a few moments to organize her thoughts. "Darnell, go through all her social media connections. Look for any suspicious activity or threatening messages. Anything that raises a red flag."

"Yes, ma'am." Darnell's fingers started working his keypad.

"Granger, go through the court documents. Find out who Olivia's lawyers were and if the divorce was friendly or cutthroat."

Granger nodded.

Sidney turned to Amanda. "You're coming with me. Grab your crime kit. We're going to Olivia's house."

***

Olivia Paisley's address was in an older section of town; an enclave of bungalows built in the nineteen-sixties with small yards and towering trees.

Olivia's house looked respectably middle class, painted white with blue shutters, and rose bushes under the window.

Sidney parked at the curb. She and Amanda walked up the sidewalk, mounted the broad front porch, and rang the bell. No answer. After another attempt with no response, they began to circle the house; trying doors, looking in windows, and spotting the victim's Subaru in the garage. They reached the rear of the house and stepped into the deep shadows of the back yard. Trees and bushes created a wall of privacy around the small, freshly mowed lawn. It was deadly quiet. A patio door was open a few inches, instantly arousing their suspicion. Drawing their weapons, they approached cautiously, staying close to the wall. Sidney stole a quick glance into the house. A bedroom. No movement. She opened the door wider and announced, "Police! Anyone here?"

No response. They entered, guns raised, moving quickly through the room, checking the closet, the adjoining bath, then carefully stepping into the hallway. They swept through the back of the house; another bedroom, bathroom, laundry room. Everything tidy, no blood, no sign of struggle, until they reached the living room. Sidney's pulse quickened. Clearly, a violent crime had been committed here.

An easy chair was knocked over, an end table overturned, the pieces of a broken lamp were scattered across the hardwood floor. Most telling was the blood—only a small amount but smeared over several feet as though a body had been dragged across the floor. The attack started twenty feet away in the kitchen. A plate with a half-eaten meal sat on the island. A barstool lay on its back on the tiled floor. Next to it, red wine pooled around a shattered glass.

"Clear," Sidney said.

They holstered their weapons.

"Looks like Olivia was shot here. The killer probably got in the same way we did; the unlocked patio door. He crept into the front room, saw she had her back to him, surprised her in the kitchen. She resisted, struggled, ran into the living room. More struggle. They knocked over the lamp, the furniture. He got the best of her and shot her in the back of the head. The small amount of blood is consistent with a wound from a .22."

"Must have been terrifying."

"Yeah. Fucking terrifying," Sidney said.

"Then he dragged her across the floor to the front door and carried her body out to his truck," Amanda added. She looked calm and controlled, but Sidney detected an underlying edginess that matched her own. There was always something sinister and palpable that lingered in the air of a house where violence and death took place.

"He must have had his truck parked in her driveway," Amanda said. "He took a big chance. You think he's an inexperienced killer?

"Shooting the victim in the back of the head with a small caliber pistol sounds more professional to me. And quiet. He committed the murder at night. Darkness covered his actions. Sounds pretty smart to me."

"Maybe the neighbors saw something."

"I'll start talking to them. You need to start processing this crime scene. You can't do it alone. I'll get a team over here from county to help."

They went back outside and circled to the front of the house. Amanda grabbed her forensic kit from the Yukon, paused on the porch to put Tyvek booties over her shoes, then entered. Sidney called the station. "We have a crime scene, Winnie. Get hold of Judge Stevens. I need a warrant to search Olivia Paisley's residence and everything on her property, including her car. Have Granger pick it up and bring it over."

"Yes, ma'am. I'll get right on it."

Next, Sidney called the sheriff's office and asked for assistance. She was assured a crime scene unit would show up within the hour. She sensed a shift in the weather. The temperature dropped and the wind had picked up. In the distance, the sky was darkening over the hills above the lake.

Sidney scanned the neighborhood. Quiet. Not a soul in sight. A movement caught her attention in a window of the house next door. A curtain was pulled back and someone stood watching. The house was a twin to Olivia's, only blue with black shutters. Sidney walked up to the front door and rang the bell. The barking of a small dog grew louder and then the door cracked open. A slice of an old woman's face peeked out.

Sidney introduced herself.

The woman's eyes widened as she took in her uniform. "Oh yes, Police Chief Becker. I recognize you from the paper." The door opened wider and a Boston Terrier shot out and pawed Sidney's leg.

"Jasper, no!" The old lady scooped up the terrier and peered at Sidney through thick bifocals, her magnified eyes enormous. "I'm Edna Hobbs. Did Olivia's house get burglarized?"

"No, ma'am," Sidney said. "May I come in for a moment, Ms. Hobbs?"

The old woman frowned, but she waved her in. "Call me Edna. Let's go into the living room."

Sidney followed her down the hall to a dimly lit room furnished with furniture that looked as old as the house. The curtains were closed tight, and a musty smell lingered in the air. Edna wore a faded flannel bathrobe over faded pajamas.

"Sorry, I just woke up from a nap." Edna opened the curtains wide enough for a shaft of light to fall across the floor, then she sank into a recliner parked in the shadows. She looked frail and sickly. A row of prescription bottles sat on the end table.

Sidney seated herself across from her on the couch. Jasper hopped onto her lap. Sidney gently pushed him to the floor, but he bounced right back up and curled into a ball.

"Is Olivia okay?" Edna asked.

"We're still investigating. Mind if I ask you a few questions?" Sidney ignored the dog.

Edna shrugged. "You're here. Why not."

"Did you notice any vehicles parked at Olivia's house last night?"

"Yes," she answered without hesitation. "Her ex-husband stopped by. He stayed about twenty minutes."

"Would that be Dr. Thornton, ma'am?"

"Yes."

Sidney's antennae shot straight up. "What does he drive?"

"A big black truck."

"What time was that?"

Edna thought for a moment. "It was dark. Maybe eight?"

"Are you sure it was Dr. Thornton? Did you actually see him get out of the truck?"

"No. Just saw the truck."

It was dark, and Edna didn't actually see anyone, but Dr. Thornton was still at the top of Sidney's suspect list. He had the right vehicle, and twenty minutes was plenty of time to kill his ex-wife and cart her body out the door. "Did you see him leave?"

"No. I just heard that goddamned engine of his. Sounds like a plane taking off. He must have a penis the size of a string bean to need a truck that big."

Sidney suppressed a smile. Edna had a feisty streak. "You don't like him."

The old woman's expression soured. "Hell no, I don't like him. He's been a bastard to Olivia."

"How so?"

Edna pulled a wadded tissue from a pocket and coughed into it, then swallowed and continued. "He fought her tooth and nail in court. Didn't want to give her a penny. She put all her savings into the down payment on the house. She finally settled with him, just to get something to live on."

"Was he abusive?"

"He never hit her. But he wasn't a prince, either." Edna leaned forward and said in a hushed tone, as though the walls had ears, "He cheated."

"Did she tell you that?"

"No. Wilma did." Edna coughed again, blew her nose. "Sorry. Emphysema. Don't ever smoke, dear. You pay the price later in life. Wilma lives across the street. They were in the same book club."

"Did Olivia work?"

"No. She used to do some kind of work with kids. But she had to stop."

"Why is that?"

"Threats."

"What kind of threats?"

Edna wheezed, and went into a coughing fit. Her face and neck turned crimson. "You'll have to ask Wilma," she choked out.

Sidney needed to end this interview. Clearly, talking aggravated Edna's condition. "One last question, does Olivia have any family living in town?"

"None. Parents are dead. No siblings." She squinted through her thick lenses. "Is Olivia dead?"

"Sorry, ma'am. I can't disclose any information right now."

Edna's face screwed up with anger. "He killed her, didn't he? That bastard husband of hers!"

"As I said, I can't disclose any details." It wasn't looking good for the doctor. A hostile divorce and bitter wrangling over money was a powerful motive. Sidney kept her suspicions to herself and gently shoved Jasper to the floor. "Thank you for your time, Edna. You've been very helpful. Please don't get up. I'll see myself out."

"Wilma lives in the pink house," Edna called after her.

CHAPTER SIX

FROM THE OUTSIDE, Alpine Ridge looked like a charming one-story residential building, surrounded by large maple trees and lush green lawns. Inside, the doors locked after someone entered, and an alarm sounded if an unauthorized person exited. Selena pressed the code into the keypad, entered the lobby, and heard the door click behind her. She crossed the floor to a young woman named Micky, who sat behind the reception station talking on the phone. She had spiky magenta hair, purple fingernails, and a yellow dress with white polka dots.

While waiting, Selena's gaze swept across the lobby that had a warm, homey atmosphere. Overstuffed couches and chairs were arranged to allow pathways for wheelchairs and walkers, vases of fresh flowers sat on coffee tables, and a side table was stocked with coffee and cookies.

Rows of folding chairs had been placed around a grand piano that took up the middle of the floor and gray-haired seniors started filling the seats. A plump, red-haired woman crossed the lobby, seated herself at the piano and began playing *Singing in the Rain*.

Micky hung up the phone. "Hi, Selena. I'll tell Richard you're here." She entered the manager's office, then motioned to Selena.

Richard Miller stood when she entered and reached across his desk to grasp her hand. Fortyish with horn-rimmed glasses, he wore casual business clothes and an appropriately solemn expression. "Have a seat, Selena."

Richard sat forward in his seat and folded his hands on the desk. "I know why you're here. I'm sure it came as a shock that your mom left the premises this morning." He paused, as though searching for the right words. "This is the fourth time Molly has managed to leave the building. And today, she took Ray."

"So you're saying it's her fault?" Selena asked. "You're blaming the patient?"

Richard held up his hands. "Hold on, Selena. That's not what I'm saying.

I just want to emphasize that getting out of the building is an exception, not the norm. No one else has ever left on their own. This is the fourth time in the three years she's been here."

Selena sensed the presence of someone in the doorway before Richard glanced up with a touch of alarm. "Mr. Abbott ...."

Selena flinched. She scoped out the man standing there in seconds: tall, silver haired, expensive tailored suit, more distinguished than handsome with a Roman nose and intelligent gray eyes.

Micky stood behind him, frowning. "Sorry, Richard. I told him you were with someone."

"Please come in, Mr. Abbott. Can we get you coffee, tea?" Richard said in a supplicating tone.

"Or a cold drink?" Micky asked in a softer tone, realizing her mistake.

Abbott waved her away like she was an annoying gnat. He took the seat next to Selena and his cool gray eyes locked on hers. "I overheard your conversation. So it was *your* mother who took my father on a shopping spree this morning." His voice was smooth and cultured, with a trace of iron.

"Actually, it was your father who took my mother," Selena said evenly.

"Your mom has a history of escaping. The only resident here who has ever accomplished that feat. She's clever. She helped my dad ring up quite an expense. Maxed out his credit card."

"Anything bought by your father will be returned," she said, bristling. "It was his idea to dress my mom up as Catwoman and parade her downtown."

"Catwoman?" He looked puzzled, then the steeliness returned to his eyes. "I don't care about some silly costume. I'm concerned about the diamond bracelet and ring he bought at Saffron Jewelers, to the tune of twelve thousand dollars."

Selena's mouth dropped open.

Abbott glanced at Richard, expecting some intervention. The manager looked as shocked as Selena.

"My mother wore no jewelry when I found her at the coffee shop. She showed me everything your dad bought her. No jewelry. She has Alzheimer's, Mr. Abbott. Mom's like a child. Easily manipulated. Your father has her convinced that he's her husband who died four years ago. She calls him Clarence, my dad's name."

The room went quiet. Abbott leaned back in his chair and gave Selena a penetrating stare. She sensed a methodicalness to his thinking, as though he was carefully assessing her character. That unnerved her a little, but she held his stare, and stated the obvious. "Ray had the credit card. He's responsible for any purchases."

Abbott drummed the armrest with long, elegant fingers, his nails perfectly manicured.

"Did you speak with the salesperson at Saffron's?" Richard finally joined the conversation.

"Of course I did," Abbott said curtly. "She had no idea they were memory-impaired. My wife and I have made a number of purchases at Saffron's. The saleswoman had no qualms about Ray when she learned he was my father."

Selena thought of the Rolex watch and diamond earrings Abbott bought for his young mistress, who became a victim of the serial killer. The Rolex alone must have cost upwards of twenty grand.

"Ray and Molly have periods of lucidity, and can be quite convincing," Richard said.

"I want their rooms searched," Abbott clipped. He was a man who was accustomed to giving orders and taking control. "If the jewelry isn't found, someone may have stolen it. Possibly someone who works here. In which case, we're looking at grand larceny."

"One step at a time, Mr. Abbott. Let's start with a search of the rooms." There was intensity in Richard's eyes, and also a shade of anxiety. The morning's debacle made him look less than competent.

Selena needed to make sure her mom remained an innocent bystander. "I'll search my Mom's room."

"Someone not involved should do that," Abbott said pointedly.

"What do you mean not involved? I'm my mother's guardian. I am involved."

He gave her another one of his icy stares.

"Are you suggesting I would cover up for her? Or that I would steal the jewelry?"

"Now Selena, that's not at all what he meant," Richard said in a placating tone.

"I'm suggesting it would be in everyone's best interest if we maintained impartiality," Abbott said evenly. "In the event this becomes a criminal case."

Abbott had a smooth, polished manner, and an air of untouchable superiority. He also had a reputation for being a ruthless businessman. As the former CEO of NetStorm Electronics, he was known for seizing or steamrolling smaller companies to eliminate competition—destroying careers and marketplace diversity in the process. Yet he and his wife were received like royalty at the elegant charity functions they sponsored. It sickened Selena that the allure of power and money could whitewash unscrupulous dealings.

During her investigation of the serial killer known as "The Collector," Sidney had uncovered many of Abbott's slimy secrets. He routinely cheated on his wife, and his affair with Sammy Ferguson, one of the victims of the serial killer, had been described as sadistic. At the time of her death, the young woman had been hiding from Abbott. His tailored suit and manicured hands did not disguise his vile nature.

"You can witness the searches. Ray and Molly should be listening to the concert in the lobby right now, so this is a good time." Richard picked up the phone and asked Micky to recruit a couple of caregivers to conduct the searches. "Have them come to my office immediately."

Selena stepped into the hall and spotted her mom sitting in the first row, dressed in jeans and a pullover. Ray was seated next to her, holding her hand. They looked relaxed and content. Even a casual onlooker could see that they shared a deep affection for one another. Molly had a newfound glow that had been absent since her husband died. Selena was warmed by the simple sweetness of the moment.

Abbott came and stood next to her. There was something dark and heavy in his presence. His eyes narrowed when he located Ray and Molly and his mouth dipped into a scowl. "We need to have my dad reassigned in the dining room. He was doing fine until they moved him to your mother's table."

With mixed feelings, Selena nodded. It was for the best. She wanted to avoid all future encounters with James Abbott and keep her mother off his radar. Hopefully their parents would forget about each other if kept apart.

Riley and Tyler crossed the lobby, and with Micky in tow, joined the group outside the office. Richard explained that they needed to conduct searches. "Tyler and I picked up Ray and Molly from the coffee shop this morning."

"Did you see Molly with any jewelry?" Abbott asked, watching them keenly. "At the coffee shop or in the shuttle bus?"

"Jewelry?" Riley looked puzzled. "What kind of jewelry?"

"A diamond ring and a bracelet."

"No. That, I would have noticed."

"Molly did have a shopping bag, though," Tyler added.

"Micky, I want you and Riley to search Molly's room for the bracelet and ring," Richard said. "Selena will be observing. Find that shopping bag. I'll go with Tyler and Mr. Abbott to Ray's room. Let's go down the back hall so Ray and Molly don't see us."

The building was a square configuration that wrapped around a central courtyard. A connecting hallway ran down three arms of the building with apartments on both sides. The lobby, dining room, and offices were located on the fourth side. It was a layout that residents could easily navigate, both mentally and physically. The courtyard had trees and flowers and a gazebo, which residents could access anytime. Other than that, they were confined to the building unless checked out by a relative.

The three men entered a room halfway down the first hall. The women continued, turned the corner, and entered Molly's studio apartment three doors down. Simply furnished, a bed with a gaily colored spread and throw pillows hugged an alcove on the left. A small sitting area faced a TV on the right, and colorful prints hung on the walls. Photos of the Becker family lined a bookcase, with Clarence Becker front and center in his uniform. A big window faced the courtyard where Selena had planted Molly's favorite flowers, and birds fluttered around the feeders Sidney hung in the tree branches. The two sisters made it a cozy oasis where Molly felt comfortable and safe.

Micky and Riley started searching the sitting area while Selena watched.

"So let me get this straight," Riley said, "Ray bought diamond jewelry for your mom this morning?"

"Yeah. At Saffron's," Selena said. "To the tune of twelve thousand dollars."

Micky paused and whistled. "Holy heck!"

Riley's brow lifted in surprise. "Wow. That's nothing to sneeze at. But it's pocket change to Abbott." She lifted cushions off the couch, replaced them. "Figures. It had to be something big to get Abbott over here. He hardly ever visits Ray."

Selena frowned. "Sorry to hear that."

"He has more money than God," Micky said, on her hands and knees, sweeping her hands under the furniture. "He doesn't like someone one-upping him. Using his father is using him."

Riley sighed. "I already see Richard losing his job. Hope there isn't more fallout than that."

"It sucks that Abbott picked Garnerville for his real estate projects," Micky said.

"Got that right." Riley walked to Molly's closet, pulled open one of the sliding doors, and started pushing hanging clothes aside. "By the time he's done, quiet little Garnerville will be a playground for rich people."

"And the rest of us will be pushed into the fringes," Micky added.

The two young women, who probably lived paycheck to paycheck, continued to express their vexation as they worked. Selena also heard anxiety in their voices. Garnerville had always been stridently blue-collar; mostly ranchers and lumber mill families. But twenty years ago the economy rapidly declined as lumber jobs went away. During the last decade, the economy rebounded. Out of towners started discovering the town's rural beauty and charming historical downtown, and Garnerville transformed into a vacation destination. Dusty shops and eateries turned into trendy coffeeshops and upscale boutiques. Tourist dollars revived the economy, much to everyone's relief and gratitude. But now the townsfolk wanted to preserve Garnerville's small-town lifestyle by limiting growth, before its allure was paved over, and before the rising cost of living drove working class families from the neighborhoods they grew up in.

Riley slid open the other closet door and pulled out a shopping bag with The Pink Pussycat logo on it. She held it up triumphantly. "Got it."

Riley reached in and brought out the leopard printed nightdress and bottle of massage oil. Then she pulled out a smaller bag with the Saffron Jewelers emblem on it. Inside were a rectangular box and smaller ring box.

Selena held her breath.

Except for the cotton padding, both boxes were empty.

"Damn. That would've been too easy."

"Let's search the rest of the room," Riley said, equally frustrated. "Maybe we'll find it."

A thorough search produced no results. Dispirited, the women retraced their steps back to the office where Richard and Abbott waited in the hallway.

"No luck?" Richard asked grimly.

"No luck," Micky said, handing him the shopping bag. "The empty jewelry boxes are in there, along with the purchases from The Pink Pussycat."

"I profoundly apologize for all of this trouble," Richard said to Abbott, ignoring Selena completely. "I'll make sure nothing like this ever happens again."

A hard expression tightened Abbott's lips. The icy stare he leveled at Richard made him flinch.

"I'm going to do your job for you," Abbott said. "And make sure the security here is bulletproof. Even Houdini wouldn't escape."

The group in the hall avoided meeting Richard's gaze. Selena felt embarrassed for him. "I'll run out and search the shuttle bus for the jewelry," Riley said.

Micky scurried back to cover the front desk.

Though she disliked Abbott intensely, Selena was grateful he had fought the battle for her. An upgrade in security was a pressing necessity.

Linda Berry   42   *Cold Revenge*

"I need to get back to work," Richard muttered. With a dark melancholy hanging over him, he stored the shopping bag in his filing cabinet, then sank into his chair behind his desk.

Abbott watched the concert in the lobby with his hands on his hips. His jacket opened enough for Selena to see the handle of a Glock poking out from a shoulder holster. Why was he carrying a gun?

He caught her stare, quickly lowered his arms, and said stiffly, "Let's talk to our parents. There's a chance they'll remember something."

Slim to none, Selena thought.

Not waiting for an answer, he pressed a hand to the small of her back and guided her into the lobby. His fingers moved to the curve of her hip and felt uncomfortably intimate. She quickened her step, moving away from his touch. He let his hand drop, but not before it caressed the contour of her backside. Inwardly, Selena cringed.

CHAPTER SEVEN

THE DARK CLOUDS speeding over the hilltops had reached Olivia's neighborhood. There was another gust of wind and Sidney heard a buckle of noise in the distance. Thunder. The smell of rain was in the air.

The house across the street from Edna's was painted hot pink with white shutters. It looked glaringly out of place in the conservative neighborhood of muted colors: a landmark that could probably be seen from space. Flowering shrubs and spring flowers grew in abundance and scented the air as Sidney hiked up the sidewalk. The door opened before she reached the porch and a woman wearing pink sweats greeted her with a smile. Middle-aged, she had pleasant features, dimples, brown eyes, and curly gray hair. "Hello, Chief Becker."

Responding to Sidney's blank look, she added, "I'm Nurse Wilma Cox, from the hospital."

Sidney pictured the woman in scrubs and the image of a friendly, competent nurse sprang to mind. "Of course, Wilma. You always wear pink scrubs."

"Yep, that's my trademark. I'm very fond of pink." She ushered Sidney into the house and into the warm kitchen that smelled of cookies and coffee. "Have a seat. Can I talk you into a freshly baked chocolate chip cookie and coffee?"

Sidney smiled. "Absolutely. Smells heavenly." She sat at the small round table and took in the room, accentuated with pink dish towels and pink flowered curtains. Watery gray light filtered through the window, which had a good view of Olivia's house. A sheet of lightning pulsed, brightening the kitchen for a split second.

"Storm's coming in. A doozy." Wilma poured two mugs of coffee from a fresh pot on the counter, and set down a platter of cookies. She sat across from Sidney, looking settled in and ready for a long chat with an old friend.

Wilma added cream and sugar to her mug and stirred. Sidney did the same. They both bit into a cookie. The chocolate was warm and gooey. The coffee was rich and strong.

Wilma's eyebrows arched and she asked eagerly, "So, what the heck is going on across the street? What has the doc done now?"

"The doc?" Sidney asked. "What's he done before?"

"Whatever he can to make Olivia's life miserable. Constantly stirs up trouble." Wilma snuffled a bitter laugh. "I've advised Olivia many times to call the cops, but she won't. Is that why you're here? Did she finally call you?"

"What kind of trouble has he stirred up before?"

Wilma puffed out an exasperated breath. "Well, he's kidnapped the dog a few times. They share custody. But he doesn't return Cooper when he's supposed to. Plus, he's come over and looked through the letters in her mailbox. She had to get a P.O. box in town. Then, of course, there's the time he chopped down one of her trees in the back yard when she wasn't home. Her favorite plum tree. Just malicious. A juvenile delinquent in a grown man's body. Hard to believe he's the same super smart doctor in charge of the ER. Jekyll and Hyde." She sipped her coffee and gazed at Sidney over the rim of her cup. "He's got a problem with boundaries."

"In other words, he's stalking her."

"Oh, yeah." Wilma's expression got serious and intense. "What's he done this time? I called Olivia, but no one answers."

"Did you see anyone outside her house last night?"

"Yeah, Thomas. I saw his truck. Figured he was returning Cooper."

"What time was that?"

"Hmmm. I was watching the news, so I'd say just after eight."

"Did you actually see him go in or come out?"

She squinted, thinking. "No. I came into the kitchen about a half hour later for a snack, and his truck was gone."

"Are you certain it was his truck? Could you see his license plate?"

She frowned slightly. "No, didn't see his plate, but who else would it be? She didn't get many visitors. Especially people who drive loud, noisy trucks."

"Edna mentioned you and Olivia are close. Did you know her when she was a social worker?"

"No. Just since she moved across the street. I invited her to join my book club. She fits right in. Smart. Loves books. Super friendly."

"Do you know why she quit her job?"

A shadow passed over Wilma's face. "Yeah. She was getting threats.

Scared the bejeebers out of her."

"From who?"

"That's the scary part. She didn't have a clue. Just creepy messages sent to her office. After she quit, they stopped coming."

"Do you know what they said?"

"Yeah. Something to the effect of "Stop destroying people's lives," or "I'm going to get even," or "You'll pay for this." Olivia was with Thomas at the time. He told her to ignore them. Can you believe it? Ignore them! Instead, she quit her job. Said she was afraid to be in the office alone. Afraid to walk out to her car at night."

"Why didn't she report it to the police?"

"She did. Your predecessor, Idiot in Chief Bill McKlusky, also told her to ignore them. That man did everything wrong while he was in office. That's why he only lasted eight months."

They both took a moment to finish their cookies and sip coffee. "Great coffee."

"French roast. I grind the beans fresh."

"Yum. So rich. Do you work with Thomas?"

"No. I work days. He works nights. I leave as he arrives. I'm off weekends. He works Sunday through Tuesday."

"So Thomas was off last night."

"Yes."

"Edna said Thomas cheated on Olivia. Know anything about that?"

"Oh, yeah. He was a serial offender. She found him out several times over their ten-year marriage, but the last time was the final straw. Poor Olivia. He was doing it with Michelle Bukowski, a nurse half his age. She was married, too! Can you believe it?" Anger flared, then dimmed in her dark eyes. "What a louse. Thomas has a very good reputation as a doctor, but no one has a clue what he's like outside of work."

A stalker, a cheater, and a perpetual harasser. The case against him was gaining strength. Thomas needed a damn good alibi. Sidney glanced out the window and saw Granger's patrol truck pull to the curb behind her Yukon. He had arrived with the warrant. She drained her cup and stood to leave. "Thank you, Wilma. You've been very helpful."

Wilma wrapped a dozen cookies in foil and handed them to Sidney.

"That's so nice of you," she beamed.

"I appreciate what you do. Cops don't get enough credit." She walked Sidney to the door and her brow creased into multiple folds. "So you're not going to tell me what's going on with Olivia?"

"I'm sorry. We're in the middle of an investigation."

"Jesus." Wilma's mouth twisted in a bitter grimace. "I hope he didn't kill her."

CHAPTER EIGHT

TAKING A BRIEF intermission between tunes, the pianist sat leafing through a music book. The audience of forty seniors was quiet except for the soft rustle of people shifting in their seats.

Ray and Molly glanced up as Selena and Abbott approached.

"James? James …." Grinning broadly, Ray instantly rose to his feet.

Confusion appeared in Molly's eyes. She blinked hard, as though willing herself to recognize James Abbott.

Ray embraced his son warmly. When they pulled apart, Selena was startled to see actual emotion on James's face. A fleeting expression of sorrow.

"Where ya been, son?"

"Sorry I haven't been around for a while, Dad. Work is all-consuming."

Ray dismissed his son's sentiment with a wave of his hand, and chuckled. "Love means never having to say you're sorry." He turned to Selena and pumped her arm energetically. "Welcome. So nice to see you, Reese."

James frowned at the mention of his wife.

Realizing his mistake, Ray asked, "Who is this vision of loveliness?"

"For heaven's sake, Clarence. It's Selena."

"Of course." Ray smiled at Selena. "I see the resemblance now. As beautiful as her mother."

Selena looped an affectionate arm around her mother's shoulders and kissed her upturned cheek. She caught a hint of the gardenia soap Molly had used for years.

James pulled two folding chairs over and he and Selena sat facing their parents. After a few minutes of small talk, James brought up the subject of their trip to town, framing it in the context of an adventure.

"Yes, that was fun, wasn't it dear?" Ray said to Molly. "Remember our cappuccinos on the patio?"

She beamed. "And the flowers in the park."

"You bought Molly some nice presents," James said.

"Yes. Yes, I did."

"A leopard nightgown," Molly smiled. She brushed the top of her head. "And cat ears."

"And jewelry," Selena said calmly.

Molly frowned and shrugged.

"Do you remember the nice jewelry you bought Molly, Dad?"

"Hmmm. Did I?" Ray thought for a moment. "Ah yes, a tiara, wasn't it? Yes, that's it. A tiara for my fair lady. The poor little flower girl who became a princess." He grinned and recited a line from the song "The Rain in Spain" from My Fair Lady, using a cockney accent. He suddenly sang the verse and motioned for Molly to join him.

She didn't pick up her cue.

"Once again!" Ray said, mimicking Professor Higgins.

Molly drew a blank.

He cheerfully sang it again.

Then she sang it too, laughing.

"She's got it! By George, the flower girl has got it!"

It warmed Selena's heart to see her mother laughing at Ray's silly antics. "I loved that movie," Selena said. "Audrey Hepburn and Rex Harrison."

"Dad!" James's said sharply, stifling the cheerful mood. "Focus. Do you remember buying a diamond bracelet and ring for Molly?"

"A bracelet? A ring?" Ray's smile disappeared and for a moment he looked thoroughly confused. He scratched his head, thinking, then he looked at Molly. "If I didn't, I want to. Would you like that, Molly? A diamond ring?"

"Yes," she said. "I would love it."

"Isn't she lovely?" Ray said, meeting Molly's eyes in a lingering gaze.

Matching spots of color materialized on her cheeks.

"Where've you been all my life, gorgeous?" he said with a Brooklyn accent.

"With you, silly."

"Forever." Ray lifted Molly's hand and kissed it like a dashing knight of old.

Molly was still full of life and passion, and Ray knew how to tap into it and bring it to the surface. He was a godsend. The last four years had not been kind to Molly. In addition to losing her husband of thirty-five years, the woman known as Molly Becker was self-destructing in slow motion before her very eyes. Then, three years ago, for her own safety, Selena and Sidney had made the painful decision to move her from the home she loved into this facility.

Miraculously, Ray had appeared like a beam of sunshine, eradicating Molly's sorrow and boredom. Even with his limited abilities, he managed to be funny, upbeat, and charming. What he and Molly found together was tender and endearing. Selena now believed that separating the two would be an act of cruelty.

She glanced at James Abbott, expecting to see a softening of his attitude, but something close to fury shone in his eyes. Fury! The man could not put his own interests aside to support his father's happiness. He met Selena's gaze and a wall instantly came down over his emotions. His face went blank. But she had caught a glimpse of something hidden underneath—a kind of deformity to his character.

Abbott rose to his feet in one smooth motion. "I have to get back to work, Dad. Nice to meet you, Molly."

"Let's not say goodbye, son. But simply, 'See ya soon,'" Ray said cheerily.

"See ya soon, Dad."

"Walk with me," Abbott said to Selena. An order.

"I'll be right back, Mom."

They crossed the lobby, and again Abbott's fingers found the curve of her hip. At the front entrance, she roughly pushed his hand away. The man made her skin crawl.

He turned to face her, a harsh smile twisting his lips. "This is a great place for seniors with memory problems, Selena. Safe. Clean. Good food. Top notch caregivers. The best facility in the three-town area."

"We're very lucky to have it here," she said, wary.

"Your mother is very pretty. As are you." His eyes flickered over her face, specifically her eyes, then her mouth. He appraised her openly, as though she were a particularly fine cut of steak. There was entitlement in that stare.

It felt invasive and rude, and it angered her. "What do you want, Mr. Abbott?"

"I'm on good terms with the Alpine Ridge board members. I have sway with them. A case could be made that your mother poses too great a risk to remain here as a resident."

Selena's breath caught. "Is that some kind of threat?"

"It's a statement of fact." He glanced at his watch. "I'm running late for a meeting, but if you'd like to discuss it further, we could meet later for a drink."

"Today isn't good for me," she said coldly.

"Tomorrow?"

"I'm busy."

"Maybe you need time to think it through." His smile lingered, but his eyes were cold and calculating. His voice roughened. "Whatever you and your mom are up to with my dad, it isn't going to happen."

"What could we possibly be up to?"

"Clearly, my dad has a fixation with your mom. Considering how delusional he is, he could easily be pushed into believing he's in love with her. He might even be persuaded to marry her. I'm instructing the staff to keep them apart at all times. I hope you will respect my wishes. Don't encourage them."

Selena held her tongue, though she wanted to lash out at him. He made it sound like she and Molly were co-conspirators, manipulating Ray. Did he imagine they were scheming to swindle money from Ray's fortune? Even if Ray and Molly were to marry, it would pose no threat to Abbott. In all likelihood, he was the executor of Ray's estate, and he probably had legal safeguards in place that were equal to Fort Knox. He sounded more delusional than his father, but with paranoid underpinnings.

"As far as the jewelry issue," he continued. "I told the saleswoman to keep it quiet. But I want this theft to be thoroughly investigated. Someone stole twelve grand from my dad. I intend to get it back. You can relate that to your sister."

So Abbott knew who Selena was, and he knew that her sister was the Chief of Police. Not surprising. He made it his business to know the power players in town.

"Lovely woman," Abbott murmured, the coldness in his eyes warming for a moment. He reached out and brushed a wisp of hair from Selena's cheek.

She slapped his hand away.

Abbott's eyes narrowed.

"Maybe your tactics work on other women, but they won't work on me. I'm a cop's daughter. I know the law. You've laid hands on me twice. That's a misdemeanor assault. I'm sure it's been recorded. This place is full of cameras."

Abbott stood motionless, his face hardening.

"And your attempt at extortion is bullshit," Selena continued. "It doesn't hold water. Regardless of your influence in town, no board in their right mind would throw my Mom out. There would be a ton of bad publicity, as well as a lawsuit." She paused a few beats for effect. "Threaten anyone in my family again, and your wife is going to get a surprise visit."

His eyebrows shot up. "What's that supposed to mean?"

"I know a few things about you and Sammy Ferguson."

"Look who's talking bullshit," Abbott said, his voice as sharp as a knife edge. His eyes locked on hers, waiting to see if she'd crack. She held his gaze. He turned abruptly, plugged a code into the keypad, and strode out into the bright afternoon sunshine.

"Cold-blooded bastard," Selena said to his back as he crossed the lot to his gleaming black Mercedes. She rubbed her cheek with her sleeve, wiping off the feel of his touch. To threaten her in one breath, and intimately invade her space in the next, was a tactic used by sexual abusers. Abusers channeled their need for dominance through a steady dose of intimidation, breaking down a woman's resistance little by little.

***

Unnerved, Selena called Granger on speed dial.

"What's up?" From his tone, she knew he was busy with work and others were within hearing range.

"Do you have a minute?"

"A quick minute."

Selena related the abbreviated version of the mornings' events, starting with Ray and Molly's escape, the loss of the diamond jewelry, and Abbott's threat to evict Molly. That was enough for Granger to process for now. She kept silent about Abbott's lewd behavior towards her.

"He accused you of manipulating his father?" Granger said, astonishment in his tone. "He threatened your mom?"

"Yes."

Anger fused into his words. "I'd like to take his head off."

"Get in line. Tread lightly, Granger. Abbott's ruthless. He has ties to half the business people in Linnly County. Everyone wants a slice of his real estate projects. That gives him a lot of power. If he wanted to, he could make trouble for you, or Sidney."

Granger listened silently, but Selena could almost feel his anger coming through the phone. "Tell me you'll be careful," she said.

"I'll investigate quietly," he said, his voice controlled. "Does your sister know about this?"

"Not about my interaction with Abbott."

"She needs to know."

"I'll call her soon."

Even when he was preoccupied, Granger's voice had a calming effect on her, as though casting a net of protection around her. "Talk later," she said, and disconnected.

CHAPTER NINE

RAGGED STORM CLOUDS congealed overhead, darkening the afternoon. The air felt heavy with moisture. Sidney had everything under control at the crime scene. Two forensic techs from county, dressed head to toe in Tyvek, were helping Amanda process Olivia's house. It didn't appear to have been burglarized. Her credit cards and a hundred dollars were in her wallet, and expensive items in her jewelry box were untouched.

Sidney and Granger had split up, interviewing neighbors on opposite sides of the street. He was still in the last house on the block. Sidney tried for the fifth time to contact Dr. Thornton by phone. Still no answer. She left another message. Darnell had gone by his residence, a small condo near the hospital, but found no one home, and his truck was missing from the carport. As soon as she hung up, her phone buzzed. *Selena.*

"Got a minute?" her sister asked.

"Just. You talk to Richard?"

"Yeah, I talked to him. And to James Abbott."

"That, I wasn't expecting. Fill me in." As she listened to Selena's update, Sidney's emotions came to the surface in a rush of fury. Holy Hell. Abbott had bullied her sister, touched her inappropriately, and threatened to evict their mother! This was goddamned personal. Abbott was going to war with her family.

"You there?" Selena asked.

"Yeah, I'm here." Sidney inhaled and exhaled slowly. "I need to think. My impulse is to throw his ass in jail. Let him rot without food or water."

"Wish you could," Selena said hotly.

Sidney took some time to work through the heat of her emotions, to look at the full picture and allow the threads of reason to knit together. "We can't go to battle with Abbott. It won't end well. Not with Mom caught in the middle. He's taken measures to keep her separated from Ray. Let's see how that plays out. Hopefully, out of sight, out of mind."

"Hopefully. Though I like the jail option much better."

"Me, too."

"I told Granger about the missing jewelry."

"I'll get him working on it. As far as Abbott touching you, he and I are going to have a conversation. Soon."

"No need. I put him in his place," she said adamantly. "Let's just get his freaking jewelry back and be done with him. He's the kind of guy who will hurt you just because he can."

With everything Selena had been through in the past few years, she didn't need to be in Abbott's crosshairs. Sidney needed to do her job. Which was protecting the public, and especially Selena. He would definitely get a piece of her mind.

"Promise me, Sid."

"I need to get back to work. We'll talk later." Sidney disconnected and called Dr. Linthrope.

Stewart Wong answered.

"How're you guys doing over there?"

"I have info for you. Dr. Linthrope is just finishing up the autopsy. Come watch if you want."

Sidney didn't enjoy watching corpses get sliced and diced, but she did have a scientific interest in what a body could tell about a killer. She had grown an emotional shield years ago. The horror of violent death could still shock her, but it didn't prevent her from doing her job. "I'll be right over."

Granger was heading back up the street. A light drizzle drifted through the landscape of giant maple trees carrying the sodden, earthy smell of rain. Sidney saw the shine of moisture on his uniform.

"Anything?" she asked.

"Nothing new. Most neighbors didn't know Olivia. She kept to herself. The few that did corroborated what we already know. So far, all arrows point to Dr. Thornton."

Sidney had gotten the same response. "Yeah, and I still haven't been able to get hold of him. For now, we're done here. Selena told you about the missing jewelry?"

"Yeah, and about Abbott's threat." Anger momentarily flared in his eyes, but his voice was controlled.

"Do some quiet investigation in town. Go by Saffron's and check out their CCTV."

"Copy that." Granger's gaze dropped to the gift of Wilma's cookies she held in her hand. She folded back the foil and held out her hand. "Fresh from the oven."

He helped himself to two. "No one gave me any goodies."

"Did you smile?"

"I may have forgotten to."

"Smile. People talk more. And give you goodies."

His handsome face cracked into a grin.

"While you're in town, stop in at The Pink Pussycat. Try to keep your mind on business."

He gave her a little salute, a whole cookie shoved in his mouth, and mumbled, "That's the plan."

***

The rain fell softly, almost soundlessly, and occasionally, lightning pulsed in the zinc gray sky. Intermittently, the wipers swept away the rain jeweling Granger's windshield. Careful not to openly advertise that a cop was conducting police business at Saffron's Jewelry, he parked a half block away down Main Street. In a small town like Garnerville, gossip seemed to pass from mouth to mouth faster than by electronic transmission.

He entered the high-end store and removed his shades. Bling was everywhere, safely displayed behind glass cases lining three sides of the shop. Gold, diamonds, silver, and precious gems sparkled brilliantly under the soft ceiling spotlights. Sophia Gambolini stood behind a counter assisting a young couple. Dressed in expensive sportswear, they had the look of out of towners. All three turned and glanced at Granger, taking in his uniform, and Sophia smiled. "I'll be right with you."

Disinterested, the couple turned back to Sophia.

While growing up, Granger had known most of Garnerville's residents, at least by sight. But dozens of wealthy strangers had moved to town, buying lakeshore and mountain properties as second homes. Tourists crowded shops and cafes, which was great for the overall economy, but Granger believed the town had reached its maximum capacity for growth. James Abbott had other ideas. The wealthy CEO had swooped into the area like a vulture, building a monstrous vacation home in Maple Grove, and grabbing up every lake shore property he could get his hands on, so far only on the south shore.

Granger's parents had always been involved in the town's civic affairs, and now that his dad had Parkinson's disease, the responsibility of leadership had been passed to him. He and other concerned townsfolk were organizing, getting petitions signed by the hundreds, preparing to fight Abbott with every legal maneuver possible.

Anger tightened Granger's gut the more he thought of the wealthy interloper. Now Abbott was taking interest in his girlfriend's family, and threatening Molly's future at Alpine Ridge. Granger needed to get this jewelry issue resolved quickly and move the Becker family off Abbott's radar.

Putting a lid on his anger, Granger occupied himself by looking at engagement rings studded with diamonds. He imagined slipping one on Selena's left hand. Though they'd only been dating for six months, he knew he wanted to marry her. His parents had made a commitment for life, married for over three decades, and Granger was ready to do the same. Unknown to Selena, as a wedding gift, his parents were giving them a hundred-acre parcel of the family ranch. They could build their dream house, she could have all the animals she wanted, and Granger would be close enough to his ailing father to share the burden of his care. Hell, he'd marry Selena tomorrow. But she was as skittish as an unbroken filly, ready to take flight the second he made a wrong move. After what she'd been through with her ex, followed by her close call with a serial killer last fall, she needed time to heal, to learn how to trust a man again. Granger was patient. He knew how to be gentle, how to listen, how to intuit a woman's needs even when her verbal communication was cryptic. He had faith that if he didn't make any major missteps, Selena's trust in him would grow, and she would eventually come around.

Sophia handed back the man's credit card. All smiles, the couple walked past Granger, the young woman clutching a bag in her hand.

Sophia was an elegant woman in her sixties, with dark eyes and Mediterranean coloring. She locked the door and turned over the CLOSED sign in the window. Sophia and her husband opened the shop six years ago. After Antonio died of a cardiac arrest, Sophia pulled herself together and kept the business running. From the number of tourists marching in and out, she appeared to be doing quite well. Her business benefitted from the wealthy vacationers streaming into town, yet she was one of the most passionate members of the anti-growth movement. Her son, an ivy league lawyer, was on their advisory team.

Sophia turned to Granger with a stricken look on her face. "Am I in trouble for selling that jewelry to Ray Abbott?"

"No. Of course not. You did nothing wrong."

Looking tense, she shoved her hands into the pockets of her sweater. "James is not the type of man you want to get on the wrong side of."

"Don't worry about Abbott," he said. "Let's just get his father's jewelry back. Think carefully, Sophia. Was anyone else in the shop while they were here?"

She nodded. "A few people wandered in and out. No one I recognized. Tourists."

"What about outside? Anyone hanging around?"

"There are always people on the sidewalk, Granger. I really didn't pay that much attention. But I have security cameras. Inside and out."

"Good. I'm going to need those DVDs. I'll review them at the station."

"Let me get them for you." Sophia left the room and returned minutes later with the DVDs in hand. "Ray and Molly got here around ten-thirty. They stayed about a half hour. Such a dear, sweet couple. I didn't have a clue they were impaired. He's so upbeat. So unlike his son."

"A heart beats in his chest, you mean?"

She smiled thinly. "Exactly."

CHAPTER TEN

SIDNEY CROSSED THE LOBBY of the small community hospital to the elevator and descended to the basement. Her footsteps sounded hollow in the tiled hallway as she passed the open door of the forensic lab. Inside, Stewart Wong was at his workstation, his head bowed over a microscope.

An astringent chemical odor reached her nostrils as she pushed through one of the double doors and entered the morgue. The spotless room was equipped with cold storage compartments, a cleanup area, and two stainless-steel slabs in the middle of the room. One was currently occupied by the body of Olivia Paisley.

Wearing green scrubs and nitrile gloves, Dr. Linthrope was sewing the post-mortem incisions with thick twine using standard baseball-style stitching. The two arms of the "Y" ran from each shoulder joint and met at mid-chest, with the stem running down to her pubic region.

"Hello, Doc," Sidney said, getting a closer look. The side of Olivia's face that had been attacked by crows looked like something out of a horror movie. Her colorless body was now an empty shell, drained of blood, stripped of larynx, organs, and brain. Olivia obviously had been devoted to staying physically active. Her limbs were toned and well-muscled.

"Ah, Chief Becker," the doctor said with his normal good cheer. "Just finishing here." He stripped off his gloves and disposed of them in the hazardous waste bin. "I have some interesting findings. As suspected, the gunshot wound was the cause of death. A .22 round can kill, though unreliably. In this case, most of the bullet's inertial energy was expended penetrating the skull. Not having enough energy to penetrate the other side, the bullet bounced around inside the cranium, causing extensive damage to her brain." He pushed his wire-rimmed glasses higher on his nose. "That isn't her only injury." Linthrope turned Olivia's head to the left, and then to the right, revealing regions of extreme swelling and discoloration. "She has contusions and abrasions of the scalp which you can clearly see in these areas where I've shaved her hair. Her fractures are complex, suggesting a lot of force, and multiple impact points."

"Consistent with someone slamming her head against the hardwood floor?"

"Yes. Indeed."

"Any sign of sexual assault?"

"Not that I could see. There's no bruising or tearing. I swabbed for fluids and lubricants. We also found debris under her fingernails. It could be skin tissue from the suspect. We'll see what comes back from the lab." Linthrope walked over to a countertop, picked up an evidence bag and handed it to her. "Check out Ms. Paisley's personal effects."

Inside was a Cartier watch, a diamond ring, and a gold chain with a diamond pendant shaped like a heart. "These look valuable. Money and other valuables were left in her house. Burglary obviously wasn't the motive. His intent was murder. And he made fast work of it. He was only there for twenty minutes."

"Plenty of time to kill her," Linthrope said.

"The message he put in her mouth speaks of revenge. Slamming her head against the floor suggests a lot of pent up rage."

"Revenge is certainly a force for violence," Linthrope agreed.

"He shoved the wadded note in her mouth to degrade her. He made her pay. But for what? What did this woman do to him to trigger such violence?"

"The million-dollar question." Linthrope leaned against the counter and crossed his arms, looking relaxed. "How'd he get into her house?"

"He probably came in through an unlocked back door. He attacked her from behind while she was eating dinner. She put up a hell of a struggle." Sidney's eyes met his. "What's her height and weight?"

"Five feet eight inches. One hundred and forty pounds."

Linthrope lifted his brows in inquiry.

"Tall for a woman. She looks physically fit. Our suspect has to be pretty strong." Sidney was quiet for a long moment, thinking. Dr. Thornton was around six foot two. In good shape. Certainly capable of overpowering Olivia. "The killer managed to enter, commit murder, and cart Olivia's body out without being seen. He blatantly parked in her driveway, like he didn't care if his truck was seen."

He looked thoughtful, his bushy white brows knitting together. "Or he was driven by impulses he couldn't control."

"Evidence points to her ex-husband. But the killer could also be someone she worked with as a social worker. She received ominous threats a few years back. Removing children from abusive parents, some with crippling addictions, can leave bitter feelings behind."

"Not easy working with families in crisis."

Sidney cleared her throat. "When will we have results from the lab?"

He shrugged. "Not sure. Stewart can tell you more precisely."

"Thanks, Doc. I'll go see what he has for me." Sidney walked down the hall to the lab and found Stewart at his workstation writing reports. "Hey, Stewart."

He looked up and nodded toward the table in the corner. "Pull up a chair."

They both seated themselves.

Stewart leafed through a sheaf of printouts and pushed a page across the table to her. "Toxicology report. No drugs. No alcohol. Miss Squeaky Clean." While she read the report, he added, "No prints were found on the coin in her pocket. It was wiped clean, which suggests the killer placed it there, not the victim."

"Did you identify it?"

"No. Nothing like it in the system. The lab might have better luck." He placed another printout in front of her. "I ran our suspect's boot prints through the database. You've got yourself a pretty classy killer. The manufacturer of his hiking boots is Vitalia. A designer out of Tuscany. The price of their footwear starts at a grand and goes up from there. Our suspect's boots are part of the Tuscany Royal line." Stewart slid a color printout across the desk. "This is from the website."

Sidney looked at the photo and read the ad copy beneath it. "Camel leather. Impressive. High end. Something a doctor could afford."

"But then again, he could have gotten them at a thrift store."

"True, but if we bring in a suspect wearing these boots, the chance of him being the killer is pretty damn high. All we have to do is find him. When will we have results from the lab?"

'Don't know. They're backed up. Olivia's house is being processed. Whatever samples are being collected will also go to the lab. Should get results over the next few days."

Sidney's frustration built as she thought of the evidence sent to the lab, including the cigarette butt, possible urine sample, and the note found in Olivia's mouth. "Dammit."

Stewart arched a brow.

"It's damn irritating that critical evidence that could ID our suspect is just sitting there. And we're forced to wait."

Stewart sighed. "That's the name of the game. Pick a number. Then hurry up and wait."

"In the meantime, this guy could kill again."

They sat in silence for a moment, Sidney stewing in her exasperation.

Stewart's fingers drummed the table for a moment, then he scraped back his chair and walked to his workstation. "I know a guy who knows a guy. I'll make a call. See if I can put a rush on the cigarette butt, at least."

"Thanks, Stewart," she beamed him a smile. "Maybe it'll be my lucky day."

CHAPTER ELEVEN

THE RAIN FELL in hard, fat droplets, sluicing down the windshield and dancing on the pavement. The wind had picked up, as well, and Granger's truck shuddered under the impact. Through the rain-mottled glass, The Pink Pussycat looked like it might be a European tea shop with its cottage style architecture, lead paned windows, and colorful flower boxes. The front lawn was a whimsical maze of topiaries carved into animals—a bear, a rabbit, a mouse. The sex shop did a bustling business and the ten-car parking lot was full.

Granger hurried inside. Shoppers, mostly women, milled about, browsing through racks of sexy apparel and filmy lingerie. Some perused shelves stocked with oils, creams, and colorful packages of condoms. A few women shot him curious glances. He felt a little bit out of place in his uniform and position of authority. While craning his neck to spot the owner, he nearly knocked over a headless manikin wearing a transparent bra and panties.

He spotted Bridget helping a couple in an adjoining room that was stocked with an impressive array of sex toys. Trim and leggy, she wore a Catwoman costume that fit like the skin on a hot dog, leaving little to the imagination. He couldn't help but wince, thinking of Molly parading downtown in the same outfit. Granger and Bridget had been classmates at Garnerville High School. Back then, she went by her birth name, Penny Wilcox, and she had been a quiet bookworm with thick glasses and limp brown hair. At eighteen, she went to Paris as an exchange student. She returned four years later, reinvented as Bridget Martine, sporting a sexy new look and a sexy new husband, Pierre Martine.

Granger found Pierre behind the counter assisting a lanky young man with a flaming red mohawk. Pierre wore a black leather vest over his bare chest, a silver-spiked dog collar, and black leather chaps over his skintight jeans. Handcuffs hung from his belt and fake tattoos of busty women decorated his muscled arms. Pierre handed a bag to the young man, then smiled at Granger with a flash of impossibly white teeth. "Ah, Officer Wyatt," he said with a heavy French accent, reading Granger's name tag. "You got my message."

Granger arched his brows. "What message?"

Pierre frowned slightly. "The message I left at the station."

"Sorry. We've been busy with a big case. What message?"

"About the jewelry."

"You have the diamond jewelry?"

"Yes, of course. The older couple left it here." Pierre opened a drawer and pulled out a small box. Inside, a diamond ring and bracelet sparkled brilliantly.

Granger sighed his relief. "Where was it?"

"The woman left it in the dressing room. Fortunately, Bridget found it before a customer did. Who knows what a stranger would have done. We have things go missing all the time."

"Have you reported the thefts?"

"Too small to report. Five dollars here, ten dollars there. It's an expense we have to absorb."

"Thanks for taking care of this, Pierre." Granger shoved the jewelry box into his breast pocket. "If you catch someone in the act of stealing, contact us. Next time call 911. Those calls, we always get."

"I'll do that."

Granger turned and bumped into a pretty young woman standing directly behind him. "Sorry."

"No problem, officer," she said with a flirtatious smile. Her eyes scanned him from head to toe. "I like the uniform. Very convincing. That gun looks real."

Granger's face warmed. "It is a real gun, ma'am. I'm a real cop. Have a good day." Dodging her, he left the shop, his mind on work, ignoring the rain. He thought about all the time and stress that could have been avoided if someone had returned Pierre's call this morning. He climbed into his truck and called Chief Becker.

She answered after one ring. "Yeah, Granger."

"I've got the jewelry."

"Fantastic."

"Pierre left a message at the station this morning. Too bad no one returned that call."

"Yeah, well, we've been a little busy. That's the reality of being understaffed. The lab is backed up, too. Seems to be an epidemic."

"Something's gotta give, Chief. We need more manpower. Hope it doesn't take a casualty to get our elected officials to take notice."

"I'll bring it up, again, at the next council meeting. Come back to the station and put that jewelry in the safe. Call Abbott. Tell him we're returning the jewelry to Ray tomorrow. It was charged to his card. It's his property."

"He ain't gonna like that."

"Tell him to come talk to me. Then I can throw some questions at him about his threats to Selena."

"I'm on it, Chief."

***

As Sidney disconnected, the storm hit with a vengeance. Booming thunder walloped the sky and rain slashed her office windows. Above the roar she heard a sharp knock on the frame of her door. Swiveling around, she saw Darnell standing in the doorway, and waved him in.

"It's really coming down out there," he said, hands resting on his duty belt.

"Pigs and cows." The window shuddered from the impact of a strong gale and the lights in the room blinked on and off. "Hope the town doesn't lose power. What's up?"

"I spoke to one of Dr. Thornton's colleagues at the hospital. I found out he's up at the monastery."

"The Buddhist monastery on Elderberry Ridge?"

"Yes, ma'am. He lives there part-time. He's training to be a monk."

"For real?"

"For real."

She shook her head. Truth was stranger than fiction. "Good job. He's our main suspect."

"Should we head up there, Chief?"

"In this weather? Hell no. It's miles of dirt road, which will be turning into mud. I need you to rustle up our reserve officers. Everyone needs to be out on patrol tonight. We're going to have cars in ditches, trees down on roads, fender benders. It's going to be a long night."

Granger paused in her doorway in a dripping slicker. "Abbott's bringing Ray in tomorrow. The jewelry's in the safe."

"Don't bother taking off that slicker. We're all heading out into the storm."

***

Selena accompanied Ray and Molly to the movie room that featured four rows of cushioned seats, a big screen TV, and free popcorn. Dirty Harry was the selected film. Ray knew most of the lines, and he wasn't shy about reciting dialogue right along with Clint, using an array of different accents. He was highly entertaining. Molly and Selena laughed through most of the movie. When they came out of the theater it was 4:00 p.m. "Will you join us for dinner?" Ray asked Selena. "Starts at 4:30."

"Happily," Selena said. "I'm going to run home and get out of these yoga clothes. I can only take Spandex for so long." Outside, rain snapped off the pavement, plinked the hoods on cars, and carried the faint odor of ozone. Lightening cracked open the sky followed by the distant boom of thunder. Selena stepped into the torrent and was soaked by the time she reached her Jeep. When she returned to Alpine Ridge a half hour later, she was comfortably dressed in jeans and an oversized green sweater that came to mid-thigh.

As soon as she entered the dining room, Selena spotted Molly, seated at a new table on the north end of the room, facing the lobby. She could just barely see the back of Ray's head. He was sitting at the south end of the room, facing the courtyard. About twenty tables filled the floorspace between them, each seating two to four people.

Plastering a fake smile on her face, Selena seated herself next to her mother.

After greeting Selena with a radiant smile, Molly's gaze swept over her two new tablemates. To her left sat a scrawny man wearing a turtle-neck sweater and a ball cap that read WWII Veteran. Across the table sat a woman with thinning hair and translucent, milky-white skin. She wore a bib with teddy bears and bunnies on it.

"Who are you?" Molly asked the man in a mildly accusing tone.

"I'm Major Fred," he said congenially. "This is my nurse, Tricia. Ready for rations, Tricia?"

The old woman nodded. "I want soup."

"Where's Clarence?" Molly asked, frowning. "Why are you in his seat?"

"This is my seat," Major Fred said huffily. Spots of color bloomed on his pale cheeks.

"You're at the wrong table," Molly insisted, her voice rising.

He shot Molly an irritated look. "No, ma'am. I've sat here for fifty years. Since the end of World War II. Right Tricia?"

The old woman nodded. "I want soup."

Molly locked eyes with Selena and her voice pitched a few decimals higher. "Where's your father?"

Selena recognized the symptoms of an escalating emotional event. She searched her mind for the best response before Molly reached the tipping point. "It's okay, Mom. Dad's just running an errand." Lame.

Molly's frown deepened. "But he was just here, in the lobby."

Spotting Molly's distress, Riley made her way to their table and said brightly, "We have meatloaf, tonight, Molly. Your favorite. With gravy and mashed potatoes."

"I want soup," Tricia said.

"Okay, Trish. What about you, Major Fred?" Riley asked, not losing her cheerful stride. "Want the meatloaf?"

He glanced warily at Molly. "We have an enemy at the table. A femme fatale."

"Where's Clarence?" Molly asked, her voice vibrating, tipping upwards in volume. She rolled back her chair and stood scanning the dining room. Selena rose with her. She and Riley took positions on each side of Molly.

"He's in his room," Riley said sweetly, putting a gentle hand on Molly's arm. "Let's go visit him, okay?" Selena took her other arm and they tried to steer her away from the table.

"Clarence!" Molly wrenched herself free, her voice in full panic mode. "Clarence!"

The soft murmur of voices in the dining room ground to a halt and graying heads turned in their direction. At the end of the room, Ray turned in his seat wearing a concerned look on his face. He rose to his feet with unusual grace for a man his age.

"There he is!" Molly cried. She half marched, half jogged across the room, weaving around tables. Physically, she was in excellent condition. "Clarence!"

Riley and Molly followed, matching her stride. Heads in the room swiveled to follow their passage.

"There you are, my angel." Ray put a protective arm around Molly's waist and pulled her close. "I wondered what happened to you."

Molly's eyes were moist. "I was so worried."

"There, there. It's all right." Ray's voice was quiet, almost a murmur. "Did they put you at the wrong table, too?"

Molly sniffed and nodded, her normally sweet expression serious and intense.

Observing his tenderness and her mother's immediate, calm response, Selena was awash with shame. Every day, Molly struggled to hold on to bits of memory that slipped through her fingers like sand. Selena detested dishonesly, yet here she was, deceiving the most innocent of people.

"Riley said you were in your room," Molly said. "Selena said you were running an errand. But you're here in the dining room. It's very confusing."

A muscle worked in Ray's jaw and his eyes hardened as his gaze landed on Selena. "Why did you tell your mother I wasn't here? Why would you deliberately mislead her?"

She took a deep breath and let the air out slowly. "A mistake."

"What's the meaning of this?" A scowl darkened Ray's handsome features. "What are you two playing? I demand an explanation!"

It didn't sound like Ray was quoting movies. Instead, Selena caught a glimmer of the powerful businessman he once was, taking control of a bad situation. Selena's natural impulse was to make a full confession, to inform Ray that his son was the instigator.

Riley piped up first, saying gently, "I'm so sorry for putting you at the wrong table, Molly. I promise, it won't ever happen again."

The entire staff had been given instructions to keep the couple apart. Riley was ignoring orders. And rightly so. It was unethical to expect caregivers to participate in deceitful behavior. Especially behavior that clearly hurt their patients.

"You didn't answer my question," Ray said sternly.

Selena's stomach tightened, and again she was tempted to blurt out the truth.

"It came from management, sir," Riley said.

"Management?" Ray looked thoughtful, as though he was weighing the information over in his mind, then his gaze sharpened on her. "Do you want to know who the boss is here, Riley? I am. I pay the bills. I pay your salary. I make my own rules about how I choose to live here. And the same goes for Molly. If anyone messes with her again, someone's head is going to roll."

"Yes, sir. I completely understand."

After a tense silence, Ray turned to Molly and his expression softened. He pulled out a chair for her. "Have a seat, my dear."

"Are you staying, Selena?" Molly smiled sweetly. It appeared all was right with the world again. "I'd like you to."

"Of course, Mom," Selena said, infusing brightness into her voice. "Thanks for your help, Riley."

"I'm off in ten minutes," Riley said. "Looks like everything's under control. For now." She smiled at Ray and gently touched Molly's shoulder as she said her goodbye. Clearly, she felt great affection for the couple.

A rolling boom of thunder drew everyone's attention to the windows. The view of the courtyard was obscured by rain slashing the glass. The storm drummed the roof. The lights flickered off and on and a collective gasp went up from the residents. After a long moment of silence everyone resumed eating. Molly's eyes were locked on the windows. Ray squeezed her hand. "You okay?"

"I'm worried about Sidney," Molly said. "She's a cop. She's probably out there in the storm."

"I'll go by the station, Mom, and drop off some dinner," Selena said. "I'll make sure she's all right."

"Thank you, Selena." Molly's expression relaxed.

"The weather report said the storm will peter out tonight. Tomorrow will be a warm, sunny day."

Molly smiled.

Thank god the weather was changing for the better. Selena intended to drive up to the monastery with Lalisa in the morning. She looked forward to watching the best young archers in Bhutan practice their sport. A good way to clear her head after the day's heightened drama.

CHAPTER TWELVE

FEELING AS MISERABLE as a wet dog, Sidney sloshed through numerous puddles to reach her patrol truck parked in the middle of the road. The blue and red strobes reflected on the glistening asphalt. Water ran down her hooded yellow slicker as she revved up the engine and switched on the wipers. For a minute she watched the work crew laboring in the shimmering rain. The situation was under control. Chainsaws were growling as they cut through the second half of a giant fir tree that fell across Main Street. One lane was now completely cleared. For the last hour she and Amanda had stood in the downpour detouring cars to side streets. Thankfully, the brunt of the storm had passed. The gale force wind had weakened, and the rain was down to a drizzle.

The clock on the dash read 10:15 p.m. At this time of night, traffic was at a minimum. Businesses had closed up shop except for two bars at the other end of town. Darnell was wrapping up a two-car collision with minor injuries. Three reserve officers were working on other incidents, mostly cars stuck in mud.

Sidney headed back to the station, buzzed herself into the building, and peeled off her slicker. Amanda slogged in right behind her and hung her dripping slicker next to Sidney's. They had already put in a twelve-hour shift, fatigue was setting in, and the night was young.

"Let's get some hot coffee and thaw out," Sidney suggested.

"Best idea I've heard all evening," Amanda said. "Hope some cookies are left. I'm starving."

They'd had no time for dinner.

A surprise waited in the conference room. A note from Selena was taped to the fridge. *Heat up for 15 minutes in the microwave. Enjoy!*

Sidney pulled out a huge rectangular casserole dish and stripped back the foil. Lasagna! "Wow. It suddenly feels like Christmas. Selena's lasagna is from my mom's old recipe. Melts in your mouth."

Amanda said. "Let's nuke that baby, before I'm forced to eat it cold."

Fifteen minutes later they were slapping hot gooey cheesy squares on their paper plates. The smell in the room reminded Sidney of home when her whole family lived together. Sitting down with her meal, she dialed 9-1-1.

Jesse answered. "9-1-1. What's your emergency?"

"We need help in the conference room," she said in a tense tone.

"Right away, Chief." Jesse's eyes widened behind his glasses when he burst into the room and spotted the lasagna. "Smells great. I'm starving."

"Grab a plate. Help yourself."

Sidney was on her second helping when Granger sauntered in, his face and hair dripping. "Boo-yah! Whose fairy godmother dropped by?"

"That would be Selena."

Granger needed no invitation. He crossed the room, dished out a manly portion, and joined them at the table. Drops of water slid from his hair down his face and plopped on the table.

"Don't you believe in using the hood of your slicker?" Jesse asked.

"Sometimes I forget. I get busy," Granger said out of one side of his mouth, his cheeks packed with food. "I grew up ranching. I've helped deliver calves in the middle of the night in rain, snow, hail, you name it. Weather doesn't faze me much."

"Good. Cause you just volunteered to respond to the next car stuck in mud," Sidney said with a grin.

Granger shoved another forkful of food into his mouth and made the okay sign with his free hand.

Rancher. Marine. A good man to have on the job, Sidney thought. And in the family, too, if Selena ever came around.

***

Arriving home after midnight, Sidney brushed her teeth, peeled off her clothes, and yanked a nightgown over her head. That used up the little bit of energy she had on reserve and she plopped into bed, useless. Still chilled to the bone from working out in the damp cold, she listened to the rain softly drum the roof while waiting for sleep.

Her phone buzzed on the nightstand. It was her boyfriend, David. The fifth call that day that went unanswered. Eight months ago, when she walked into David's art studio to seek help on a murder case, she had no idea her life was about to radically change. His expertise in art symbology uncovered an important lead in the case. Their immediate attraction to each other evolved into a passionate love affair. They met most afternoons at his house on the lake, for lunch, sex, and privacy, while his son was at school. This morning, she had fired off a three-word text, "Can't meet today."

David's twelfth hour call wasn't unusual. He routinely called at the end of her shift to say goodnight. She slid her finger across the screen and murmured. "Hey, David."

"You okay?" he asked. "I've been calling all day. I had to talk to Winnie to learn you're still alive."

"I'm alive, just barely. Sorry I didn't call. We had a homicide, first thing. Kept us on the move all day."

"A homicide?"

"Yeah. A woman was found dead in a field."

"Any leads?"

She stifled a yawn. "Nothing to run with. Then we were out in the storm all night. I feel like a drowned rat."

"A stressful day. Want me to pop over and give you a massage?"

"So sweet." Memories of yesterday's lovefest warmed her, and she indulged in a moment of wistful yearning. "But your talent would be wasted. You'd be working on a corpse."

"Romantic thought."

"Honestly, David. I'm a hair away from being dead to the world. Catch you mañana?"

"Mañana," he said softly.

CHAPTER THIRTEEN

WITH HIS FEET spread apart in a solid stance, Karune gripped the center of the bow with his left hand and held it at arm's length in front of his face. The three middle fingers of his right hand held the end of the arrow in place while pulling back the string until it was taut.

The early morning quiet was abruptly shattered. A throng of crows shot up screaming from the treetops. He flinched as he released the arrow. It sliced through the air wildly off course, sailed high above the target, and disappeared into the forest behind the range.

Karune turned sharply and peered through the tunnels of shadow and sunlight between the trees. Barely discernible stood a dark figure of a man, watching him. Silent. Motionless. Abruptly, the man vanished.

A chill pricked Karune's scalp. Who was this man? This trespasser? What was he doing here at this early hour, in this remote location in the Oregon mountains? No one was allowed on grounds without an invitation. Karune scanned the expanse of lawn leading up to the old Buddhist monastery on the crest of the hill, half concealed by giant oaks and maples. The only movement came from the multitude of colorful prayer flags fluttering in the wind.

No one else was around. No one else had witnessed the trespasser. The other boys were asleep on their cots, still recovering from their journey from their tiny village in Bhutan. If the monks had not graciously offered to host them they would not have been able to come to Oregon to compete.

Karune barely slept. Though small in stature, and the youngest of the boys aged twelve to fourteen, he was the most gifted archer, and the expectations of his village weighed heavily on his shoulders. At the crack of dawn, he had hurriedly dressed in his hand-woven tunic and slipped away from the dormitory to practice. An hour had passed. The sun, just skimming the treetops, was now bright in his eyes.

Karune considered fleeing back to the massive stone walls, but he needed to retrieve his arrow. His father's death left the family tight on money. To buy his bamboo bow and arrows, handmade by a master craftsman, his mother and sister had gone without necessities. The arrows were irreplaceable. The blessing of the head lama of his valley's dzong imbued them with magic. The arrows found their target as though propelled by radar.

Upon arrival two nights ago, the boys had been warned by an elderly monk not to leave the immediate grounds. It would be easy to become disoriented and lost. The looming forest frightened Karune. So lush. So thick and tangled. Filled with unfamiliar sounds and smells. A sharp contrast to the starkness of his village, where vistas stretched across many hills and valleys to the snow-covered peaks of the Himalayas.

Karune breathed deeply, summoning up his courage. What of the mysterious man? Surely if he stayed alert, and listened, he could locate his arrow quickly and run back to the safety of the range. With his bow and quiver slung over his shoulder, he used stepping-stones to get to the opposite bank of a rushing creek, then hiked into the towering trees. The air was cool, and the path was damp from the storm that swept through during the night. The trees glistened and the branches still dripped from the runoff. The air smelled of pine sap and mulch.

Certain he was in the area where his arrow landed, he left the path and trekked through the underbrush, following the curve of the creek. He folded back large wet leaves to view the forest floor and scanned the trunks of colossal trees.

He sensed rather than heard a presence behind him. Turning, he saw a tall grim man with a scarred forehead standing behind him, utterly motionless, long arms at his side. He had dark, matted hair, and wore dirty pants and a frayed flannel shirt. One sleeve was rolled up and Karune saw more scars spread over his forearm. The man's deep-set eyes seemed to look at him from another world.

Karune felt a deep stab of terror. Before he could react, the man tore the bow from his shoulder, then his fist smashed into his face. White-hot pain exploded behind his eyes. Karune stumbled and fell. Warm blood ran into his mouth and down the sides of his face. Daylight blinked on and off. He was vaguely aware of the man standing over him, lifting a weapon.

The man grunted, then crashed to the ground like a fallen tree. Somewhere an animal moaned. Or was he dreaming? Karune surrendered to a darkening void. The morning faded to black.

***

"Karune ...."

"Karune ...."

Faraway voices pulled Karune from a deep sleep. A throbbing pain in his skull pulsed down the back of his neck. His mouth felt dry and he craved a sip of water. Above were leafy branches and clear blue sky. What was this place? Where was he? He sucked in a ragged breath and tried to get his bearings. Then the memory of his attacker came crashing back. He jerked his head to the left, then to the right, but the strange man was nowhere in sight.

"Karune ...."

"Karune ...."

The voices were calling him. He sat up to a wave of dizziness. He wiped his mouth and blood smeared over the cuff of his tunic. His nose felt both tender and numb. Blood had congealed around his nostrils. His fingers moved over his cropped black hair and found a knot on the back of his skull, but no open wound.

"Karune ...."

"Karune ...."

The voices grew louder.

"Over here ...." he cried hoarsely. Gritting his teeth, he got to his feet holding onto a sapling for support. "I'm here." Feeling lightheaded, he watched three monks weave between the trees, their vibrant scarlet robes a vivid contrast to the green and brown of the forest.

Seeing the presence of the monks calmed him. Monks were the most revered men in Bhutan, next to the king. They lived austere lives devoted to spiritual practice. Karune felt a hot flush of shame for disobeying the head monk's order. He came into the forest alone and attracted bad karma to their holy grounds. He got what he deserved. Karune shuddered, remembering the vacant look in the stranger's eyes. More punishing, he had lost his most precious possession; his bow. Even as he felt the sharp pain of loss, he spotted the beautifully carved bow lying on the ground under fern leaves. Relief flooded his system.

The three men approached Karune. Like the monks of Bhutan, they had cleanly shaved faces and closely cropped hair. Two looked American and the third looked Bhutanese. The tallest of the three had blue eyes and fair hair.

"My name is Thomas," the tall monk said. He nodded at his companions. "That's Tashii and Sunni. Your nose is bleeding. I'm a doctor. I'm going to touch your face. Okay?"

Karune nodded.

The man put one hand under his chin and tilted his head back. Karune hissed out a breath when Thomas's fingers traced the outline of his nose.

"Sorry, son. I know it's tender. Good news. It's not broken. Now, follow my finger."

Karune did as he was told, his gaze locked on Thomas's finger as it slowly moved from side to side, then up and down. "Is your vision blurry?"

"No, sir."

The tall monk then examined the back of his skull.

Karune winced.

Thomas smiled kindly. "You have a nice lump, but it's not serious. We'll get an ice pack on it. Now, tell me what happened."

"A man hit me." Karune looked down, his face heating with shame. His eyes filled with tears and he trembled as he relived the attack.

"It's okay," Thomas said. "You're safe now. Tell me about this man."

"He was tall and dirty. He had scars on his arm and face. His eyes looked like a ghost. I heard him fall down. Then an animal started crying." He paused, trying to remember. "I may have been dreaming."

"Why were you in the forest?"

"I lost an arrow …."

The monk met his gaze and said gently, "I'm sorry the man attacked you, Karune. But understand, you did nothing wrong."

Karune sniffed and wiped his eyes, grateful he wasn't being scolded.

Thomas turned to the other monks and his blonde brows came together in a frown. "Sounds like the man was living in the wild."

"He wasn't in his right mind, that's for sure," Tashii said.

"Clearly," Thomas agreed. "Hmmm. I see your bow is still here. Sunni, why don't you start walking the boy back to the dzong. Tashii and I will scout around a bit."

Sunni had cropped red hair, green eyes, and fair skin covered with freckles. He smiled warmly, "Can you walk okay?"

"Yes. I think so."

"Easy does it." Sunni picked up the bow, took Karune by the arm and directed him back the way they came.

Seconds later, Tashii exclaimed in a shocked tone, "Over here, Thomas."

Karune stopped in his tracks and turned back. Partially hidden from view, the two men were at the creek pulling something out of the water. Thomas squatted for a long moment, then shook his head and stood. The two monks spoke quietly, then the tall monk caught up to Karune.

"It's the bad man, isn't it?" Karune asked. "He's dead?"

"I'm afraid so," Thomas said.

"Was it a tiger?"

Thomas said quietly, "We don't have tigers in Oregon. The man's time had come to pass into another world. His soul is now at peace." He directed his gaze at Sunni. "I'm going up ahead to notify the authorities. Make sure Karune gets a good breakfast, and an ice pack. Don't let him sleep. We need to make sure he doesn't have a concussion."

Sunni nodded. "I'll take good care of him."

With a last gentle glance over his shoulder, Thomas set off at a good jog, dodging trees, disappearing into the forest.

CHAPTER FOURTEEN

THE CELL PHONE buzzed on the nightstand and aroused Sidney from a deep, dreamless sleep. Reluctant to fully waken, she reached out and groped for the phone with her eyes closed. As police chief of her small town, she was always on call, and not answering wasn't an option.

The screen read 8:00 a.m. and the call was from her dispatcher. Groan.

"What's up, Jesse?" she asked hoarsely, blinking against a single shaft of light coming through the blinds.

"Sorry for the early call, Chief, but we have another homicide."

"Where?" She sat up, wide awake.

"Up at the monastery."

The monastery? "Who's the victim?"

"Appears to be a transient. He has a wound on his back. I just notified Dr. Linthrope. He and Stewart Wong will meet you at the station. A monk named Thomas called it in. He's waiting to guide you into the woods."

"Thomas Thornton?"

"Yes, ma'am."

Thomas Thornton! Hell of a coincidence. Two homicides in two days. The monastery was on the other side of Lake Kalapuya halfway up a mountain. The two victims were found miles apart, yet here he was, right in the middle of another murder. Never trust a coincidence as being random, her dad used to say. They often turned out to be important links in a murder case. "I need Amanda and Darnell up there, too. Also, a K-9 unit."

"I'll get right on it."

The only access to the monastery was a narrow, twisty, road. A good half hour drive. Sidney took a two-minute shower, pulled her hair into a ponytail, and dressed in a clean uniform. She added her armored vest and duty belt, then grabbed her gun off the nightstand and slipped it into its holster. Appropriately bulked up, she flew down the stairs. "Got coffee?" She bypassed Selena, who was sitting at the table reading the paper with Chili on her lap. The other three cats were catching sunbeams on the Asian carpet.

"Whoa there, cowgirl. Whose house is on fire?"

Sidney was already pouring coffee into her travel mug from a fresh pot. "Looks like we have another homicide. Up at the Monastery."

"For real?"

"For real." Sidney added milk to the mug and a whopping tablespoon of sugar, screwed on the top, and shook. Unlike Selena, who was a certified health nut, Sidney appreciated sugar and fat in her diet. Selena, she reasoned, ate enough fruit and veggies to last them both a lifetime.

"Who's the victim?"

"A man. Sounds like a vagrant."

"What's a homeless guy doing running around in the woods at the top of a mountain?"

"Not staying alive, obviously."

Selena tightened the belt on her chenille robe and trailed Sidney through the laundry room to the back door. "Lalisa and I are heading up there this morning."

"No. You're not. I'm conducting a murder investigation, not a field trip."

"We can lend a hand with the boys. Keep them calm."

"What boys?"

"The boys who live there. Hello. Training to be monks?"

Sidney drew a blank. "Didn't know there were minors up there."

"Lalisa's nephew is one of them. It's his birthday. You probably also don't know that the monastery is hosting an archery team from Bhutan. All boys. They'll be competing here in Oregon."

"Best if you don't come up."

"Hmmm. Sounds like you want to be the boss of me today."

"Don't." Sidney gave Selena a glance that held a warning. "A killer is running loose."

With a mischievous smile, Selena pulled an amethyst crystal on a silver chain from around her neck and tucked it into Sidney's breast pocket. "You've been working hard. You're stressed. This will protect you from psychic attacks and negative energy."

Sidney believed her bulletproof vest and Glock pistol would protect her, but she patted her pocket and smiled back. She gave Selena a quick hug before stepping outside into the brisk morning air.

***

Dr. Linthrope rode up Elderberry Road with Sidney, while Stewart

Wong followed in the Coroner van. Sidney heard gravel striking her wheel wells and the Yukon vibrated when hitting stretches of rutted road. The forest was thick and lush, arching over the road, and spring flowers burst in vibrant colors on the forest floor. A stunning nature outing even though the end game was a murder investigation.

After sharing the few facts she knew of the case, Sidney and Linthrope lapsed into silence, devouring cheese danishes the good doctor brought, and sipping coffee. The morning light haloed the doctor's electric hair and winked off his glasses. He wiped his hands with a napkin and shoved it into his takeout cup. "It's been a while since I've been up here. I always meant to come back, but you know, life gets in the way."

"You were up here removing a body?"

"Oh, no. Not business. It was personal. After Nora died …." Linthrope was quiet for a moment and Sidney waited politely. He was reliving memories he wasn't sure he wanted to share. During her tenure, she and the doctor had cultivated a respectful friendship. But he was from an older, more formal generation, where men had been taught to be strong, and not share their grievances. Linthrope had never invited her to call him by his first name.

He glanced out the window and continued. "After Nora died, I became despondent. My lifelong companion was gone, along with the life we built for forty-five years. Grief does inexplicable things to the psyche, Chief Becker." The doctor's expression was uncharacteristically somber. "I knew I needed to recalibrate. The world spins at a dazzling speed, and sometimes it seems we're barely holding on. Slowing down, focusing on the beauty of simple things, can be restorative. Coming up here for a meditation retreat was just what I needed."

"Sounds very peaceful."

"Oh, yes. It was definitely peaceful. The monks are accepting and nonjudgmental. Though I'm a Christian, I feel an affinity for their version of Buddhism. The purity of it. A doctrine of basic goodness. This sect was started by monks from Bhutan seventy years ago."

"Where's Bhutan?"

"In the Himalayas. A tiny country that was isolated from the rest of the world for hundreds of years. Unadulterated. Still mostly untouched by what corrupts societies elsewhere in the world."

"We could all use a dose of that." Sidney spotted a wooden archway up ahead and read the sign as they got closer: Elderberry Habitat of Peace and Divine Love.

Lining the road, dozens of colorful flags fluttered briskly in the wind.

"Prayer flags," Linthrope said. "It's their custom to write a prayer on a flag, then let the wind send it out into the world. They have these throughout Bhutan."

"Nice tradition," Sidney said, driving beneath the arch. The forest opened to a wide-open vista of hills and valleys, and far below, she could see Garnerville nestled in the foothills. Slow moving clouds cast massive shadows over the earth. The land was carved into a patchwork of farmland and flower gardens and men dressed in maroon robes with shorn heads tended the fields. In a grassy pasture, a monk rolled hay bales off the back of the truck to a herd of goats and horses. Several young monks smiled and waved as she drove by. Charmed, she waved back.

On the crest of the hill stood a solid two-story stone building that looked part fortress, part castle. It was protected by a massive stone wall and shaded by giant maples and oaks. They parked their vehicles in the lot and Dr. Linthrope and Stewart rolled a gurney out of the back of the van. Sitting on top was a folded body bag and Stewart's forensic kit.

A tall monk, fortyish, with cropped blonde hair and blue eyes, stepped from the shadows and approached them. He wore a maroon robe with a crimson wrap draped over one shoulder.

Thomas Thornton! On the drive over, Sidney had ruminated about how to handle him. As her prime suspect, he needed to be questioned about Olivia, but muddling the two murders would complicate matters. Better to deal with the one at hand, and then question him later about Olivia. In the interim, she'd catch him with his guard down and sneak in a few questions. "Hello, Dr. Thornton."

"Hello, Chief Becker." He shook Sidney's hand, and nodded to Linthrope and Wong, with whom he was well-acquainted. "Up here, please call me Thomas."

"So you're a monk?" Sidney asked. "You live up here part time?"

"Yes. On my days off. This is my other life. A way to de-stress from the ER."

"The ultimate escape. Been up here all week?"

"Yes."

"Quite a drive up here. You need good transportation to get up that road. You must have a truck."

"I do. But I rarely drive it. I use my motorcycle to get up and down. Much easier."

Hmmm. Thornton had an alibi. But was it bulletproof? Was someone else using his truck? A killer? Sidney would have to verify his alibi.

Stewart cleared his throat and shifted from foot to foot with obvious impatience. "Where's the crime scene, Doc?"

Thomas gestured toward the woods. "This way." He led them down the hill past the long stretch of lawn that was an archery range. They left the gurney at the edge of the woods, and then single file, entered the forest. Shafts of light fell through the leafy canopy, spring flowers and ferns grew vibrantly, and the air smelled of pine and mulch. Last night's storm left the forest damp with a scatter of puddles across the earth.

Thomas explained that a young boy on the archery team had been in the woods looking for a stray arrow. He was attacked by a strange man and knocked unconscious. The man was subsequently killed, but the boy had no recollection of how it happened. Thomas paused in a grove of towering ponderosa pines and pointed to a tree of enormous breadth that was surrounded by ferns and moss-covered rocks. "Karune was attacked at the base of that tree."

"Is he okay?" Sidney asked.

"Physically, yes," he said. "A terrible thing, though, his second morning in America, to have this experience."

"Of course."

"The body?" Stewart said.

"Over there by the creek, just beyond the tree. We found him face down in the water. I pulled him out and turned him over, but he was dead."

"Too bad you moved him," Stewart said in a disapproving tone. "You tampered with a crime scene."

"I did what doctors are trained to do," he said in his defense. "But we have a video. Tashii documented everything." Thomas pulled his phone from a pocket, brought up the video, and handed it to Sidney. Stewart and Linthrope stood on each side and they watched it together. The visual was clear. Tashii had kept the phone steady. The video showed the man's head and shoulders immersed in a calm inlet of the creek. Thomas gently pulled him onto the bank. Blood was spread over a large portion of the back of his shirt. Thomas turned him over. The victim's dark hair was slicked back, face white, lips blue. Thomas went through the motions of checking his vitals, then the video ended.

"This was helpful, Thomas," Sidney said. "We'll need a copy."

"Of course."

"We'll take it from here," Stewart said, looking impatient, clearly wanting to get to work.

"Two other officers should arrive shortly, and a K-9 unit," Sidney said.

He nodded. "I'll direct them in."

"Please don't leave the grounds. We need to talk."

Thomas nodded again and left.

All three donned gloves and began assessing what had happened. They located the smaller imprints of the boy in the moist debris, and the larger prints of the man, indicating where he had entered the grove and caught the boy by surprise.

Stewart squatted on his haunches, examining the ground at the base of the tree. "See this depression in the pine needles? Here's where the boy fell and hit his head. And here, just a few feet away, is where the man was attacked and hit the ground. There's a fair amount of blood." Wong paused to take photos, the flash illuminating the earth with bursts of light.

Sidney and Linthrope peered over his shoulder and saw blood smeared over the leaves.

"See these drag marks?" Stewart said. "He was injured, but he tried to get away, dragging his body through the brush." Stewart intermittently paused to place evidence markers and take photos. They moved slowly through sunlight and shadow, sidestepping the man's tortuous trail of crushed flowers and ferns. As they edged toward the creek, small creatures skittered away under the brush.

They reached the body on the creek bank just as the doctor had left him. He lay on his back, hands at his sides, face turned away. His gray streaked hair and soiled clothes were still wet. Flies had found their way to the blood-stained earth and buzzed noisily over the corpse.

After Stewart took pictures from several directions, Linthrope crouched over the man and turned his face up, looking for any sign of trauma. Sidney got her first good look at him—the scarred forehead, the deep-set brown eyes staring vacantly. Her breath caught. "Christ. I know him. This is Max Stevens. A private investigator."

Both men stared up at her with surprised expressions.

"How well did you know him?" Linthrope asked.

"He's a friend. We worked a case together last year. Before going private, he was a cop for twenty years." With a piercing sense of loss, Sidney remembered Max's professionalism and good-natured personality. "See those scars on his face and hands? He got those saving a mother and baby from a burning car. He was a good P.I. Specialized in missing persons."

"Sorry, Chief." Sympathy surfaced in the doctor's eyes behind the professional calm. "A shock to find a friend this way."

She nodded, swallowing hard.

"What was he doing up here in the woods, looking like a bum?" Stewart asked. "Why did he attack a kid?"

"Did he have emotional problems?" Linthrope asked.

"Not that I ever saw. But clearly, he wasn't in his right mind." Sidney exhaled sharply, thoughts circling in her mind, piecing together the events leading to the murder. "Who was the third person up here? The killer?"

"Maybe someone from the monastery," Linthrope said. "Defending the boy from Max."

"Maybe," she said.

"Well, let's see what killed him. Help me turn him on his side." Linthrope waved away the flies as they turned him. He lifted the victim's bloodstained shirt in the back, revealing an open penetrating wound just inside the right shoulder blade, about an inch wide. "Stab wound. Looks deep. He may have a collapsed lung." They gently laid him flat on his back again. "Most likely, cause of death is massive hemorrhaging. If drowning didn't kill him first."

"Why would he crawl into the creek?" Sidney mused out loud.

"Clearly, he wasn't in his right mind. Could be drug induced, or he was experiencing a psychotic episode. We'll find out more from a tox screen. As soon as the body is identified, we'll start the autopsy. Should have results later today." The doctor sighed. "Stewart, let's get him in the bag."

While they transferred Max to the body bag, Sidney started nosing around the base of the giant tree. She found more large impressions, probably made by Max, and the boy's smaller prints, but no prints from a third person. The knife may have been thrown from a distance. Even without prints, the K-9 unit should have no trouble picking up the killer's scent.

CHAPTER FIFTEEN

"HEY, CHIEF," Darnell's voice rang out. "We're here."

Darnell entered the grove with Amanda following right behind, a crime kit gripped in her hand. Their crisp uniforms stood in stark contrast to the peaceful nature setting. Both gazed past Sidney with open curiosity, their eyes landing on Stewart and Dr. Linthrope.

"I'm sorry to say the victim is someone we know," Sidney said quietly. "Max Stevens."

They both stood speechless, eyes widening. "The P.I.?" Amanda asked.

"Yeah."

Darnell shook his head, a bit dazed. "Jesus. Poor Cecille."

They had all worked on a case with Max last year. At its completion, they celebrated with a home cooked meal prepared by his wife of thirty years. Cecille was an upbeat, energetic woman who did a lot of volunteer work in town. They had two adult kids and three grandkids. Sidney's heart weighed heavily. Tragic news would be delivered today that would permanently alter the lives of Max's family.

"Where's the K-9 team?" Sidney asked. "We've still got a hot crime scene here. The killer might still be within catching distance."

"They're sending two dogs from Jackson. Thirty minutes out," Darnell said.

"Damn." With a suspect on the move, every minute counted.

"Ditto that. What can we do to help?" Amanda asked.

"Cordon off the area around this tree, all the way over to the body by the creek. Search the surrounding area for anything the suspect may have dropped."

"Will do." Amanda opened her kit and pulled out a roll of yellow crime scene tape.

"Darnell, let's help Stewart and the doc carry Max."

The four of them carried the body bag out of the woods and strapped it onto the gurney. Out in the full sun there was a discernible rise in temperature. The day was warming up. Squinting in the bright sunlight, Sidney pulled on her shades and the procession started up the hill. Red winged blackbirds swirled up from the trees along the creek, darting like arrows into the deep blue sky. The beauty of the place failed to lift Sidney's spirit. A good man, a good cop, had been killed under strange circumstances. Alone in the woods and out of his mind. Attacking a child. She was hung up by the suddenness of it, the senselessness. A family was about to go into mourning.

As she trekked up the hill, her skin crawled with the eerie feeling that a killer might be observing their ascent.

***

Thomas stood watching on the crest while the gurney was loaded into the van. Stewart and Dr. Linthrope climbed in and drove away. It unnerved Sidney how motionless he could be—a dark silent presence. The boys were no longer in the fields, and Sidney was thankful they didn't witness the removal of the body.

She called Granger, who was off duty. They'd both put in a lot of overtime yesterday and were the last ones on the job last night. This morning she allowed him to sleep in, but now she needed her whole team on board.

He picked up after three rings and answered sleepily, "Morning, Chief."

"We have another homicide, Granger."

"Jesus," he said, alert. "Where?"

"Up at the monastery."

"The monastery?" He paused a beat, letting it sink in. "You want me to come up?"

"Not yet. First, I need you to visit the victim's family. They need to know."

"Who's the victim?" he said with a hint of apprehension.

"Max Stevens."

Dead silence for several long moments. "Christ … Max?"

"I'm afraid so." Relaying tragic news to family members was an excruciating part of the job, and one that Sidney usually took upon herself. When the victim and his family were friends, it tore your heart out. "Sorry, Granger."

"No problem. I'll take care of it."

Sidney filled him in on the details of his death. "When you talk to Cecille, see if she knew what case Max was working on, and why he was up here. Also, ask if he was on any medication. She'll need to identify the body soon. Doctor Linthrope needs to start the autopsy."

"Got it."

Sidney clicked off and gestured to Thomas. "Do you mind answering a few questions?"

"Not at all."

She, Darnell, and Thomas moved out of the heat into the shade of a giant oak tree, seating themselves on wooden benches. In his monk garb, the doctor looked totally harmless. Handsome. Charming. But Sidney knew his true character. He had stalked Olivia and made her life miserable and he may have murdered her. But that homicide would have to be put on the back burner for now.

Darnell whipped out his notepad and pen and sat poised to take notes.

Sidney started off with innocuous questions. "How many people live up here?"

"Six adult monks, permanently. I'm part time," Thomas said. "We maintain the property and supervise and teach the students. Nine boys live here full time. Monks in training, ranging in age from nine to fifteen. Four are American, five are from other countries. I'm the only monk who leaves the grounds to go to work. The others go to town on occasion to buy supplies. And there's Chimi, the cook. We're currently hosting an archery team of eleven boys from Bhutan. They were all asleep when Chimi woke them for breakfast, except for Karune. His cot was empty. The cook promptly notified Tashii, who woke Sunni and me, and we set off looking for him."

"What time was this?"

"Seven. We got down there within minutes. The attack probably took place between six-thirty and seven."

"Who are the administrators?" Sidney asked.

"Wangchuck, our divine teacher, and head monk. Dorji is the main administrator. He runs things. Yeshey is his assistant. Handles the finances."

"Where do you fit in?"

"Definitely the bottom tier, with Tashii and Sunni. We've been here two years or less. We're novices." He half smiled. "Hopelessly ignorant. We go through the motions of spiritual practice every day, hoping some stray beam of enlightenment will fall upon us and lift us out of bondage."

Darnell stopped writing and looked up, "What do you mean by bondage?"

Thomas's blue eyes ignited with some inner passion and his voice warmed with sincerity. "Slavery to the senses. The cravings of the mind. The addiction to stimulation, be it from food, drink, drugs, sex, TV. Name your poison. Most people live their lives lurching from one moment of self-gratification to the next. Never realizing that true peace resides within."

"Tell me about Wangchuck," Sidney said, guiding him back to the case. She wanted answers. They were conducting a murder investigation, not attending a spiritual retreat.

"Wangchuck's been here since day one," Thomas said. "One of the original founders. The only one still living."

"From seventy years ago?"

"Oh, yes. He's ninety-two."

Sidney's skepticism edged into her voice. "And he's the head guy?"

"He's quite capable." Thomas smiled, a mysterious light in his eyes. "The mind is stronger than the physical body."

Ignoring Thomas's philosophical waxing, Sidney immediately ruled the old man out as a suspect. "Is the cook a monk?"

"Chimi? No. But she is a Buddhist. She's been here for over thirty years. She's approaching sixty and is close to retiring, and she has health issues."

"What kind of health issues?"

"Arthritis. Her hips, her knees. They're giving out on her. We take turns helping her with meals and cleanup."

Another suspect ruled out.

Watching Thomas openly, letting him see her do it, Sidney announced she had identified the dead man. "He's a private investigator. Max Stevens. A personal friend."

Thomas blinked and diverted his eyes for a moment, then met her gaze. A dull luster replaced the spiritual glow in his eyes. "My condolences," he said.

"Did you know him?"

His eyes narrowed. "No."

"Is there any reason why a P.I. might be investigating someone up here?"

He cleared his throat. "Not that I know of."

"Does anyone have a police record?"

Thomas hesitated for several seconds before answering. "I, uh, I can't answer that. I don't know everyone's personal history."

Couldn't answer, or wouldn't? Thomas was covering for someone, or himself. Sidney arched an eyebrow, giving Thomas her best clinical stare. When she gave space to someone who was reluctant to speak, they usually got nervous and started filling in the blanks.

It was quiet, except for the scratching of Darnell's pen on his pad.

"I suppose it's possible someone may have a criminal background," Thomas finally said. "People come to this way of life from different paths."

"Anyone you might suspect?"

Looking as though he were deep in thought, Thomas flicked a bit of dust from his robe. "I really can't say."

"What I'm going to need, Thomas, is a list with the full legal names and birth dates of all the monks who live here. Not their Buddhist monikers. And their social security numbers. We'll have to run background checks. I need to talk to all of them. They'll have to account for their movements this morning."

Thomas's shoulders visibly stiffened. "You can't possibly think one of the monks had anything to do with the murder?"

"This is standard procedure. We need to rule everyone out."

"You're on the wrong track, Chief. I know these people. No one here is a killer."

"Then they have nothing to worry about." She held his gaze and saw something in his eyes she didn't like. A glint of anger. Then it was gone. He attempted a smile, but it didn't look genuine.

"I'll get you a printout of the names from the office."

"My officers will want to talk to the boys who live here. Several were out in the fields this morning. Maybe one of them saw something. As their guardians, one of you will have to be present."

"I can arrange that. They'll be finishing their morning meditation in a few minutes." He gestured toward the entrance. "Let's head into the prayer room."

Amanda was walking briskly up the hill. They waited for her to join them.

***

Thomas led them to a tall wooden door set into the mossy stone wall that encircled the front of the monastery. He punched numbers into a code box and the gate clicked open. They stepped into a large courtyard bordered on two sides by a terraced building. Sidney had the heady feeling of stepping into another world. Gone was the exterior appearance of a Catholic monastery of European origin. Here the roofline had been modified to look like a Tibetan temple. Ornately carved woodwork disguised the original stone walls and was painted with mosaics of dragons, birds, flowers, and animals. The muted earth tones blended well with the surrounding forest. A soft drone of chanting voices poured out into the courtyard, accompanied by drumming and cymbals.

They crossed the area to a plain wooden door and Thomas removed his sandals. "If you'll wait here for a minute, I'll get a printout of those names for you." He disappeared inside, returned a few minutes later, and handed the list to Sidney. She folded it into a square and tucked it into her pocket. Then he led them to another door, this one taller and intricately carved. He opened it and stepped to one side. "Shall we?"

Following his example, they removed their shoes and stepped past him. After her eyes adjusted to the dim lighting, Sidney saw she was in a large, narrow room. Down the middle aisle, two rows of boys sat cross-legged on mats facing each other with their eyes closed, reciting Buddhist mantras. A few youths beat drums and chimed cymbals. The hypnotic chanting reverberated through the room and wisps of smoke from incense hung in the air like mist. The effect was mystical, otherworldly. At the end of the aisle, an old monk sat on a raised dais, his withered face and neck shrunken into his robes. He had to be Wangchuck. Next to him, on a lower dais, sat another monk, an American man.

Then the chanting stopped.

In the sudden, stark silence, the youths opened their eyes and began to get to their feet. Like boys anywhere, they broke into small groups, talking and joking and laughing. The youths at the end of the room wore muted knee-length tunics, and several young monks in red robes gathered around them, peppering them with questions. When she looked for Wangchuck the dais was empty, and the American monk stood against the wall, expressionless, silently watching.

"The boys in the tunics are the archery team," Thomas said. "They're revered like baseball players are idolized here."

"Which one is Karune?"

"He's not here. He's resting."

Thomas gestured and the American monk padded over to join them. "This is Yeshey," Thomas said to Sidney. "He'll sit in with the boys during your questioning."

Yeshey, the financial administrator, nodded but said nothing. He was a slip of a man, maybe five feet-five, early thirties, with a slender build, green eyes, and delicate features.

Thomas addressed everyone in the room. "May I have your attention?"

Young faces turned to Thomas and the officers with open curiosity.

"I have sad news," Thomas announced. "A man died in the forest this morning behind the archery range."

His words were met with looks of surprise and concern.

"Who died?" An older boy asked, dark eyes open wide.

"No one from the monastery. The man lived in Garnerville."

Expressions of relief passed over their faces.

"These police officers are from Garnerville." Thomas introduced them, gesturing to Darnell and Amanda. "Officer Wood and Officer Cruz want to speak to everyone except the archery team. I know you boys are eager to go practice on the range. Now would be a good time. Please wait for me in the courtyard and I'll take you down. These officers are our guests. Please treat them with courtesy and answer their questions as best you can."

"A word of caution," Sidney added. "While we are conducting our investigation over the next few days, please don't go into the woods. Stay in groups outside. Keep an eye on each other."

The room broke out in soft murmurs as the archery team padded outside. When the door closed behind them, the remaining eight boys gathered closer, their beautiful crimson robes blending together, their well-scrubbed faces curious and alert. Several smiled shyly when Sidney caught their eye. The boys immediately gathered around Amanda and Darnell, showing interest in their duty belts. Smiling, good-natured, Darnell and Amanda gave them a quick show and tell, pointing out their handcuffs, radio, pepper spray, taser, and things they carried in the leather pockets. A good icebreaker.

"Robocop!" one youngster said.

"Go ahead. Make my day." An older boy said with a German accent.

The others laughed.

Obviously, the boys weren't cut off from American movies.

Thomas turned to Sidney. "I'll take you to the adult monks." He guided her through an arched doorway, down a long hall lined with doors, and into a large, sunny room that overlooked the valley below. Silk tapestries hung on the walls depicting dragons and images of Buddha, and richly colored handwoven rugs covered the wood planked floors.

Wangchuck sat cross legged at the end of the room, his withered arms and big knuckled hands holding a worn, leather-bound book. Thick glasses were perched on his nose and a tea pot and cup sat on the low table in front of him. Dorji sat beside him.

Sitting as still and silent as a photograph, two monks sat on either side of them, their hair shorn, their bodies draped in traditional red robes. They all appeared to be calm and self-possessed, eyes bright, faces glowing with good health. There was a feeling of lightness and peacefulness in the room, as though the weight of gravity didn't apply here.

Thomas's baritone voice interrupted the deep quiet as he introduced everyone. The monks nodded, greeting Sidney in soft tones with pleasant smiles. They looked like the personification of gentleness—incapable of harming any living creature, let alone killing a man in cold blood.

Thomas gestured to a cushion in front of Wangchuck's table. "Please be seated, Chief Becker."

Sidney seated herself and Thomas left the room to join the archery team.

"Thank you for your time," Sidney said, conscious of her uniform and her persona of authority, feeling like a heavy presence in the room. In contrast to their tranquility, she felt an intense sense of purpose, and a deepening dread that always accompanied her during a murder case. Now she was juggling two homicides. Two victims. Two killers were at large. They needed to be apprehended before they killed again. "If you don't mind, may I ask a few questions?"

Wangchuck put down the book, his magnified eyes peering through his glasses, and spoke with an accent. "Please, Chief Becker. We want to help. We are all shocked and saddened to hear of this poor man's death."

"I'll need to speak to you one at a time, maybe in the hall."

Tashii was the first to follow her into the passageway, out of the hearing of the others. Sidney took out her notepad and pen and explained who the dead man was, then she proceeded to ask rudimentary questions.

Tashii reaffirmed that he had been wakened by the cook, then he quickly woke Sunni and Thomas, whose rooms were directly across the hall from his, and the three hurried into the forest and found Karune, then discovered the body.

"Were Sunni and Thomas sleeping when you entered their rooms?"

"Yes. I could hear Thomas snoring when I opened his door. And Sunni looked as though he woke from a deep sleep. He had wrinkles on his face from the pillow."

It seemed unlikely that Thomas or Sunni killed Max. The timeline was off. Tashii entered their rooms at seven. To have killed Max and provide a cover, the suspect would have had to race back up the hill at breakneck speed then bury himself in bed with seconds to spare.

Sunni followed. He had the same story. Though several men had visited the monastery recently and participated in their meditations, no one looked like Max. And no stranger had been seen lurking in the forest, watching the monastery. The monks appeared to be responding truthfully. She saw none of the nervous tics that indicated someone was lying. Dorji was next. Sidney recalled he was the chief administrator who oversaw all operations. Middle-aged with a round, pleasant face, he looked Bhutanese. Deep lines radiated from his eyes and framed his mouth. "Could you please account for your whereabouts this morning?" Sidney asked. "It would help me put together a timeline of the murder."

"Wangchuck and I were eating breakfast in the dining hall between six-thirty and seven," Dorji said, with an accent matching Wangchuck's. "We always eat before the boys rise."

"Thank you."

Wangchuck came out last. He was astoundingly spry and focused for a man his age, and his beatific face seemed to glow with an ageless wisdom. Sidney felt some kind of energy emanating from him that was strangely beautiful, and a sense of serenity descended upon her. As she questioned him, she found herself smiling into his eyes. His responses corroborated Dorji's.

Sidney and Wangchuck reentered the room to find the monks had quietly reassembled in their previous places.

Only one monk was unaccounted for. The diminutive monk in the hall with the boys. "Where was Yeshey this morning?" Sidney asked.

"He usually eats with us, but not this morning," Dorji said.

"Did anyone else see him?"

No one had. Sidney paused to jot down notes and was interrupted by Dorji.

"Do you believe this was a random murder, Chief Becker?"

"Hard to say. We're still investigating."

Dorji's dark eyes shadowed, and a trace of concern edged into his voice. "What can we do to keep the boys safe?"

"Have them stay in groups at all times. No one should enter the forest for any reason until the killer is in custody."

"Can a policeman stay here in the meantime?"

Sidney sighed. "I have a small department, and we're stretched thin as it is. But I'll talk to the county sheriff. He might be able to spare an officer."

"Thank you. Thank you," Wangchuck said. "Bless you, Chief Becker. Bless your officers. Please tell the family of the dead man that we will pray for them." He pressed his hands together and raised his fingertips to his forehead.

The other monks did the same, raising their hands in prayer and murmuring blessings.

Tashii escorted Sidney outside to the front of the monastery, where Darnell and Amanda waited under the oak tree. The feeling of lightness that had enveloped her in the presence of the monks dissipated, and the solidness of the world came back into sharp relief.

Tashii left to join the archery team on the range.

"You get anything from the boys?" Sidney asked.

"Nada. Just a bunch of sweet kids." Amanda chuckled "No one saw a stranger on the grounds that look like Max."

"There was one boy who seemed evasive," Darnell said. "He looked nervous, and never said a word, other than telling me his name and that his family lives in Garnerville. I tried to coax him, but he just looked away when I asked him a direct question." Darnell read from his notes. "His name is Nopadon Preeda. His aunt is Lalisa Preeda. Isn't she tight with your sister?"

"Yeah, she is. Close friends since grade school. They were going to come up today. I discouraged it. Looks like they're going to get their wish. If they're here, Nopadon might talk." Sidney pulled the folded printout of names from her pocket and handed it to Darnell. "Better run backgrounds on these names."

"Copy." He took the list and walked to his patrol car.

CHAPTER SIXTEEN

GRANGER PARKED his department vehicle on a leafy, tree-lined street three blocks east of downtown. The Stevens's ranch-style home looked peaceful in the late morning sun, set back from the street behind a manicured lawn and colorful rhododendron bushes. He saw Briana's van parked in the driveway and was grateful Cecille would not be alone. A dull dread had been growing in his chest on the ride over, and now his stomach twisted into a tight knot as he climbed the front porch and pressed the doorbell. His news would be an explosion coming out of nowhere that would shatter the lives of this whole family. His shoulders stiffened and he braced himself.

Cecille opened the door with a look of surprise, hoisting one of her grandkids on one hip; a toddler with curly blonde hair. A youthful-looking woman in her fifties, Cecille wore faded jeans and a pink T-shirt, her shoulder-length brown hair brushing her shoulders.

"Granger, what a nice surprise. Are you looking for Max?"

"No. I've come to talk to you, Cecille." His solemn expression and quiet tone forewarned her of dire news.

Her eyes widened. "Is Max okay?"

"We better sit down."

"Who is it, Mom?" Briana appeared behind her mother's shoulder and peered at Granger, taking in his uniform and serious expression. In her mid-twenties, with her mom's coloring and unfussy beauty, she too, immediately picked up on the gravity of his visit. "What's going on? Is Dad okay?"

"Come in, Granger," Cecille said soberly. "Let's go into the living room."

He stepped past mother and daughter and plopped into the nearest chair, which faced the fireplace and big screen TV, remembering too late that it was Max's recliner. He pictured Max sitting there, relaxed, a beer in his hand, enjoying the comfort of friends and family. Max had been an affectionate, easy-going guy with a playful sense of humor that kept his grandkids in stitches.

Cecille and Briana sat opposite Granger on the couch, their expressions apprehensive. The toddler squirmed to get down. Cecille released him and he started plowing a toy truck over the carpet, saying, "Vroom, vroom."

"Please, Granger, tell me Max is okay," Cecille said.

Granger had learned over time that it was best to be honest from the get-go, give the family whatever information was available that wasn't classified. He needed to tell them the truth about how Max had died. His throat had closed up, but he forced out the words. "I'm sorry. Max was killed near the monastery this morning."

Caught-in-the-headlight stares from both women faced him for several long seconds.

"What happened?" Cecille asked in a shocked whisper.

"We believe he was stabbed." He swallowed. "I'm so sorry for your loss."

Their shocked expressions melted into abject grief. Both women dissolved into tears, gripping each other's hand. The tears turned to choked sobs, Cecille hiding her face behind a veil of hair, and Brianna walking to the window with her hand pressed to her mouth, her shoulders shuddering.

For what seemed like an eternity, Granger sat pinned to the chair, motionless. He'd been in this position too many times, watching the worst kind of grief play out, waiting to see if a family needed to be alone, or if they wanted to talk.

The toddler started crying and Briana lifted him in her arms, her wet cheek pressed into his curls. "It's okay, baby," she said softly, returning to the couch and sinking next to her mother. She pulled crumpled tissues from her pocket and handed one to Cecille.

Cecille blew her nose and wiped her tears with trembling hands. "Who did it?"

"Unknown at this point. I'm sorry, but we're still piecing together the investigation. Maybe you can help us. Are you up to answering a few questions?"

She nodded, her eyelids pink and puffy.

Granger took out his notepad and pen. "Do you know why Max was up at the monastery?"

"No." Cecille chewed her bottom lip, trying to compose herself, but still, her voice came out shaky. "Max often went up Elderberry Ridge to camp and fish. Not to go to the monastery. He left in our camper three days ago. He was supposed to come home today."

"Dad liked being in the woods. It's his therapy," Brianna said, eyes filling with tears. She paused and looked away for a moment, then continued. "He did say he'd be doing a little business while he was gone."

"What kind of business?"

Brianna shrugged. "I don't know."

"I assume he meant paperwork," Cecille said. "What else would he be doing up on a mountain?"

"Everything about his business will be on his laptop," Brianna said. "Dad documented everything."

"Do you know what case he was working on?"

Cecille frowned. "He'd been very secretive about it. He said he needed to be careful."

"Careful?"

"He didn't want to step on the wrong toes. I think there were influential people involved who might not appreciate what he was digging up."

Granger paused to take notes.

"Do you think that has something to do with his death?" Brianna asked.

"It's too early to tell. When was the last time you spoke to him?"

"Max normally called every night, but I didn't hear from him last night."

"So two nights ago, he seemed fine?"

"Yes. We spoke around eight."

Granger jotted down a few more notes, then lifted his head. "One last question. Was Max on any medication?"

"No," Cecille asked. "Why do you ask?"

"Just a routine question."

"Where is he?" Cecille said, eyes misting again. "We want to see him. All of us."

"He's at the morgue. I can drive you."

"I'll call my husband and my brothers," Brianna said. "And tell them to meet us there." She left the room holding her little boy close.

Gently excusing himself, Granger stepped outside, made a call to Sidney, and relayed the new information.

"Hmmm. So he was fine two days ago and was supposed to come home today. Judging from his disheveled appearance, my guess is that he went off his rocker sometime yesterday. I wouldn't be surprised if he spent the night in the woods. We need to find his camper and his computer. That should tell us who Max was investigating, and who this person is that he felt threatened by."

"And what he was drugged on."

"You're going to be busy with the Stevens family for a while," she continued. "But call Selena. Have her contact her friend, Lalisa, and bring them both up here. We need some help getting Lalisa's nephew to talk to us."

"Yes, ma'am."

"And please give my condolences to the Stevens family."

Granger hung up and called Selena next.

"Hey," she answered. "You up at the monastery?"

"Not yet. That's why I called. We need your help. We think Lalisa's nephew knows something, but he won't talk. Maybe you and Lalisa could come up and help us out. Put the boy at ease. You can both ride with me. I'm taking care of some business right now. So maybe in an hour?"

"Of course. I'll call Lalisa. Call me when you're ready to head up there."

CHAPTER SEVENTEEN

SIDNEY SAW DARNELL walking back from his patrol car where he'd been on the computer.

"Their backgrounds came up clean, Chief. Just some traffic tickets. A few of them have been off the grid for so long, their records are immaculate."

Before Sidney could decide her next move, she spotted two Dodge Ram trucks heading up the drive. Finally, the K-9 units had arrived. She recognized the same two handlers she worked with yesterday. Deputies Kyle Mumford and Maria Sanchez. They pulled into the lot and parked next to Sidney's Yukon.

Dressed in their brown uniforms, the two handlers walked to the rear of their vehicles and lowered the tailgates. Bruiser was the first to jump out of his crate. Maria's fierce looking black and tan German Shepherd, Poncho, jumped out next. Poncho specialized in sniffing out drugs, weapons and other criminally related items, and attacked suspects on command. He was also an ace at searching for suspects.

The two handlers clipped fifteen-foot leashes to their tracking harnesses, and looked up when Sidney and her officers approached, all three armed with AR-15 assault rifles. When working, a handler's full attention was on the animal, looking for signals that he was closing in on a suspect. A handler had to be accompanied by at least one armed officer, whose sole responsibility was to keep him safe.

"Can't believe we have another homicide," Maria said. "Who's dead?"

"A private investigator. Max Stevens. Stabbed in the back. We have a murder suspect on the loose, presumed armed. The victim had been roaming the woods in some kind of altered state. We need to trace his movements back to his camper. Max was a cop for two decades. We need to find his killer."

Four alert faces stared back at her. The tension the five officers shared was palpable. The dogs were panting and pulling on their leashes, ready to get to work.

Because bloodhounds were known for their ability to discern human scent over great distances, even days later, Sidney chose Bruiser for the job of tracking Max. "Kyle, Amanda, go with Bruiser to locate the camper. He has a white ford pickup and a silver Airstream. Maria, Darnell, and I will go with Poncho to hunt down the suspect. Everyone ready?"

Heads nodded.

"Let's roll."

They walked briskly down the hill to the left of the archery range where several adults and young monks were gathered, watching the archery team at work. Sidney heard arrows slicing through the air, and thunks as they hit their targets, followed by unanimous cheering. She was dumbstruck by the remarkable skill of the archers. The boys consistently hit a narrow target about one foot wide by three feet tall at a distance of over four hundred and fifty feet—longer than a football field.

"Holy smoke," Kyle said. "Are you kidding me?"

His words expressed Sidney's sentiments exactly.

"We need to sign them up for the sniper team," Maria quipped.

They entered the cool shadows of the forest and hiked to the grove where Max had been killed. "It's a good thing we had that storm," Kyle said. "Damp air holds the scent better."

"Glad something's working in our favor," Sidney said. She directed Kyle to the trail of Max's dried blood on the crushed leaves. Bruiser seized on the scent immediately and was off like a racer, bulldozing through a sea of fern and brush. Kyle was pulling back on the leash so he and Amanda could keep up.

"And away they go," Darnell said.

Trying to determine where the killer stood when he attacked Max, Poncho moved in concentric circles. Finally, with an excited squeal, he picked up a scent. With his nose hovering inches above the ground, the German Shepherd quickly led them out of the forest. Against the sound of the archer's arrows hitting their mark and the cheers of spectators, the canine unit sprinted past the archery field back up the grassy slope. They came to an abrupt halt at the wooden entry door in the stone wall. They were all breathing hard. Poncho whined and pawed the door, keen to get inside. Maria pulled him back and looked at Sidney for direction. Sidney didn't have the keypad code.

Thomas came charging up the hill from the range below, panting, looking alarmed. "What are you doing up here?"

"A suspect entered the premises this morning," Sidney said. "What's the code?"

"That's impossible. Your dog's following the wrong scent." Pressing his lips together in a tight line, Thomas stepped in front of them and crossed his arms. A human barricade. "Do you have a warrant?"

"Open the door! Now!" Anger edged into her voice and her words were sharp and clipped. "You're interfering with a peace officer."

"I'll take you inside," a gentle voice said. Dorji had come up quietly behind them. Eyebrows drawn together, he shot Thomas a questioning look.

Thomas didn't budge.

"You can move, or we can move you," Sidney snapped.

A moment of silence fraught with tension stretched between them. Thomas gave Sidney a cryptic, yet borderline predatory look. She sensed layers of tumultuous emotions swirling beneath his façade of a holy man. The robe and shorn hair now seemed like a costume—just a role he was playing.

"You're a hair away from getting arrested," Darnell growled, stepping forward. Thomas was four inches taller than the young officer, but Darnell was all muscle, and his brawn could easily back up his words.

"I'm sure this will be a dead end," Dorji said. "But we won't impede your investigation. Isn't that right, Thomas?"

Thomas muttered something unintelligible, the blade of anger barely sheathed in his voice. He lingered for another second, then reluctantly removed himself from their path.

"The code is 2-4-6-8. We keep it easy for the boys." Dorji punched in the four digits and pushed open the door.

Tense with excitement, Poncho leapt into the courtyard. Nose to the ground, he crisscrossed the paving stones, tracking a scent that seemed to linger everywhere—clearly, the scent of someone who lived here. That unnerved Sidney. The suspect was one of the monks.

Picking up a fresh scent, Poncho let out a low whine and shot across the courtyard to a corridor that ran the length of the building. The officers ran behind him at top speed, their boots sounding hollow on the paved walkway. The corridor opened to the back of the monastery and looked over miles of hills and valleys. Poncho was leading the team directly to a large weathered barn at the bottom of the hill, its double doors wide open. A flatbed hay truck was parked outside, partially blocking the view of the entrance.

As they drew closer, the sound of a motor revved up. Dressed in black leather and a black helmet, a rider flew out of the barn on a motorcycle. He made a sharp turn, fishtailed in the mud, and tore out of the barnyard into one of the planted fields. His bike bucked like a bronco over the furrows, tearing through the neat rows of crops. One buck sent something flying off the back of the bike. Motor screaming, the cyclist reached the grassy pasture and picked up speed, scattering the panicked goats and horses in every direction. The cyclist then disappeared into the forest that bordered the meadow.

The canine group stopped in their tracks on the hill.

"Dammit!" Sidney cried. "That's probably our killer."

Poncho was straining on the leash.

"There's no way we're going to catch him on foot," Amanda said.

"No, we've lost him," Sidney said. "Check that field. Something flew off his bike. While you're at it, do a search of the barn. I need to put out an APB."

Maria loosened the leash and Poncho tore down the hill with the two officers straining to keep up.

Anger sparking, Sidney ascended the hill and marched back to the courtyard where the two monks stood waiting. Dorji looked anxious. Thomas wore an implacable expression, his hands calmly folded in front of him.

"Who just took off on that motorcycle, Thomas?" Sidney growled.

Thomas shrugged. A small smile appeared on his face and was gone so quickly she wondered if she imagined it. Her anger rose, and she got in his face. "You delayed us purposely, so your friend could get away."

"I have no idea what you're talking about."

"Who was he?"

"That had to be Yeshey," Dorji said, eyes wide with surprise. "He's the only one that wasn't down at the range."

And the only one that didn't have an alibi this morning. Sidney pulled the printout from her pocket and quickly unfolded it. "Yeshey's birth name is Terry Woodbridge."

"Yes, that's correct." Dorji shook his head, as though trying to clear it. "This makes no sense. Yeshey would never hurt anyone."

"Dorji, look at me. Think. Where would Yeshey be heading?"

He met her gaze, blinked several times, and said, "I don't know. There's a maze of trails back in there. Cave systems, too. A person could easily hide out for days, even weeks."

Holy hell! Sidney restrained herself from cursing in front of Dorji.

"Please, don't hurt Yeshey." Dorji looked deeply troubled. "He's a gentle, kind person. If he killed that man, there's a good reason."

With effort, Sidney pulled herself together and tamped down her fury. "Dorji, we never use force unless absolutely necessary. Who's the owner of the motorcycle?"

"It's mine," Thomas said. "That's how I get to and from work."

"Did you give Yeshey the keys?"

"He had permission to use it whenever he wanted. He knew where the keys were."

"Give me the make, model, year, and license number," she said, whipping out her notebook and pen.

"It's a BMW 1250 GS. Year 2018. Personalized license is B Buddha."

Sidney's small department was overtaxed, and she needed help. She contacted the sheriff's office, requested an All-Points Bulletin, and described the suspect and motorcycle. "We could use some air support up here, and we need a perimeter around the base of Elderberry Ridge."

Even as she hung up, Sidney didn't hold out much hope. They were dealing with thousands of acres of forested hills. There were meadows, open fields, and a network of hiking and biking trails, all easily accessible by motorcycle. But the APB would go to all local and county enforcement agencies, and the information would be entered into the national data base. If Yeshey got through the local dragnet, a highway patrol officer a hundred miles away, or even in another state, could conceivably bring him in.

Darnell and Maria emerged from the corridor and joined them. Poncho now looked relaxed; his job completed. But the two officers looked tense, and Darnell held four evidence bags. She recognized the folded robes of a monk in one, and a black pouch the size of a shaving kit in another. "This robe was lying in a heap in one of the stalls," he said. "Yeshey must have changed there. This black pouch is what flew off his bike in the field." Darnell held up two smaller evidence bags. "These were inside it."

One held a cell phone. Sidney's pulse quickened when he handed her the other. Inside was a knife with a double-edged blade—a tactical combat knife, perfectly balanced, designed specifically for throwing. It looked lethal. If this was the murder weapon, in the hands of a skilled knife thrower, Max didn't stand a chance. The blade was wiped clean. "We'll get it to the lab. See if there's trace blood on it. Stash these evidence bags in your truck, Darnell."

"You had no right to look in that bag," Thomas said. His face had drained of color, and he stood very still, as though fighting not to show emotion.

The man was infuriating. Why was he so willing to obstruct her investigation to protect Yeshey, incriminating himself in the process? For the moment, Sidney ignored him. "We need to search Yeshey's room, Darnell."

"You have no right to go into his room," Thomas said, inserting himself between Sidney and Darnell. Color had returned to his face in angry red blotches.

Sidney's anger flared. "Thomas Thornton, I'm arresting you for obstruction of an officer and aiding and abetting a fugitive. You're a co-

conspirator in a murder." She nodded to Darnell. "Cuff him."

The tall monk's threatening expression melted into one of stark surprise, then alarm.

Darnell cuffed his hands behind his back and then proceeded to search him, running his hands the full length of his torso and legs.

Thomas's face flushed crimson and the cords in his neck bulged. "You can't do this. I did nothing wrong!"

"Put him in your patrol truck," Sidney said.

"My pleasure. Get moving." Darnell grabbed the tall monk by the arm.

Thomas continued to vent. "This is police harassment. Dorji, call my lawyer!"

Sidney heard his muffled cries even after the courtyard door shut behind them. Sitting in a cage in a patrol car might induce his willingness to cooperate. Back at the station, she would finally get her chance to grill him about Olivia Paisley.

"Chief Becker," Maria said. "I'd like to go back to the crime scene in the woods and have Poncho do a thorough grid search. Maybe the killer left some other evidence."

"Great. Do it."

With a little salute, she and Poncho headed out of the courtyard, breaking into a trot.

Dorji, who had been a silent witness to the drama, looked a little shell shocked. Murder, cops swarming the grounds, a beloved monk turned fugitive, and another blatantly and angrily obstructing the law, could do that to a person. He stood in silence until Darnell returned.

"Dorji, would you please take us to Yeshey's room?" Sidney said.

"Of course." He shook his head. "That knife can't be Yeshey's. That's just impossible. And I don't know what got into Thomas. I apologize for his behavior. I've never seen him like this. This whole business has everyone on edge."

Sidney felt sympathy for Dorji. The tranquil, quiet world of monastic living was experiencing a seismic disruption. They followed the monk down the corridor, through a door, and into a long hallway. Sidney and Darnell tucked their sunglasses into their breast pockets and let their eyes adjust to the dim light.

"Our living quarters," Dorji said with a wave of his hand. "On the right, each adult has his own room. The boys are in dormitories on the left." He paused outside the third door and a shadow darkened his eyes. "I've never intruded before upon a monk's privacy."

"A man was murdered, Dorji. These are not normal circumstances."

Dorji nodded and opened the door.

Darnell and Sidney entered a ten-foot square room, furnished with a single bed and a straight-backed wooden chair in front of a desk. Two open doors revealed a small bathroom and a tiny closet. Nothing hung on the white-washed walls. *Asceticism at its best.* Here lived a person who resisted the material temptations of the modern world.

As they donned nitrile gloves, Sidney felt Dorji's gaze on her back from the hallway.

"What are you looking for?" he asked.

"Anything to clue us in to where he may have gone. Thank you for your help. We're good here."

Dorji took his cue and left.

Darnell searched the drawers in Yeshey's desk. "One pen. One pad of paper. Nothing else. Man, he lived like a monk," he said with a chuckle.

"Better him than me. Take away my creature comforts over my dead body."

While Sidney examined the bathroom, Darnell picked up the half dozen books on the desk one by one and shook out the pages. Nothing. The bathroom was just as austere—one toothbrush and a tube of toothpaste in the mirrored cabinet over the sink—and a bar of soap, shampoo, and conditioner in the shower. Life reduced to bare necessities. Jail offered more amenities. Wanting to get Yeshey's DNA filed with CODIS, Sidney sealed Yeshey's toothbrush in an evidence bag. It would prove useful if the monk had been arrested in the past by a different authority.

Darnell pulled back the covers and the mattress and shook out the pillow.

Sidney examined the closet. Four monastic robes hung neatly from hangers. In addition, there was one set of street clothes that Yeshey must have worn during his infrequent trips to town; Docker pants and a long-sleeved polo shirt. Three pairs of shoes lined the floor. Sidney scoured the walls with a flashlight beam, then moved the shoes to one side, and spotlighted the floor. One floorboard was a bit higher than the others. Pulling out her utility knife, Sidney pressed the sharp blade into the groove, eased it under the board, and lifted. It gave. Setting the board aside, she aimed her beam into a small recess. "Hmm. Got something." She scooped out a letter-sized envelope, slid her blade under the sealed flap and pulled out a folded yellowed document and a dog-eared driver's license.

The license was sixteen years old and belonged to Tammy Schaffer. The photo depicted a pretty young woman with long, tawny, hair. Five-foot-five, twenty years old. Sidney recalled the features of the diminutive monk when she met him in the hall with the children, and she stared long and hard at the photo, superimposing Yeshey's delicate features onto Tammy's. Holy hell. It was a good match! She unfolded the document, which was a birth certificate for Tammy Schaffer, dated thirty-six years ago.

"What is it, Chief?" Darnell came up behind her, holding something in his hand.

"Either Yeshey has an identical twin sister," she quipped. "Or he's not the man called Terry Woodbridge. As a matter of fact, he's not a man."

"That explains what I just found," Darnell said.

Sidney focused on the item in his hand and her brows lifted in surprise. "It's a home pregnancy stick."

"It was in the waste basket wrapped in paper. It shows positive."

"Holy Hannah." Sidney locked eyes with Darnell. "That explains why Thomas is so protective. He knows Yeshey's a woman. Seems they're having an affair. He may or may not know she's pregnant, but most likely, he's the father. We need to update that APB and run a background check on Tammy Schaffer."

**

Sitting in her Yukon with Darnell, Sidney ran a check on Tammy Schaffer on her computer. It turned out the woman had racked up an impressive relationship with the law. "She's a fugitive," Sidney said. "Sixteen years ago, at the age of twenty, she skipped out on a drug and attempted murder charge."

"Murder?" He whistled. "No wonder she changed her name and gender. She's been hiding from the law."

"Can't say I'm surprised," Sidney said. "After learning she's an ace knife thrower, and seeing how she handled that bike, nothing would surprise me about Tammy. She couldn't have picked a more remote location. Damn brilliant, actually. If not for this whole episode this morning, she could've lived out her life here."

Sidney made a call to the sheriff's office and updated her APB on Tammy Schaffer.

CHAPTER EIGHTEEN

AMANDA AND KYLE followed Bruiser through acres of towering Douglas Fir and meadows thick with lupine and paint brush. Max's trail meandered restlessly, with no logic to it, and Bruiser revisited the same section of forest several times. Clearly, Max had been stumbling around in some kind of mindless stupor.

They trekked up a steep bluff composed of enormous boulders that had an abrupt drop off of several hundred feet. Amanda's gaze swept a rumpled landscape of ravines and crevices and forest that stretched to infinity. The air was hot and still and smelled of damp earth. No sign of a camper. No movement except for a hawk lazily riding a thermal.

The distant sound of a rotor beat grew louder, and a chopper swooped over the treetops. It hovered above the ridge, checking them out, then descended to the valley below, sweeping past the monastery and over the forest to the south.

"Looks like a manhunt is in the works," Kyle said.

"Let's hope all this manpower pays off," Amanda added.

Bruiser picked up Max's scent and they were off again.

Thirty minutes later, hot and sweaty, breathing hard, they paused to rest by a stretch of creek where the water cascaded over a series of shallow falls. The bank was imprinted with the tracks of various animals coming to swill the cool, clear water, including deer, a coyote, and a black bear. Birds flittered over the small recesses in the boulders where water collected, drinking and bathing.

Kyle worked out of the backpack's shoulder straps and unzipped a pocket. He pulled out trail mix and two bottles of water, which he shared with Amanda. He tossed a few treats high in the air. Bruiser performed impressive pirouettes to catch them neatly in his jaws. Kyle and Amanda laughed. The hound looked anything but graceful with his big floppy ears and layers of loose skin moving with the momentum. Entertained, sitting next to Kyle on a mossy downed tree, Amanda washed down the trail mix with gulps of water. "Thanks, Kyle. I needed that."

Kyle chuckled. "You were looking a bit wilted around the edges. I figured it was either feed you or carry you."

She lightly punched his arm. "I could outlast you any day of the week. Another couple of hours of this and I'd be signaling the chopper to airlift you to safety."

"We'll see who gets airlifted."

The satellite phone buzzed in a pocket of her tactical vest and she yanked it out.

"Yeah, Chief."

"We got a suspect on the run." Chief Becker's voice sounded urgent. "Be on the lookout for the monk known as Yeshey. She's been identified as Tammy Schaffer."

"Yeshey is a woman?" Amanda asked, incredulous.

"Yes. Dressed in black leather, black helmet, riding a black BMW motorcycle. License plate is B Buddha."

"Copy that."

"Any luck locating that camper?"

"Not yet."

"Keep me posted."

"Copy."

"Did I hear right?" Kyle asked when Amanda clicked off. "One of the monks is a woman?"

"You heard right. Now a fugitive named Tammy Schaffer, wearing black leather and riding a BMW motorcycle. License plate is B Buddha."

"This case gets stranger by the minute." Shaking his head, Kyle slung his backpack over his shoulder. He gave Bruiser a command and the canine lurched into action.

Bruiser randomly wove between brush and trees for another twenty minutes, then he lifted his muzzle from the ground, ears straight up, and shot off in a straight line. Trying to keep up, Amanda and Kyle trotted behind. They moved through the brush at a good clip until he brought Bruiser to a halt at the edge of a small clearing. Max's travel trailer and white Ford pickup were parked next to a calm inlet of the creek.

"Hallelujah," Amanda said, grinning.

"Bonanza," Kyle said, grinning back. "Good job, Bruiser."

Amanda saw that Max had taken great pains to conceal his presence behind a thick copse of aspen trees. "To reach this clearing, Max had to leave the main road and drive a mile down that overgrown fire road."

"He was hidden away, but someone knew he was here," Kyle said.

"Yeah, someone who wasn't too happy." From where they stood near the creek, the peaceful setting showed signs of an intruder, and a skirmish. Two camp chairs were overturned next to a firepit, and the door of the camper stood wide open.

Amanda called the Chief and relayed the troubling news.

"Doesn't sound good," Chief Becker said. "A forensic specialist from county just arrived. I'm sending him your way to help process the campsite. We need to recover Max's computer and phone. Look for any sign that he may have been drugged. Stay alert. A killer's out there."

"Copy. Will do." She recited their coordinates, clicked off, and turned to Kyle. "A CSI is heading our way. We need to process the area. Looks like you're going to be here for a while, standing guard."

"No problem." He flashed her a smile. "We leave together. Let Bruiser clear the camper." He gave the bloodhound a long lead and stepped into the clearing.

The camper was an Airstream Sport about sixteen feet long, its aluminum siding shining in the dappled light. Amanda unclipped her sidearm from its holster and raised it to eye level. Through the opened door immediately to the right, she saw a dinette. To the left, a bedroom. A sink, stove, and small fridge shared the compact space directly ahead.

"Police," Kyle called out. "Anyone in there? Come out now."

No response.

Kyle unleashed Bruiser and the canine shot into the trailer like a bullet. He came back out seconds later wagging his tail. Empty. But Amanda needed to be doubly sure. Pulling booties from her duty belt, she slipped one over each shoe. "I'm coming in." Gun held high, she entered. The tiny bathroom was empty. A double-size bed filled the bedroom wall to wall. Nowhere for an intruder to hide. She holstered her weapon.

Her gut tightened when she saw that the small, crowded camper had been searched. A couple drawers had been yanked open and the cushions were askew around the dinette table. A power cord was plugged into a socket at the dining nook, but the tabletop was bare. No computer. No phone. Who knew Max was in this remote location? Who drugged him? Until the tech arrived with a crime kit, there wasn't much Amanda could do except start a search. "Wait out there, Kyle. Don't move around."

"Yeah, I know. Walk in a straight line back to the periphery."

Amanda smiled. Every person walking through a crime scene increased the risk of contamination. She pulled nitrile gloves from her duty belt and snapped them on, then whipped out her cellphone and systematically began taking photos of the interior of the camper in slices. She spent fifteen minutes searching every inch of the trailer. No phone. No computer. The keys to the truck were hanging on a hook by the door. Amanda searched every conceivable hiding place in the Ford pickup. Nothing of consequence.

Amanda took more pictures as she made her way through the campsite. Max had not been here solely on business. A hammock had been strung between the trunks of two lodgepole pine trees and an open novel laid face down on the canvas. A fishing pole and tackle box sat on a wide tree stump next to the camper. Max may have gone fishing at one of the alpine lakes. A moment later, that was confirmed. Flies buzzed over a frying pan on the blackened grill of the firepit. Inside was a fish fillet. A fork and antler-handled hunting knife rested in the pan. A half empty bottle of Budweiser sat on the ground next to the pit. That told her the skirmish happened while Max was preparing dinner.

Amanda was struck by a sudden, piercing sense of loss. She pictured the easy-going private investigator enjoying his quiet getaway in the great outdoors; fishing, reading, eating in the crisp mountain air—never realizing it was his last night on earth—that he would never see his family again.

Amanda studied the area around the firepit where a coffee pot sat on the grill next to the frying pan. She noted the position of the two chairs that had been knocked over. Why two chairs? Did Max have a meeting with someone out here? Did the meeting turn violent? The surrounding carpet of pine needles showed some disturbance, which could have been caused by two men shoving each other or even wrestling on the ground. She looked more closely at the firepit and her heart skipped a beat. Unmistakably, there was blood spatter on a few of the rocks and the coffee pot. Someone sustained a wound here. Gunshot wound? Stab wound? A knuckled fist to the face? She photographed everything.

When she made her way to the road, overgrown with wild grass, she found a small patch of muddy earth where tire impressions overlapped those made by Max's vehicles. A car had been parked here. The tread of one tire was clearly defined. A plaster cast was needed. Hopefully, there would be a unique characteristic to the tread that could link the visitor to the campsite, if need be. Amanda took photos.

A white county SUV bumped up the road and parked a distance away. A stocky, round-faced man with thinning gray hair got out carrying a forensic kit. He wore Chino pants, a blue button-down shirt, and a pistol in a shoulder holster, even though he was a civilian. Amanda instantly recognized Calvin McConnell, the best tech she'd ever worked with next to Stewart Wong.

She'd been crouched over the fire pit, taking photos, but stood to greet him.

"Really, Amanda? A cellphone?" Calvin said. "I've got the real McCoy right here." With a cocky grin, he patted the digital SLR camera hanging from his neck.

She grinned back. "I've never been so glad to see a crime kit. My fingers are itchy."

"So you only love me for my crime kit?"

She gave him an affectionate clap on the back. "Let's get to work. There's plenty to do."

"Right. Skip the small talk. No 'how are you, Calvin? How're the wife and kids, Calvin?'"

"You can start by making a cast of these tire tracks," she said, focused. "Then collect some blood samples from the firepit and bag those blood-spattered rocks."

"Everyone's fine," Calvin said. "Thanks for asking."

Her attention was diverted to a dense copse of poplar saplings on the other side of the creek. From the corner of her eye she had caught a movement. A darting black shadow. Amanda stood motionless for several long moments.

"See something?" Kyle asked, joining her. At his side, Bruiser stood at attention, his ears straight up, staring in the same direction.

"Not sure. I may just have the jitters."

"It's probably just a bear. Or a cougar."

"That's supposed to make me feel better?"

"They're more afraid of you than you are of them." Kyle got out his high-powered binoculars and scanned the woods. "Don't worry," he smiled. "I'll protect you."

She rolled her eyes and went back to work.

Calvin took photos of the tire tread, then he used a hardening spray to set the print before pouring in the casting material. Amanda rummaged through the crime kit, grabbed evidence bags and the fingerprint kit, and headed for the camper. Inside, she picked up two cups from the sink and placed them in separate bags. They would be analyzed at the lab for the visitor's DNA and any trace of mind-altering drugs. Minutes later, Calvin joined her, and the two shared the crowded space as best they could, looking for trace evidence and dusting for prints.

Through the opened door, Amanda saw Kyle walking Bruiser along the creek, staring into the forest, his gun held down at his side. She didn't like being out in the woods. A killer with malicious intent had all the advantage, hiding behind cover while they operated out in the open. The sooner they were all out of here, the better.

CHAPTER NINETEEN

AT THE SOUND of gravel crunching, Sidney looked up from her computer as Granger's truck pulled into the lot. He killed the engine and through the windows, she recognized his two passengers—Selena and her friend, Lalisa.

Selena smiled and gave a little wave, unable to hide her enthusiasm. Fate had inserted her, once again, into one of Sidney's murder investigations. In all fairness, as strapped for manpower as the department was, Selena's help in the past had proved extremely useful. Like Sidney, she had inherited the itch under the skin to solve a good mystery. Growing up, sitting at the dinner table as willing hostages, the two sisters were challenged by their police chief father to solve notorious murders. He fed them oblique clues, which they cobbled together to come up with a construct of an investigation. It could take days, even weeks, to solve a case. But their tenacity paid off— they always got their man—maybe with a little too much help from dear old Dad. The process taught them critical thinking and encouraged them to see what wasn't apparent but lurking in the realm of shadow. Her father helped to hone Sidney's sixth sense, or gut instinct, which served her well when she became a cop. Selena's gentle nature didn't steer her down the same path, but she'd always had a keen desire to be a part of Sidney's support team.

They climbed out of the pickup and Selena introduced Lalisa, an athletic and striking dark-eyed woman. Like Selena, she wore jeans, a T-shirt, and hiking boots. She carried a small gift-wrapped box. Selena held up two bulging paper bags.

Sidney recognized the logo on the bags immediately. Pickle's Deli. Inside those bags were sandwiches that were two inches thick, packed with hickory smoked ham and melted cheese on rye. And, on the side were the best Kosher pickles this side of the Cascades, full of salt, dill, and garlic.

Sidney realized she was starving. She didn't need to ask Granger and Darnell if they wanted to eat. While they rummaged through the bags, Sidney turned to Lalisa and said cordially, "Thank you so much for coming."

"Whatever I can do to help." Lalisa scanned the woods. A vertical line deepened between her brows. "It's horrible to think a man was killed up here. Selena said you think my nephew may be able to help you. Nopadon is very shy, but he'll open up to me. Where is he?"

"The boys just went in for lunch."

"I'll go check on him. Why don't you guys eat while the boys are busy? There's a small meditation room off the courtyard just to your right. It's quiet. We'll meet you there in twenty minutes."

Sidney and her group sat in the shade of the oak tree and packed away their sandwiches in record time.

"That was great, Selena. We were running on empty."

"Can't let you guys run yourselves into the ground," Selena said, sending Sidney an accusing stare.

Rightfully so. Sidney would have barreled through the day without eating.

Granger sat next to Selena, knees touching, their eyes sometimes locking in a lingering stare.

Sidney smiled. Granger was slowly melting down her sister's resistance.

Sidney gulped water from her bottle, screwed on the top, and glanced at the monk sitting in the cage of Darnell's truck. His posture rigid, face set in stone, Thomas was unrecognizable as the friendly doctor who eased the suffering of patients in the ER. She wrapped up the other half of her sandwich, grabbed a cold bottle of water, and handed them to Darnell. "Better check on Thomas. Walk him around. See if he needs a bathroom break, and if he's cooled down enough to eat."

***

The meditation room was small with hazy light filtering through a single window. Floor cushions lined three walls, facing an altar covered with dozens of candles in small colored jars. A silk tapestry above the altar depicted the Buddha sitting in a forest surrounded by birds and animals. The smell of incense, burned in this small space for decades, seemed to permeate the walls.

Sidney and Selena kneeled on cushions and sat back on their heels. The peaceful ambience of the room resonated at some deep level and quieted Sidney's mind, taking her swirling thoughts to a lower tempo.

"Don't these people believe in furniture?" Granger grumbled, as he tried to find a sitting position that didn't make his duty belt and gun holster ride up. He finally decided to just stand near the door.

Lalisa arrived shortly with Nopadon, and both conformed their bodies into cross-legged postures. She and Selena sat like bookends on each side of the boy, offering a protective buffer.

Nopadon's gaze quietly swept the room, flickering over Sidney and Granger. With his dark-brown eyes and intensely serious expression, he could have been Lalisa's younger brother. There was no mistaking the family resemblance. His gaze landed on the gift his aunt held on her lap.

"This is for you," she said with a grin, handing it to him. "Just a little something. You're twelve years old!"

His slender fingers unwrapped a plain cardboard box. Inside, wrapped in tissue, he found a pair of in-ear wireless headphones. He looked up at her and beamed. "Awesome, Aunt Lalisa. So cool. Just what I wanted!"

Though he had an accent, Nopadon sounded like an American boy. Sidney wasn't surprised. All the young monks had smartphones, and social media allowed kids around the world to share universal pop language and culture.

"You can pair it up with your phone," Lalisa said, her dark eyes gleaming.

He leaned over and kissed her cheek. The shift in his manner from solemn to lighthearted paved the way for Sidney to begin her conversation. "Thank you for meeting with us, Nopadon," she said, her tone and expression friendly. "Happy Birthday! Do you mind if we ask you a few questions? Then you can go test out your earphones."

He nodded, his smile fading.

Sidney asked a few simple questions to put him at ease: How did he like America? How was the food? Was he excited about the archery competition coming up? He responded with enthusiasm to all the questions. Nopadon was an exceptionally bright boy with a good command of English.

Then Sidney slipped in a question about Max. "I'm wondering if you noticed this man at the monastery the last few days. Or in the woods?" She brought up a photo of the P.I. on her phone and held it out to him.

The boy stared at the photo for a long time. An aura of apprehension settled over him.

Lalisa put her hand on his shoulder and said gently, "It's okay, Nopadon. You can tell us."

After a couple of beats, he said shyly, "Yes. I saw him when I was in the woods yesterday. I was picking bear's garlic and spicy wild ginger for the cook." Nopadon swallowed. "He scared me."

"Why did he scare you?" Sidney asked.

"He was standing behind a big tree, like he was hiding. Just staring at something. Not moving. But then he brought a camera up to his eye and I realized he was a photographer. I was going to leave, but then I heard two people talking. I walked around some bushes to get a better look, and I saw two monks. At first, I couldn't see who they were. It scared me that the man was hiding from them. Like he was a spy."

"Then what happened?"

"The two monks walked between the trees and I saw who they were."

He went silent again.

"Who were they, Nopadon?" Lalisa asked.

The boy stared at his hands for what seemed like minutes, then his expression gradually changed, morphing from one emotion to another, finally settling on sadness.

"What's wrong, sweetie?" Lalisa said. "Don't be scared. It's okay. You can tell us. Who were the monks?"

He raised his head. His eyes were sad, and they glistened in the filtered light. Tears. His mouth opened and closed, and he finally choked out the words, barely above a whisper. "Thomas and Yeshey. They were kissing. Monks aren't supposed to be romantic."

Lalisa took him in her arms and he hid his face in her shoulder. "True, monks aren't supposed to be romantic. But Monks are people, Nopadon," she said softly, stroking his head. "People aren't perfect. Monks aren't perfect."

That's for sure, Sidney thought. When Tammy Schaffer was eighteen, she made very grave mistakes. Racking up a string of felonies. For sixteen years, she posed as a man, deceiving the monks who trusted her. And Thomas was complicit in her deception. He knew she was a woman. How long were the two engaged in a secret relationship? What was their game? Were they sincere practitioners of monastic teachings, or were they both playing the roles of monks in order to keep her safely hidden? Now that Tammy's cover was blown, Thomas's motivation for obstructing a homicide investigation and helping her escape became crystal clear.

"Can you tell us what happened next?" Sidney asked. "Did the man take pictures of Yeshey and Thomas?"

Nopadon pulled away from his aunt and wiped his eyes with his fingertips. He cleared his throat and said hoarsely, "Yes. Then he pulled some branches apart so he could get a better shot. His backpack fell off his shoulder and made a loud noise. Thomas and Yeshey stopped kissing and looked right at him. They looked really surprised. The man grabbed his backpack and ran. Thomas chased him. I ducked down in the bushes. I just wanted to be back at the monastery. After a long, long time, I looked up. No one was there. I didn't hear anyone. So I ran really fast back up the hill and stayed in the dormitory until dinner. I was so scared, I left my basket behind. When I went to the dining hall a couple hours later, the cook came out and thanked me. She said Yeshey brought my basket to her."

"So they knew you were in the forest."

He nodded, biting his lip.

"Did they say anything to you?"

"No. I've avoided them." Nopadon's dark eyes grew large. "Now that man is dead. Did Yeshey and Thomas kill him?"

CHAPTER TWENTY

AMANDA AND CALVIN finished their collection of evidence and were packing their gear when two roll-back tow trucks arrived. They parked, brakes groaning, and Calvin helped negotiate Max's camper and truck onto the flat beds. They would be transported to a secure lot and processed more fully.

When the trucks with their heavy cargo were well on their way, Amanda sighed with relief. The entire time they were working she'd been on edge, her senses on high alert, tuning in to any sound or movement that forewarned of an attack. It wasn't until they were in Calvin's SUV driving away from the campsite that she inhaled her first easy breath. She rolled her shoulders back and forth, releasing some of the knotted tension, and pulled out her phone.

"Yeah, Amanda," Chief Becker answered, all business.

"We just finished up over here."

"Good. Max was seen taking photos. Did you find his camera?"

"No camera, no phone, no computer. But we did find blood and two used cups in the sink. Which might give us prints or DNA."

"Get them to the lab." Chief Becker exhaled sharply. "I just got word that Tammy Schaffer was spotted twenty miles east of Garnerville. Officers pursued but she dodged off the main road into the forest again."

"She's wily."

"Like the Roadrunner. We're wrapping things up here at the monastery. We'll clear out when you return."

Very good news to Amanda. "See you in a few."

***

Maria and the German Shepherd had no luck finding anything else at the original crime scene, but Poncho did find Karune's missing arrow; a great relief, she was certain, to the boy who was attacked. She and Kyle were the first to head back down the hill, followed by the vehicles of Calvin

McConnell, Darnell, and Amanda.

Granger opened the passenger door of his patrol truck for Lalisa. She scrambled in and was strapping on her belt when Sidney stopped at the open window. "Thanks so much for coming up. Nopadon's input was really useful."

"I'm happy to help. I'll sleep easier knowing Yeshey's off this mountain. I still can't believe it. I've known him ... I mean her ... for years. She seemed like such a gentle, kind person."

"Too bad she didn't just turn herself in," Granger said, opening the back door for Selena. "She only made it worse for herself when she's caught."

Selena reached over and slipped her hand into his, and with a teasing smile, gave it a little squeeze. He responded with a slow, sexy smile. Her stomach did a little seesaw. No man should be that ridiculously attractive. "Think you'll be off work in time for dinner tonight?"

"Hope so. Let's play it by ear." He stole a little kiss, and she climbed into the cage.

***

Sidney was immediately flagged down by Winnie when she returned to the station. "James Abbott is in the conference room. Been waiting for forty-five minutes. His dad's with him."

"Thanks, Winnie." Sidney silently groaned. In light of the homicide investigations currently consuming her department's time and manpower, Abbott's problem with his father's jewelry purchase wasn't close to being high on her list. But, like a mosquito bite that kept on itching, he wasn't going to go away. She'd give him ten minutes, tops. His baritone voice filled the hallway before she entered the room, barking at someone on the phone. He had made himself at home, briefcase open on a chair, papers spread across one end of the table.

She glanced at the crime board, which she had forgotten to flip over before leaving the station last night, but Winnie had saved the day by turning it to its blank side.

A handsome older man sat with his head resting against the wall, eyes closed, gently snoring. So this was the man who had captured her mother's heart. Ray. Dressed in a blue golf shirt and tan pants, he was probably in his early seventies. He had a tanned face and a thick head of silver hair that matched his son's. A warm tenderness swelled in Sidney's heart when she thought of the loving relationship Ray and Molly could have, if Abbott would just step out of their way.

Abbott put up a finger when she walked into the room and kept on talking in a heated tone. Right now, when every minute counted, Sidney could make better use of her time than eavesdropping on his conversation. She walked into the hallway and entered the bullpen, the common area where her three junior officers had staked out their respective real estate. The station's cramped quarters, a bit rundown from overuse, was thoroughly inadequate for the amount of work her department put out every day. Amanda and Darnell sat at their desks which were butted against each other, their fingers busy on their keyboards. Granger's empty desk was shoved against the wall in the far corner. They both focused their attention on Sidney.

"Where's Thomas?" During her drive, Sidney had gone over her line of questioning, and had determined how to integrate inquiries about both murders without frightening Thomas into silence.

"You mean stone man?" Darnell asked. "He's in the sweat box. I offered him your sandwich, but he gave me the silent treatment. Just sat there like a statue. Apparently, he enjoys playing martyr."

"You get everything to the lab, Amanda?"

"Yep. Dr. Linthrope will be done with the autopsy around three."

Sidney glanced at her watch. It was 2:45 p.m. "Thomas is going to have to wait. Let him stew in his own juices until I get back."

Abbott appeared in the doorway. With his strong features, impeccably tailored suit, and confident persona, he looked as stately as a diplomat—far too elegant for the shabbiness of the station, but Sidney knew his well-crafted appearance was camouflage for his corrupt nature.

He glanced impatiently at his watch, then caught her eye. "Can we get the jewelry, Chief Becker?" he clipped. "I'm running late."

"Darnell, get the release form and the jewelry for Mr. Abbott, please." She and Abbott reentered the conference room. He had packed his briefcase and was ready to grab the jewelry and go. Ray had not moved and still snored, asleep in his seat.

"Dad." Abbott shook Ray's shoulder. The old man's head nodded forward, chin to chest. "Dad," he said louder, shaking the old man a little harder. "Dad, wake up."

Ray lifted his head and blinked, as though coming out of a trance. He looked up into the face of his son, but his eyes didn't focus.

Darnell walked in and placed the form and jewelry box on the table. Sidney gestured for him to stay.

"Stand up, Dad." James helped Ray to his feet and the old man shuffled to the table, then slumped into a chair. James pushed the form toward his father, pulled a gold pen from an inside pocket of his jacket, and pressed it into Ray's hand. "Dad, you're at the police station. We're picking up the jewelry. Remember? We talked about this on the drive over. You need to sign this form." He pointed to the signature line. "Right here."

"Hold on a second, Mr. Abbott." Sidney sat next to Ray. Up close, she saw that his pupils were dilated. She asked in a gentle tone, "Ray, do you know where you are?"

"You're at the police station, Dad," Abbott said tersely.

"Please step into the hall, Mr. Abbott." Sidney shot him a no-nonsense look and he retreated to the hall, but stood watching from the doorway, impatient, arms crossed.

"Ray, do you know why you're here?" Sidney asked.

With a mystified expression, Ray looked from Sidney to his son.

"To pick up the jewelry," Abbott said.

"To pick up the jewelry," Ray repeated.

Sidney quelled her anger. Clearly, Ray was sedated. "Your father seems disoriented."

"He's got memory problems, Chief Becker. He's subject to confusion. That's why he lives at Alpine Ridge."

"Did you give him something?"

Abbott sucked in a breath, exhaled sharply. "Yes. Some medicinal pot. Just to calm him down and get him over here. He didn't want to come."

"I'm sorry, but I can't release the jewelry to Ray when he's in this state of mind."

"Are you kidding me?" Outrage edged into Abbott's voice and he approached in a menacing manner. "I cancelled important business appointments to get him over here."

Darnell took a step forward and Abbott halted halfway to the table. "Let's just get the damn form signed," he said.

"I'm sorry for your inconvenience," Sidney said firmly. "But Ray needs to be cognitive before he signs anything."

Abbott's grey eyes matched his tone, hot with anger. "What's the problem? Do you really think I need to rob my dad of twelve thousand dollars? For Christ's sake. Get real. Let him sign the damn form!"

"In the future, do not administer any kind of drug to your father," Sidney said in a carefully controlled tone. "His caretakers at the center work closely with his doctor, and not even a vitamin can be given without an MD's consent." She nodded to her junior officer. "Darnell, will you help Mr. Abbott take his father to his car?"

"Yes, ma'am." Darnell helped Ray to his feet and they slowly shuffled into the hallway. Sidney watched, noticing that Ray looked extremely fit for a man his age. Selena said he and Molly walked all around town before ending up at the coffee shop. There was no reason why he should be dragging himself over the floor as though he was at death's door. Sidney looked forward to meeting the poor man when he was back to his normal self. When she turned back to Abbott, he was watching her with a reptilian stare that looked deadly, ready to strike. It made her skin crawl. "One more thing, Mr. Abbott," Sidney stated coldly. "Don't threaten my family again. It won't go well for you."

After leveling a stare at Sidney that clearly told her to fuck off, Abbott grabbed his briefcase and left.

***

Sidney crossed the lobby of the small community hospital and took the elevator to the basement. This time yesterday, she was viewing the body of Olivia Paisley. Hard to believe that Max would now be occupying that sterile metal slab. She took a deep breath, steeling herself, then pushed through one of the double doors and entered the morgue. She approached the slab and sucked in a breath as she confronted Max's remains in the unforgiving bright light. The colorless body bore no likeness to the warm, easy-going man she had known as a friend and colleague. Staring at his corpse, Sidney shuddered, and the emotion she'd kept buried all day surfaced. Tears stung her eyes as more memories flashed. She recalled Max playing with his grandkids in the backyard, and the steaks he grilled for her whole department to celebrate the closing of his case. He was always cheerful, fully enjoying the warmth of family and friends.

Linthrope was washing up at the sink. He dried his hands with paper towels and joined her at the slab. Beneath his cumulous of white hair, his face sobered at her expression, and he asked gently, "You okay, Chief?"

She nodded, ignoring the queasiness in her stomach. "Yeah, I'm okay. It's just a shock to see a friend this way." She blinked back tears, swallowed, and said hoarsely, "Let's proceed, Doc. What did you discover?"

"As suspected, Max suffered massive blood loss from the knife wound." Linthrope cleared his throat, and his voice resumed its normal tone, calm and professional. "The wound was made by a double-edge, six-inch blade, consistent with the knife you turned in. A fairly heavy throwing knife. The heavier the knife, the more impact it has on the target. A heavier knife will also allow you to hit a target that's further away. To hit Max with accuracy from a distance of even ten feet, and have the whole blade embedded, you have to know what you're doing."

"So the suspect had training throwing knives."

"Yes." Linthrope pushed his glasses higher on his nose. "It appears the suspect approached Max as he tried to crawl away and pulled out the knife. That sealed his fate. The knife acted as a plug. Once it was removed, his blood poured out, thus the trail of blood all the way to the creek."

"So COD is the knife wound."

"Yes and no. That would've killed him within minutes but crawling into the creek expedited the process. He gulped in water and drowned."

"Double whammy."

"That's not all." Linthrope lifted Max's head and turned it to the left, revealing a region of extreme swelling and discoloration. "Max sustained a violent blow to this side of his skull the night before he was murdered, which caused increased pressure and swelling in his brain."

"So he was running around seriously injured."

"Right. In desperate need of medical attention. A traumatic brain injury can change a person's state of consciousness. Resulting in unusual behavior such as profound confusion, agitation, anger, and combativeness."

"So you're saying his head injury caused his violent behavior?"

"Yes. His tox screen showed no medications, and no psychoactive drugs. Just a low level of alcohol. Which would have induced relaxation, not violence."

"What caused the head injury? There were signs of an altercation at his campsite. And blood spatter."

"Hard to say. He may have been struck by a blunt object, or he may have fallen and hit his head. One thing is certain, the blood on the firepit isn't his. There are no open wounds on his body other than the knife wound. It appears Max inflicted an injury on the person who visited his campsite."

"So we have DNA from his visitor." She sharply exhaled. "But the lab is backed up. Why does this sound familiar?"

He shrugged. "We do what we can. Now it's out of our hands."

Sidney was quiet, thinking of her friend's ill-fated last night alive, roaming through the forest severely injured and delusional. The next morning, unfortunately, Max came upon Karune and attacked him. Then he, himself, was attacked. Stabbed. Dying, he crawled to the creek and drowned. A nightmare.

"Knife throwing." Linthrope shook his head. "Not something you'd expect from a peace-loving Buddhist monk."

"Yeshey is not your normal monk. For one thing, Yeshey is a woman."

Linthrope's bushy white brows lifted in surprise. "Yeshey is a woman?"

"Yes. Her name is Tammy Schaffer."

"Holy mackerel. She passed for a man all these years? Well, I'll be damned."

Sidney quickly brought Linthrope up to date on what she knew about Tammy, and added, "She's now a fugitive. Skipped out on drug and murder charges sixteen years ago."

"I'll be damned," Linthrope repeated, adjusting his glasses. "Well, let's go talk to Stewart and see what he's got for you."

They walked down the hall and Stewart lifted his head from his microscope as they entered the lab. "Have a seat."

She and Linthrope took seats at the small table in the corner.

Dressed in a white lab coat over gray slacks and loafers, Stewart picked up a file and an evidence bag containing a phone, pulled out a chair, and joined them. He opened the file, lifted the top sheet of paper, and cleared his throat. "First, Max's toxicology report showed no drugs or medication in his system. Blood alcohol level was .04 percent, the equivalent of about two drinks for someone his size. Secondly, Yeshey's real name is Tammy Schaffer. Her prints are in the system. Now, the knife. Prints confirm that it had been in Tammy's possession. There are traces of blood on the blade. The lab just needs to confirm it's Max's, Chief Becker."

Sidney sighed her relief. "So we may have our killer. Got any results from the campsite, Stewart?"

"Not much. Most of it's at the lab. As you can expect from a family man, there were a number of fingerprints, clothing fibers, and hair samples in the camper and truck. It'll take a while to rule out his family members. We pulled fresher prints from the armrest of one of the camp chairs, but they don't match Tammy. There were no matches in AFIS, either." He looked up at Sidney, his eyes grave behind his glasses. "Sorry. That's the long and short of it."

"Darn. What about the phone found in her black bag?"

Stewart held up the phone. "It has two sets of prints. One matches Max. One matches Tammy."

"So the phone belonged to Max?" Sidney said with a touch of excitement. "Why did Tammy have it? Did she pick it up after she killed him this morning? I need access to everything on that phone. It could have all kinds of valuable info on it. When will you have phone records for me?"

"I can get an IT guy working on it. Should have results in a few days."

"Darnell's an IT guy. I'll take it."

Stewart slid it across the table. "I put a rush on the cigarette butt found at Aspen Lake. The DNA result might come in today. Tomorrow at the latest."

"Did the tire tread tell you anything?"

He pulled out another sheet of paper. His dark eyes scanned the sheet and he started reading. "It's a high performance, all terrain Goodyear Wrangler DuraTrac. High end. Expensive. The preferred tire for souped-up trucks." He met her gaze. "There are unique characteristics attributed to wear and tear of the tread."

"Each tire wears down differently over time," she said.

"Yep. If we find the truck, we can match the tire to the impression."

"Why does that sound familiar? The boots at Olivia's crime scene were high end. Her killer drove a truck. These are high end tires. From her neighbor's account, the engine sounded like a plane taking off. Sounds souped-up to me. Could Max's visitor be Olivia's killer?"

Both men were quiet, thinking. Linthrope scratched his head. "It's a leap. Nothing else connects the two murders."

Stewart shrugged and ran a hand through his short-cropped black hair. "Until we have more evidence, we have a bunch of puzzle pieces that don't fit together. At this point, it looks like we have two separate murders. Two killers."

"I agree. Two killers. Two murders. But somehow both homicides are related. There's a link. A glaring link. Thomas. But the connecting dots have yet to materialize." She glanced at her watch, then smiled at the men, grateful to have a team of their caliber here in town. "I have to get back to the station. Thanks for your excellent help."

Both men nodded, returning her smile.

CHAPTER TWENTY-ONE

SIDNEY LEFT THE MORGUE, her brain a vortex of swirling thoughts. She drove down Main Street, and by habit, observed the tourists idling on the sidewalks, looking for anything out of the ordinary. People were browsing shop windows, eating ice cream cones, sitting on the patios of cafes—peacefully enjoying a beautiful day. The sun drifted in and out of billowing white clouds and Lake Kalapuya reflected the deep blue of the sky. A few sailboats drifted lazily on the currents.

Lights glowed from inside the Art Studio and Sidney caught a glimpse of her boyfriend, David, dressed in jeans and a T-shirt, talking to a handful of students. His class ended fifteen minutes ago. The image of the coin found in Olivia's pocket suddenly popped into her mind. On impulse, she pulled over and parked. The studio door opened, and people streamed out onto the sidewalk. She waited until the last straggler left and David was locking the front door.

His brown eyes brightened when he saw her, and he opened the door, grinning. "Hey, beautiful." He pulled her into his arms, and the familiar warmth of his body calmed her. "I didn't think I was going to see you today. This is a nice surprise." He softly kissed her lips and released her. His eyes narrowed. "You look seriously stressed."

"That's putting it mildly. Would you believe we have another homicide?"

His brows shot up. "Jesus." He studied her for a long moment. "You better come into the kitchen. Let me make you a cappuccino and we'll talk about it."

They crossed the large classroom that smelled faintly of oil paint and turpentine. Art of every kind hung on the walls; charcoals, pastels, watercolors, oils. David led her into a back room equipped with an updated kitchen. Modern-style chairs were arranged around a rustic wood table, tasteful art crowded the original red brick walls, and the cement floor was stained wine red and polished. David pulled two white porcelain cups from a cabinet and turned to a commercial-size coffee machine that took up half of one counter. The smell of strong coffee filled the room and the machine hissed as David crowned each cup with a cloud of steamed milk. With his back to her, he asked over his shoulder, "I'm afraid to ask, but who's the victim?"

"Max Stevens."

With a sigh, he set one of the cups in front of Sidney and settled next to her. "My worst fear was that I might know him. Thank God I don't."

Sidney's eyes filled with tears.

"Oh my god. You did."

Sidney sniffed and nodded. Tears streamed down her face and she wiped them with her fingertips. In addition to discovering Max, it had been doubly stressful trying to maintain her composure in front of her officers all day. They were a team. What they accomplished was the result of their collective effort. But she was the leader. She was used to taking charge and solving problems. Her show of strength held the team together. But finally, with David, she could be herself, let her emotions rise to the surface, show her vulnerability.

"I'm sorry, Sidney." He covered her hand with his and they sat for a long moment in silence. "Want to talk about it?"

In a shaky voice, without going into detail, Sidney related the basics.

He listened attentively with an expression of empathy. A gift David had.

As she spoke for the next few minutes, she pulled herself together, until her voice was calm and controlled. "I think you might be able to help me with something."

"Name it."

Sidney pulled out her phone and swiped through her photos until she found the coin. She held out the screen. "Maybe you can tell me about this."

David leaned forward in his seat and his eyebrows arched. As an art historian who studied symbology, his interest was clearly piqued. "This is interesting. It's a very good reproduction of a rare 9th Century Viking coin. The symbol is a Valknut, or the 'Knot of the Slain Warrior.' The three interlocking triangles represent a certain type of connectivity of everything, infinity and immortality. It's also an aid for reincarnation, cyclical relationships, and a talisman to ward against evil."

"Hmm. It does all that?" She smiled. "I should get one."

A flicker of amusement touched the corner of his mouth. "Me, too."

"So where would I get something like this?"

"Depends. There are cheapies you can order off the internet. But I believe this one came from a collector of coins, or maybe of Viking artifacts. Cheapies are usually perfectly uniform, stamped from the same mold. This is a reproduction, but a good one. And it looks very old. See the rough texture? The rough edges? Those are characteristics of hand tooling. If you want, I could send it out to my antiquities contacts to see if anything about it raises a flag."

"That would be really helpful." Sidney texted him the photo and heard his phone ping. Frowning, she wondered what the coin's significance was to Olivia's killer. What was he trying to communicate by putting it in her pocket?

"Hey, earth to Sidney. You look a million miles away."

"Sorry." She cradled her mug in her hands, sipped her cappuccino, and let out a sigh of satisfaction. "You make a mean cup of java." She drained her cup and the foam tickled her upper lip.

David gently wiped a speck of foam from her mouth with a finger. "When will I have you all to myself again?" he asked. "I miss our afternoons."

As she met the brown eyes she'd lost herself in so many times, she felt a warm stirring of affection. She couldn't help the surge of attraction she felt for this man. He had a tanned face, pleasant features, and dark hair that curled around the back of his collar. "I don't know. Two homicide investigations can really take it out of a girl."

"Promise me you'll take time to eat and sleep."

"I'll put it on my calendar." She smiled. "As much as I'd like to stay, duty calls. Crime never sleeps."

Sidney followed David to the front door, enjoying the visuals. Lean build, broad shoulders, cute butt. They indulged in a sweet kiss and then she was out the door into the real world again, putting on her practiced cop façade.

***

Standing in the audio room, which was no bigger than a broom closet, Sidney stood with Amanda and Darnell, watching Thomas through the one-way mirror. In the small cinder block room under the glaring fluorescent lights, the tall monk looked out of place in his flowing crimson robe and sandals. Most suspects looked tense or nervous, or feigned a calm while a sheen of nervous sweat told otherwise, but Thomas sat as still and tranquil as the Buddha himself. His eyes were closed, and his cuffed hands looked relaxed resting on the scarred metal table.

Darnell thumbed a few buttons. "Audio and video are ready to go."

"Good. Let's go in, Darnell. Take notes."

Darnell pulled a notepad and pen from his breast pocket and followed her into the windowless room. They scraped back metal chairs and seated themselves.

"How are you doing, Thomas?" Sidney asked gently.

Thomas opened his eyes and looked like a man coming out of a trance. His gaze swept past Darnell and landed on Sidney, holding her stare without looking the slightest bit nervous, or angry.

Sidney let her face slide into a professional mask and kept her voice carefully polite. "Can we get you a cup of coffee? A soft drink? Water?"

"Water, please."

Sidney nodded toward the mirror where Amanda stood on the other side. She entered with a pitcher of water and three plastic cups, placed them on the table, and left. Darnell poured water into the cups. Thomas immediately lifted his cup in his cuffed hands and emptied it. Darnell refilled it.

Thomas wiped his mouth with the back of his hand. "Are these cuffs really necessary?" He seemed to view his presence there as a colossal waste of time. "I'm a monk. I preach peace and non-violence. Do you really see me as dangerous?"

I see you as someone with a lot of motive. "Sorry Thomas, just procedure. Officer Wood advised you of your Miranda rights in the patrol car. Is that correct?"

"Yes," he murmured.

"Having those rights in mind, are you willing to talk with me now?"

"Of course. I have nothing to hide."

The monk's stress level appeared to be low. Sidney needed to keep it that way. Remembering how volatile he was at the monastery she needed to proceed with sensitivity. One murder at a time. If he knew he was a prime suspect in Olivia's murder, he might spook, lawyer up, quit talking, and they'd be dead in the water.

First, Max. Sidney began by asking him neutral questions. How long had he been going to the monastery? What led him to become a monk?

Thomas had a natural tendency to preach, and for several minutes he recited his spiritual beliefs and his teaching methods with the boys. Sidney and Darnell nodded, encouraging him. Then Sidney steered him to the events of the morning.

Thomas's expression changed to one of deep concern, and he stated how shocking the murder was, and how nothing even remotely that violent had ever happened at the monastery before. "It's going to take time for the climate to return to normal. To a state of tranquility. I just hope it doesn't have a lingering emotional impact on the boys."

"Time heals everything," she said softly. After pausing a few beats, she continued. "Help me understand what happened today. Tell me about Yeshey. It seems you two have a very close friendship."

"We do."

"You felt a great need to help him. You felt he was in danger."

He rubbed his forehead with his finger, the handcuffs clinking. "You have no idea how wrong you are about him."

"I want to understand. We came on pretty strong, with the dog and three heavily armed officers marching up to the monastery. That must have been pretty frightening."

"It was. I thought you might hurt him."

"That's why you helped him get away."

"I did what I had to do." He held her gaze with intelligent blue eyes, his voice polite but essentially unapologetic.

"Help me understand, Thomas, why you had to do that."

"For one thing, you were hunting him down like he's some kind of rabid killer. He's not."

"Tell me more about that," Sidney said gently.

"Yeshey was protecting Karune." He spoke in a quiet voice, almost a murmur. "If Yeshey didn't have a knife, and if he hadn't acted, that strange man might have killed the boy."

"How do you know this?"

"He told me later. After I contacted you. That's when we devised a plan. If you guys caught wind of his involvement, his best recourse was to escape."

Sidney glanced at Darnell and he gave her a subtle nod of acknowledgement. Thomas had just confessed to aiding and abetting a felon in a murder case. He was digging a hole he wasn't coming out of. She wanted him to keep digging.

"What happened exactly? In the woods."

He rubbed his hands over his face, suddenly looking haggard. "Yeshey was walking in the forest. Something he did every morning. He was alarmed when he spotted Karune out in the woods alone. Before he could say anything, he spotted the man."

"The stranger."

"Yes, the stranger. He looked like a tramp. And he was acting strangely, hiding behind a tree. He lurched at Karune and slammed his fist into his face. The boy went down hard and hit his head. Then the man raised a piece of wood to club the boy. Yeshey acted instantaneously. Most likely, he saved Karune's life." Thomas's voice softened, and sorrow settled in his eyes.

"Yeshey was devastated. He's terribly, terribly sorry for the man's family."

"Yeshey didn't want to kill the guy, he just wanted to stop him from hurting Karune," Sidney summarized, maintaining a sympathetic tone, offering a rationalization for Yeshey's crime. Her role as an interrogator was to appear to be a friend, not a moral judge. "Why did he pull the knife out of the man's back, Thomas?"

"For one thing, he knew that no one could survive that kind of injury. His first instinct was to get out of there. Not leave any evidence behind."

Sidney shivered, picturing a small boy who just suffered a head injury, lying unconscious on the ground. And Max crawling through the brush, moaning, trying to save himself. The killer yanked out the knife, then ran. Cold blooded. Yeshey's instinct was to save herself, not Max or Karune. "If Yeshey acted in defense of the boy, why didn't he just turn himself in?"

Thomas retreated into silence, a faint frown touching his lips. A full minute passed.

"Talk to me, Thomas," she said in a soothing tone.

Thomas stared at his hands. Another minute passed. Sidney needed to break the logjam. "Thomas, we found documents when searching Yeshey's room. We know her real identity is Tammy Schaffer."

He was quiet for a few beats, staring at his hands, then he looked up. "Since you know her identity, you must also know why she ran."

"Clue me in, Thomas," Sidney said. "I want to fully understand."

Leaning back in the metal seat, his gaze sharpened. "Tammy has been in hiding for sixteen years. She didn't want her cover blown. Her life was at stake. I have no doubt she'd be dead right now if certain people knew where she was." Thomas glared, looking at her and Darnell like they were the enemy. "I had to give Tammy time to make a clean getaway before you broadcasted her name all over the state. Which by now I'm sure you've done."

"Who are these people?"

"Traffickers. Drugs. Sex. You name it."

Darnell jotted notes on his pad, his eyebrows drawn together in concentration.

"Why would they still be looking for Tammy after all these years?"

"These are the kind of men that never forget a betrayal." Anger leeched more aggressively into his voice. "They butcher people without blinking an eye. They'd make sure Tammy died a slow, agonizing death."

Sidney was silent, sifting through his words. "Who specifically are we talking about, Thomas?"

He avoided her eyes, focusing on his tightly clasped hands.

"Talk to me, Thomas."

"Even if I could trust you, which I don't, what could you do? You're a small-town cop. Tammy is up against a well-organized cartel. If they wanted to, they could mow down your whole department in a heartbeat."

Sidney exchanged a glance with Darnell. His face was inscrutable, the line of his jaw hard. Like Sidney, he found the story suspicious, if not ludicrous. "I want to help you, Thomas. And Tammy. But I need to know the facts. Tell me about the role Tammy played."

He leveled a cold stare at her. She could feel the skepticism on him. His expression went through several transformations until his shoulders sagged. He looked like a man in deep despair.

"How did Tammy become involved with these traffickers?"

"She'd been an addict. She bought and sold drugs. One of her clients ripped her off. To get his money back, her dealer farmed her out for sex. Tammy got arrested by a vice cop posing as a John." Thomas's blue eyes held a sharper scrutiny as he stared at Sidney and Darnell, gauging their reaction.

Sidney sat quietly, absorbing the shock of his words, wearing her practiced sympathetic expression.

"Tammy was given a chance to redeem herself and she took it. She became an informant and wore a wire." Thomas paused, his voice holding more anger. "Do you know how dangerous that is? The courage it took? She got some vile people off the street."

"You're right. Tammy is a brave woman," Sidney said. "I understand that you want to protect her. You know where she is, don't you, Thomas? We can help her. We can offer police protection."

"Yeah, that's what that detective told her. Trusting him almost cost Tammy her life. Someone in the department leaked the location of her safe house. Probably him."

Sidney's body tensed and a she felt unease in her stomach, right before she looked at Darnell. He was staring hard at Thomas. Accusations of a cop being dirty were not taken lightly. Tammy's old case would need to be evaluated, though her story sounded like the product of a wild imagination. Sidney's eyes narrowed. "Who was the detective?"

Thomas stared at his hands and refused to answer.

"Tell us where she is, Thomas. We'll help her."

No response.

Sidney came at him from a different stance. "Yesterday, you and Tammy were spotted in the woods kissing. You two were in a relationship. Want to tell me about that?"

His jaw clenched and unclenched. "Nothing to tell. We love each other. Plain and simple. We've kept it secret for months. For reasons just mentioned."

"It isn't entirely true that you and Tammy thought the stranger was a tramp, is it? You caught him watching you. Correct?"

"Spying, more like it," Thomas said, agitated. "Taking photos. He scared the hell out of Tammy."

"Must have made you mad."

Thomas leaned forward, a scowl darkening his features. "What do you think? Some strange man in the woods. Taking pictures. She thought he was associated with the cartel. The people who want her dead."

"What did you do?"

"I followed him."

"To his campsite?"

He sat straighter in his chair and cleared his throat. "Yeah, I followed him to his campsite. But I didn't do anything. I needed to think. I went back to the monastery and had dinner. I returned later that evening and confronted him. I wanted to know who the hell he was, and why he was spying on us. He told me he was a P.I." Thomas exhaled a long, ragged breath. "A private investigator, just as Tammy thought. I admit, anger got the better of me. I demanded he tell me who hired him. He said it was confidential, and I better get the hell out of his campsite."

"What happened next?"

"Nothing. I left."

"That's not entirely true, is it, Thomas?"

Thomas licked his lips, took a sip of water, then wiped his mouth with the back of one hand.

"Did you have an altercation?"

He wouldn't meet her gaze.

"Did you take his camera and computer?"

Finally, his eyes locked on hers. "I saw his camera sitting on the stump by the trailer. I grabbed it and made a dash across the clearing. But he caught me by the arm and slugged me. I shoved him back and knocked him down. I dropped the camera. But his phone fell out of his pocket. Before he could get to his feet, I grabbed his phone and ran. But he wasn't hurt when I left."

"So it's your blood we found at the campsite?"

"Yeah, maybe. My nose bled when he hit me."

She held up the evidence bag holding the phone that Tammy left in the barn. "Is this Max's phone?"

"Yeah. I gave it to Tammy. We thought we'd try to find out who hired Max."

"And you didn't take his camera or computer?"

"No." His brows suddenly lifted. "Oh, I just remembered. Right at the end of our scuffle, someone drove up in a black truck. He was watching us from the cab."

Sidney's adrenaline spiked. *A black truck.* "Did you recognize him?"

"No. I just caught a glimpse before I ran. He wore a bill cap. Shadowed his face."

"Thomas, think very carefully. Could that have been your truck?"

He looked taken aback. "My truck? No. My truck is at home in my carport."

"Where were you the night before last?"

"At the monastery."

"Can anyone verify that?"

"Yes. I was in the dining hall having dinner. Everyone can verify that."

"What time was that?"

"We eat at five."

"And after dinner?"

"I was with Yeshey. In her room. All night."

"Hmmm. Did anyone else see you?"

"No. We didn't advertise that we were together."

Sidney ruminated on that. Thomas's only witness was on the run. Not that Sidney would trust Tammy anyway. Lovers, more likely than not, covered for each other. His involvement in her escape, and his unwillingness to divulge her location, revealed his commitment was to Tammy, not to obeying the law. Sidney and Darnell locked eyes for a moment. Thomas did not have an alibi for the time of Olivia's murder. And he just admitted his truck may have been at Max's campsite. Maybe Thomas was the one who drove it there.

"Does anyone else have permission to drive your truck?"

"No." He narrowed his eyes and looked pointedly from Darnell to Sidney. "What's with these questions? Why do I need an alibi?"

Sidney watched him carefully. "Olivia's neighbors believe they saw you at her house two nights ago. Your truck was parked in her driveway."

His body tensed at the mere mention of her name. "Did Olivia say that? That's utter nonsense. I was with Tammy."

Sidney didn't answer.

"Don't believe a word Olivia says. She's been trying to screw me ever since the divorce.

If there was a truck at her place, it wasn't mine."

"How would you describe your relationship with your ex?"

He shrugged. "What you would expect, I guess. We were civil to one another."

Stalking and constant harassment hardly sounded civil. "If you don't mind, Thomas, tell me how much alimony you pay Olivia."

He scowled. "Too freaking much."

"May I have a figure?"

"What's going on here? What's with all these questions about Olivia? What did she tell you?"

"Bear with me, Thomas. I'll explain in a minute. I just have a couple more questions. Can you tell me about the threats Olivia was getting a couple years back? Before she quit her job?"

He blew out a breath and looked at the ceiling, thinking. "Haven't thought about that in a long while." His eyes met Sidney's. "She got five or six nasty letters over a period of three months. At first, she just tossed them out. They were unpleasant, but not threatening. That changed. The last three frightened her."

"What did they say?"

"Don't remember exactly. But she was called a bitch, and a monster. She was accused of destroying the sender's life, and her life would be destroyed in return. And that she was going to pay. She reported the letters, but the cops said there was nothing they could do. They had no return address. No fingerprints. No way to trace them. That seemed to be the catalyst for a major overhaul in Olivia's life. She quit her job, declared she wanted a divorce, and moved out. All within a two-week period. I think she was trying to become anonymous." He huffed out a weary breath. "The rift between us had been widening for a long while, but getting that last letter put her over the edge."

"Where are these letters?"

"She burned them when she moved out."

Great. "Did she have any idea who sent them?"

He shrugged. "Could have been any number of people. People were upset with her all the time." He narrowed his eyes, concentrating. "You know, there was one person in particular. A guy with a foster kid. He berated her every time she went to check on the boy."

"Why?"

"Said the state wasn't paying him enough."

"What was his name?"

"I don't know."

"Know anything about the kid?"

"He was a teenager. I believe Olivia said he was sixteen or seventeen."

There was silence in the room as Sidney reflected on his words.

"So what's going on with Olivia? Why all these questions?" Thomas frowned. "Is she okay?"

Sidney inhaled deeply and slowly exhaled. "Thomas, I'm sorry, but Olivia is dead."

The monk sat pressed back in his chair as though he'd been struck, his eyes wide with shock. "Oh my God. Olivia's dead? What happened?"

She studied him—every nuance of expression. His reaction looked genuine, but guilty people could be convincing actors. Award winning, in fact. "Olivia was murdered. By someone driving a black truck. And your truck is not in your carport."

"My truck's gone?" He looked dazed, as though her words made no sense. As though he was trying to transition from shock to rationality.

Thomas knew the symptoms of shock. He'd been witnessing various states of shock in the ER for years. Was this an act?

"Then ... if it's my truck .... It's been stolen," he stammered. "Olivia's killer is driving my truck ...."

Sidney could see the wheels turning in his head. As he sifted through their conversation he realized the implications of what he'd said. "You think I killed Olivia!" His gaze locked on Sidney, a touch of panic in his eyes. "I'm not saying another word. I want my lawyer."

Sidney nodded to Darnell. "Will you kindly book Thomas? See that he has a nice cell for the night."

"Got it," Darnell said.

Thomas stiffened, his features hardening, but he left the room quietly. "I want to talk to my lawyer." She heard him repeat it to Darnell in the hall. Sidney knew that was the last she would see of Thomas for a while. Once he had a lawyer, she might as well throw in the towel. He would easily make bail in the morning. She probably wouldn't hear another word from him until they were in court.

The questioning had gone better than she hoped. Thomas had done an excellent job of incriminating himself, and Tammy. A mountain of evidence pointed directly at him as Olivia's murderer. Men had been convicted on far less. Still, Sidney had a niggling feeling in the back of her mind. She suspected that there was a lot more going on than what had floated to the surface in the interview. She picked up Thomas's empty cup with a pencil and dropped it into an evidence bag, sealed and labeled it.

CHAPTER TWENTY-TWO

SIDNEY WALKED into the hallway and entered the bullpen. Amanda sat over her computer. Granger, too, was hunched over his desk in the far corner. They both focused their full attention on Sidney.

"Amanda, get this cup with Thomas's DNA over to Stewart. Tell him we need a rush on it, and on Tammy's toothbrush. We need to compare their DNA to what we collected from the suspect at Aspen Lake."

"Granger, go pick up a couple of large pizzas. We're all meeting for a briefing in the conference room as soon as you get back."

Sidney entered her office and sank into her leather chair. She had an Everest of paperwork to catch up on. Even with two investigations going full steam, reports still needed to be filed. The bane of all cops.

Darnell walked into her office a few minutes later, his brown eyes playful. "Thomas is booked and settling into his new digs. The luxury suite."

"Full amenities." She smiled, picturing the station's two cells; stripped of everything but basic needs. The luxury suite was one foot wider than the economy suite.

"He's in a state of shock."

"A small locked room with bars will do that to you."

"He said it's like a cage in a zoo. Having the toilet out in the open is degrading."

"Poor baby. Where he's going, he better get used to it."

"Amen."

***

Winnie had started a crime board for Max next to Olivia's, including photos of the crime scene and Max's campsite. Sidney went over every scrap of physical evidence they had collected that day, plus the information elicited from all the monks—and specifically, Thomas.

Her authoritative voice and manner did the trick. Everyone hurriedly finished eating pizza and cleared the table.

"Right now, a mountain of evidence points to Thomas and Tammy as murderers and co-conspirators. Thomas has motive for killing Olivia. He was obsessed with her. Couldn't seem to let her go. He constantly harassed her, went through her mail, and was upset about alimony payments." Sidney paused and sipped her drink. "Tammy had motive for killing Max. Supposedly, according to Thomas, she thought he was hired by someone scheming to kill her."

"I think she may have been more concerned about her cover being blown," Amanda said. "And her ultimate arrest."

Darnell leaned back in his seat, tapping a pen on the table. "That story she fed Thomas sounds like really bad pulp fiction. Cooked up to hide the fact that she's a fugitive."

"She had him by his little dark curlies," Granger said. "One gullible dude."

"Another intelligent man derailed by a woman's wanton charms," Amanda said, with a tilt to her lips.

Granger rolled his eyes.

"Stumbling upon Max attacking Karune may have been her lucky break," Darnell said.

"Justification for murder. No witnesses. She could have made up anything."

"She may have wanted him dead," Amanda said. "You never pull a knife out of a victim. That's often the only thing keeping them from bleeding out."

"To jerk the knife out of Max's back while he's still crawling away speaks to mindset," Sidney added, her chest tightening at the image of Max on the slab. "And a callous disregard for a mortally wounded person. Not to mention leaving Karune there unconscious."

"Tammy may have been justified in throwing the knife," Amanda said. "But her actions thereafter just made her a murderer."

"While that's true, a defense attorney could easily argue that she didn't realize that. That she'd only thrown at targets before, and that she panicked. We'll have to wait and see how it plays out in court."

"Well, we all agree on one thing," Granger said. "Tammy's a suspect for murder and Thomas is a patsy."

"Don't give Tammy all the credit," Sidney said. "Thomas may be just as coldblooded."

"While we're waiting for lab results, what do we do next?" Amanda asked.

"Follow other leads," Sidney said. "Darnell, we need Max's digital footprint for the last few weeks. All email, text messages, and phone records. We need to find out who his client was. Cecille said he'd been very secretive about it. He said he had to be careful."

"Careful?" Darnell asked.

"Yeah. He didn't want to step on the wrong toes. I think there are influential people involved who might not appreciate what he was digging up."

"Sounds ominous."

"Yeah, it does. First, try the easy way. Call Cecille. See if she knows her husband's password. As backup, and to protect our asses in court, call Judge Blumenthal and get a warrant."

"Will do."

"Amanda, I want you to call Social Services. At night, they have an intake supervisor. Have him go through Olivia's old client files. See if she red-flagged anyone. Look at disgruntled foster parents who had a teenage boy."

"Got it."

"Granger, I want you to find out where Tammy got popped last. That's most likely the jurisdiction that worked her case. If she was involved with an actual cartel, this could get really complicated. No doubt, state lines were crossed, which means the FBI would be involved in some capacity. The DEA could be involved regarding the drugs, and ATF may be involved regarding weapons."

"Complicated is right," Granger said, shaking his head.

"The key players could be in jail, retired, or dead. We might be chasing smoke here, but if there's even a thread of truth to her story, we need to know."

"Yes, ma'am."

Sidney picked up her soda and sipped until the straw gurgled on the bottom of the glass.

The three officers sat waiting, still watching her.

"What are you all waiting for? Dessert?" Sidney half smiled. "Dismissed. Get to work."

***

After her fingers had clicked the keyboard for an hour, Sidney rubbed her tired eyes and stifled a yawn. Exhaustion was wearing her down. Not enough sleep. She needed a strong dose of caffeine. She pushed her chair away from the desk and made her way to the break room with her empty cup. With her jumbo-size coffee mug filled to the brim, Sidney encountered Granger in the hallway, notepad gripped in one hand.

"Just coming to see you, Chief." He exuded energy and his blue eyes sparkled. A good sign. Sidney led him back to her office. They took their seats and she fortified herself with a gulp of strong coffee. "Okay. What do we have?"

"Tammy's convoluted story about her past is pure fiction, as we suspected. No cartel. No Fed involvement. No safe house. No prostitution arrest. No wiretap. I contacted Detective Dan Bunker who worked her case in Crestview. Small town near the Idaho border. Population around fifteen-hundred residents. He was a patrol cop at the time. We went back through her rap sheet. He remembered her because she skipped out of town, and she told fantastical stories."

Sidney cocked an eyebrow. "Why am I not surprised?" In their line of work, cops were told every kind of fabrication imaginable. "If the mind can think it, the mouth can spout it. What's the real lowdown?"

Granger crossed an ankle over a knee, scanned his notes, and read. "Tammy was born and raised here in Garnerville. Got into the drug scene as a teenager, which landed her a couple of stints in juvenile detention. Her mom sent her to Crestview to live with her dad. At eighteen, she had another drug bust. She had graduated to heroin. She turned in her dealer and got a lighter sentence. Afterwards, she stayed clean; waitressing, going to night school, attending substance abuse meetings. Three months later, she nearly OD'd on smack. Tammy had complained of a shower leak, and lucky for her, the apartment manager dropped by to repair it after dinner." Granger looked up and met Sidney's gaze. "He found her sprawled in a chair a hair away from dead. Her roommate wasn't so lucky. He was unconscious, the needle still in his arm. They rushed him to the ER, but he didn't make it. Her prints were found on the drug paraphernalia. His weren't. She did the deed that killed him. They got Tammy on a drug bust and murder. So that's why she's been hiding out. And why she skipped on us."

"Serious charges. Probably would have been reduced to manslaughter. With a good lawyer, she may have gotten a light sentence."

"Too bad she ran." Granger flipped to the next page of his notes. "It's her cover story that made the detective remember her. Tammy claimed she didn't hit up anyone. Two men broke into her apartment at gunpoint and made her hit up her boyfriend. Then they held her down and did the same to her. She didn't recognize them because they wore ski masks."

"You kidding me? That's pretty damn creative."

"Needless to say, no one believed her. Next day, when she was released on bail, she skipped, never to be seen again, until today."

"Hmmm." Sidney mulled over his words. "So grandiose stories were sprouting in her mind even back then. She had a nice little gig up there at the monastery. It's too bad Max had to die for us to finally find her."

"When Thomas finds out she's been playing him he might not be so gung-ho about protecting her."

Sidney took a sip of coffee. "We can only hold him until his bail hearing in the morning. He'll make bail easily. We'll have to set it up with his lawyer to go at him again."

"That would be Terry McAvoy. Coming down from Portland in the morning."

"What about Tammy's mom?" Sidney asked. "Did you get an address?"

"Yep."

"Okay. You better head over there. See what she has to say. Maybe she knows where her daughter's hiding out."

Sidney's phone buzzed. It was David. She held up her index finger to Granger. "Hey. What's up?" she said, using her professional tone. She was in efficiency mode.

"You're busy," David said. "I get it, but I have some info on that coin."

"Great. Shoot."

"There's a collector of old coins right here in Garnerville. I'm not saying the coin came from him, but he may know other collectors in the tri-town area. His name's Mitch Turner."

Sidney wrote down the address and phone number, and said lightly, "That's a big help, David. Appreciate it."

"For you, doll, anything," he said with a wise guy accent, and hung up.

Amanda breezed in and Sidney motioned for her to take a seat next to Granger. "What do you have?"

"The intake supervisor at social services was more than happy to help, considering they lost an excellent employee because of those threats. He gave me a half dozen names of folks that Olivia flagged." Amanda passed over the list.

Sidney scanned the list. Her eyebrows shot up when she got to the last name. "Hmmm. Mitch Turner. David just told me this guy collects old coins. Let's see what Mr. Turner has to say for himself." She called Turner's number, got an "out of order" response. "Disconnected." She glanced out at the night sky. It was late for a house call, but there was a nagging voice in her head that would not be ignored. "Never underestimate a coincidence. Turner is a foster dad that Olivia had issues with, and he collects old coins." She stood and motioned to both officers. "Alert Darnell. We're all heading over there. We leave in five minutes."

***

Strobes flashing, Sidney and Granger took the lead in the Yukon. Amanda and Darnell followed behind in his patrol truck. The forest streaked by in a dark blur. The address was located on the north side of the lake in an older neighborhood. The houses sat on large lots tucked into the woods. "The address is Deer Creek Road," Sidney said. "Remember Jethro Dunn, aka the Hulk? We busted him for drunk and disorderly, and for beating his wife."

"Not something you forget. The guy's like a side of beef. I remember we tasered him, and it still took three of us to get him cuffed and stuffed. Glad tonight isn't a repeat."

"Me, too. So far, he's managed to keep his nose clean. Looks like he's Turner's immediate neighbor. They're the only two houses on the cul-de-sac." Sidney switched off her strobes as she turned onto a narrow road that looked like a pale gray snake in the darkness. "Should be right around this next bend." As she rounded the curve her headlights captured a bulked-up man rolling a big plastic trash can down to the end of his driveway. He lifted an arm to block her brights.

"Speak of the devil," Sidney said, pulling over and switching her headlights to normal. Darnell pulled in behind her. "Wait here," she told him by radio. The moment she opened the door a frigid breeze smacked her in the face. The crisp clean air had the scent of pine and wood-burning fires. She and Granger approached the grizzly-sized man who stood around six and a half feet tall and was built like a linebacker. He wore a red-plaid flannel shirt, a blue down vest, and black sweatpants. He lowered his arm, revealing a round, fleshy face with loose jowls that rivaled a bulldog. A knit cap crowned his skull down to his eyebrows. His small dark eyes squinted at her and blinked in recognition.

"Hello, Jethro," she said, friendly.

His eyes flicked from her to Granger and back, not too pleased to see them. "Long way from town, Chief Becker. What brings you out this way?" He looked and sounded sober, to her relief.

"Thought maybe you could tell us a little about your neighbors," she said.

He looked surprised, and a little relieved. "Not much to tell. Mitch lives with his wife, Becky. They're very quiet. Keep to themselves."

"They have a foster son?"

"Luca? He left home more than a year ago. He's away at school somewhere."

A brisk wind picked up. Sidney zipped her jacket and pulled her woolen cap down over her ears. Granger shoved his hands into his pockets. Spring might be here, but the weather at night still held the chill of winter. "Their phone's out of order. Is that unusual?"

"That don't sound right. He has a little business out of the house. Needs his phone for work."

"What kind of guy is Mitch?"

"A royal pain in the ass. Complains about everything. Borrows tools and doesn't return them. I avoid him now."

"Does he appear to be violent?"

"Violent? Hmm. He gets pissed off easy. Don't know about violent, though."

"Have you seen the Turners lately?"

He scratched his head. "Hmmm. Now that you mention it, I haven't seen Becky for a while. As for Mitch, I've seen his rickety old pickup truck go by."

"What color is the truck?"

He shrugged massive shoulders. "I don't know. Light blue. Gray."

"When was the last time you saw him?"

"Yesterday."

"Thanks for your help."

Sidney and Granger climbed back into the Yukon and the two patrol vehicles headed down the driveway at the end of the cul-de-sac.

"What do you think about Turner?" Granger asked.

"I think it's strange that his phone is out of order. Something isn't sitting right with me."

Sidney spotted the one story, ranch-style house up ahead between the trunks of towering trees. A soft light shone from a single room in front of the house. She got on the radio to Darnell. "Let's park back here and walk in."

They exited their vehicles, pulled out their flashlights, and advanced up the driveway. Behind her, Darnell's and Amanda's boots crunched on the gravel. The smell of damp vegetation closed in around them. Wind rustled leaves and the tree branches creaked overhead. When she reached the sidewalk leading to the front door, she saw a curtain move in the front window, then the light went out, plunging the yard into total darkness.

The muscles in Sidney's neck tightened. "Someone in there doesn't want to talk to us."

"I don't like it," Granger said. "I'm getting the heebie jeebies."

"Me, too," Amanda said.

Sidney gestured to Amanda and Darnell. "You two circle around the back."

Sidney and Granger mounted the porch, stood on either side of the front door, and she rang the bell. No response. She banged loudly with the brass knocker. "Mr. Turner, it's the police. Please open the door."

No response.

They heard a booming crash inside the house and glass shattering. Sidney spoke into her mic, her heart thumping wildly, "Someone's in trouble. We're going in. Watch the back of the house."

She and Granger whipped out their weapons and held their flashlights against their Glocks. Granger tried the door handle. It was unlocked. Feeling her adrenaline humming, Sidney nodded. Pistols held in a two-hand grip, they entered and made a slow orbit through the living room, scanning it in slices, missing nothing. "Clear," Sidney said.

They did the same in the dining room and kitchen. "Clear."

A faint creak came from the back of the house. They whirled toward the sound and followed their beams back across the living room. Sidney inched to the hallway and panned the opening without exposing her body. A room on both sides, then the passageway made a sharp right turn. No cover. A funnel. The suspect could come out with an automatic weapon and mow them down in a heartbeat. Her heart picked up speed.

Granger's mouth tightened. He nodded.

Slowly and methodically they advanced down the hall as one unit. Sidney's muzzle pointed to the right, with Granger behind her left shoulder covering the length of the hall. Heart knocking like a parade drum, she opened the door on the right, entered briskly, gun arm going from left to right. No movement. A bedroom. Unmade bed, clothes draped over an armchair. A few clothes in the closet. "Clear."

Granger entered the room on the left while Sidney covered the hall. His beam darted over the walls and furniture. An office. Empty. "Clear." He stepped back into the hallway, beads of sweat on his upper lip, and fell behind Sidney.

At the turn in the passageway, Sidney stopped and listened. Dead silence. Arms extended, both hands on their pistols, they slipped fast around the corner and confronted the source of the crash. A large cabinet had been turned over and blocked their path. Glass and books were strewn everywhere.

Sidney heard a window open in a room to the left. She smelled the stink of gasoline before she saw flames leaping through an open doorway on the right. A fire was dangerously out of control, following a generous trail of liquid fuel. A roaring inferno burst into the hallway and a dense plume of hot air and smoke spread across the ceiling. In an instant, Sidney and Granger were engulfed by a deadly cocktail of hot gases. Flames spread over the walls racing toward the living room.

Amanda's urgent voice screamed over her radio. "Fire! Get out! Get out!"

Suddenly blinded, aware that survival time was less than a minute, she and Granger darted back down the hall. Compounding the heat was the dense smoke cloud hovering a few feet above the floor that billowed in front of them.

They stumbled into the living room, bumping into the couch, knocking over a coffee table, tripping over a lamp, trying not to suck in smoke. Totally disoriented, desperate to escape, they sank to all fours. Their hands hurriedly felt along the carpet until they hit a wall. But which way to the door? Granger went in one direction, she in the other. The room was turning into an oven. She heard flames licking the walls. Trying not to panic, eyes shut tight, lungs screaming to gulp in a breath, her fingers frantically groped along the floorboard. She was perilously close to dying, her lungs about to burst. Smoke and intense heat could kill her before the fire ever reached her. She heard the front door open off to her left, then Granger's hand came out of nowhere, grabbed her arm and pulled. Seconds later they burst out into the frigid air, gasping for breath.

Outside, they sank to their knees, coughing, lungs burning, uniforms damp with sweat. Sidney's eyes stung and tears streamed down her cheeks. The icy air pricked her skin like needles. She could barely breathe. But she was limp with relief, grateful to be alive. Through blurred vision she saw smoke billowing out of the open door and flames leaping through the living room.

The growl of an engine suddenly roared to life and a huge black truck rounded the back of the house and thundered past them down the driveway. Brake lights flashed before it bounced and skidded around the curve, followed by the sound of rubber squealing as it hit the road.

"Jesus. A black truck," Sidney wheezed. It hurt to talk. Her vision was too blurry to see the driver or read the plates. The back of her throat was so dry she could hardly swallow.

Darnell and Amanda sprinted around the opposite side of the house.

Sidney waved them on. They hopped into his truck and peeled out in hot pursuit, siren screaming, strobes lighting up the surrounding forest. Amanda would already be on the radio, calling in the pursuit and the fire department. As a result, every law enforcement officer in the county would likely be hauling ass towards the suspect.

The glass windows shattered as the oxygen was virtually sucked out of the living room. Balls of fire and flames exploded out of windows and doorways. Fed by an abundance of fuel, the flames roared, snapped, and hissed, leaping high above the roofline. She and Granger backed away from the searing heat out to the driveway. Sidney's chest tightened, and it grew worse as she watched the fire engulf the house. Every scrap of evidence that could possibly identify a brutal killer was going up in smoke.

The paramedics arrived first. Working fast, the two men sat Granger and Sidney down on the open end of the rescue truck. They applied oxygen masks, wrapped them in blankets, and checked their vitals. Though trembling from shock and cold, Sidney could finally breathe freely. Next to her, Granger's body sometimes shuddered, and his eyes were red rimmed, but he gave her a thumb's up. She met his gaze above the plastic mask and smiled her gratitude. His eyes crinkled at the corners, smiling back. They had nearly been swallowed by the burning jaws of death, and barely, just barely, escaped from being incinerated.

Within minutes, three wailing fire trucks arrived, and firemen jumped into a state of organized chaos, silhouetted against the flames. With ringside seats, sucking in blessed oxygen, Sidney and Granger watched the animated drama. Everyone was in emergency mode, operating at hyper speed. Even as the hoses fired cannons of water at the structure, missiles of debris shot from the roof, which was starting to cave in on itself.

The investigation of the Turner home disaster would now be transferred to the fire inspectors and the crime scene unit.

CHAPTER TWENTY-THREE

A MURDER SUSPECT had just tried to kill two police officers. Every available cop in the county was out there, responding to the chase, and no one was going to give it up until they had to. After a pursuit at breakneck speed for miles, Darnell and Amanda lost eyes on the suspect. The black truck veered off the highway and gained ground by tearing across a rugged meadow of rye grass and nettles. The clincher came when it barreled into a rocky, fast moving stream and crossed easily to the other side. Darnell's old department Ram truck braked at the bank, no match for the suspect's souped-up vehicle with a suspension lift system and custom wheels and tires. The truck was a tank. Darnell zoomed up and down country roads, crisscrossing miles of territory surrounding the stream. Sidney and her officers stuck to the radio until final word came down two hours later. There had been no sightings whatsoever of a souped-up black truck on the highways and public roads. The suspect had vanished.

***

Darnell and Amanda returned empty handed and dispirited. Their vexation was contagious, and a dark pallor hung over the station. Hopefully the APB would bring results once daylight hit. A black truck could blend in with the forest at night, but it would stand out like King Kong during the day.

When asked why they didn't see the suspect leave the house, Amanda said they were distracted by the flames leaping out of a window on the east side of the house. The suspect apparently climbed out of a window on the west side of the house, got to his truck parked behind the garage, and peeled out before they could round the house.

Revisiting the aftermath of the evening's events, they hunkered down in the conference room. Thoughts of the calamitous night swirled in their minds. Trying to save her voice, Sidney spoke very little, but stood in front of the crime board and pointed to the notes she added in the margin. They could only assume that the escape vehicle was Thomas's stolen truck, driven by Olivia's murderer—which meant Thomas was innocent, since he was locked in a cell here at the station. And most likely, the suspect was Mitch Turner. With everything incinerated in the house, Sidney prayed CSI would get a sample of his DNA to match what they had at the lab, possibly from the old truck that Jethro Todd described. Another question loomed large in their minds—where was his wife? Where was Becky Turner?

Sidney dismissed them at midnight. Everyone had earned a good night's sleep. They'd convene in the morning at 10:00 a.m.

From her office window, Sidney watched Granger climb into his patrol truck drooping with fatigue; something she'd never witnessed before. Young, strong, mentally tough, a former Marine, he always seemed inexhaustible. Tonight, she understood the emotional strain that two murders in two days—one a close friend and fellow cop—had put on everyone, in addition to working long hours. Sidney, too, felt weary to the bone. She reeked of smoke and her respiratory system was stinging from smoke inhalation.

One last thing had to be taken care of. A press release. Shoulders sagging, stifling a yawn, Sidney entered her office and got to work. There was no doubt that two murders and two killers on the run were sure to attract local attention. Sidney carefully worded the release to minimize the impact, substituting "suspicious deaths" for "murders"—keeping it all low key—and not associating one event with another. Hopefully, that would buy her time. From past experience, she knew that once the town was overrun by reporters, she and her officers would be stalked mercilessly, and her investigation would be severely hampered.

Sidney did a final edit and sent the release to Mayor Burke's office. His administrators could massage the language a little before releasing it to the local press, if they wished. Thankfully, since Garnerville's newspaper had shut down last year, the local press consisted of one small newspaper in Jackson: The Bugle. The editor and his two reporters were less skilled at investigative reporting than covering rotary events and seasonal festivals. They would downplay the tone, Sidney hoped, wanting to keep the "big" story to themselves as facts emerged.

David had called and left three messages. Too tired to think or string sentences together, she texted him that she was out of commission, and would talk tomorrow.

***

Sidney was surprised when Selena met her at the back door in the laundry room.

"Thank God you're okay!" Her sister attached herself like a huge barnacle and spoke into Sidney's hair, her voice breathy and emotional. "Granger told me what happened. It really gave me a scare. I came so close to losing you both!"

"He's fine. I'm fine. Truly." Sidney gently rubbed her sister's back. They stood together for several long moments and it was immediately comforting for both of them. "There, there. Everything is fine."

Eyes moist, Selena pulled away and straightened her shoulders, and Sidney watched her struggle to regain her composure.

Sidney remembered the amethyst on the silver chain Selena gave her that morning to ward off psychic attacks and negative energy. With a wry smile, she pulled it from her breast pocket and held it out, dangling from her fingers. "Thank you. You were right about this. It saved my life tonight."

Putting on a wobbly smile, Selena pulled the chain over Sidney's head, positioning the stone at the base of her throat, and met her eyes. "Keep it. Don't ever take it off." Then she wrinkled her nose, her voice almost back to normal, and a little bossy. "I love you Syd, but you stink to high heaven. You cannot enter the house with toxic smoke and chemicals all over your uniform. Strip off your clothes and I'll wash them for you."

Sidney did as she was told, emptying her pockets of pen and notepad, a spare cuff key, some loose change. She unbuckled her duty belt and hung it on a peg, removed her boots, then stripped down to her bra and panties. She loved it when someone else took charge when she was brain-dead.

Holding Sidney's jacket and uniform at arm's length, Selena tossed them into the washer. "Here, put this on." She handed her the fluffy pink flannel robe and matching bunny slippers she gave her for Christmas.

Once enveloped in the soft flannel and huge slippers with bunny ears and whiskers and goo-goo eyes, Sidney's tough cop persona melted away and she felt like a child. A giant child.

Selena sat her at the table in the dining area. There was a setting for one, complete with her mother's good crystal, china, and linen. Tantalizing aromas reached Sidney's nostrils from something in a cast iron pot on the stove. "What smells so freaking good?"

"Lamb stew," Selena said from the kitchen, and added with a touch of sarcasm, "I made it for Granger, but our date didn't pan out. A couple of murders ruined our plans." She set down a bowl of stew and a plate of biscuits covered with pats of melting butter, poured Pinot Noir into a crystal glass, lit three of her vanilla candles, and turned off the light. "Why let a romantic evening go to waste? Now eat up. I have a hot scented bath waiting for you upstairs with fresh rose petals floating on the water."

"Did I die in that fire and float to heaven?"

"No wisecracks about dying," Selena gently scolded.

"Deal." Sidney sighed her pleasure as she ate the delicious stew, but she couldn't help feeling sorry for Granger, who was going home to a cold bunkhouse and a frozen dinner. She would have to make it up to him. A warm wave of affection filled her heart. Tonight, he did what he was trained to do. He saved her life. She was proud of him, and her whole team, who had put in long hours without complaint. Every day, her officers acted selflessly and courageously, maintaining that thin blue line between a safe society and anarchy. They felt more like family to Sidney than co-workers.

She finished her food and sipped the last of her wine. "I'm ready to soak in that hot bath," she said to her sister who was putting food away in the kitchen. "But I may get so relaxed, you'll have to fish me out later."

"Or I could just leave you in there all night."

Sidney gave her a mock frown.

Selena laughed. "I'll run up and check the temperature."

***

The buzz of her cell phone woke Sidney at 9:00 a.m. She felt weighted down like an immense log at the bottom of a lake, and she didn't want to fight her way to the surface. Too heavy. Too much work. Never had she been so tempted to ignore a call.

The buzz grew louder. She surfaced in increments of consciousness. Her fingers found her cell and she peeled back one eyelid. It was her dispatcher. Groan. "What's up Jesse?"

"Sorry, Chief, but you're needed at the Turner house ASAP. We have a situation."

Situation was a code word for something she didn't want to hear. "Spell it out, Jesse."

"H-o-m-i-c-i-d-e," he said, taking her literally.

What the hell? Another homicide? First thing in the morning? The third day in a row? This was starting to feel like "Groundhog Day," only there was nothing funny about it. With a grim premonition, she asked, "Who's the victim?"

"The crime scene people found a woman's body out behind the house. They believe it's Becky Turner."

Of course it is.

"The fire inspector already alerted Dr. Linthrope and Stewart Wong. They're on their way. Do you want any of our officers out there?"

"Sounds like there're plenty of bodies on the scene already. I'll go check it out and take it from there. Thanks, Jesse." Sidney cast her gaze toward the window. A light drizzle streaked the glass and the sky was a deep leaden gray. Perfect. Matched her mood exactly.

***

A light rain fell, and black, swollen clouds were racing in from the west. A bigger storm was on its way. Sidney steered the patrol vehicle down the narrow gravel driveway and parked behind the coroner's van. A white sedan from county was also parked on the shoulder. A fire department vehicle was heading out and the fire inspector, looking exhausted, shot her a little salute as he passed. Protected by a hooded yellow slicker, she exited the Yukon and got her first look at the remains of the Turner house. A blackened husk, its damaged limbs pierced the sky, and its interior was filled with heaps of charred debris. A burnt, pungent smell hung in the air. The whole structure was cordoned off by yellow tape. A sudden gust of wind blew a shower of raindrops into her face.

Calvin McConnell, the crime scene specialist who helped Amanda process Max's campsite, stood in the driveway talking to Linthrope and Wong. Rain sluiced down the hooded slickers they wore over their field clothes. Wong gripped his crime kit and a folded body bag was tucked under one arm. Despite the circumstances, they greeted Sidney pleasantly as she approached.

"So, we meet again," Linthrope smiled. "Too soon. With all these homicides, Garnerville is starting to feel like a big city."

Sidney smiled back. "Too soon is right. Let's pray this isn't the new normal, Doc."

"The CSI unit was here most of the night," McConnell told her. "They were about to leave when one of them found the body, quite by accident. I came in to relieve them. We're assuming it's Becky Turner, but who knows at this point."

The sky continued to darken, as if the elements were gathering to unleash an assault.

"Let's get moving before the brunt of the storm hits," she said. To punctuate her words, a vein of lightning brightened the sky, followed by a clap of thunder. The air seemed to shiver, and she caught a whiff of ozone.

"I'll walk you back to the body." They circled the house and McConnell pointed to a row of willows and low bushes that wound across a neglected lawn towards the tree line. "There's a stream back in there. That's where we're headed." They passed a two-car garage and a large utility shed filled with tools and equipment. A small Honda CRV and an old pickup truck were visible through the open doors. "Those are the Turner's vehicles," McConnell said. "They've been thoroughly processed. Good thing it's a detached garage or it would've burned, too. Right now, the trace DNA we found inside each car can help to identify them. The suspect had his black truck hidden behind the garage when your officers were back here last night."

They crossed the grass and entered the woods. Rain pattered on the leaves overhead. A layer of damp leaves underfoot muffled the sound of their steps. The path ran parallel to a clear, gurgling stream which disappeared on occasion behind tree trunks and bushes.

"No wonder no one found her. What was the tech doing back here?"

"He was wandering along the trail to clear his head. Been a long night."

They arrived at the edge of a small rectangle of leaf-strewn turf cordoned off by yellow tape. Partially hidden by brush was a rocky overhang that protected the alcove beneath it from rain. "I didn't touch the body," McConnell said. "But I processed the area around it."

"Find anything?"

"Besides a lot of blood? Yeah, a cigarette butt. Looks fresh."

"Marlborough, with a filter?"

"Yeah." He looked thoughtful. "Not your first experience with this killer."

"DNA will tell," Sidney said. "But it's highly improbable the cigarette butt is a coincidence."

"I also got plenty of blood samples from the leaves and grass."

The dark red color of the leaves caught Sidney's eye. They should have been green. In the dreary light, there was no doubt that it was blood. Looking around, she saw more blood smeared over leaves. The green grass, too, was spattered with rust-colored flecks.

"A lot of blood," Linthrope said. "She must've been killed here."

"No doubt," McConnell said.

Sidney and the two men snapped on gloves. Stewart started taking photos, the bright flash pulsing over the ground.

"A warning; it ain't pretty." McConnell lifted the tape and they entered the crime area.

The woman lay wedged on her back between the earth and a ledge of stone in the back of the alcove, her hands at her sides. She wore black pants, a red sweater, and white gym shoes that were stained with blood. Judging by her blood-soaked hair, which covered her face, she appeared to have been struck about the head. Stewart took photos as Linthrope examined the body. He moved her sweater sleeves up to her elbows and studied her skin and hands. "She has restraint marks on her wrists, old and new. Appears she was held captive somewhere for some time. Possibly weeks."

Sidney leaned over his shoulder and saw bruising and red welts banding her wrists.

"Her body's fairly fresh," he continued. His bushy brows knit together but he spoke in a professional tone, with no hint of emotion. "Time of death is within the last twenty-four hours. No defensive wounds, which would suggest she may have been bound when brought here. Unable to defend herself."

Sidney compiled mental notes, keeping her feelings separate from the process of observation. But her poise deserted her when Linthrope drew aside the matted hair to look at the woman's face. A gasp escaped her lips. No stranger to violent death, she still was not prepared. The victim had been beaten beyond recognition and her head was twisted around at an unnatural angle.

"Her neck is broken," Linthrope said. "And she sustained multiple traumatic injuries to her face."

Sidney hoped the broken neck killed her, quickly, before she was subjected to the savage beating. She shuddered, thinking of the feral brutality of this killer, who possibly was Mitch Turner. To kill Olivia, he had smashed her head repeatedly onto the floorboards, but her face was left untouched. More intense rage had been unleashed on this new victim, and the killer exhibited a compulsive need to obliterate her face; her identity. Did he have a stronger hatred for this woman, possibly his wife, or was his thirst for violence escalating?

Thunder boomed out again like a great bass drum and the rain grew heavier, now penetrating the tree canopy, plopping on their slickers. The patina coating the leaves was smeared by falling raindrops and the dry crust was reverting to liquid form, running like fresh blood. Fortunately, the scene had already been processed and they weren't losing evidence.

"Let's get her to the lab and out of this weather," Linthrope said. Stewart bagged her hands and head to preserve trace evidence, then the four of them lifted the body into the long black bag and zipped her in. The silence around them was filled with the sound of dripping water.

Casting about, Sidney noticed a tiny patch of flattened grass beyond the yellow tape—then another a couple feet beyond it, and another beyond that—the size of boot prints, leading in the direction of a birch tree. Its pale trunk was partly screened by the undergrowth. She worked her way round the ring of grass until she reached the birch, where she crouched down, parting the branches of a laurel that was growing wild beside the bank. "Come take a look at this," she called, her adrenaline spiking. The men came to peer over her shoulder. The trunk had been scored by deeply etched grooves; a strange design carved with a sharp instrument. "Recognize it?"

"Yeah," Stewart said, his camera flash popping. "The same symbol that was on the coin in Olivia's pocket."

"A Valknut," she said. "The knot of the slain Viking warrior. It represents infinity and immortality, and wards against evil."

"It didn't ward off this evil," McConnel said dryly. He peered at the carving more closely. "The wood's still white. The bark's been stripped recently. He must have carved it yesterday after killing the woman."

"Whoever murdered this woman also killed Olivia," Sidney said. "This symbol ties both crimes together."

"Indisputably," Linthrope said. "At the lab, we'll check her pockets for a coin, and see if a note was placed in her mouth."

A heavy curtain of rain descended through the flimsy canopy of leaves. They each grabbed a corner of the body bag and trekked out of the woods, the rain drumming a melancholic harmony suitable for a funeral march.

CHAPTER TWENTY-FOUR

SIDNEY FOLLOWED the coroner van back to town, then veered off on Main Street and pulled in at the station. The rain had ceased, and the sun was trying to break through a seam in the clouds, shooting out weak shafts of light. She had missed the morning briefing she scheduled with her officers. After hanging up her slicker, Sidney walked to the doorway of the bull pen and gestured to Amanda and Darnell who sat hunched over their computers. "Quick word."

"We got another homicide, Chief?" Amanda asked, rising from her desk.

"Jesse told us," Darnell said. "A Jane Doe at the Turner property."

"Yeah. It could be Becky Turner."

They followed her into the conference room and stood waiting for instruction as she poured a cup of coffee at the sideboard. Sidney turned, stirring cream and sugar in her cup. "What do we know about the Turner's foster son, Luca Ashe?" Sidney asked. "He needs to be notified of her death."

"At this point, nothing. Never looked into him."

"Amanda, I want you to go to Social Services. Look through all of Olivia's files. Go back years, if necessary. I want to know everything about this kid. What other foster parents he stayed with. What his personality's like. His current address."

"I'm on my way." She walked briskly from the room.

"Darnell, get on social media. Find out everything you can about Luca Ashe."

"Copy that."

"Granger at the Schaffer farm?" Sidney asked.

"Yeah, he just called in. He left from home about ten minutes ago."

***

Granger pulled up in front of a small white farmhouse surrounded by flower-specked meadows and a pasture occupied by goats. Tender green shoots sprouted from the dark, rich furrows of a vegetable garden. He glanced at the sky. The rain had stopped and sunshine broke through the thinning clouds, bathing the fields in late morning light. He sat for a moment, gearing up for another long day of police work. The toxic smoke he inhaled last night really did him in. He showered and did a faceplant in bed at 11:00 p.m. and slept straight through to 8:00 a.m., then he got up and did his ranch chores before dressing in his uniform. He was mentally and physically fatigued, and his lungs and throat still felt raw and irritated.

Across the clearing, he spotted a woman in an oversized slicker entering a weathered barn, followed by two ranch dogs. Granger hurried after her and found her dumping a bucket of food scraps over a rail. On the other side was an enormous white pig, nursing a large litter of squirming piglets. The sow had droopy ears and a long body covered in fine hair. With loud grunts of satisfaction, she shook off the babies and attacked the food scraps ravenously.

"Mrs. Schaffer," he called as he entered.

The dogs rushed at him, wriggling and barking and wagging their tails. The woman turned, alarmed when she saw his uniform, then her face went blank. "Down, Rascal. Down Bandit." She pushed back her hood and he saw she was middle-aged with gray hair and pleasant features.

"Good morning, Mrs. Schaffer. I'm Officer Wyatt." They shook hands. The dogs pranced around him, sniffing with curiosity, then settled down. "That's a handsome sow," he said. "American Landrace, isn't it?"

"Yes, that's Duchess. She's too smart for her own good. Thinks she's queen of the dogs. Keeps them in line. Sneaks into the house whenever she can." Mrs. Schaffer's gloved hands reached into the pile of squirming piglets and scooped one up; white with black spots, small eyes, pink snout. She cuddled it as one would a puppy.

"Damn, he's cute," Granger said fondly, scratching its head. "My family owns the cattle ranch a couple miles down the road. We have lots of animals, but no pigs."

"The Wyatts. Of course. I know your parents. Weren't you overseas?"

"Yes, ma'am. I've been back a year."

"Oh, that long. I didn't know. Haven't seen your parents in a while. How's your dad?"

"He has his good days and bad." For decades, Granger's parents had been very active in the town's civic affairs, but Parkinson's disease had forced his dad to drop his volunteer activities one by one. Granger's mom stayed home most of the time to care for him.

"And now you're a policeman. Your parents must be proud."

"Yes, ma'am." Granger hesitated a moment before changing the subject and dropping the bomb. "I wonder if I can ask you a few questions. We're in the middle of an investigation up at the monastery."

Her soft gray eyes immediately narrowed, and she looked at him with heightened alertness. She said nothing but waited for him to continue.

"Mrs. Schaffer, we know Tammy's been in hiding up there for the last sixteen years." *Boom.* "A man was murdered up there yesterday. We have evidence that points to Tammy. There's also evidence that she killed him to protect a child."

The woman showed no surprise, no reaction whatsoever, other than a tension along her jawline. She knew. Tammy must have been in touch with her. But she said nothing, still waiting.

"Every cop in the state will be looking for her. I'm concerned, ma'am, because if we don't find her first, she might not fare too well as a dangerous fugitive on the run. We'd like to bring her in peacefully. Treat her fairly. Give her a chance to tell her side of the story."

Mrs. Schaffer was slow in responding. She stared at the ground and the silence between them lengthened.

"City people don't understand country folk," he continued. "Our motivations. Our dispositions. Tammy's been hidden away from the world for sixteen years. She's led a peaceful life. She's quiet. Sensitive. If this ends up in court, the fact that she's stayed out of trouble for years, and worked with children, will soften a jury's attitude towards her." Granger waited, giving the woman time to process. This was a matter of monumental consequence. The fate of her daughter hung in the balance, and if not handled well, it could end very badly. "You may as well talk to me. Her cover's blown. She'll never be anonymous at the monastery again."

The woman stared off into the distance and her fingers rubbed the head of the piglet mindlessly, but finally, she met his eyes and said quietly, "You better come in the house and have a cup of coffee. Call me Alice."

"Call me Granger."

They shared a wry smile.

Minutes later she had stepped out of her mud-caked boots on the porch and lost the raincoat, and he was seated at a scarred oak table in a sunny country kitchen. Mrs. Schaffer had a slim, wiry build, and was dressed for farm work in Carhartt pants, a flannel shirt, and thick wool socks. She poured two mugs of coffee at the counter and placed them on the table with a plate of glazed doughnuts, then seated herself across from him. They both stirred in cream and sugar and Granger bit into a doughnut. Alice's hands, free of the gloves, were calloused and dry, the nails cut down to the quick—the rough hands of a laborer. He figured she put in long, hard days working her spread. "You have help running the farm, Alice?" he asked with a note of real concern.

"I have Pedro. He's old but he's a good worker." She sipped her coffee. "My granddaughter, Riley, helps when she can, but she has a fulltime job at Alpine Ridge. Care worker. Putting herself through school."

"That's admirable." He knew Alice only had one child; Tammy.

They sat in silence for a moment, and then he steered the conversation back to Tammy. "So Tammy has a daughter. You raised Riley?"

"Someone had to. Tammy got pregnant when she was sixteen." Alice's face hardened momentarily, and she continued in a no-nonsense tone. "She wanted an abortion. We're Christian. I told her it was out of the question." She met his gaze. "Something in her changed about that time, Granger. She became a different person. Withdrawn. Quiet. Depressed. Started doing drugs; not good for her, and certainly not good for the baby." Alice's back stiffened, and he detected a steely determination in her tone. "I sent her to live with her father in Crestview. He's a disciplinarian. Tammy stayed off drugs until the baby was born. I got custody of Riley." Alice cleared her throat. "When she turned eighteen and could do what she wanted, Tammy moved in with some lowlife and started using again."

"That's when she got into trouble again," he said.

She nodded, and a shadow of sadness crossed her face. "As you know, not too long after moving in with Conner, he died of a drug overdose. It wasn't her fault the dope was bad. Conner consented. He had a choice. I have no idea what happened after that. She disappeared. Fell off the face of the earth. Years went by. Terrible, terrible years." Alice's eyes suddenly teared up and her voice quivered. "Her dad and I didn't know if she was dead or alive."

Alice spoke of her daughter with grave tenderness. The difficulties one faced with family, sharing their shortcomings, their pain, was the most piercing kind of hurt a person could endure. Watching the slow decline of the robust, indestructible cowboy his father once had been had caused Granger to shed tears many times.

"Sorry." Alice swallowed and took a long moment to pull herself together. Wiping her eyes with a napkin, she continued. "The only thing that got me through those hard years was Riley." She lifted her mug and her eyes warmed over the rim. "Riley's a beautiful girl. Caring. Thoughtful. Never a lick of trouble. She blessed my life." She drained her coffee, got the pot from the counter, and refilled their mugs.

"Thank you. Good coffee." Granger polished off his doughnut, talking out of one side of his mouth. "When did you learn Tammy was at the monastery?"

Looking evasive, Alice puffed up her cheeks and blew out a long breath, stirring cream into her cup. "Oh gosh, let me think. Time flies, doesn't it? I'd say about ten years ago."

Granger thought she was stalling, taking time to choose her words carefully. If she admitted she knew her daughter was a fugitive from the law, she'd be incriminating herself as an accomplice.

"She had a monk drop off a letter," Alice continued. "Needless to say, I was beside myself with surprise and happiness. It was as though a ghost came back to life. I started visiting her up there. We took many, many long walks through the woods. It took a long time for me to come to terms with what she did—running away, letting her dad and me be eaten up with worry. She wouldn't tell me why she changed her identity, only that I had to keep her secret. I learned to accept it."

Alice looked away as she spoke, and Granger determined she was lying. But he couldn't prove it, and he didn't want to. He wasn't going to arrest a woman for protecting her daughter. For sixteen years, Tammy had kept her nose clean, practiced nonviolence, and contributed to the welfare and education of boys.

"It's been wonderful having my daughter back in my life. She was off drugs and at peace with herself. That's all that mattered to me." Alice's brow furrowed and her gray eyes clouded with worry. "That's all gone now."

"If Tammy turns herself in, faces her charges, she could put this all behind her," Granger said gently. "If it was proven that she acted in defense of the boy, the prosecuting attorney would take that into consideration, possibly with good results for Tammy." There was no getting around that she threw a knife into a man, pulled it out, didn't administer aid to the boy or the man, and left the man there to die while she fled the scene with the weapon.

"Everything would go back to normal," Alice said wistfully.

No, Tammy's life would not go back to normal. She would be extradited to Baker County where she would have to face her charges in Crestview. With a good lawyer, those charges could possibly get dropped to involuntary manslaughter.

"How did Riley feel about her mother pretending to be a man, and secluding herself at the monastery?"

"I'm not sure what passed between them. But Riley was sworn to secrecy back when she was ten years old. She and Tammy have a close, loving relationship. Riley went up to the monastery regularly. She's a practicing Buddhist."

"Alice, did Tammy talk to you about the man who died?"

"No. And I don't want to know. It's too horrible." She stared into her cup, then she lifted her head and met his eyes. "What was he doing up there?"

"He was a private investigator. Obviously investigating Tammy."

Alice's eyes widened with surprise.

"His name was Max. He sustained a head injury the night before he died, and he was running around delusional. The next morning, he attacked a boy. Tammy acted to save his life." He paused to let her digest that. "Do you know anyone who may have hired Max to find your daughter?"

"No. Of course not," Alice said without conviction. She averted her eyes when she answered, and her fingers played nervously with her napkin.

Granger suspected she knew something that frightened her. "Think carefully, Alice. If someone is after her, we need to know. We can stop him before he hurts her."

Alice stared at her mug and shrugged. She wouldn't look at him.

"Can you help us bring her in safely? Once in our custody, she'll be protected."

Finally, Alice met his gaze. "I don't know where she is. That's the truth of it. If I did, I'd tell you."

"But you do know who may be looking for her."

She shook her head.

"If someone is after Tammy, they may come after you and Riley, too."

Alice's face showed alarm. She stared at her cup, chewing her bottom lip.

They sat in silence.

"If you talk to me, Alice, I can help you."

"I have to get back to work," she finally said in a dismissive tone.

She wasn't going to talk. Not yet. "If you think you're in danger, it would be wise for you to stay someplace where you're safe."

"I have a sister in Jackson," she mumbled. "Maybe Riley and I will go visit for a couple of days."

"Can you give me her number, and yours, in case I need to get hold of you?" he handed her his notebook and she jotted down the numbers. Granger stood to leave, placed his card on the table, and added earnestly, "Do the right thing, Alice. Please call me if you hear anything from Tammy."

CHAPTER TWENTY-FIVE

THE FAMILIAR ASTRINGENT CHEMICAL ODOR immediately hit Sidney's nostrils as she entered the morgue. Dr. Linthrope was at his station suited up in scrubs, gloves, and a surgical cap. The remains of Jane Doe lay on the metal slab, her nude body opened from the clavicles to the pubic bone. Some of her organs were on a cutting board and the doctor was snipping open the stomach with a pair of surgical scissors.

"Morning, Doc," Sidney said with a slight grimace.

Linthrope glanced up. "Ah, Chief Becker," he said cheerily. "Not used to seeing you in the middle of a postmortem." He poured the stomach contents into a plasticized paper carton, then he moved to the end of the slab and the woman's ruined face and shaved head came into view. Sidney felt her cheek twitch, an involuntary muscle reaction.

"I have good news for you. We've ID'd our mystery woman from her fingerprints. As we suspected, this is Becky Turner."

"That's good news, Doc," Sidney said. "Did you find a coin, or a message in her mouth?" Sidney asked.

"Yes, indeed. Both. I turned them over to Stewart. You'll have to go visit him at the lab. But while you're here, let's go over what I have so far." Linthrope peeled off his bloody gloves and dropped them into a red biohazard bag, then snapped on a fresh pair. He waved his hand over the victim's shaved head. "As you can see, there are multiple contusions and lacerations on the scalp. Let's get under the skin and take a closer look." With one swift sweep of the blade Linthrope cut from behind one ear, over the crown, and down to the back of the other ear. Then with a tug and a wet, ripping sound, he peeled the scalp free of the crown and forehead, and folded the flap down over the face.

Jesus. Sidney clenched her jaw.

Linthrope peeled the other half of the scalp backward, folding it down to the nape of the neck, so that the entire top of the skull was exposed. He gestured for her to come take a closer look. She saw that a number of holes marred the cranium, each about the size of a quarter with small fracture lines radiating outward.

"Needless to say, cause of death was blunt-force trauma. We have multiple impact points and complex fractures, suggesting a lot of force at high velocity. I believe a common workman's tool was used. Probably a hammer."

"The murder was premeditated," she said. "Why else would he have a hammer out in the woods?"

"I agree," Linthrope said. "He killed her execution style. The angle of the holes on the crown indicate he was standing above her. I'd say she was kneeling, probably with her hands bound behind her back. Then she fell to the ground and he continued the assault while straddling her."

"He just kept hitting her?" she asked, masking her revulsion.

"Yes."

"What about her broken neck?"

"That, and the facial injuries were sustained postmortem."

"So she was dead by the time he got to her face." Thank God.

"She was probably unconscious after the first two blows to the head," Linthrope said. "I'm sure we'll find fractures on the facial bones matching those on the skull. Explains why there was so much blood at the crime scene."

"He was caught up in a frenzy of brutality," she said.

"Driven by rage."

"What can you tell me about the injuries on her wrists?" Sidney asked.

Linthrope lifted the dead woman's right forearm and pointed with his index finger. "See these old scars? At some point, she struggled to free herself, but eventually gave up. It takes a couple of weeks for wounds like this to scab over, heal, and leave these kinds of scars. She could have been held captive for two to three weeks." He pointed to other injuries on her wrists that were red and swollen. "These welts and abrasions are recent. I found tiny synthetic fibers in the newer scrapes. A common type of material that can be found in rope at any hardware store. Aside from the blood in her hair, I found spider webs, insect parts, and clumps of dirt. The hair was matted and hadn't been washed for weeks. The same goes for her body. Unbathed. I took swabs and hosed her down before I started working on her. My guess, she was held in a shed or basement with an earthen floor."

Sidney was quiet, ruminating on the hell the women endured doing her last weeks on earth. "Anything else you can tell me, Doc?"

"No other injuries to her body. No sexual activity. She was

undernourished, so her captor didn't feed her well, or she refused to eat. We've yet to analyze her stomach contents, skimpy as they are." As he spoke, one of his gloved hands cradled the woman's head, the other held a Stryker autopsy saw. "I'm just about to open the cranium. Then I'll be removing and weighing the brain."

Not something she needed or wanted to see. "I'll head over and see Stewart."

Dr. Linthrope's bushy white brows came together and he said solemnly, "Stewart has some surprising news for you."

Surprising? What did that mean? She hoped that was a good thing.

As she walked out, she heard the whine of the Stryker saw, and then the sound of the oscillating blade grinding through thick bone.

***

Stewart sat hunched over a microscope, wearing a white lab coat over jeans, a collared shirt, and loafers. He gave her a cursory nod, grabbed a couple of evidence bags, and joined her at the table. "Okay, we have a number of things to go over," he said soberly. "Let's start with Becky Turner. First, here's the note we found crumpled in her mouth. It's a match to the one recovered from Olivia. Looks like the same paper, same handwriting. Same message." Stewart slid the bag across the table to Sidney. "We're waiting on final results from a handwriting expert."

The crumpled paper had been smoothed out to form a perfect square. Like the other note, the handwritten words slanted slightly to the left. Sidney read the words out loud.

Killing you was the purest love I've ever known.
The sweetest revenge.

The hair stood up on the back of her neck. "Creepy. He got off on killing her. The same with Olivia."

"So it appears."

"His taste for extreme violence suggests he's a psychopath. A highly functioning psychopath. He had the foresight to write notes in advance of his murders, and arm himself with a hammer, in Becky's case. Premeditated murder."

"Yep. Plain and simple." Stewart cleared his throat and slid the other bag across the table. "Here's the coin we found in her pants pocket."

"Another Valknut symbol," Sidney said, examining it. "A match to the other one. Why does he include this coin? This symbol? Did he think it would help his victims in the afterlife? Is it some kind of redemption after his act of violence?"

He didn't answer. How could he? Who knew what motivated a twisted mind?

"Any prints on the coin?"

"No," Stewart said.

She frowned. "Did you get anything back from the evidence you put a rush on?"

"Yes." He studied his notes for a long moment, then met her gaze, matching her frown. "Extraordinary results came back."

Sidney sat waiting, her antennae straight up.

"The urine samples collected at the site at Aspen Lake are definitely human. Here's the surprising thing. It's from a female."

"What?" Sidney's brows lifted in surprise. She thought for a long moment. "Is it from the victim? Did he let Olivia pee?"

"No. It's not from Olivia."

She sat quietly at the table, then asked, "Could the killer be female? Or did he have a female partner? An accomplice?"

Stewart shrugged, and pushed his glasses higher on his nose with an index finger. "We can't identify the source at this time. We're still waiting to get a bunch of DNA evidence back from the lab."

"Damn," Sidney said. "Same old story. While valuable evidence sits at the lab, we're investigating with our hands tied behind our backs."

An awkward silence hung in the air.

Stewart stared at his notes.

"What's going on with you? What's with all these dramatic pauses?" Sidney asked impatiently.

"When you came in," Stewart said, clearing his throat again. "I was examining the cigarette butt we found today on the Turner property. Physically, it's a perfect match to several found in the ashtray of Mitch Turner's truck. It's also a match to the one found at Aspen Lake."

"So Mitch Turner is our killer?" she asked.

"That's what the killer wants us to believe." Stewart's brown eyes shadowed behind his glasses. "This is going to blow your socks off. The DNA from the Marlborough butt found at Aspen Lake has no match in the system. But we do have a DNA match right here in the lab. It matches the headless John Doe found three weeks ago up at Steelhead Lake."

Sidney sat back in stark surprise. Her thoughts started whirling, trying to make sense of it, trying to fit pieces together. "That means our John Doe is most likely Mitch Turner. Dead for several weeks." She shook her head.

"Both husband and wife are murder victims, identified on the same day. Becky Turner was taken hostage about the same time we found his remains. Which points to the same perpetrator for her abduction, and both murders. Now we've drawn a link between their murders and Olivia's. One killer, three murders. The bad news is that the suspect's in the wind and we have zero leads."

"And he's playing you."

"You're right," Sidney said. "He planted those cigarette butts at each crime scene. He may have planted the woman's urine, too, just to thumb his nose at us."

"He's having fun at our expense," Stewart said, and added gravely, "A warning; this killer is smart, unpredictable, and exceptionally dangerous. He has a good understanding of how to cover his tracks. The Turner house was incinerated. Not a lick of evidence will be obtained from it. Both coins were wiped clean. No prints. No DNA. We've collected a bunch of fingerprints and other samples from the two cars, the shed, and the garage. But we may not find a thing associated to the killer. He's careful. Watch yourself. He's already tried to kill you and Granger once. Don't give him another chance."

She was touched by his concern, and said with a wry smile, "Careful is my middle name."

**

Sidney left. As she pulled into the station and parked, her phone buzzed. It was Deputy Kyle Mumford. "Hey, Kyle. What's up?"

"Afternoon, Chief. I'm meeting up with Deputy Bryce Dixon, the handler for the cadaver dog. We're heading up to Steelhead Lake to search for John Doe's missing skull. Anyone over there want to join us?"

"Yeah, me. He's not a John Doe anymore. He's just been identified as Mitch Turner."

After a moment of surprise, Kyle answered. "As in the Mitch Turner whose house burned down? And who kept all the cops in the county chasing ghosts last night?"

"The very one."

He whistled. "Now corpses drive. Can this week get any weirder? Look, we'll be up at the lake at two."

"I'll meet you up there in the parking lot."

CHAPTER TWENTY-SIX

SIDNEY WORKED in her office until all of her officers had returned to the station. By early afternoon, she had everyone assembled around the table eating sandwiches from Pickle's Deli and sipping drinks. To expressions of shock, she briefly described the feral ferocity of the attack on the woman found that morning, identified as Becky Turner.

"We need to find this guy before he kills again," Darnell said with an edge of anger. "Put him in a cage for life."

"Or stick a needle in his arm," Amanda said emphatically.

"That's not all," Sidney continued. "We have an ID on our John Doe. He's Becky's husband, Mitch Turner."

"Mitch Turner?" Amanda said with astonishment. "Holy smoke."

Granger's brows lifted in surprise. "So he's not our killer."

"No. It appears he's also a victim. Here's more interesting information—the cigarette butts found at both crime scenes were planted. They came from Mitch Turner. And the urine found at Aspen Lake came from a woman, but not Olivia. That means our suspect may have a woman companion or accomplice, or he may be screwing with us, planting more false evidence." Sidney intermittently worked on the crime board as she talked, pinning up new photos. When she finished, she gave her officers time to process the new information. "So what do we know about Luca Ashe, the foster son? He needs to know his foster parents are dead. Let's start with you, Amanda. What did you find at social services?"

Amanda opened a file folder and cleared her throat. "After reading through all of Olivia's files, I started getting a picture of the Turner family. They lived a quiet, private life, supported by Mitch's home business—selling coins and other items on eBay. As far as Luca, he didn't seem to have, or want, a relationship of any kind outside the family. A few folks with kids his age invited him to birthday parties, and sports activities in town, but he always declined, saying he was too busy with schoolwork." Amanda passed out a few head shots of Luca. "Sorry, these photos are several years old."

Sidney pinned one to the board. Luca Ashe was a gaunt teenager with pale blue eyes, tawny hair, a scrawny neck, and protruding ears. Nothing about him was distinctive. He was the kind of person who could all but disappear in a crowd.

"He was underweight and undersized for his age," Amanda continued, reading from her file. "He was a quiet introvert. But sometimes he had explosions of temper and had physical skirmishes with other kids, which resulted in him having three different foster families in his first ten years. His doctor experimented with anti-anxiety meds, and Zoloft seemed to finally keep his moods in check. Luca was with the Turners for eight years, from age ten to eighteen. He left a year ago. He got the same kind of reports from Olivia year after year. Being in a quiet home seemed to be the ticket. The Turners home schooled him, so he wasn't active in sports or other activities that attract boys his age. He loved cats. The Turners had three, and they all ate and slept in Luca's room. His room was full of books, and he went to the library frequently. That seemed to be his main escape from home. He wanted to be a lawyer, and from all accounts, he's away at school."

"Any reports of trouble?"

"Only one." Amanda took a minute to review her notes. "When he was seventeen, Luca confided in Olivia that he'd had an incident with a neighbor named Larry McKenna. He brushed it off, but Olivia was concerned enough to pay McKenna a visit. He told her he frequently hiked out in the woods, and sometimes took his dog off leash. A few times, he came across Luca on the trail. Luca was always alone, but he habitually carried a big tabby cat in his backpack, with just its face peering out. The man often attempted to engage Luca in friendly conversation, but the boy put his head down, mumbled something unintelligible and hustled away. Once, McKenna's dog jumped up on Luca, trying to sniff the cat. The cat jumped out of the backpack and high-tailed it up a tree. The dog clawed the tree, barking. Luca started screaming obscenities at the dog, and he kicked it a couple of times. The man had to grab Luca by the shoulders and jerk him away. Then Luca attacked McKenna. Though scrawny, he got in a couple of good punches, and gave the man a nosebleed. Larry and his dog, who was limping, got the hell out of there. When he reported the incident to Mitch Turner, he smoothed it over, saying Luca would have a good talking to, and he gave McKenna a valuable replica of an old Norse coin. Worth a couple hundred dollars." She looked up. "So essentially, Mitch bought him off."

Sidney's antennae shot straight up. "A Norse coin? That could be a

Viking coin."

"Yep. Here's a photo."

The coin had a crude image of a Viking ship on it.

"So Mitch Turner did trade in Viking coins," Sidney said.

"Yes. The man said Mitch gave him a few to choose from."

"Any other complaints about Luca?" Sidney asked.

"No, only from Mitch Turner, who constantly complained they weren't being paid enough to care for him. Olivia's notes stated that the boy never complained, and said he was fine, and he liked living with the Turners. The only other glimpse anyone caught of him was sitting in the passenger seat of Mitch Turner's truck. Coming or going on the road." Amanda frowned. "His existence appears to be one of isolation. Cut off from the world. He must have been lonely. Can't help but feel sorry for him."

"I don't feel sorry for him," Darnell said. "Sounds like he has a violent streak."

"He was protecting his cat from a vicious animal," Amanda said. "We're only hearing one side of the story. Luca definitely had emotional problems, but the meds kept it under control." She pulled a couple more photos from the folder. "Here are pictures of Luca posing with the Turners."

The Turners were as nondescript as Luca—a middle-aged couple with graying hair and bland clothing. Mitch was tall and lean with deep-set eyes and a thin mouth. Becky was a head shorter, and plump with a plain face. Sidney recalled her undernourished corpse. She had lost considerable weight during her captivity. In each photo, the Turners stood like bookends on each side of a young adolescent boy in front of a Christmas tree. The head of a tabby kitten poked out from the top of the boy's shirt and his hands supported its weight.

"Posing is right. No one is smiling. No one is touching. They look grim," Sidney said.

"Guess no one said cheese," Darnell said, passing one of the photos to Granger.

"Look how tenderly he's holding that cat," Amanda pointed out.

"Right. Like he's protecting it," Granger said. "Maybe it was his Christmas present."

"Did he get any therapy?"

"Nothing is mentioned in his files."

"It looks like this kid just disappeared into the bureaucratic woodwork," Sidney said soberly. "Social workers are overloaded with cases, they give their attention to the kids that squawk the loudest. So where is he now?"

"No one knows. They stopped keeping tabs on him when he left the Turners, and effectively, dropped out of the system."

"Are these the only pictures they had? Nothing recent?"

"Chief," Darnell interjected, his brown eyes more intense than usual. "I searched the internet and found a few things on Facebook, posted over the last six months, when Luca opened his account for the first time. There's no trace of him anywhere else."

Sidney sank into the chair next to him and leaned forward. Amanda and Granger leaned in from behind their shoulders. There were a half dozen images of a young man dressed in long sleeved shirts and jeans. In every shot his face was shadowed by a bill cap and a close-cropped beard. He held one or more cats, three in total, sitting in a bedroom with bare walls. In others, he was alone in the woods.

"All these photos look like selfies," Darnell said. "No friends. That's really unusual."

"Hmm. There are no photos of him with his foster parents, either, or even their house," Granger said.

"Maybe he didn't like the Turners," Amanda said.

"Maybe." Sidney rubbed her forehead with her fingers. "What else do you notice in these photos?"

"He bulked up," Granger said. "You can see his shoulders are broader, and his biceps are sculpted."

"What shows of his face, it's fuller," Sidney said. "He put on quite a bit of weight, and it looks like it's all muscle." She squinted at one of photos. "His wrist is turned but it looks like he has a tattoo. Can you focus in on that?"

Darnell enlarged the photo five hundred percent and centered in on Luca's wrist.

"Holy hell," Sidney breathed. Unmistakably, in bold black ink, a Valknut symbol was visible on Luca's wrist. "It's a Valknut." Sidney stood up and paced, rubbing her chin. "A lot of arrows are pointing at this kid right now. In addition to the tattoo, Luca had a close relationship with all three victims. Mitch Turner collected Viking coins, which may very well have included the Valknut coins."

"The killer stayed at the Turner house," Amanda said. "Luca certainly knew the lay of the land."

"He's strong enough to have carried Olivia out to the middle of that field," Darnell said.

"Do we have a current address?" Sidney asked. "The name of a school?"

"No. And I looked," Darnell said. "He wants to stay anonymous."

"We don't have a good photo of him," Amanda said. "He's deliberately hiding his face, so no one can see what he looks like."

Sidney rubbed the back of her neck. "I suspect the Turners' killer may have been the man who attacked Max up at the monastery. A black truck was seen up there. The driver wore a ball cap. Did you find anything on Max's phone, Darnell?"

Darnell shook his head. "He kept his business separate from his private life. Everything he had on social media is about friends and family. But there's a number that appeared a few times recently in his phone records. The last time was the night that Max met with someone at his campsite and was attacked."

"Did you trace it?"

"Untraceable. It's a burner phone. It could be Max's client."

"Until he comes up with a bulletproof alibi, Luca Ashe just became our prime suspect," Sidney said. "We can assume the guy in the black truck is Luca. Somehow, he's connected to Tammy and Max. He stole Max's laptop and camera. He doesn't want to be identified. Judging from the trail of bodies he's left behind, Luca would have no qualms about killing Max to keep him quiet."

"He may have tried to kill him that night, but Max got away."

Sidney nodded. "Max was hit on the head. Sound familiar? That seems to be Luca's M.O."

"Did we get any prints off the camp chairs?" Granger asked.

"Yeah. A bunch. Stewart is still ruling out Max's family. I told him to compare fingerprints to anything found in the Turner vehicles. Also, we should have the DNA results from the cups found in the camper sink and Tammy's toothbrush today or tomorrow."

"Why would Luca be trying to find Tammy?" Darnell asked.

"Good question," Sidney said. "The scary thing is, he got close. He stole Thomas's truck. Somehow he knew Thomas had something to do with Tammy. Max must have told him. One thing's for sure. If Luca's looking for her, she's in imminent danger."

"We need to find her before he does," Darnell said.

"Darnell, put an APB out on Luca Ashe. Medium height. Muscular. Light blue eyes. Protruding ears. Wears ball caps. Nineteen years old. He may be driving the black truck everyone is looking for. Give them the license plate of Thomas's truck."

"Copy." Darnell left the room.

Sidney's gaze landed on Granger. "What did you get from Alice Schaffer?"

Granger related the facts he got from Alice regarding Tammy and her daughter, Riley. "Alice knows something. I'm sure of it. But she's scared. Enough to keep her from talking. I don't think she knows where Tammy is, but I may have her convinced to call me when she does."

"What's she scared about?"

"I don't know."

"Right now, she's too close to this investigation. She and Riley need to stay somewhere safe until we bring Luca in."

"She's going to go stay with her sister in Salem."

"Good. I'm heading up to Steelhead Lake to meet Kyle. He got hold of a cadaver dog."

"You may need my help, Chief," Granger said with a look of concern. "That's treacherous country up there. Steep. Still covered in ice and snow. You'll need snowshoes."

Sidney took in Granger's face, his eyes still a little bloodshot and puffy from last night's fire. He sat slouched in his seat, his muscular legs angling out sideways into the room. He fared more poorly than she had, gulping in more of the toxic gases. But he had a steely glint to his blue eyes, and he looked determined. Sidney, too, was burned out, operating on fumes, and she didn't have very much experience walking in snowshoes, but she was just as determined. She never asked anyone to do more than she was willing to do herself. "You're on, Granger."

Standing by the sideboard, Sidney poured a fresh cup of coffee and took a sip. She needed to fortify herself with a strong dose of caffeine. "I really want that skull," she mused. "It might tell us something. Every single clue is a puzzle piece that gets us closer to the complete picture. Gets us one step closer to the killer." She pressed a lid on her cup. "Grab your winter gear. Let's roll."

CHAPTER TWENTY-SEVEN

A LIGHT SNOW had fallen the night before, and as they drove into the higher elevation, the forest glistened and shimmered under deeper mounds of white. Sidney pulled into the lot by the boat ramp at Steelhead Lake and parked next to Kyle's Search and Rescue truck. Forested hills rose on three sides of the lake to form craggy peaks that pierced a cloudless sky. The lake had thawed to a deep cobalt blue though the water along the shoreline was still frozen solid. The subdued color of the landscape and the vapor rising off the lake gave the place a serene, mystical quality.

"I forgot how beautiful it is up here," Sidney said.

"Awe inspiring," Granger acknowledged.

Kyle and another officer were sitting on the open end of their truck strapping on their snowshoes. Sidney and Granger stepped out into the frigid air and did the same. They all wore knit pants, parkas, knit caps, gloves, and wrap-around sunglasses. They greeted one another with warm smiles and Kyle made introductions. The handler was Deputy Bryce Dixon, who looked fortyish and had a muscular build. He opened the crate and a large black and tan German Shepherd jumped out, wearing snow booties and a waterproof vest. Immediately, the dog looked keen and alert, his intelligent brown eyes scoping out the people and the landscape. "This is Trooper," Bryce said.

"Maybe you've heard of Trooper, the wonder dog," Kyle said. "Last year he found four corpses buried twelve feet deep in a killer's back yard."

"I did hear about that. Job well done." Sidney smiled. "The trainers did an amazing job with him, Bryce."

"Yeah, training me was the hard part. I had to learn how to let him do his job. Trooper is a loyal partner and a hard worker. He can be fierce, and he'd take a bullet for me in a heartbeat. But he's also gentle. Great with my kids." Bryce snapped the leash on the dog's harness. "Did you bring something that belongs to Turner?"

Granger lifted an evidence bag that held one of Turner's gym shoes.

They had stopped by the morgue to pick it up.

"Perfect. That will be loaded with scent." Bryce stuck it in his backpack then lifted the pack over his shoulders. "Let's hike to the spot where Turner's remains were found, then I'll get Trooper plugged in."

"It's on the other side of the lake," Kyle said.

They walked single file with Kyle in the lead, everyone digging in with their poles. Sydney was next, then Granger, and Trooper loped alongside Bryce in the rear. The effects of the warming season were on full display. The surface of the snow was slushy in the sun and multiple gullies streamed across their path from snowmelt in the higher slopes. It was colder and drier beneath the trees, and the snow squeaked beneath their snowshoes. Snow crystals sifted down through the branches, and they could hear water dripping throughout the forest.

Kyle set a fast pace, and after a mile, Sidney was perspiring beneath her clothes. She concentrated on the narrow trail that snaked through the forest while listening to Bryce and Granger. They kept up a steady conversation, first talking sports, then veering into the art of finding corpses.

"That's amazing that Trooper found those bodies under twelve feet of earth," Granger said.

"That's nothing. Cadaver dogs have found corpses that have been buried for hundreds of years, as deep as fifteen feet. Or even a body under thirty meters of water."

"No shit?"

"No shit. Trooper can even detect the difference between human and animal remains. Using his strong sense of scent, he can work through the woods and ignore decomposing squirrels and birds while honing in specifically on the scent of a deceased human."

"For real?"

"Yeah. For real. Human bodies decompose in five stages, and each produces different odors. A whopping total of 424 different chemicals are released. Corpses in the ground and above ground rot differently and give off different smells."

"Didn't know that." Granger sounded impressed.

By the time Kyle brought them to a halt, Sidney had conjured all the images of rotting corpses she could handle. Ten years as a homicide detective had given her firsthand experience, up close and personal. She wrinkled her nose, remembering.

The forest of ponderosa pine opened to a wide, snowy meadow and under the sun, the surface snow was slushy. Rivulets of water rushed downhill making gurgling noises.

"Scattered over this meadow is where we found some of Turner's ribs, an arm bone, and a leg bone with the shoe still on it," Kyle said. "All the bones had various bite marks and the flesh had been gnawed off. The rest of him we never found."

"Let's see what we can do today." Bryce took off his backpack and pulled out the bag holding Turner's shoe. He opened it and Trooper took in long, deep sniffs, then with his nose grazing the surface, he started traversing parts of the meadow. He gracefully bounded through knee deep snow and the team followed behind. After ten minutes, Trooper stopped with a few short whines, tail wagging.

"He's got something." Kyle and Bryce removed folding shovels from their packs and started digging, slowly and carefully.

Sidney suppressed her excitement.

A foot down they struck pay dirt. Bryce gently lifted the top of a long bone that looked like a human tibia. As he brushed away the snow, they saw the whole foot was attached, wearing a sock and shoe—a perfect match to Turner's. Kyle lifted it triumphantly and everyone grinned, slapping Bryce on the back and showering praise on Trooper. The dog pulled back his lips in what appeared to be a satisfied grin. Small wins like this were the rewards for long hours of police work.

"We just might find that freaking skull after all," Granger said.

"You had doubts?" Bryce asked in a mocking tone.

"We haven't found it yet," Sidney interjected. "Let's not get ahead of ourselves."

"You're right," Bryce said. He placed the bone in an evidence bag and stuffed the bag in his backpack. "One bone at a time."

Trooper was eager to get back to work.

***

After two hours, they had meandered through the forest and found more bones, bagged and distributed to all four backpacks, almost completing Turner's skeleton. But no head, and the sun had sunk behind the tree line, casting the meadow in deep shadow. The forest had also darkened, with just an hour of filtered light still available. A noticeable chill had descended as well. Trooper wanted to take them deeper and higher into the forest. The group did a quick pow wow. "What do you think?" Kyle asked.

"This is pretty strenuous for Trooper," Bryce said. "He's been bounding through snow for over two hours, subjected to constant cold." He blew out a breath. "I don't know."

"What if we carry him back to the truck?" Sidney suggested. "I hate to give up on that skull. Trooper looks pretty enthusiastic to me. Can we give it another twenty minutes, tops?"

"I'm up for it," Granger said. "I'll carry him back."

Everyone looked at the dog. He was pulling on the leash, eager to take them up the hill.

"I think he'll be okay," Bryce said, looking at their faces, which reflected the same enthusiasm as the dog. "Let's go." He gave Trooper a long lead on the leash, and the shepherd was off like a bullet, with Bryce doing his best to hold him back.

The terrain grew steeper and more rugged with jagged boulders at times blocking their path. Not to be deterred, Trooper led the team over or around them. There was no sound—no wildlife, no wind rustling or whistling through branches—just the snow squeaking beneath their snowshoes and the stabs of their poles. The frigid air made Sidney's nose drip while beneath her clothing, she was sweating again.

They followed Trooper around some immense, craggy rocks and came face to face with a stunningly beautiful ice cave. The mouth of the cave was almost clenched completely shut by icicles that hung like glistening daggers. The basalt rock walls had slicked over with thick layers of ice, and delicate snow-covered formations had formed on the roof. Up here, Sidney recollected, during an especially bitter winter, the wind and cold combined to form small ice caves, usually just tall enough for a man to walk into upright, and not more than five yards deep. But this one was deeper and higher. The interior was a tunnel and their flashlight beams reflected on a far wall about fifteen yards in.

Trooper sprinted to the mouth and disappeared through a gap in the dagger-like teeth. He peered out at them, barking excitedly.

"Something's in there," Bryce said, his eyes animated. "Trooper's really excited. But I can't recommend anyone going in. I don't need to tell you, at this time of the year, everything's thawing out. The floor and walls inside that cave, and the roof, could be unstable. The floor could be concealing a crevice, or deep hole beneath it."

"If the skull is in there, once this cave collapses, it could be crushed. Or buried. We may never retrieve it," Sidney said. "I'm going in."

"No more than two people should go in, otherwise we're putting stress on the entire structure," Bryce warned.

"I'm going in, too," Granger said, without hesitation. "Let's break off some of these icicles and make a decent entryway."

Bryce called for the dog to come out, then he and Kyle brought out ice axes and started chipping away at icicles that weren't support pillars. When a hole was large enough to duck through, they handed their axes to Granger and Sidney, should they be needed inside.

"Don't walk on anything that isn't one hundred percent solid," Bryce warned. "Follow in the leader's tracks from a safe distance, and for God's sake, err on the side of caution."

"I'll go in first," Granger said. "Let me get ten feet in front you."

Sydney waited, then went in. Everything was dark except for what their beams illuminated. The interior of the cave was constructed of multiple layers of ice in luminous colors of blue. The cyan light reflecting off the frozen walls gave it an eerie, otherworldly hue. Everything was wet and dripping. Water oozed down the walls and there were puddles on the icy floor. A sudden loud, sharp crack blasted through the tunnel.

Granger let out a long, low whistle. "Damn."

"Holy hell." Sydney's chest tightened. What if it caved in on them?

Granger kept walking, his beam scouring the slick walls until it reflected off the end. His beam spotlighted something partially encased in the ice a few feet off the ground. "See that?"

"Yeah. It's yellow and green. Definitely manmade."

"I'm going to chip it out." He made his way to the end of the tunnel and under the light of both beams they saw what it was—a backpack. "What the hell?"

"What the hell is right. Is Turner's head in there?"

"We're going to find out."

"Careful." Sidney approached and took photos while Granger worked, chipping delicately.

The thick layers of ice above them groaned and let out a deafening crack.

"Okay, that's it." She stepped away from him. "This place isn't safe. We need to leave. Now." The muffled sound of her voice made her feel claustrophobic, but she willed herself to stay calm. The air closed in around her, thick and heavy. Her blood pounded in her ears.

"I almost have it," Granger said urgently. He chipped away more ice, aggressively, and finally, with a forceful tug, he yanked the backpack out of the wall. Huge cracks appeared where the backpack had been, spreading like lightning across the wall and up to the ceiling. The ceiling groaned. "Let's get the hell out of here!"

They both turned and ran as fast as snowshoes would allow. Granger tripped and hit the floor behind her and slid five feet forward. Sidney turned to help him, her heart hammering her chest. A chunk of ice the size of a refrigerator hit the floor behind him with an ear-splitting crash, burying him in ice splinters and crystals. Sidney worked frantically to help him dig himself out and he emerged like some kind of shimmering iceman; every inch of him white. She yanked him to his feet.

A series of rumbles above them were thunderous.

They ran.

The mouth of the cave was just feet in front of them. Behind her, Granger dove for it, grabbing Sidney and carrying her along with him. They flew out of the entry hole and tumbled down the face of the hill as the cave imploded, sounding like a bomb going off. Chunks of ice shot off like fireworks and cascaded down on the surrounding area, hitting the ground like stones.

Everyone ran, covering their heads, and they rounded one of the immense jagged boulders, which offered a protective barrier. Panting, they stood catching their breath, listening to the continuing demolition of the cave. Finally there was dead silence except for their ragged breathing.

"Everyone okay?" Kyle asked, his eyes large.

Sidney nodded, breathing deeply, heart racing, though one arm had taken a painful hit from an ice projectile. She'd have a few good bruises to show for her effort.

"Yeah," Granger gasped, his chest heaving from the burst of speed and adrenaline. He was still covered with shavings of ice from his burial in the cave, his eyelashes and eyebrows were white. "How's Trooper?"

"He's fine," Bryce said. The dog sat at attention beside him. "I told him to leave the area when we heard the first big crack. I can't believe you stayed in there. I thought for sure we'd be doing a search and rescue."

Granger held up the backpack like a trophy. "We got this."

"What kind of crazy are you two?" Kyle shook his head, and grinned. "Well, let's see what's in there. I'm going to laugh my ass off if it's some kid's schoolbooks."

With a look of distaste, Granger held out the pack. "Anyone want to do the honors?"

Bryce stepped forward and took the pack. "It can't be any worse than the corpses we find. At least it'll be frozen. No smell." He set it down, unzipped the top, and looked inside.

Everyone watched with rapt attention.

He looked up, his expression inscrutable, then he grinned. "It's a human head, all right. I can see the hair on its crown. Good job, you two fearless idiots."

A few moments of jubilation were shared, then everyone became aware of the darkening sky, and determined it was time to get down the hill.

"You guys have some weird kind of killer out there," Kyle said as they hiked.

"That head was deliberately severed from the body and put into that cave," Bryce added. "Why?"

Sidney shrugged. "Can't quite figure this guy out. He's a vicious psychopath, for sure. And also a trickster. Likes to put obstacles in our path. Misdirect us. Let's hope this is Turner's head, and that it tells us something important when we get it back to the lab."

Dusk settled around them and the forest took on ominous shapes and shadows. They all felt the night chill penetrating their clothes. With their backpacks stuffed with human bones and a human head, they hit the lower trail leading back to their vehicles.

Back at the SUV, Sidney called ahead to the morgue to ensure that she caught Stewart and Dr. Linthrope before they left for the night. "Tell Doc we found more of Mitch Turner's bones," she told Stewart. "And a frozen head. Hopefully, his."

"You've been busy," Stewart said, sounding impressed.

"Never a dull moment."

Her second call was to her dispatcher. "Hey, Jesse, any chatter out there about Luca Ashe, or the big monster truck?"

"Nada, Chief. Right now he's a ghost."

CHAPTER TWENTY-EIGHT

STEWART AND LINTHROPE were waiting in the morgue when they arrived. While Stewart snapped photos, Sidney and Granger removed the bones from the four backpacks and lined them up one by one on a metal slab. Each evidence bag was labeled and dated, and Sidney had documented the locations with photos from her phone.

"Here's the head." Granger lifted the evidence bag holding the backpack found in the cave.

"Put it on the other slab," Linthrope instructed, snapping on a pair of gloves.

Everyone moved to the slab in the middle of the room.

"Since the head's been frozen, it should be intact, which will tell us a better story than any of those bones," Linthrope said with enthusiasm. "I'm eager to have a look."

Sidney was conflicted. On the one hand, she didn't want to see a decapitated human head emerge from the backpack. That image would be imprinted in her memory for life. On the other hand, she was seized with a strong desire to learn something new about her case. What could this head tell them? What clues did it hold?

Linthrope gingerly withdrew the backpack from the evidence bag, then unzipped the top. Granger and Sidney stood motionless; their eyes trained on the opening. Sidney held her breath.

Very gently, Linthrope withdrew the head. Viewed from the back, she saw the gray hair was matted with blood—an ominous forewarning. Carefully, the doctor laid it down on the slab, face up. Sidney and Granger both inhaled sharply. Turner's face was covered in blood. Two medallions covered the eye sockets and the mouth gaped in an expression of agony. As Stewart's camera flash pulsed, Linthrope peered inside Turner's mouth with a pin light, and stated calmly, "His tongue's been cut out. Hmmm. There appears to be a message crammed down his throat." Linthrope inserted forceps, carefully pulled out a wadded ball of paper, and laid it on a clean cutting board. He carefully smoothed it out using two pairs of tweezers and the familiar slanted handwriting materialized. "Same killer," Linthrope murmured, and then he read out loud:

The longer the vengeance is drawn out, the more satisfying it will be.
-Old Viking Saying-
Killing you slowly was the sweetest love I've ever known.
Rot in Helheim for eternity

Sidney shivered. "His statement of brutality is followed by a statement of exhilaration, same as with the women. This time it sounds like he tortured his victim. Drew out his death."

"Interesting," Stewart said, unaffected, lowering his camera. "In Norse legend, when a Viking dies honorably, he goes to Valhalla. If a Viking dies dishonorably, he goes to Helheim—also known as the Realm of the Dead—where he's forced to tread through icy lands where no fire can live. One is always cold and hungry. Only terror and torment can be expected."

"How do you know this?" Sidney asked.

"Haven't you seen the movies "Outlander" or "Beowulf," or the TV series "Vikings?"

Stewart was met with blank stares.

"So dishonorable Vikings went to icy lands where no fire can live," Sidney said. "Speaks to why Turner's head was left in an ice cave."

"But why cut out his tongue?" Granger asked.

"Speak no evil," Stewart said. "Viking vengeance."

Sidney studied the embossed symbol on the twin medallions. A serpent in the shape of a circle grasped its tail in its mouth. "I'm afraid to ask, but what's with these medallions?" Sidney snapped a couple of photos with her phone. "They're pressed deep into his eye sockets. Why do I have a feeling his eyes are gone?"

"Let's take a look." Linthrope lifted the edge of a coin with a tweezer.

Sidney diverted her gaze.

"Yep. Gouged out."

"See no evil," she said. "Check his ears, Doc."

Linthrope shone a pin light into both ear canals. "They've been punctured repeatedly."

"Hear no evil," she and Granger said in tandem. Her junior officer was quiet, and Sidney sensed his tension. She too felt tense, and bone weary. Two near-death experiences—one by fire and one by ice—and the stress of witnessing the violent attacks on victims by a psychopath, were catching up to her. Luca was still out there, free to kill again.

Granger met her eyes, concern on his face. "Let's take a break, Chief. Get a cup of coffee. It's been a long day."

"Good idea," Linthrope said gently, watching her. "Why don't you go up to the break room? Let me get to work on Turner's head and catalogue these bones. I'll send over my report in the morning."

Stewart escorted them upstairs to the hospital break room. They all grabbed a cup of coffee and sat under the bright fluorescent lights at one of two small tables. The coffee revived Sidney a bit and she asked hopefully, "Did any lab results come in, Stewart?"

"Yes, one thing. We have a match to the urine collected from Aspen Lake. It came from Becky Turner."

Sidney's brows lifted in surprise. "I didn't see that coming."

"Little freak," Granger growled. "He collected his foster mom's urine while he held her hostage. Then dumped it at the lake to mess with us."

Sidney sighed her relief. "I'm just glad it's hers, and not some female accomplice. We don't need another Bonnie and Clyde running loose around the county, creating double trouble."

Granger's brow relaxed a bit. "Yeah. It could always be worse."

Stewart added, "I'll have the results from Tammy's toothbrush and the cups in Max's camper in the morning."

"Great. Thanks, Stewart. We'll catch up mañana."

They walked outside and climbed into the Yukon. Sidney's stomach growled and she realized she was ravenously hungry. All that hiking on an empty stomach had burned through the little bit of fuel she kept on reserve. Granger looked equally drained. She pulled up next to his truck in the station lot. "I bet you're starving."

"I could eat." He smiled and his blue eyes warmed.

"Go home. Eat. Sleep."

"What about you, Chief?"

"I'm just about ready to call it a night myself. First, I'm going to go in and check on Darnell and Amanda."

"Give Selena a hug for me," he said with a touch of yearning in his eyes.

"When we break this case, you're coming over for dinner." And private time with Selena, she thought. She'd make sure she and David were out for the night.

***

Her two junior officers were hunched over their computers, filing reports.

They both looked relieved when Sidney dismissed them. She had Winnie call out reserve officers to cover their patrols that evening. No one had gotten more than a few hours of sleep since the discovery of Olivia's body. Amanda and Darnell both had spouses and toddlers at home, whom they hadn't seen much of in three days. She needed highly functioning officers in the morning, and that came with a good night's sleep and a few hours of quality time with family. Before she headed home, Sidney called David from her office.

He answered on the second ring, and asked with a note of worry in his voice, "How're you holding up?"

"Tired. But okay. Making progress. I could use your input on something."

"Sounds promising. Does that mean I get to see you?"

"I have just enough energy to drive home. If you don't mind meeting me there …."

"Sure. Can I bring you dinner?"

She smiled. David always wanted to feed her. She missed his wonderful cooking. Right now she needed time to morph from Chief Sidney Becker, law enforcement officer, to Sidney Becker, civilian and girlfriend. "Thanks, but Selena will have something waiting. Give me a half hour to eat and take a shower."

"You got it. See you then."

***

With her hair damp around her shoulders and Chili purring on her lap, Sidney sat at the table in her soft chenille bathrobe. Somewhat revived after finishing the leftover lamb stew, she was nursing a cold Corona when David arrived. When she met him at the front door, he pulled her into his arms and held her close. "I've missed you," he murmured. His mouth found hers and they kissed. His gentle kiss deepened, stirring the undercurrent of longing she always felt for him. Sidney stroked his back for a moment, feeling the lean muscles under his shirt, then she led him back to the dining room.

Wearing big potholder mittens, Selena greeted David cheerily from across the island in the kitchen as she pulled a sheet of cookies from the oven.

He draped his jacket over the back of a chair and settled next to Sidney, his knee pressed against hers. His warm brown eyes flicked over her face. "You look positively done in." He moved her wet hair aside and planted a kiss on her neck. "Can I give you a back rub later?"

"I thought you'd never ask," she answered softly, breathing in his comforting scent. Her shoulder muscles were as tight as corded rope and he had the fingers of a magician. His presence beside her felt reassuring and calming, and for the first time that day, she felt her tension easing.

David squeezed her hand and called out to Selena, "Are those chocolate chip cookies I smell?"

"Yep, gluten free." She brought out a plate of cookies and set them on the table. "Almond butter, quinoa flour, maple syrup, and dark chocolate."

David grabbed one and pulled it apart, then dropped it. "Ouch." The warm chocolate oozed out on the plate.

"Give them a minute," Selena said. "They're hot."

"Yeah, I noticed."

"Get the burn kit," Sidney teased.

David rolled his eyes.

"Need milk?"

"You know I do."

"I have cashew, flax, or coconut. Pick one."

"Hmm." He lifted a brow and thought for a moment. "I'll try cashew." He went for the cookie again, this time popping half of it in his mouth. David was Selena's biggest fan. He loved her healthy concoctions. Sidney had to admit, her sister was an alchemist, making ingredients like hemp and flax and chia actually taste good. He ate the other half. "Five stars, Selena."

She beamed, dropping off his glass of milk, then she headed upstairs with the four cats bounding after her.

"Hmmm, I can't resist." David ate another cookie, washed it down with a gulp of milk, and smiled at Sidney. "Okay. I'm burning with curiosity. What do you need my help with?"

Sidney picked up her phone and scrolled through the grisly photos of Mitch Turner's head. She picked one that didn't show his bloodied face and gaping mouth; just a close up of a medallion. "Can you tell me anything about this symbol? Is it Viking related?"

David's eyes sparkled with enthusiasm. "Is it ever. This is an interesting case you're working on. First the Valknut coins, now the Jormungand. Both rich in Viking symbolism."

"The what?"

"Jormungand. In Norse legend, Jormungand was a poisonous serpent; so enormous, his body encircled Midgard, or the entire world. Thus, he could grasp his own tail in his mouth. Jormungand was the enemy of Thor, God of Thunder. The serpent rose from the oceans during Ragnarök, or the end of days—equivalent to the Christian apocalypse—and spewed toxins and poisons into the air. The seas boiled and the earth quaked, and the stars fell from the sky." David glanced at her with a glint of humor. "You look totally mystified. You've never heard this folklore before, have you?"

"No. I've been deprived." One corner of her mouth tilted up. "Keep going."

"According to old Norse poems, Thor met his death during the battle of Ragnarök. He and the snake were locked in combat until Thor dealt several death blows to the serpent with his hammer. But Thor was covered in poisonous venom. He walked nine paces and fell dead."

"So that was the end of Thor and the world?" she asked, frowning.

"The end of Thor, yes. The end of the world, yes and no. The world and its inhabitants were destroyed, and it led to the death of several gods, including Odin and Thor. Natural disasters submerged the world in water, but a new world surfaced, beautiful and green and fertile. Miraculously, and conveniently," he chuckled, "Líf and Lífþrasir, a human couple, managed to sleep in a magic tree through the end of the world. They emerged to discover that everything they'd ever known was destroyed. Then, like a post-apocalyptic Adam and Eve, the responsibility of populating a new world fell upon them."

"Which they did."

He laughed. "Yes, quite happily, I'm sure."

"That's an interesting story," Sidney said, her thoughts turning to Luca. "I'm wondering why the killer I'm pursuing finds it relevant."

"The medallion was strategically placed with his victim?"

"Yes." Remembering Turner's gouged eyes and other mutilations, Sidney carefully hid her emotions, but David had a unique ability to read her. He gave her an assessing glance that invited confidences, but she didn't elaborate. As much as she trusted David, this was police business. When the killer was safely apprehended, she would be free to share more details.

"There are several meanings we could derive from this symbol," he said, moving on. "But the most obvious, is that it tells the story of the death of a glorious warrior, Thor, who sacrificed himself for the birth of a new world."

"And he killed a monster that lurked in the sea, hidden from the world."

"Right."

"Maybe my suspect associated himself with Thor—a heroic figure who rid the world of a dangerous monster."

"The monster being his victim."

"Yes." Hidden away in Turner's house, who knew what ghastly things, real or perceived, Luca was subjected to. Puzzled, she added, "But in the end, Thor dies."

"True," he said, "But your killer also left the Valknut coins with other victims. Correct?"

"Yes." And he wore a Valknut tattoo.

"That signifies reincarnation, immortality," David said. "Protection from evil. And now with the monster's death, a shiny new world will open up to him."

Sidney sighed, suddenly too tired to theorize further.

David's expression softened and his thumb brushed her cheek. "Hey, let's get you to bed. I owe you a backrub."

"Are you staying over?" Sidney yearned to be held in David's arms. She needed an escape from the horror of the last few days.

He smiled. "I didn't bring my toothbrush for nothing."

CHAPTER TWENTY-NINE

WHEN SIDNEY ARRIVED at the station at ten o'clock, she was surprised when Winnie informed her that Stewart was waiting in the conference room. What was so important that it couldn't wait? She found him sitting at the head of the table looking over his notes, an empty coffee cup sitting in front of him. "Hey, Stewart." Her curiosity piqued; Sidney seated herself next to him. "Sorry to keep you waiting. You have something?"

He glanced up; his brown eyes animated behind his glasses. "Yes, ma'am. I have lab results from Max's campsite."

She sat in rapt anticipation.

"A fingerprint lifted from the armrest of a camp chair matches one found inside Mitch Turner's truck, on the inside of the glove compartment. Could've been there for years, hidden away where someone washing the truck wouldn't reach it. Doesn't match Mitch or Becky Turner. No match in the system."

Her heart picked up a beat. "Luca used to ride in Mitch Turner's truck as a passenger. He could easily have put that print in the glove compartment. This is the first piece of tangible evidence that may connect Luca to Max."

"Actually, I have more evidence that places him there. We got a surprising result from the DNA pulled off the cups found in the sink. One cup is a match to Max. The other is a familial match to the DNA pulled off of Tammy Schaffer's toothbrush. A male."

Sidney sat still for a moment, not sure she heard right. "So the DNA on the cup is from a male who is related to Tammy?"

"Not just related. It strongly suggests that the male who visited Max is Tammy's son."

Sidney stood and paced, her heart racing as she processed the information. "Luca is Tammy's son? She had two babies out of wedlock? Wait a minute. Riley and Luca are the same age. The only reasonable explanation is that they're twins."

"So it appears."

Sidney exhaled slowly, pushing this new piece of evidence around in her brain, analyzing how it fit into the whole puzzle. "Thanks for getting this over to me."

"You bet." Stewart pushed his report across the table to her and said with a wry smile, "I have to get back to work. I have a pile of bones to go through, thank you very much."

"Yeah, sorry about that."

"Dr. Linthrope said to tell you he'll have the results from Turner's head later this morning." He tossed his cup in the trash and left.

With her adrenaline humming, Sidney called her three officers into the room and delivered the startling news that Luca was Tammy's son and Riley's twin.

They sat in stunned silence.

"Alice raised Riley, while they gave up her twin brother at birth," Sidney said. "Luca got the short end of the stick. He ended up with a family he hated enough to murder."

"Holy moly," Amanda said. "We already suspected that Luca hired Max. Now we know why. He wanted to locate his birth mother."

"He's a vicious killer," Darnell said. "His reason for finding Tammy can't be good. If he found out she kept his sister, but gave him up, and he ended up in foster care purgatory, that would make him pretty damned angry."

"He attacked Max and stole his camera and computer," Granger said. "He wanted complete anonymity. Probably so he could get close enough to Tammy to kill her."

"It's fortunate Tammy took off from the monastery when she did," Darnell said. "Or she might have ended up being Luca's fourth victim."

"We don't know why he's looking for her," Sidney said. "But we need to find her before he does."

"Now I know why Alice was so dodgy when I questioned her," Granger said. "She knew about Luca all along."

"We need to question her again, and make sure that she and Riley are safe," Sidney said.

"I'll call Alice right now. She said she and Riley were going to stay with her sister, Dottie Cox, in Salem." Granger plugged in the phone number, put the phone on speaker, and they listened to it ring twelve times before he hung up. "Let me try her sister." He plugged in another number.

"Hello, this is Dottie," a woman's voice answered.

"Mrs. Cox, this is Officer Granger Wyatt with the Garnerville police department. I'm calling for Alice Schaffer."

"Alice isn't here."

"She told me she and Riley were coming to stay with you for a few days."

"They're coming this afternoon."

Granger frowned but he spoke calmly. "Have you talked to either of them today?"

"No. I've just been getting their voicemails." A touch of panic entered her voice. "Are they okay? Alice said someone might be after them."

"We're heading over there to check on them, Mrs. Cox. In the meantime, if you hear from her, please tell her to call us." He hung up.

"Everyone, saddle up," Sidney said, her gut tightening. "We're heading to the Schaffer farm. Now!"

***

Sirens wailing, strobes pulsing, Sidney punched the gas pedal and accelerated through an endless corridor of trees. Forest rushed by on both sides of the highway and grey asphalt vanished beneath her tires. In the rearview mirror, she saw Darnell's lights flashing behind her as his truck hugged a curve, keeping pace with the Yukon.

The forest dropped away and they drove into open farm country. Sunshine broke through the thinning clouds, bathing the fields and houses in morning light. Sidney reduced her speed, turned into a driveway, and drove past a pasture occupied by goats. The two vehicles parked in a clearing between the weathered barn and a small white house. At first, everything looked quiet and peaceful, then Sidney noticed that the front door of the house stood wide open. "Check the barn," Sidney said urgently into her mic to Darnell and Amanda. "We'll check the house."

The clearing offered no cover from a shooter who might be hiding. Everyone exited, pulled out their sidearms, and hurried out of the direct line of fire to the shelter of the structures.

"Police! Anyone home? We're coming in." Sidney and Granger cautiously entered the house with guns raised to eye level. They moved through a sunny kitchen, then a dining room, and discovered Alice lying in the middle of the living room floor with blood pooling around her head. They quickly cleared the two bedrooms in the back of the house and holstered their guns. Sidney grabbed a hand towel from the bathroom, and they rushed back to examine the injured woman. Alice had a weak pulse and raspy breathing. "She has a wound above her left ear," Granger said.

Sidney pressed the folded towel to the wound while Granger pulled gloves and a pressure bandage from his duty belt. He snapped on the gloves, ripped the packaging from the bandage, and placed the pressure bar directly over the wound. Alice moaned when Granger wrapped the bandage around her head. The bar pushed against the wound, applying enough pressure to stop the bleeding. "Her wound is fresh," he said. "Her attacker must have been scared off by our sirens."

"Lucky for her." Sidney called for an ambulance and was barely off the phone when Amanda's voice came over her mic. "Chief, we have a farmhand in the barn with a head injury, but he's conscious. He was attacked by a young guy driving a black truck."

Luca.

"Bring him into the house. An ambulance is on the way. Any sign of Riley?"

"He said she left for work at seven-thirty. Darnell called to tell her to stay put until we arrive."

"Good move." Sidney heaved out a tense breath, thankful Riley hadn't been home. Luca left wreckage everywhere he went. Family included. He had no problem assaulting his grandmother. She called the sheriff's department and put out a new APB on Luca and the black truck. Luca had managed once again to elude capture, but in the light of day, he might not be so lucky driving around in a monster truck.

Amanda and Darnell entered the kitchen supporting a swarthy, white-haired man and helped him sink into a chair at the table. "This is Pedro Gonzales," Amanda said. "He has a nice lump on his head, but no open wound. This is Chief Becker."

Weather worn, face deeply creased, Pedro nodded, rubbing his head. "Is Alice okay?"

"We think so. An ambulance is on the way," Sidney said. "Amanda, look in the freezer, get Mr. Gonzales some kind of ice pack. Darnell, did you get hold of Riley?"

"No. But the woman at the front desk said she'd give Riley the message to stay put."

"Okay. Go pursue. Look on all the backroads."

"Copy." Darnell rushed from the kitchen.

Sidney sat next to the old man, and said gently, "Mr. Gonzales, can you tell me what happened to you and Alice?"

"Call me Pedro." The old man cleared his throat, and said gruffly, "I was working in the barn. Some guy drove up in a noisy black truck, about twenty minutes ago. He knocked on the door, then went into the house. There was something off about him. I can't say what." Pedro stopped talking when Amanda handed him a bag of frozen peas. He pressed it against his crown, winced, and continued, "I headed for the house and I heard him yelling when I came into the kitchen. He was in the living room, holding Alice by her shoulders. She was crying, trying to talk. He started shaking her, screaming into her face." Pedro paused and swallowed hard, his Adam's apple crawling the length of his throat. He switched the hand holding the frozen peas.

"Take your time, Pedro," Sidney said. "Get him a glass of water, Amanda."

Amanda filled a glass, then carefully placed it into the farmhand's big knuckled hand. He gulped a third of it and placed it on the table. "Then the guy hit her on the head with something. Maybe the butt of a gun. I don't know. But Alice went down. I grabbed the first thing I could find—a lamp—and charged him. He turned and knocked it out of my hand like it was nothing. He was really strong, and fast. He whacked me on the head. I kicked him in the crotch, and he buckled over. I managed to get out of the house. That's when I heard your sirens. Far away. I felt all woozy. My knees were weak, but I made it to the barn and fell into a pile of hay. I heard the guy's truck peel out. Your sirens got louder. Thank god you came when you did. He would've killed us."

"Your quick action probably saved Alice's life," Sidney said gently. "If you hadn't distracted him, he might have hit her again. Can you describe him?"

Pedro nodded. "Young. Maybe nineteen, twenty. About five foot ten. Big. All muscle."

"Did you see his face?"

"Yeah. Clear as day. His hat fell off when I kicked him. He had blue eyes. A beard that was a few days old. Short brown hair, big ears."

Sidney pulled out her phone and brought up the photo of Luca as a teenager. "Is this him?"

"Yeah," he said instantly. "That's him. Though his face is fuller."

"You're sure? Take your time."

"I'm sure. Same nose. Same eyes. Same ears."

The distant sound of a siren grew piercingly loud, then Sidney heard a vehicle brake to a halt in the driveway, followed by doors slamming. Amanda ushered two paramedics into the kitchen, one carrying a medical bag. The room suddenly felt small with five people in it.

"We have a woman with a severe head injury in the living room," Sidney said. "And Pedro, here, took a good thunk on the head."

"We'll look at the woman first," the taller of the two men said. They walked swiftly past the table. Moments later, the same paramedic strode past them, grabbed a stretcher parked on the porch, and steered it into the living room.

Sidney refocused on the farmhand. Color had come back into Pedro's face and his eyes looked livelier. She asked gently, "Are you up for a few more questions?"

"Yeah," he said with a touch of anger. "I want you to catch the culo that hurt Alice."

"Good. Do you remember what the guy was saying to her?"

"Yeah, I do. When I came into the kitchen he was yelling 'where's my mother? Tell me, or I'll kill your whole family.' Then he started screaming, 'who's my father?'" Pedro made a circle at his temple with his index finger. "He's loco. Crazy. He made no sense."

"Did Alice answer him?"

"I don't know. She was blubbering. Crying." Pedro thought for a long moment, blinked, and met her gaze. "When he asked who his father was, she said something like 'range rabbit,' or 'ingot,' or 'nugget.'"

"Hmmm." Sidney wrote the words in her notebook, then looked up at Pedro and smiled. "Thank you. You've been very helpful."

Granger and the shorter paramedic rolled a stretcher into the room carrying Alice. She was covered with a blanket, wore an oxygen mask, and had an IV tube snaking from one hand.

"How is she?" Sidney asked.

"She took a good blow. We'll know more when she gets a CT scan." They rolled Alice out of the house and the other paramedic crouched in front of Pedro. "Sir, my name is Michael. I'm going to shine a light in your eyes. Could you please follow it?" He proceeded to shine a penlight into the old man's dark eyes and moved it from side to side. Pedro's eyes darted from left to right. Michael asked him what year it was and who was the current president. The old man answered with clarity. "No concussion," Michael said. "But we'd like to check you out more thoroughly at the ER." He smiled. "Want to ride in the back of the bus with Alice?"

"Yeah," he said emphatically. "I want to stay with Alice."

"Do you have a key to the house?" Sidney said. "We're going to lock up when we leave."

"Yeah." He nodded to a handbag sitting on the sideboard. "Her keys are in there. And her phone. We better take it."

Sidney locked the kitchen door, then she and Amanda watched as the two patients were situated in the ambulance. "Go with them," she said to Granger. "Stay at the ER. The second Alice is able to talk, call me. That woman knows exactly who Luca is. It sounds like Tammy's old boyfriend who OD'd, Conner, may not be his father after all. I'd guess that Alice knows who is, and she may have just put him in imminent danger by telling Luca."

"Yes, ma'am." The ambulance engine was idling, ready to leave. Granger hopped into the back, Sidney shut the doors, and the big vehicle pulled out of the clearing.

As Sidney and Amanda were walking to the Yukon, a distant explosion disrupted the silence of the morning. They jerked their attention toward the sound, just northeast of the barn, and saw plumes of thick black smoke billowing into the sky, probably about four miles out. "What the hell? Let's check that out."

***

Accompanied by police chatter on the radio that identified the explosion as a vehicle fire, Sidney raced to the location with the siren wailing. When they arrived at an open meadow bordered by a wall of thick forest, they saw a vehicle the size of a pickup truck engulfed in flames and clouds of smoke. The fire truck had not yet arrived, but several sheriff deputies and Darnell were already at the scene, attempting to manage the blaze with the extinguishers they carried in their vehicles.

Sidney spotted a couple of deputies on the fringe of the woods, trampling through the bushes along Wild Rabbit Creek. One of them was Kyle Mumford, trailing his bloodhound, Bruiser. Sidney and Amanda grabbed the two extinguishers from the back of the Yukon and joined the fire brigade. The inferno snapped and roared, and the heat was intense, radiating a good twenty feet in every direction. The most they could do was control the rash of fires igniting the surrounding grass. Within minutes a fire truck arrived, and they all backed away, allowing the firefighters to do their job. The firemen wrangled a hose from the truck and shot a powerful geyser of water directly at the blaze.

Sidney finally had the opportunity to separate Darnell from the chaos of the emergency, and he confirmed what she already suspected.

Darnell wiped sweat from his brow with the sleeve of his jacket. "That's the truck Luca was driving, Chief."

"Figures. He's an ace at destroying evidence. We'll get nothing from that truck. What happened?"

"I crisscrossed a few back roads and spotted his truck about a half mile in front of me on Alfalfa Road. By the time I reached this meadow, the truck was on fire and Luca had disappeared. These deputies responded to your APB and were right behind me. Kyle got here minutes later." He exhaled sharply. "Man, I almost had him."

Sidney glanced toward the creek. The deputies had migrated into the woods and were searching through the overgrown terrain, following in the direction of the K-9 unit. "Luca's on foot. We're joining the K-9 unit. This may be our lucky day."

**

Sidney and her two officers grabbed their AR-15 semi-automatic rifles from their vehicles and joined the manhunt, everyone staying close to the edge of the shallow creek. On the opposite side, the woods came down to an overgrown pathway that ran along the bank. The path, dark as a tunnel, ran beneath a dense canopy of big leaf maples and quaking aspens. She peered downstream, but her view was impeded by thick undergrowth and overhanging trees.

The ten-person unit split into two groups, each following the waterway on different sides. The going was slow. The hound lost the scent repeatedly. He stood sniffing the air, his body tense, his long ears lifting and falling, then at a moment's notice, he shot into the creek to the other side, only to reenter the water further downstream. The smaller team of four crisscrossed the creek trailing Bruiser, hobbling across stones, using fallen logs as a bridges. As part of the larger team, Sidney and her officers were spread out in the woods, keeping a vigilant eye in the event Luca decided to become a sniper. A carpet of damp leaves underfoot muffled the sound of their steps.

Every time Bruiser lost the scent, they lost precious seconds. The seconds added up to minutes. Luca's lead was steadily growing. Tensions were running high. Sidney heard a few cops curse under their breath.

Then the scent disappeared completely. With his nose hovering inches above the ground, the hound moved in widening circles, searching for a trace of odor. Bruiser and Kyle were fifty feet behind Sidney on the opposite bank when something caught her eye. She went down on her haunches and pushed some branches aside.

"See something?" Amanda asked, joining her, squinting at the ground.
"Wow."

Imprinted in the damp earth was a well-defined and distinctive boot print. Sidney recognized it immediately. It was a perfect match to the print discovered in the field where Olivia Paisley's body was found. The logo was clearly visible. "Over here!" Sidney yelled. Kyle and Bruiser headed in her direction at a run.

"This connects Luca to both crime scenes," Sidney said to Amanda as the handler and hound splashed across the creek. "Take a few shots of it."

With an excited squeal, Bruiser seized on the scent and was off like a racer, bulldozing through a sea of fern and brush while Kyle strained to keep up. Everyone else fell into line behind them, trotting. The dense canopy of foliage deepened as they sprinted further into the forest. Bruiser led them through ferns and low, stunted bushes that filled the spaces between the trunks. Sidney had to watch for branches clawing her uniform and whipping back in her face.

They came to a spur of woodland spilling down from the slopes of Black Bear Peak. Bruiser lifted his muzzle from the ground, visibly excited. Kyle loosened the leash and the hound shot off in a straight line. The scent was stronger. They were gaining on their fugitive. The trees thinned and they began wading through waist-high ferns that stretched unbroken on either side of them. Trekking uphill was strenuous work. Bulked up with body armor, their shirts sprouted stains and their faces shone with sweat. They were all breathing hard.

Then Bruiser quickly led them to a clearing of grass and wildflowers. On the other side of the clearing were lines of aspens, their leaves blowing silver and green in the gusting wind. A dense growth of saplings filled the spaces between their trunks, forming an impenetrable screen.

As they stepped out from the shade of the trees into the sharp light, it was hotter than hell. They stepped back into the shadows. The hound strained on the leash, wanting to lead them directly through the middle of the meadow. Kyle held him back. They turned their gazes up the slope where rocky outcroppings rose above the tree line. A killer with malicious intent might be up there, watching, waiting. He would have all the advantage, hiding behind cover while they were out in the open. Bruiser stood at attention, staring in the same direction, whining with anticipation.

Kyle scanned the area above with his binoculars.

"See anything?" Sidney asked.

"Nope."

"Should we spread out? Head up there?" A female deputy asked.

Before Kyle answered, a familiar sound came to their ears, borne on the breeze; the oiled click of a rifle-bolt being drawn back. Then the silence exploded.

CRACK! CRACK! CRACK!

The shots came in rapid succession and the ground beside Sidney erupted. She and Amanda dove behind the nearest lodgepole pine tree. Safe behind the massive trunk, she turned to Kyle just as bullets slammed into his chest. The impact threw him backwards. His armored vest had caught the bullets, but he lay flat on his back, his face white and shocked. He moaned as Sidney and Amanda each grabbed one of his feet and pulled him to safety. The earth where he had lain leaped into the air.

They quickly identified the source. The rounds weren't coming from up on the peak, but from the grove across the clearing. Sidney felt the familiar heaviness in her chest, the pounding of blood in her temples that came with abrupt and sudden danger. In an instantaneous clatter of metal, she and every other cop raised their rifles. A hurricane of bullets blasted the grove. Chunks of steel-jacketed lead flattened against trunks and the surrounding rocks with a deafening clamor. The smell of gunpowder tainted the air.

The senior deputy signaled for them to stop, and yelled, "Luca, give it up. You're outmanned. Come out peacefully. Save yourself."

Luca unloaded his weapon, shooting wildly, rounds ripping up the earth. He may have been wounded. His precision was way off. But he was making a statement.

The deputy signaled. The cops also made a statement, responding with an earsplitting show of force. A continuous burst of automatic fire was unleashed into the grove. Chips of bark exploded like wayward missiles. Branches splintered and rounds thudded into tree trunks. Again, the deputy signaled for the fire power to stop.

The shots rang in Sidney's ears for long seconds, then gave way to a deafening silence. Gunsmoke drifted in the air. The deputy's voice sliced into the quiet. "Luca, put down your weapon. We don't want to hurt you."

No response for ten long seconds. Then a hoarse voice carried across the meadow. "I'm coming out. Don't shoot. I'm hit."

Sidney's heart thumped in her chest as a figure materialized between branches of green and silver leaves. The man who stepped into the clearing was of medium height, muscular build, dressed in jeans and a T-shirt, with prominent ears poking through limp brown hair. Luca. He walked unsteadily, one muscular arm raised, the other covered in blood, pressed to his side.

"Turn around," the deputy yelled. "Walk back towards us."

The young man complied, stumbling a few times.

"Lay on the ground, spread eagle," the deputy shouted when he got within fifty feet of their position.

Luca sank to his knees, then did a faceplant in the grass, groaning.

Four deputies rushed over. One cuffed his hands behind his back while the other three provided cover. They weren't taking chances. Every officer there had been fired upon. If Luca had his way, several would be dead. Only then did they turn him over and begin to assess his injuries.

Sidney released the grip on her rifle, wiped her sweaty hands on her pants, and took her first easy breath since the shooting started. She and her two officers joined the group surrounding Luca. Two men hurriedly treated his gunshot wounds; one to his right side, one to his shoulder. The female deputy was on her satellite phone, urgently calling for Med-Evac.

With Bruiser at his side, Kyle trudged out of the woods, grimacing, his face stained with dirt and sweat. He gripped his vest in one hand. "Man, I thought I was a goner, but this thing saved my life. It caught a couple rounds." In response to their looks of concern, he added with a determined expression. "I'm okay."

"You don't look okay," Amanda said.

"You've got to be hurting like a sonovabitch," Sidney said. "When my vest caught a single bullet last year, it felt like a sledgehammer." Vests offered protection against projectile penetration and fatal wounds, but the kinetic energy of the bullet always resulted in shock and minor injuries.

"Never said it didn't hurt." Kyle gave them a wobbly smile.

"You're going to have extensive bruising, and possibly, cracked ribs," the senior deputy said. "You're getting on that chopper. They'll give you morphine."

"Man, I could use it." He sank to his knees, then lay back on the grass, clenching his teeth. Sidney felt for him.

Minutes later, the distant sound of a rotor beat grew louder, and a chopper swooped over the treetops. It hovered above the clearing, then descended to the middle of the field. The wind from the rotors flattened the grass and it rippled outward in waves. Two paramedics leaped out and the cops moved aside to let them take over. They worked quickly and methodically to stabilize Luca, administering an IV and oxygen mask.

"How's he doing?" Sidney asked anxiously.

"Not good. But no major organs were hit. He'll make it."

Luca was loaded into the chopper, and then Kyle climbed on board. The cops on the ground stood watching in the rotor current, hair flying, shirts snapping back, while the bird lifted into the air and disappeared over the trees. They were a hot, sweaty lot, and it would be a long hike back to their vehicles, but the morning's accomplishment erased some of the tension from their faces. The elusive and brutal murderer, who had evaded them at every step, was finally in custody. Luca's killing spree was over.

CHAPTER THIRTY

HOT AND SWEATY, Sidney wanted to stop at home to grab a shower and a fresh uniform, but a few minutes from town she got a call from Granger. He told her Alice Schaffer was recovering at the ER. She was going to be okay.

"Good to know," Sidney said. "I'm heading over."

"Where've you been all morning?" he asked.

"Hunting down Luca." To Granger's exclamations of astonishment, Sidney related the details of their high-octane morning. "He was airlifted to Jackson Hospital for surgery. The Jackson department is helping us out. A guard will be posted at his room twenty-four seven. As soon as Luca's able, we'll go talk to him. He's got a lot of blanks to fill in."

"Great. So while you guys were out seeing all the action, I was here nursing grandma."

She chuckled. "That's the way the chips fall. I'm pulling into the ER lot. See you in a sec."

The small ER was spotless and smelled of antiseptic. A good section of floorspace was divided into curtained cubicles. Normally, it was unoccupied half of the time, especially during the day, but a young boy was getting stitches on his forehead in one partition. Wearing a worried expression, his mother gripped his hand and hovered over him and the doctor. No other medical personnel were present.

At the sound of Sidney's approaching footsteps, Granger stepped out of another cubicle.

"How's she doing?" Sidney asked, her voice low.

"She has a mild concussion. Because of her age they want to keep her here for a few hours for observation."

"Is she talking?"

"She's been in and out of sleep. I've let her rest, but the doctor said we can talk to her." Granger held the curtain aside and they both entered.

Alice looked small in the white hospital bed, her head and shoulders propped up by pillows. Her hands were folded over the sheet and the IV tube and oxygen mask were gone. A clean bandage was wrapped around her head and her face was drained of color.

"Alice," Sidney said quietly, then a little louder, "Alice."

The woman opened her eyes, looking groggy, and she took a few moments to focus and respond. "Hello, Chief Becker." She swallowed, licked her dry lips. "Thank you for saving my life." She looked at Granger. "I should have listened to you when you told me to leave. But Alpine Ridge couldn't find anyone to replace Riley on short notice. We were going to go today."

"I understand," Sidney said gently. "How are you feeling?"

"Like a heavy weight is pressing against my head. I've had worse. Been kicked by cows and horses in my day. I'll live. How's Pedro?"

"He's okay. They released him. He went back to the farm."

"I hope he takes it easy."

"Alice, we need to talk about what happened today."

She nodded and murmured, "I know."

"We know that it was Luca who attacked you. We also know he's your grandson."

Alice's eyes widened. "You know about Luca?" She closed her eyes for a long moment. When they blinked open a look of deep remorse shadowed her face. "That's been a dark family secret for nineteen years. One I'm deeply ashamed of. How did you find out?"

"It wasn't easy," Granger said. "When we spoke at your house, why didn't you just tell me about Luca?"

Alice frowned, as though not comprehending. "Why would I tell you about Luca? I had no idea who he was until he barged into my house and identified himself. I was stunned. And scared half to death. He's a lunatic. I had no idea where he's been his entire life, or how he found me."

"When we talked, you looked like you were holding something back. Something that worried you," Granger said. "I thought you knew who was looking for Tammy."

"I didn't know it was Luca. I suspected someone else."

"Who did you think it was, Alice?" Sidney asked softly.

Alice bit her bottom lip. "I swore I would never tell. But now I'm scared."

"Did you think it was Luca and Riley's father?"

She looked down at her tightly clasped hands, then back at Sidney. "Yes."

"Did you give his name to Luca?"

Tears sprang to her eyes. "Yes." Tears streamed down Alice's face and she impatiently knuckled them away. Her eyes locked on Sidney's. "His name is James Abbott."

Sidney felt a tremor of shock and her mouth fell open. *James Abbott!* She would never have strung Tammy and Abbott together in the same thought. How did two such disparate worlds collide—a multi-millionaire CEO and a small-town teenager? The man had a predatory nature. The notion that he had sex with Tammy when she was a teenager alarmed her. Sidney recalled that Tammy was pregnant when she was sixteen. In Oregon, an individual was legally incapable of consenting to sexual intercourse if under the age of eighteen. The law mandated that even if Tammy willingly had sex with Abbott, it was not consensual. That made Abbott a statutory rapist! Sidney caught a look of stark surprise on Granger's face as well. But this was not the time to bring up rape. She had to keep Alice talking.

"It's because of James that we were forced to give Luca up." Alice started weeping.

Moved, Sidney put a hand on her arm, and said gently, "It's okay. It's okay."

After a full minute, Alice managed to choke back her sobs and sputter out her words. "James wouldn't take responsibility. Tammy was useless. On drugs. Luca was a special needs baby. He was born with a club foot, which meant he'd have to have surgery, then wear a series of casts for months, or years. I wanted to take them both, but I couldn't manage two babies, and the farm. It was too much. I had to let the baby boy go."

"James never helped with child support?" Granger asked, his voice rough with indignation.

She nodded her head. "He gave us a lump sum of cash. In exchange, Tammy and I signed an agreement never to contact him or tell anyone he was their father. But the money didn't go far." Alice sniffed and Sidney handed her a few tissues. She blew her nose, wiped her eyes, and continued in a shaky voice. "The ranch was failing, I had to use the money to prop it up. Make it sustainable. Which it is today. But it takes a lot of hard work. Constant hard work. I've thought about selling it many times. I'm getting too old to keep it going."

Sidney gently steered her back on track. "Does Riley know Abbott is her father?"

"No."

"So she's caring for Ray at Alpine Ridge, not knowing he's her grandfather."

"Yes. Funny how fate is. She loves that old man."

"Pedro told us that Luca also wanted to know where Tammy was. Did you tell him?"

"No. Never," Alice said emphatically. "I would die before I'd give my daughter up. Now she's in danger. We're all in danger from Luca."

"No, you're not. Luca's in custody. He was shot in a manhunt this morning. He's in surgery at Jackson Hospital. Then he'll sit in a cell. He'll never hurt anyone again."

"Thank God ...." Alice whispered. "There's something very, very wrong with that boy."

"Alice, you need to tell us where Tammy is."

She let out a weary sigh. "I don't know where she is. That's the god honest truth. All I know is that she's with Thomas. Someplace safe."

"She and Thomas are both fugitives from the law. If she's brought in by another agency, anything could go wrong."

"She's safe," she sniffed. "They won't find her."

As Sidney suspected, Alice knew where her daughter was. It was time to pull out her wild card. Sidney stated calmly and firmly, "For Tammy's sake, and the baby's, let us bring her in."

Alice frowned. "What baby?"

"Tammy's pregnant, Alice."

Alice's brows shot up in surprise. "Tammy's pregnant?"

"Yes."

"Oh my god. Thomas and Tammy are going to have a baby? I'm going to have another grandchild?" Her face went through a mix of expressions—surprise, joy, and finally wariness. "If you bring Tammy in, she'll have her baby in jail ...."

"If we don't, she may have her baby alone, without medical care. That puts her and the child in danger. With a good lawyer, Tammy could get a reduced sentence. She could do limited jail time. Imagine how her life would change for the better once she's put all of her mistakes behind her." Sidney paused, giving Alice time to process what she said.

"That would be great for the whole family. But I honestly don't know where she is. Thomas has a cabin somewhere remote. They don't even have electricity. All I know is that it's on a little lake." She swallowed. "But she'll call me. She knows I'll be worried sick until I hear from her."

"We'd like to put a trace on your phone, Tammy. That would give us a location. Will you let us do that?"

"Yes." She nodded to her handbag sitting on a chair. "My phone's in there."

Sidney fished out her phone and sat it on the table next to the bed. "Keep it with you at all times."

"Want me to get a warrant to tap her phone?" Granger asked quietly.

"You read my mind."

Footsteps were heard coming through the front door, then an anxious voice called out. "Where's my grandma? Alice Schaffer?"

"That's Riley," Alice said.

Granger stepped out of the cubicle. "Your grandma's in here." As footsteps hurried toward them, he opened the curtains on two sides to make more room. Sidney didn't recognize the pretty young woman who rounded the curtain. She usually picked Molly up in the lobby of Alpine Ridge and took her home for visits. She didn't know most of the care workers. Riley had a slender build and a long blonde braid, and at the moment, she looked frantic. "Grams, are you okay?"

"My head hurts like heck, but I'm okay," Alice said weakly.

Riley placed a hand on top of her grandmother's. "What happened? The cop said someone attacked you and Pedro. Is Pedro okay?"

She nodded. "He's fine. He's back at the farm."

"I was so worried, but they said I had to stay at Alpine Ridge. They were hunting the guy who attacked you." She glanced at Sidney. Her eyes were an unusual shade of blue, almost violet. "You caught him?"

"Yes."

"Who is he? Why did he attack Grams and Pedro?"

Sidney exhaled. "I think the answer would be best coming from your grandmother."

Silence stretched in the room as Riley trained her gaze on Alice. The old lady's brow creased, and she chewed her bottom lip, staring at her hands.

"Grams, who is he?" Riley asked again, impatient.

Alice met her granddaughter's eyes. "I just don't know how to tell you this. It's been a secret for nineteen years. I've never said it out loud before, until today."

Riley's shoulders stiffened as she braced herself for bad news. "For god's sake, Grams. Tell me who he is."

Alice swallowed. "His name is Luca. He's your brother."

Riley stared blankly. "I don't know what that means."

"You were born with a twin brother. He was given away at birth. We kept you."

A visible tremor passed through the young woman's shoulders and her mouth fell open.

Alice kept talking, her words hurriedly strung together, as though she just wanted to get the dark secret out in the open. She related every detail—Luca's club foot, Tammy's drug use, and her own inability to care for two babies. "I had no idea what happened to him. I was stunned when he stormed into the house today and told me who he was. He started screaming. I was so scared." Alice's hands gripped the sheet and her eyes filled with tears. The emotional ordeal was taking its toll. She choked out her next words. "He wanted to know where his mother was."

Riley's eyes had remained wide with shock. She blinked, trying to comprehend. "Jesus. You didn't tell him, did you?"

"No. Never. That's why he hit me."

Riley stood frozen, clearly in shock. An uncomfortable silence lingered between the two women. "How did he find out Mom was hiding at the monastery?"

"Luca hired a private eye to track her down. That's how he found me, too."

"Jesus. Mom had twins. I have a brother. Poor Luca." Riley looked at Sidney. "When can I meet him?"

"That's not a good idea, Riley," Alice said. "He's violent."

"Maybe he has a right to be," Riley said. "Who knows what drove him to be that way."

"Listen to your grandma," Sidney said. "Luca didn't just hurt Pedro and your mom. He murdered three people."

"What?" Riley sank into the chair by the bed, a look of incredulity on her face. "Are you sure?"

"Yes. We have plenty of evidence."

"Who?" she whispered.

"His social worker, and his foster parents. Plus, he tried to kill a bunch of cops this morning."

"I can't believe this is happening." Riley's shoulders slumped, and she shook her head. "It's a lot to process. I have a twin brother who's a murderer. Jesus." After a long pause, she said, "I need to get back to work."

"Are you sure that's a good idea?" Granger asked gently. "You're in shock."

"Yeah," she said quietly. "I need to have some distractions, right now." She looked at Sidney. "It's Ray's birthday. We planned a big bash for him. Music and everything. I know it would mean a lot to Molly if you and Selena were there."

Sidney and Alice locked eyes and the same thought passed between them. Riley needed to know who her biological father was, and that Ray, the man she was so fond of at Alpine Ridge, was her grandfather. Sidney shook her head no. It was too soon. Riley just had the shock of her life. One was enough.

"We'll be there. What time?"

***

When Sidney and Granger arrived at the station, they spotted several live news TV satellite trucks parked on Main Street. Townspeople and tourists milled on the sidewalk, wearing astonished expressions as a swarm of people surrounded the Yukon. Sidney could hear their excited voices through the closed doors. Through some kind of electronic telepathy, the media always managed to catch wind of a story—this time before the townsfolk even knew the bare facts. Reporters and men carrying cameras on their shoulders blocked the driveway to the back lot, so she gave her siren a couple of blasts. The majority jumped back, startled, and she pulled over and parked on the road.

"Wait here, Chief," Granger said. "I'll come around to your side and keep them away from you."

"Thanks, but I'll handle it," Sidney said. She had years of experience dealing with the press in Oakland. She climbed out of the vehicle and the crowd surged forward. A half dozen microphones were thrust in her face. "If you want a statement, stand back," she said assertively. "Or I'll go inside."

The crowd fell quiet.

"Please get out of the street. You're blocking traffic." Sidney and Granger herded them into the side parking lot, where they swirled around them in a half circle. Granger stood close to her, hands on his duty belt, ready to jump to her aid if anyone got too aggressive. The reporters started lobbing questions at her like hand grenades, again turning into an unruly throng. One question that got through repeatedly, "Do you have a serial killer in custody?"

Sidney put up her hands for silence. "I can't tell you much at this stage. We haven't concluded our investigation. What I can say is that we have a suspect in custody. We are confident that there is no further danger to the public."

Another flurry of questions came at her. "Please, one question at a time."

"Chief Becker, is it true Luca Ashe killed three people?"

"We do have three victims, unfortunately. We're still piecing details together."

"Did he kill his own parents, Mitch and Becky Turner?"

"I can't comment further at this time."

"Did Luca cut off Mitch Turner's head?"

"That's all I can say at this time."

"What about the P.I. that was killed up at the monastery, Chief? Is that killer still running around?"

"We're still investigating, but we feel the public is safe. I'll comment further as details materialize. Thank you." Sidney didn't feel that Tammy was a threat to the public. It appeared she killed Max in defense of Karune. But she was still a fugitive from the law and needed to face the consequences of her actions. As did her boyfriend, Thomas, who was guilty of aiding and abetting.

Sidney and Granger ignored the cackle of voices and the microphones thrust in their faces as they carved a path through the crowd to the back door. When they slipped inside, she exhaled a long, slow breath. "Man, what a day. I need to update Mayor Burke and warn him about what's coming down the pike—a blast of sensationalized news. The whole town is in for a shock. No one had a clue a serial murderer was on the loose. I also need to prepare Max's family. Reporters will probably show up at their door. Then I'm going to lock myself in my office and have a five-minute nervous breakdown."

"You owe it to yourself, Chief. I won't let anyone disturb you."

His voice was teasing, but Granger looked so earnest, so tense, she had to smile. "At ease, Granger. You're not in Afghanistan anymore. The Taliban are not about to blow up the station. It appears we're in a lull, between emergencies. Now would be a good time to catch up on paperwork, before the next crisis hits."

His handsome features relaxed, and he grinned back. "Copy that. I'll git 'er done!"

CHAPTER THIRTY-ONE

SIDNEY WOULD have loved to shed her police persona to attend the birthday party at Alpine Ridge; wear a dress, heels, feel utterly feminine. For the last few days, from morning until she fell into bed at night, exhausted, her uniform had been her second skin. She had continued her duties while she carefully pulled her personal self way back.

She would also have loved to release her hair from the tight bun at the back of her neck, but the demands of her job persisted, unrelenting. Now she had to be prepared, at a moment's notice, for Tammy's call to come in to Alice. In that event, Sidney would start coordinating with a tactical response team to swoop in on Tammy's location and take her and Thomas into custody.

Sidney grabbed a quick shower, dressed in a fresh uniform, and went downstairs where Selena waited in the dining room. The house smelled like fresh baking. On the table sat two beautifully wrapped gifts and a plate covered with foil.

"Great. You're ready." Selena rose from the table, shaking off Chili, who had been purring on her lap. She looked like a breath of spring in a short, floral print dress that showed off her long, toned legs. Her straight blonde hair was glossy, and her complexion glowed with good health. All those fruits and veggies were working, Sidney thought. Maybe she, herself, should eat more of the green crunchy stuff. Instantly, she wrinkled her nose, thinking of the taste and texture of kale.

Selena handed Sidney the covered plate. "Brown Butter Madeleines with roasted almonds. Mom's favorite."

"Mine, too. Can I steal one?" Here was a food Sidney could relate to.

"There's a dozen on the counter for you, which you can eat to your heart's content when we get home. Right now, we need to get our butts in the Jeep. We're late." With a purposeful air, Selena slung her handbag over her shoulder and grabbed the gift-wrapped boxes.

"Thanks for taking care of the presents," Sidney said with a touch of guilt. Buying a gift for Ray had completely slipped her mind.

Selena chuckled. "The least I could do. It pales in comparison to getting a brutal killer out of circulation. You're Supergirl and Wonder Woman combined. You set the bar pretty high, Sid."

"You don't give yourself enough credit. You're an entrepreneur. Your products, and your yoga classes make people happy and healthy. And you hold our family together. Mom and I couldn't get by without you."

"Thanks," she said with a quiet smile.

Sidney gave her a warm hug. "So, what did you get Ray?"

"Tickets to a music concert. A nice night out for him and Mom. We can take them, to make sure they don't wander off and get into trouble."

"Like buying more costumes from the Pink Pussycat?"

"Or hundred-dollar bottles of wine at the Analee's Bistro. Though Ray could afford it. But then we'd have his son all over us like a hammer on an anvil. Did he ever get the jewelry back?"

"No. Abbott brought Ray to the station all drugged up. Wanted him to sign the release. Of course, I said no. I have the jewelry with me. I'm going to ask Ray what he wants me to do with it."

"And you'll give it to him, if he wants it?"

"That's the law."

"Yep. Abbott's going to be all over you like hammer on steel."

"Yeah, he'll continue to be an ass. But he really doesn't have much say, legally. I did a little research. Ray's daughter, Lucinda, has Power of Attorney. She makes the decisions. I called her. She said Ray's credit limit has been cut to a couple grand. That will keep him from getting into too much trouble."

"She sounds amazingly reasonable. How can she and James be from the same family?"

"I got the sense that they aren't on the best of terms. Lucinda closely monitors what goes on at Alpine Ridge. A consultant is looking at how to make it escape proof."

Selena smiled. "I feel much better, now."

"Me, too. By the way, she's footing the bill for the band tonight."

***

When they walked into the dining room at the center, they were immediately absorbed into the festive mood of the celebration. Streamers hung from the ceiling, colorful balloons were tied to each centerpiece on the tables, and an exceptional soft rock band was performing a James Taylor song. A dozen care workers were busy serving appetizers and drinks to the seated residents.

Sidney scanned the gray heads and spotted the birthday boy seated at a table at the head of the room. Molly sat next to him. She and Selena sauntered over.

"Selena! Sidney!" Molly cried, a smile taking up half of her face. "My daughters are here!"

Ray immediately got to his feet. He looked dashing in gray slacks and a blue cashmere sweater over a pin-striped button-down shirt. He playfully put up his hands when he saw Sidney's uniform. "Don't shoot. I swear, I'm innocent."

Sidney laughed. "No worries, Ray. You get a free pass on your birthday."

Looking alert and energetic, he extended a warm hand, grasping both hers and Selena's in turn. Ray was a starkly different man from the hunched, shuffling figure Abbott had dragged into her office. He was tall, with straight posture, a captivating smile, and warm brown eyes. Sidney liked him immediately.

Molly stood, too, wearing a forest green dress that complimented her curvy figure and her gray-green eyes. Pearl earrings and a single drop pearl on a gold chain accented the dress. After both daughters kissed and hugged her, Ray put a hand on Molly's waist and pulled her closer. She looked radiant, like the Molly of yesteryear, before their dad died and the two used to go out on dance and dinner dates. The Becker family had been reshaped by tragedy over the last four years, but here Molly stood tonight, clearly happy, enjoying life, looking years younger. Ray's presence was an elixir.

"These are for you," Selena said, holding out the gifts to Ray.

"How nice of you girls," he beamed. "Your mother's kindness runs through your veins."

"These are for you, Mom." Sidney said. "Selena baked you brown butter madeleines."

Molly placed a hand on her heart. "My favorite. Thank you, little dove."

Sidney and Selena locked eyes for a moment. That was Molly's pet name for Selena. They hadn't heard her say it in years.

"Please, join us." Ray, a gentleman with old fashioned manners, pulled out two chairs.

Riley stopped by, pushing a cart, her cheeks flushed from all the activity. "Hi, ladies. Happy Birthday, Ray!"

"How are you doing?" Sidney asked quietly.

"I'm okay. I've been too busy to think. I'm picking up Grams when I get off work. I'm glad it's safe to go home."

Sidney took her aside, just out of the hearing of the folks at her table. "A warning, Riley. The press has gotten hold of this story. It'll be in the paper tomorrow. As of yet, they don't know Luca's related to you. Hopefully, that will never be an issue."

Her face paled, and she stood frozen for a moment. Her eyes filled with tears.

"You okay?" Sidney asked gently. "Maybe you should take the rest of the evening off."

She watched Riley struggle to gain her composure. The young woman released a deep breath and met Sidney's eyes. "I'll be okay. My shift is over in a half hour. Thank you. You've been very kind." She walked back to the cart, tossed her blonde braid over one shoulder, and resumed her role as caretaker. "Would you like some appetizers?" she asked brightly. "Some bubbly? Both?"

The tray held little plates of food. Riley pointed out the fare. "Bacon wrapped cheese bites, garlic shrimp skewers, salmon and cream cheese on cucumber, and manchego cheese, ham and olive bites."

As Sidney reseated herself, she marveled at Riley's ability to compartmentalize, to continue performing her duties under duress—something cops learned to do early on in their careers.

Suddenly, she was starving. After Riley served everyone else, Sidney said, "I'll have four plates, and the real thing to drink." The center gave Champagne to people who could handle it, and sparkling cider to those who could not.

Sidney eventually got drawn back into the festivities. Everyone at her table cheerfully ate and drank, chatting about trivia, then the topic shifted to classic movies. They found they all had a particular fondness for Marilyn Monroe movies. Ray amused them by quoting lines from "Some Like It Hot" by heart, imitating to a tee the quirks of the characters played by Jack Lemmon and Tony Curtis. Selena joined in, quoting Marilyn, imitating the blonde bombshell's breathy voice. "'I'm not very bright, I guess ... just dumb. If I had any brains, I wouldn't be on this crummy train with this crummy girls' band.'" Selena was good. Everyone laughed.

The band started playing "Sweet Baby James" by James Taylor, and several caregivers took seniors out on the floor to dance. They moved in slow motion, singing along with the band. Melodies and lyrics seemed to be embedded in the psyche of memory impaired people, outlasting all other memories. Music bypassed the brain and went straight to the heart.

The next song was "You Are So Beautiful" by Joe Cocker.

"Shall we?" Ray asked Molly.

"We shall," she said.

Selena and Sidney smiled through the whole song, watching Molly and Ray move gracefully on the floor, her head resting on his shoulder. He executed a few fancy turns and Molly followed fluidly, her years of ballroom dancing with their dad kicking in instinctively.

Later, everyone was served carrot cake and ice cream, then Ray happily opened his handful of gifts.

Selena and Sidney had worried that James Abbott might appear and spoil the party, but he never showed. He had taken Ray out for lunch, Riley informed them. They breathed easier. And so, the evening unfolded pleasantly. Sidney's concerns lifted from her shoulders. When the evening died down and most of the residents drifted to their rooms, around six-thirty, Sidney slid the jewelry box across the table to Ray. "Ray, do you remember this?"

Ray opened it, brow creasing, and for a long moment he just stared at the contents. Recognition suddenly sparked in his eyes. "Ah, yes. I do remember. I bought these for my fair lady." He turned to Molly. "Can I put them on you, my dear?"

"Please do." Ray slid the ring on the fourth finger of Molly's right hand. Then he put the bracelet around her wrist and set the safety clasp in place. The diamonds sparkled brilliantly in the soft light. Molly toyed with the bracelet, then the ring. "These are truly lovely. I'll never take them off."

Ray kissed the back of her hand, met her adoring gaze, and said softly, "You have blessed my life, Molly. You are my oasis. I will never tire of drinking in your smile, and the mystery behind your celadon eyes."

"You've blessed my life, too," she said in a tone barely above a whisper.

"Wow," Selena mouthed silently.

"He's one romantic old dude," Sidney said quietly.

In a rare show of lucidity, Ray and Molly had mostly been aware and cognizant the entire evening, and capable of managing intimacy. Sidney and Selena were in agreement that their relationship should evolve naturally and take its own course. The memories created tonight would long be remembered—a gift to both sisters. The bracelet and ring were exactly where they were meant to be.

CHAPTER THIRTY-TWO

SIDNEY ENTERED THE SMALL community hospital in Jackson at 10:00 a.m and strode down the hall to Luca's room. An officer from the Jackson police department was stationed outside his door. His name tag read Carson. "Thanks for helping us out, Officer Carson," she said. "How's he doing?"

"Showing signs of life this morning. Hasn't said zip to anyone who's male, and actually shot daggers at the doctor, a male nurse, and me. Boy, if looks could kill …." He shook his head, and grinned. "You got yourself a classic nutjob in there. But he did thank a female nurse for his breakfast. He was very polite to her."

"Thanks. Go ahead and take a break. I'll be here for a while."

"Yes, ma'am."

After the officer left, Sidney paused at the door of the dark, cramped room, and studied the young man who had proved to be so cunning and elusive. What happened to Luca, she wondered, that deformed his character and mind, and made him capable of unimaginable brutality? Judging from what the officer told her, Luca had a dislike of men. Being female might work in her favor.

He lay against the pillows in the half-elevated hospital bed with his eyes closed. His right arm was in a sling. An IV tube snaked from the back of his left hand which was cuffed to the bed. He opened his eyes as she entered, met her gaze, didn't flinch, but just stared with a calm stillness. She saw some resemblance to Riley. Luca had handsome, angular features, a close-cropped beard, and pale blue eyes. A unique feature were his ears; poking through his limp brown hair like radars.

She needed to draw him out, get a read on his personality, see how his mind functioned. "Hello, Luca. I'm Sidney Becker," she said quietly, forgoing the use of her title. The challenge would be to get him to see past her uniform, to see her as a human being, not an authority figure. "How are they treating you here?"

"I'm okay. They got me pretty drugged up. Don't feel a thing unless I move." His brow furrowed. "I'm worried about my cats. I need someone to check on them. Feed them. They'll be frightened. I haven't been home in days."

His immediate responsiveness surprised Sidney and gave her hope. His request presented a chance to make an inroad, to buddy up to him. "Sure. I'll get someone to check on your cats. Where are they?"

"At my house." He gave her an address that was in a remote location on the outskirts of town, near Jackson.

"Is there anyone who could take them during your hospital stay?" *And his time in jail, which would be substantial.* For three murders, and a dozen attempted murders, he'd probably never step outside a prison for the rest of his life. For the moment, Sidney would avoid mentioning anything that disturbing. Keep his barriers down, if possible.

"Yes. My grandmother. She has a farm. You know her. Alice Schaffer."

Sidney hid her surprise, and a suspicion that Luca might be playing her, looking to get a cheap thrill by shocking her. Or he might be delusional, or extremely clever at pretending to be. For now, she would play along. "Hold on just a second, Luca. Let me call one of my officers and have that taken care of for you."

Sidney stepped out of the room and contacted Amanda. After informing her of Luca's unusual request, she added, "Get a warrant. Search his house, any vehicles, and his property. Have animal control pick up his cats. Make sure they get to a shelter and are kept there safely until further notice." She disconnected and breezed back into the room. "That's all taken care of. Your cats will be well looked after."

Luca closed his eyes and looked relieved. He met her gaze and half smiled, and said politely, "Thank you, Officer Becker. That means a lot."

"Call me Sidney." Still trying to read him, she asked, "Do you mind if I stay awhile? We have a lot to talk about."

"Please. I welcome your company. I'm exhausted from solitude. My cats are my only company. They are good communicators, speaking through their eyes, their behavior, but I'm hungry for human conversation." He nodded toward the chair and she seated herself next to his bed.

His calm demeanor did not surprise her. His manner of speaking did. Rather formal for someone who was still a teenager. And educated. Apparently, the Turners did a good job homeschooling him. Sidney had questioned many killers in her time who confessed to their crimes without a twitch of emotion, even when describing gruesome details. Would Luca be the same? "Do you mind if I record our conversation?"

"Go ahead."

Once her phone was set to record, Sidney advised him of his Miranda rights.

"I understand. I've read lots of law books."

And no doubt books on forensics. He was an ace at destroying and planting evidence. "You mention you've been alone for some time, Luca. Why is that?"

"I needed solitude to work through the demons in my head. And to get strong. To make sure the plans I was setting in motion would go down without a hitch."

"Want to tell me more about that?"

"Where should I start?" he asked. "No doubt with the Turners. You want to know what my life was like, how I was treated. You looked at my files at Social Services and saw that I was satisfied with my living arrangement." He gave her a penetrating stare. "Nothing could be further from the truth. Living with them unbalanced me. I was a child of ten when I was acquisitioned to their home. Innocent. Unloved. Lonely. Desperate for a place where I could fit in. But that was not to be. I have no idea what it feels like to be normal, to be part of a loving family."

Sidney listened attentively, and said gently, "I'm sorry to hear that, Luca. It sounds like you had a very lonely childhood."

"You have no idea. The only love I've ever known has come from my cats."

"Tell me what you mean by acquisitioned."

"Purchased. My services were traded for room and board, and an education of sorts."

"What services were expected of you?"

Luca looked away for a long moment. She saw his jaw clench tightly, then unclench. His face relaxed and he turned back to her, expressionless. "Most of the services I provided were acceptable to me. Labor, mostly. Mitch taught me a lot about carpentry and construction. We remodeled and added rooms to their house. Everything was beautiful. Custom upgrades throughout. We built the garage and equipment shed, as well. I liked the hard work. It was challenging and rewarding." Luca spoke in a flat voice without emotion. Sidney did not try to guide the conversation. She would allow him to lay down a foundation and get into the flow of talking before steering him to the topic of murder.

"They gave me a solid, basic education," he continued. "But mostly, I educated myself. Since I rarely left their property, the only thing I could do to escape was read. I read thousands of books during my eight-year indenture."

"Books on Vikings?"

"Oh, yes. Everything Viking. Their history, culture, customs. They were a very misunderstood people." His voice became more energized and she saw a touch of passion light his eyes. "Vikings are known for plundering, but many travelled to other countries to settle peacefully. To farm, or trade goods. They were also poets, lawmakers and artists. They were refined and well groomed. They braided their hair and wore fine cloaks and intricately crafted jewelry."

"That's interesting, Luca." Sidney meant it.

"Did you know the Vikings were the first Europeans to visit North America and establish communities?"

"No."

"Leif Erikson beat Columbus by 500 years." Luca paused, licked his dry lips, and stared at his plastic glass on the table.

"Water?"

"Please."

Sidney held the glass close enough so that his mouth could take the straw. His eyes locked on hers as he sipped, and when she pulled the glass away, he smiled sweetly, as though they had shared an intimate moment. Not sexual, but some kind of connection out of the ordinary—like a client with a shrink. Unloading his thoughts to a nonjudgmental person was perhaps producing a sense of alliance. Good, she thought. Maybe the interview would give her all the answers she needed to wrap up this case. She set down the glass. It was time to get Luca to talk about something more personal. "Tell me about your cats. How did they come into your life?"

"Payment. When Mitch saw how I loved cats, he used them to control me. I got three cats over time. As long as I did as was expected, I got to spend time with them."

"And when you didn't?"

His face altered in an instant, eyes narrowing, mouth twisting into a snarl. "Solitary confinement."

"Where were you confined?"

"The cellar of horror."

The hair stood up on the back of Sidney's neck. "Tell me about the cellar, Luca."

Luca's haunted stare went right through her. "The cellar was Mitch's private place. No one ever went down there except him and me. There was a door in a dark corner. Behind the door was a small space. No floor. No heat. No light. No stimulus. Just cold, damp, dark misery. No food, either. I got to know that room very well. Every inch of it."

A cold chill crept along Sidney's spine. "How much time did you spend in there?"

"Total days and nights? It added up to weeks every year."

"Why were you put in there?"

"Because I didn't want to be Mitch's recreation. Of course, in time, I would break down. I always broke down." His expression changed to one of self-loathing. His hand clenched into a tight fist, then slowly relaxed.

"He molested you?"

For some time, Luca didn't move. He stared off into space, as though a part of him had exited the room. Sidney sat in silence, except for the sounds filtering in from the corridor—the soft voices of nurses navigating their mobile workstations in and out of neighboring rooms.

"Luca," she said, after what seemed like minutes.

He seemed to come out of a trance and blinked when he saw her still rooted to the chair. "Sorry. What was the question?"

"Luca, did Mitch molest you?"

A sharp alertness tightened his features. She could feel the tension mounting, although he tried to hide it. "Molestation is a polite euphemism for what he did to me, Chief Becker. That's all I'll say on the subject. Ever."

As Sidney absorbed the implications of the young man's words, she could feel the emotion radiating off of him in waves. Dark. Tormented. He had just revealed that he had been tortured and sexually assaulted by his foster father, possibly for years. This was a horrific case of long-term abuse of a defenseless child. The extent of harm done to Luca was staggering. Here were the conditions that twisted his young mind, setting into motion what would be his predilection for violence as an adult. When Luca seemed to mentally leave the room for a few minutes, she sensed he was experiencing an episode of disassociation—a survival technique used by victims of extreme violence. It allowed a victim to keep functioning while being severely traumatized, or while reliving trauma.

Sidney felt a great wave of sympathy for Luca, and her immediate instinct was to offer comfort. But she was here in the capacity of a police officer, not a shrink, and it was her job to elicit a confession from a murderer. She would certainly recommend to his defense attorney that Luca be given a thorough psych evaluation. A mental health facility might be more appropriate than prison. A long moment passed before she could settle back into her role as interviewer. She continued in a calm tone, "Did Becky know Mitch locked you in that place, Luca?"

A muscle twitched near his jaw. "What do you think? Sometimes I didn't appear upstairs for days."

"Did she know what Mitch was doing?"

Sidney caught a glimpse of fury in his eyes, then it was gone. "She knew. But she played a game of sickening deception. Sugary sweet on the surface. Rotten inside."

At that point, a uniformed cop walked into the room. "I'm Officer Coulter, Chief Becker. I'm replacing Officer Carson."

Luca's expression changed swiftly, and the muscles of his face tightened into a mask of pure hatred.

"What the hell is your problem?" Officer Coulter asked him.

"Get the fuck out of here!" Luca said with such vehemence spit flew from his mouth.

Sidney caught Coulter's eye and nodded toward the door. The officer shot Luca a look of contempt and strode from the room. She couldn't blame the officer. It was known across local law enforcement agencies that Luca had tried to kill a dozen cops. There was no love lost between them.

Luca's face was a frightening mask of fury and hatred. His explosive emotion lingered and boiled, heating up the room. He turned his face to the wall, the tension stiffening his limbs, tightening his hand into a fist, bulging the cords in his neck. It was as if a demon had entered his body. This had to be the part of his personality that committed brutal murder. She waited some time for Luca to calm down. She glanced at her watch. Ten minutes passed by.

When he finally calmed, he turned back to her, his voice raw with emotion. "I'm a damaged man, Chief Becker. I know that. It hasn't been easy living with this monster inside me. What it makes me do. I'm under no illusion that I'll ever be a free man again. I should be locked up. I killed the Turners. I killed Mrs. Paisley. I attacked my grandmother and that Mexican guy. I guess I was trying to commit suicide when I shot at all those cops yesterday. But at the last minute, I gave up. Just like I always did with Mitch." He swallowed, and tears squeezed out of his eyes. "I guess death frightens me more than what I've experienced in life. I don't want to go to the same place as Mitch. He'll torment me throughout eternity." Luca stopped talking, and again Sidney waited until he appeared more composed.

"Why did you hire Max Stevens?"

He exhaled, tear tracks on his cheeks. "To find my parents. All I ever wanted, throughout my entire fucked-up life, was to meet my mom and dad. I can't explain how strong the feelings were. Most people have a history. A line back to their ancestors. The path I emerged from has been completely erased. I'm just a solitary figure floating in the universe with no more relevance than a speck of dust." He cleared his throat, his penetrating gaze again assessing her. "Do you know what that feels like? To have no connection to anything, or anyone?"

"No. I don't," Sidney said gently. "It must be gut-wrenching."

He nodded. "I couldn't believe it when Max called me and told me he found my mom. I didn't think that day would ever come. I raced up to his campsite like a madman, happier than I'd ever been."

"Did you want to kill her?"

"Christ. Of course not." Another rapid transformation in Luca's demeanor took place. His mouth turned downward and something like sorrow darkened his eyes. He made a small strangling sound, then blurted, "I just wanted to be in the presence of my own flesh and blood. Even if it was just for a few seconds, to see what it felt like to have a mother."

"What happened when you got up there?"

"Mrs. Paisley's ex-husband was there. Dressed like a freaking monk. I was driving his truck which I'd stolen the day before. He was too busy fighting with Max to notice me, until I got out and yelled at him. Then he ran. Max was lying on the ground. His head hit a rock when Dr. Thornton pushed him. I thought he was dead. So I ran into his camper and grabbed his computer. When I came out of the camper, Max was gone. I figured he must have been okay, and he went after Dr. Thornton. I took his camera and got the hell out of there." He looked at her and said with all sincerity, "Is Max okay? I still need to pay him."

Sidney ignored the question. "You were staying at the Turner's house during this time. Were you going to use Mitch's coin collection to pay Max?"

"Mitch's coins? No. My coins. After all the years of labor I did for him, it was small compensation."

"Why did you steal Dr. Thornton's truck?"

"He's a jerk. He was married to Mrs. Paisley when she was supposed to be watching out for me. Once I heard Mrs. Paisley tell Becky that her ex had been emotionally abusive. That gave me the idea. It was too perfect. I decided to cast the blame on him by driving his truck to her house the night I killed her. I knew all the neighbors would see it."

"You never told Mrs. Paisley about Mitch?"

He shook his head. "No. I couldn't. Before Mrs. Paisley's visits, Mitch rounded up my cats and locked them in that dark place. He told me he'd hang them if I ever said anything about the cellar. He said the cellar was our little secret. Man to man. His point came across loud and clear. My cats had been hurt by him before, so I had no doubt he'd kill them. So when Mrs. Paisley showed up, I talked about other things; books I'd read, and dumb crap like that. Becky always told her I was fine. That I was just quiet."

Sidney saw a tremor pass through him. "What did you just remember?"

He inhaled deeply, exhaled. "Becky and Mrs. Paisley sometimes shared this smile that was pure evil. Their faces resembled reptiles and their eyes glowed red. A serpent's tongue slithered out of their mouths. When it happened, it was quick. A blip of time. You'd miss it if you weren't watching for it. But I knew it was a signal. Both revealing their true selves to each other." After taking another deep breath of air, he continued, "They were Mitch's handmaidens, Sidney. Infected. Like Mrs. Paisley couldn't see my suffering when she got me alone?" he asked with hot sarcasm. "It was pouring out of my eyes. Screaming out of my head. In the old days, they burned women at the stake who were possessed. But those two were roaming around free. Hurting people."

Sidney sifted through the emotion in Luca's voice—grief, anger, confusion. What he felt was real to him. She made a mental note to add hallucinations to his signs of disassociation—both classic indications of PTSD. "Where did you keep Becky before you killed her?" Sidney knew the answer before he told her.

"Where do you think? She was getting an education. She was learning first-hand what I'd been subjected to for years. Only, minus the rape. She got off easy."

"Why did you kill the women so brutally?"

"You think I wanted to?" His pale blue eyes watched her, the intensity of the emotion behind them powerful. "This is hard to talk about."

Burying her disgust, Sidney touched his hand, and said gently, "I understand. Take it slow."

"My plan was to shoot Mrs. Paisley in the back of the head. Clean. Easy. But she turned and saw me before I got close enough to get a good shot. She went nuts. She knocked over her chair, threw her glass of wine at me, and ran into the living room. Then she grabbed a lamp and bashed me on the shoulder with it." He grimaced. "I still have the bruises. I was going to shoot Becky, too. But she struggled, got a leg free, and kicked me in the groin. Bloody hard. If her hands weren't tied, she would have gotten away. When they were facing death, their true selves came out. Half demon. That's when the beast inside me took over. It knows how to combat supernatural creatures. Killing those cambions was a gift I gave to the world."

Sidney felt a coldness spread through her gut as images of the women's corpses rose in her mind—Becky's obliterated features, and Olivia's crow-pecked face; the back of her head bashed in. She couldn't help but imagine the terror of their last few minutes on earth. "Why did you put the coins on their bodies?"

"I live with a monster inside me, Sidney. But I also have a saint who lives in my heart. The saint feels positive emotions. Tenderness towards my cats. Empathy. It made me show mercy. The Valknut coins ensured the women would get a second chance in the afterlife. To evolve into better beings."

"What about Mitch?"

"Mitch got the death he deserved." Luca's face contorted, and Sidney caught a glimpse of emotion so intense it chilled her. "He never showed me an ounce of mercy; not for a second. Disposing of his ghoul's head in that ice cave, pressing those Jormungand coins into his empty eye sockets, ensured that he'd rot in Helheim for eternity. The Vikings would have put his head on a spike and let it rot in the sun."

Sidney shivered, remembering the mutilated head on the slab in the morgue. "Did you send those threatening letters to Mrs. Paisley a year ago?"

"Yeah. My good side tried to warn her that I'd reap revenge someday. She could have left town. Disappeared. But the arrogant demon inside her chose to stay. It taunted me. I got the message. When it was time to act, she was part of my plan."

Sidney was sickened, but she kept her voice calm. "Why now? Why did you choose to kill them now?"

"First, I needed to get stronger. By the time I left the Turner's, I had lost twenty pounds in three months. I was too depressed to eat. I was puny in mind, body, and spirit. And I was terrified of Mitch." Almost imperceptibly, Luca flinched. She watched the muscles tighten and loosen on his face, as though he was grinding his teeth. "For months, I lived in fear that he'd find me and drag me back to the cellar. I hid out in my little house in the woods with my cats, and bought my supplies in Jackson. I started power lifting. I ate a ton of carbs and fat and put on forty pounds. I meditated to calm my anxiety. I read. Slowly, the fear I wore like a second skin began to shed. Courage grew in its place, like a shield."

Luca's tone and expression shifted. He appeared more confident. A flame burned brightly in his eyes. "It took over a year, but finally, I was ready. When I drove back to the old house, I started shaking so badly I could hardly drive. I stopped several times to fight a powerful urge to turn back. But I thought of Thor engaged in deadly combat with Jormungand. He sacrificed himself to save the world. I drew strength from that." A little smile tugged at his lips. "As it turned out, it was incredibly easy. Mitch was in the garage. I crept up behind him and swung one good hammer blow to his head. He fell to his knees. The ghoul inhabited a frail human body, after all. I had envisioned killing him for years. The beast inside me roared to life and took revenge. Mitch's blood flowed like a river. A triumphant moment, I can tell you. Viking justice."

It wasn't easy listening to Luca's confession and the details of his murders, but Sidney was grateful for his candor. Rarely did confessions go this smoothly and quickly. There was still one last thing Sidney had to clear up. "If you were so happy to meet your blood relatives, Luca, why did you assault your grandmother?"

Luca's expression looked remorseful. His eyes flicked away and then returned to meet her gaze. "I'm sorry I treated her that way. Under other circumstances, I would have been jubilant. But I'd been hunted by cops for days. I'd had a close call the night of the fire. I was jumpy as hell." A note of supplication entered his tone. "I just wanted to know where to find my mom. And who my dad was. It should have been easy. She could have embraced me; her long-lost grandson. But instead, she treated me like I was some kind of lunatic. She wouldn't tell me a thing. I admit, I was hurt and angry. I lost it."

"Were you going to kill her?"

"No. I swear." He inhaled and released his breath in a slow exhale. "But if I hadn't hit her, she wouldn't have told me anything. At least now I know who my dad is." His upper lip curled into a snarl. "James Abbott."

"You know of him …."

"Who doesn't? He's in the paper every other day. Some pompous, rich jerk. I doubt he'll want to know that his son, a serial killer, suddenly popped up in his life." Luca smirked. "Serves him right, for not claiming me. For not giving me his name."

The young man fell silent and she waited patiently for him to resume speaking. A beatific smile slowly appeared on his face and his eyes brightened. "But I know my mom is different. Tammy Schaffer. What a beautiful name. She's been a Buddhist monk for sixteen years. Did you know, Sidney, that the term Buddha literally means enlightened one, a knower?"

"No, I didn't."

"A knower. I love the sound of that. My mom practices the development of morality, meditation and wisdom. I'm so proud of her, and the path she's chosen. No doubt, she's learned the art of forgiveness. I'm her son. A mother's love is the strongest force in the universe. She'll understand what motivated my violent actions, and she'll forgive me. I know she'll come to visit me. I live for that day."

Sidney wondered if there was any truth to his prediction. A different side of Tammy had been shown to Sidney. She was a woman who ran away from her problems sixteen years ago, and lived a life of deception ever since, posing as someone she wasn't. She was a woman who practiced the art of knife throwing, and then used her skill to kill a man. For the second time, she ran, instead of facing the consequences of her actions. And now Tammy was a fugitive hiding from the law. Anytime now, Sidney would be heading up a tactical team whose sole intent was to bring her in.

Luca had made no mention of Riley. Sidney wondered if he would ever find out that he had a twin sister. That decision would be up to the Schaffer family.

CHAPTER THIRTY-THREE

AS SIDNEY DROVE HOME from the Jackson hospital, she felt a tremendous sense of release. Three horrendous murders had been solved. The public was safe again. She also felt immensely proud of her small department. Overworked and sleep-deprived, her junior officers had risen to the occasion; pushing themselves beyond their limits to get a killer behind bars. Sidney was giving her officers the evening off to spend time with their families—a reward richly deserved.

She turned her attention to the other matter that had been pressing heavily upon her. Max's killer was still in the wind. Until Tammy Schaffer called her mother and gave up her location, the investigation was essentially at a standstill.

At 5:00 p.m., Sidney entered the house and greeted her sister, who was busily at work in the kitchen. The work island was covered with ingredients and Selena was vigorously stirring something in a bowl. Humming pleasantly, she waved a hello without missing a beat. Selena had invited Granger over for dinner, and judging from the aromas wafting throughout the house, he was in for something spectacular.

Sidney climbed the stairs with two of the four cats bounding after her and turned her focus to her own personal life. She had a date with David and needed to change into civilian clothes. The intensity of the last few days stayed with her as she peeled off her vest and uniform, released her hair from the interminable tight bun, and stepped into a warm shower. Five minutes later, wrapped in a towel, she blew her hair dry and applied a touch of makeup. While dressing in a plum colored trumpet skirt, cream tunic blouse, and heels, she tried, and failed, to block the reel of crime scene images that flickered through her mind. It was pointless to try. She knew from experience that she would relive every gruesome detail for several days, until they lost their power.

Standing in front of the mirror with Chili twining through her legs and purring, she saw that her appearance had transformed. She looked feminine and appealing with her clothes clinging in just the right places and her lustrous auburn hair falling around her shoulders. But she still felt the presence of the bullet proof vest and the bulky duty belt she had worn for very long days. And she felt the weight of her responsibilities. That never went away. At any moment, an emergency call could come in, and she'd be rushing to the scene of a new crime. She prayed she would have an uninterrupted evening.

Thirty minutes later she was driving down the narrow lane that led to David's house on the lake. Thunderclouds were beginning to build to the north and west, and broken clouds scudded above the trees. Sleeves of vapor enshrouded the dock and the deep green water pushed onto the shore in waves. As she parked the Yukon, the first sheets of rain began to fall. The lake surface began to riffle and agitate. The storm released the fecund smell of the forest and the silent trees began to darken and gleam. Sidney left the SUV and hurried up the stairs to the porch.

David opened the door before she knocked, looking casual in jeans and a long-sleeved T-shirt. His hair was tousled, and his handsome face was shadowed with a day-old beard. "Hey, beautiful," he grinned. The lines she loved radiated from the corners of his eyes.

"Sorry, I'm late. I wanted to change out of my uniform."

"I'm glad you did." He moved his hand towards her blouse. She felt the cloth lift below her shoulder as he pulled her softly towards him. She snuggled closer, tilting her face up to his. He kissed her, slowly and deliberately.

"That was nice," she murmured.

He kissed her again. "I missed you."

"Me, too." Her head found the warm groove of his neck and she smelled the familiar hollow space at the base of his throat. David's scent, his warmth, felt like a refuge. There was so much about him that she wanted to learn, to grow into.

"I've got stuff cooking on the stove," he said, his voice husky.

Reluctantly, she left his arms and followed him into the kitchen. Butter sizzled in the fry pan on the stove on the granite topped island, and two pots steamed on back burners. The contents of one was flowing over the sides and hissing into the burner. David quickly removed the top and lowered the flame. Fresh salmon fillets and chopped veggies sat on a cutting board. "I'm making your favorite. Coconut lime salmon. With rice pilaf, asparagus, and green beans."

"Yum. My stomach is saying thank you."

"Let me turn down the sauce and start the fillets, then I'll sauté these veggies." David got to work, spatula in hand, commandeering three different pots. "I just pulled that bottle of wine out of the fridge."

Her favorite Chardonnay and two crystal glasses sat on the counter. Sidney poured them both a glass and they sipped while he cooked. She heard a far grumble of thunder and peered out the window at the darkening sky. Lightning flashed across the lake.

David slipped the fillets into the pan, poured in the sauce, and the aroma of lime and coconut lifted into the air. Her stomach rumbled.

"Why did I know you'd be starving?" David laughed. "Hang on. We'll be eating in just a minute."

"What can I do to help?" she asked.

"You are helping. Just by being here." He looked up and tossed her a grin. "Looking ... well, like you do."

Sidney liked the way his eyes appraised her, and the way his gaze fell to her mouth for a long moment. She was feeling better by the second. Leaning against the counter, she took in David's digs. His modern-style house was modest compared to others on the lakeshore, but it had been upgraded with cherry wood cabinets, bamboo floors, and a cook's kitchen with top-notch professional appliances. Several of his stunning landscape paintings hung on the walls in the living room, accompanied by a few pastels and oils rendered by his best students. "This is No Ordinary Love" by Sade floated through the room.

By the time the food was on the table, they were on their second glass of wine, and Sidney had transitioned into a civilian as much as she was able. David dimmed the lights. They sat with legs touching under the table, laughing softly and speaking of nothing of consequence. She loved listening to his voice, which was warm and masculine. He had the ability to make trivia sound fascinating.

After dinner she started clearing the table.

"Leave it." His beautiful brown eyes held her gaze and his mouth tipped into a sensuous smile. He took her hand, guided her into the living room, and pulled her into his arms. They slow danced to "Let's Stay Together" by Al Green. David's hands slid down her back, following the curve of her spine, and came to rest on the swell of her hips. He brushed her forehead with his lips. She lifted her face, offering her mouth. He kissed her, sweet and slow. When his mouth lifted away, she placed a hand behind his neck, and drew him gently back. They kissed hungrily, bodies pressed tightly together.

***

A few minutes later they were in his bedroom peeling off their clothes.

Sidney lay back against the pillows and pulled David down beside her. Their kisses were assertive, unapologetic. A warm current of pleasure spread to her belly and thighs as his hands explored her body, finding her sensitive areas. The room darkened to black and they lay touching each other, his hands on her hips, his breath hot against her neck. They moved rhythmically to soft moans and grunts of pleasure, his skin slick with sweat against hers.

Afterwards, it felt exquisite to lie together, satisfied, talking in soft tones, hearing his voice rumble in his chest. He liked to fold her in his arms, pulling her to him so that her back curled neatly into his chest. His fingertips moved lightly over her forearms and hands. Such a simple thing. Yet it felt like he was strumming the chords of her soul.

Outside, the rain fell softly, almost soundlessly, harmonizing with David's breathing. Sidney traveled to some distant outpost of her mind, leaping across fragments of the day, bringing moments of her workweek into bed with her. She pulled away from David, laying on her side, watching him sleep, envying his ability to turn so easily from the world.

"No, don't move. Don't drift away from me," he murmured.

"I'm right here." She spoke into the darkness of his face. "I'm not going anywhere."

He pulled her back into his arms. She rested her head against the muscles of his shoulder, smelling his hair and skin, familiar and comforting, yet not enough to block her encroaching thoughts.

"You're doing it." He opened his eyes. In the dim light, they were almost luminous. There was concern in his voice.

"What?"

"You're a galaxy away. Thinking about work. Want to talk about it?"

"No." She didn't want to share images of dead people. A mutilated head.

"I know it's been a hell of a week for you. Empty your thoughts, Sid. Let me help."

"No."

"What I'm imagining is probably worse than what you actually witnessed," he said.

Sidney sighed.

"Look, I'm not going to pretend I don't worry about you. I do. And with good reason." David suddenly sat up in bed, his voice changing, sounding troubled. "I stopped by your house this morning and had coffee with Selena."

Sidney sat up next to him, her posture tensing.

"She's worried about you, too. She told me you almost got killed three times this week. Three times! First getting trapped in a house fire. Then a collapsing ice cave. And yesterday, you got shot at by some lunatic up in the woods. And you didn't mention any of this to me. It's like we live in parallel universes."

She said nothing, just listened.

"We both know you love your job," he said. "And that's not going to change."

The concern in David's voice shook old memories loose. Sidney recalled the strain her high-risk profession had put on past relationships, several of which resulted in painful breakups—the reason she was still single at thirty-five.

"You shut me out of a big part of your life, Sidney," David continued. "You don't have to. It's your choice. Emotionally, you keep me at arm's length."

It was true that her professional life was mostly closed off to David. He was the kind of man that liked to share deeply, and he wanted the same in return, but she was unable to reciprocate. She brought her work into their relationship. It hovered around them, but she wouldn't talk about it. She always held back, afraid to fully commit, afraid David would bail like the others.

Then there was her work schedule. When she got busy, she worked around the clock. When they did manage to get together, it was on her schedule. David dropped everything to make it work, and then she was usually exhausted and wrapped tighter than a drum. He'd been making a lot of sacrifices to keep this relationship going. Her stomach clenched. Was his patience finally running out? "So what are you trying to tell me, David?"

"I admit, I'm struggling right now. Trying to figure out what to do."

"Do you want to stop seeing me?"

David sucked in a breath and went silent.

Sidney felt hot tears sting the backs of her eyes. *Here it comes.*

"Hell, no, I don't want to stop seeing you. Are you kidding me? It's tough enough seeing you as little as I do. Not seeing you at all would kill me."

Sidney breathed a sigh of relief. She wiped tears from her eyes with her fingertips.

"Hey, are you crying? Damn, I'm sorry. Come here." He curved his arm around her shoulders and drew her tightly against him. He ran his fingers along her arm again, which had an immediate calming effect.

"What I'm struggling with, Sid, is where to go from here," David continued. "I know you have a stressful job, and you work all hours, but I'm willing to put up with it. I've been thinking that we should move in together. It's the next logical step."

What? David wanted to move it with her? As she reflected on his words, a feeling of warm exhilaration spread through her body. He just confessed that he was in it for the long haul, even with all the challenges her job presented. After six months of dating, that spoke of a deepening commitment on his part, a milestone.

One thing Sidney had learned about David was that when it came to important decisions, he was thoughtful and deliberate. When they first started dating, he'd been a widower for three years. She knew David needed to make the emotional leap from his beloved dead wife to Sidney in his own time. Sidney had waited, sometimes agonizingly, for him to be the first to say, "I love you." When he did, after two months, she immediately responded in kind. There was a palpable shift in their relationship after the exchange of those three words—a deeper, warmer bond.

And now he wanted to live with her. He had given it thought. He was ready.

Sidney's mind went into instant analysis, weighing the pros and cons of cohabiting with David. On the one hand, she was thrilled beyond measure and wanted to laugh out loud, and promptly consent, but the cautious side of her nature was waving a big red flag that said, "slow down."

"Earth to Sidney," David said with a touch of humor in his voice. "Hey, I didn't ask you to solve world peace. Just to move four miles across town."

She said nothing, still thinking.

"We can start slow. Move in a change of underwear and a toothbrush."

"David, I'm thrilled that you asked me to move in with you. I really am …."

"But …."

"It caught me by surprise, that's all. And there's a concern …."

"You mean Dillon."

"Yes." Habitually, Sidney and David met in the afternoons, before she left for her night shift and his fourteen-year old son came home from school. They also saw each other most weekends —movies, hikes, sports events—and Dillon was always included. Of course, Dillon knew they were sleeping together, but in his mind, Sidney existed on the periphery of the relationship he shared with his dad. In that respect, she posed no threat. He was still feeling the ramifications of losing his mother to cancer three years ago. "Dillon's a great kid, and I adore him, but I don't think anyone is ready for me to replace Kelly."

"That wouldn't even be possible, nor is it expected. Kelly has a sacred place in our lives, in our memories. But there's plenty of room for you here, Sidney. All you have to do is be yourself. Dillon's grown attached to you. He told me so."

"Yeah, but going on weekend outings is different than suddenly having a third person living in your house. How would he view my role? As a roommate? A friend? Or an authority figure? I'm the Chief of Police. I'd be coming home in my uniform. I'm about as much of an authority figure as you can get." Sidney hesitated, then added, "Stepfamilies go through a long period of adjustment."

"I realize that," he said earnestly. "I know what I'm asking of you."

"I've never been a parent. I don't have those skills."

"I'll help you."

Sidney chewed her bottom lip. "I can't believe I'm saying this, because I would love to live with you. But I don't think we should shake things up right now. I trust my instincts, and they're telling me it's too soon. I'd like my relationship with Dillon to be on more solid ground. I'd like to spend more time with him. Maybe one on one. He needs to see me in my cop role, so that he becomes comfortable with it."

"I trust your instincts, too. Spending time with Dillon is a great idea," David said. "The last thing I want to do is pressure you. Look, I'm sorry I sprang this on you. We'll take it slow and easy."

"Slow and easy sounds good."

For better or worse, they were caught up in the net of this relationship, unable to swim away. "I want you in my life, Sidney. I'll take as much of you as I can get."

A long silence stretched between them and his warm hand came to rest on her thigh.

"It's been a tough week, but my job isn't always this demanding," she said. "We'll get our afternoons back, soon. I promise."

"How soon?"

"Very soon." An edge crept into her tone. As soon as she brought in Thomas and Tammy.

"You're the master of oblique statements," he said. "Personally, I think you could use some stress reduction in your life."

"You're right. I need to get back to the gym."

"I mean a mind and body de-stressor. Something relaxing, that pulls your thoughts away from the outside world. Like meditation, or yoga. You do realize you live with a yoga teacher, right? The yoga studio is thirty feet from your front door."

Sidney didn't like the idea of folding her body into a pretzel a hundred different ways. Jogging and pumping iron at the gym was more her thing.

"I'll do it with you," he said.

Jiminy, what this man was willing to do for her! Sidney wasn't happy about it, but if going to yoga would ease her mind, rein in her renegade thoughts, and reduce David's concerns, she felt compelled to oblige him. "Okay, I'll give it a try." She paused a few beats, then added, "I'm also going to open up to you more about what goes on at work."

"Great."

She could hear the smile in his voice.

"Want to start now?" he asked.

"Why not? What do you want to hear about first? The fire, the cave, or the mutilated head?"

"A mutilated head?" he asked with a note of stark surprise.

"Just another unremarkable day on the job." Sidney stretched her body full length next to his, and their legs entwined. She leaned over to gently kiss his exposed skin, her hair falling around her face. She could feel his intake of breath. Feeling mischievous, she started stroking him.

"You're cheating. You're trying to distract me."

"Is it working?"

In answer, he released a little moan. Then another.

It was working beautifully. David pulled her on top, so that she straddled him, and they both surrendered to her favorite method of stress reduction.

CHAPTER THIRTY-FOUR

IT WAS FORTUNATE that her whole department was well-rested. The following day proved to be stressful and demanding. A whopper of a thunderstorm moved in late afternoon, and everyone was working a double shift responding to calls for help. Selena brought bags of sandwiches to the station for a quick food break at 7:00 p.m., then everyone headed back out into the thrashing storm.

Calls finally died down after 10:30 p.m. Sidney had returned to the office and was engaged in paperwork when the call she'd been waiting for came in. "This is Chief Becker. What's up, Alice? Did you hear from Tammy?"

"Not me personally. She contacted my granddaughter. I just got off the phone with Riley."

"Did she tell Riley where she is?"

"Yeah. She's in Fall Springs. Thomas has a cabin on Mule Deer Lake." Her voice sounded strained. "About forty-five miles from here."

"You sound tense, Alice. What aren't you telling me?"

Alice hesitated, then exhaled. "Tammy said they're leaving Oregon tomorrow. I think they're heading for Canada."

Sidney felt a jolt of adrenaline. Tammy and Thomas would be on the run tomorrow. They needed to be apprehended as soon as possible. Sidney had one chance to bring them in. It had to be tonight.

"Please be careful with Tammy," Alice said. "She's armed. If she feels threatened, she'll defend herself."

"What's she armed with?"

"A Glock semi-automatic."

And, of course, her knives. Lethal weapons.

"We'll be careful, Alice. With your help, we should have her safely in custody tonight. We'll be in touch." Sidney disconnected. Urgency throbbed behind her eyes, pounding out a rhythm that warned her to get a jump on this.

Fall Springs was in the jurisdiction of the Douglas County's sheriff department. Their agency was stretched as thin as hers, with the sheriff and three deputies covering hundreds of square miles. Sidney contacted Sheriff Hank Griffin, an old friend, and explained that a murder suspect might be hiding in the woods at Mule Deer Lake Resort.

"Mule Deer Lake. Sure, I know it. Remote. There're about five cabins on that lake, from what I recall." His voice toughened. "You think you got a murder suspect up there?"

"Yeah. Tammy Schaffer and her boyfriend, Thomas Thornton."

"Tammy Schaffer?" His tone changed, his words etched with anger. "Hell. She's the woman who killed that investigator. A retired cop."

"She's the one. I need eyes on the ground. With your approval, I'd like to send one of my officers up to the lake to surveil. If Tammy's there, I'll need help. She's armed with a gun, and knives. I'll need SWAT protection for my officers."

"Go ahead and send out your officer. As far as tactical guys, you can count on our help. I have a couple of deputies who are SWAT trained. It won't be hard to get some trained deputies from another jurisdiction. Everyone wants this woman behind bars. I'll get back to you." The line went dead. Fifteen minutes later, Griffin called back. "I got a team of five men who'll join you tonight. Give us a head's up with plenty of warning."

"Will do. Thanks, Hank."

"You owe me, Sidney," he said with a touch of humor.

"Yep. I got it." Sidney disconnected and heaved out a sigh, relieved to have the manpower she needed. The tension in her shoulders eased a bit. She glanced at the window, slashed with rain. In light of the severity of the storm, all of her officers and reserve officers were still on patrol duty tonight. One of them had to be pulled in. Sidney called Granger. "How're you holding up out there?"

"I'm ready for an ark. Just helped pull a fifteen-hundred-pound dairy cow out of a muddy ditch. The farmer tried to thank me with a half-gallon of fresh cream and five pounds of butter. But of course, we can't accept gifts."

"Uh huh. That cream and butter are in your truck right now, aren't they?"

"I can neither deny or confirm."

"You better make sure some of it finds its way to Selena. I see quiche Lorraine in my immediate future."

Right on cue the storm beat a tempo on the roof that was straight out of a Wagner opera. Lightening thundered and brightened the window.

"Holy shit. The world's coming to an end," Granger wise-cracked.

"Holy shit is right. Come back to the station. Pronto. I have a gig for you."

"Copy that."

Ten minutes later Granger walked into her office in a wet slicker. Water slid off the hem leaving a trail on the floor, and beads of rain decorated the brim of his hat. "What's up, Chief?"

"We've located Tammy and Thomas. A cabin out at Mule Deer Lake Resort."

His handsome face broke into a grin. "Yowzer. We got 'em. Where the heck is Mule Deer Lake?"

"Fall Springs, Douglas County. I need you to head over there ASAP. Quietly surveil. Look for smoke coming from a chimney, a light in a window. If you spot the suspects, send me an immediate confirmation and coordinates. Then Darnell, Amanda, and I will join you. The sheriff's sending a tactical team to help us out."

His eyes brightened. When police work escalated into a crisis, Granger seemed to thrive on the challenge.

"Wait for backup," she warned. "Tammy's armed with a Glock. And she's freaking lethal with knives."

"Copy that," he said, looking undaunted. "I'm on my way."

***

As Granger drove further east into the hills, the wind and rain died down, and eventually, he moved out of the brunt of the storm. The torrential downpour eased into a gentle drumming on the roof. After reducing his speed on a pitted dirt road that bordered a pasture of tall grass, he made a hard right. Up ahead, Mule Deer Lake swung into view. The rain had ceased, the cloud cover had broken apart, and a partial moon glowed bright in the sky. Smoking in the cold, the water looked gun metal gray. A few secluded cabins squatted on the shoreline, barely visible through the trees.

Granger pulled off the road at midnight, hid his truck behind a stand of aspens, and climbed out wearing his camouflage uniform. The world looked tormented and alien in the silvered light. Wind thrashed the trees. Water dripped from branches. The big live oaks creaked and moaned. Staying hidden, he cautiously approached a cabin, first looking for vehicles, then disturbances in the earth around the entryways. Nothing. Using his flashlight beam judiciously, Granger looked into the window of the garage, and then the house itself. Empty.

It took over an hour to circle the entire lake, searching each of the five cabins. It was pitch dark and cold. A sharp wind whistled through the trees.

Not a single cabin showed a sign of life. He glanced at his watch. 1:30 a.m.

Damn. Feeling dispirited, Granger heaved out an exasperated sigh. The fugitives were not in this remote vicinity. It appeared the chief had been given false information. Granger was about to relay the disappointing news to Chief Becker when he caught a vague, unexpected scent. Mixed in with the sodden, earthy smell of rain was a wisp of woodsmoke. Somewhere, someone had a fire burning. He went into hyper focus, scanning the surrounding forest in slices. About a hundred yards from the lakeshore, he caught a sliver of something through the burrows of trees. Something that shouldn't be there. A dim, flickering light. As he crept closer, dodging between tree and bush, a structure emerged. Soft light wavered in the windows. He edged closer and the structure turned into the wall of a cabin, extremely well concealed behind dense shrubbery. Granger circled around the back and cast a beam of light through the window of the garage. Inside, an old rugged Jeep Wrangler took up the floor space. As far as he knew, Thomas didn't own a Jeep. But squeezed in next to the Jeep, he spotted a motorcycle. Tammy had escaped on a motorcycle.

Adrenaline humming, Granger crept up to a cabin window, jeweled by rain and partially fogged. Staying in the shadows, he peered into the interior. It was one room, with a small kitchen area, wood paneled walls, and rough-hewn furniture. Fishing hats and poles decorated the walls. Lining the mantle were photos of a man proudly exhibiting his daily catch. Opposite the window, the door to a small bathroom stood wide open. Pushed against the left wall was a bed occupied by two nude people who were making love. They had to be Thomas and Tammy. He ducked back into the darkness.

***

Sidney drove the Yukon with Amanda riding shotgun and Darnell in the cage. Rain sluiced down the windshield in between the wiper strokes. Eventually the storm tapered off, and heavy vapor rose off the gleaming asphalt in waves. The plan was to meet the tactical team at a rest stop a quarter of a mile outside of the resort. Granger would wait at the cabin to ensure the couple stayed put. When notified of their arrival, he'd guide them in. The two-lane county road rose through the foothills and did a few hairpins before Sidney spotted the sign that identified the Bear Creek rest stop at 2:30 a.m. She pulled into the cutout and saw five men waiting off to the side by their vehicles. Her headlights illuminated "SWAT" on the backs of their vests. They looked formidable in their camouflage military-style uniforms, ballistic vests, and helmets. Behind them, pockets of mist hovered over the creek and hung like veils in the treetops.

After Darnell alerted Granger of their arrival, Sidney and her team climbed out into the heavy moist air. Like the SWAT unit, in addition to their duty pistols, they were armed with assault rifles. The two groups came together in a circle and made quick introductions. Aside from their name tags, it was impossible to tell the deputies apart in the darkness, except for Gabriel Slade, the team leader, due to his unusual height; about six feet five. A deputy with the name tag Jenkowski stood next to him with a battering ram slung over one shoulder.

"My officer instructed us to follow the creek trail into the resort," Sidney said in a calm, professional tone. "Then take the offshoot that runs parallel to the lake. It curves around to the north end of the dock. He'll meet us there and lead us to the cabin. The female, Tammy Schaffer, is our primary threat. She's armed with a Glock 9mm semi, and she's an expert knife thrower. You need to get her hands cuffed ASAP."

"Yeah, we know who she is," Jenkowski said with distaste. "Cop killer."

"She killed one of our own," Slade said. "Max Stevens. She'll be prone on the floor before she knows what hit her."

Sidney heard the hostility in their tones and understood their sentiment. Cop killers were the most loathed of all criminals. In the heat of the moment, a cop's anger could get the best of him. It wasn't unusual back in Oakland for a cop killer to have an "accidental" fall and get booked at the station with a bloody nose or black eye. That wouldn't happen on Sidney's watch. Feeling a tightening at the back of her neck, she added, "She's pregnant."

The mood of the group changed minutely, but palpably. The two lead deputies nodded their understanding. The safety of the team was the foremost priority, but they wouldn't direct undue aggression toward Tammy.

"Here's the search warrant." Sidney unfolded the document and handed it to Slade.

He studied it under his beam and handed it back. "Perfect. We're good to go."

They stepped into single file formation with the deputies taking the lead, low mode flashlight beams pointed at the ground. Slowly and soundlessly, they made their way over the overgrown path to the lake. The tall pines soughed. A breeze slipped through the flat leaves of the aspen trees, causing them to tremble and quake. Sidney felt the moisture on her face, the only part of her body with exposed flesh.

When they reached the dock, mist had rolled over the lake, concealing most of the water. She heard waves lapping gently against the shore. Looking ghostly, Granger emerged out of the vapor and joined them. He nodded a quick greeting, and said in a low voice, "The cabin's a couple hundred feet through the woods behind me. I just left. The two suspects are sleeping. The bed is to the left of the front door, against the wall."

Knowing the location of the suspects was critical. If a flashbang made contact with someone's body, it would result in severe burns.

"Watch your step. There isn't a path." Granger turned to lead the way.

Single file, they stepped in line, everyone diligent about the placement of their feet. Sounds were amplified in the forest and carried long distances. A single sound out of the ordinary could alert the suspects. They entered the mist and visibility was reduced to about twenty feet. Sidney was immediately disoriented, her eyes glued to the vest of the deputy in front of her.

They reached the cabin, and everyone quietly fell into protocol. To protect Sidney's officers, only the SWAT team would enter the premises. Granger glanced through the window and nodded, indicating the suspects were in bed. Four of the deputies stacked up to the right side of the door while Jenkowski positioned himself to the left. Slade gave the signal. Jenkowski smashed the door open with the battering ram, then backed out of the way, and Slade tossed in a flashbang. In the small cabin, it was like a mini nuclear explosion went off. Bright light from the blast flashed in the windows. A shock wave reverberated off the walls, floor, and ceiling. A thick haze of smoke filled the room. The suspects would now be stunned, deafened, temporarily blinded, and disoriented. The SWAT team rushed into the cabin.

Sidney heard a woman screaming. The deputies were yelling, "On the floor! On the floor! Face down!"

Through the haze in the doorway, Sidney watched three deputies grab Thomas and Tammy, push them face down on the floor, and cuff their hands behind their backs. The other two men stood with guns leveled. Once the suspects were controlled and subdued, the deputies lowered their guns and did a quick search of the cabin for weapons.

Officially, the job of the SWAT team was done once the prisoners were in custody in the Garnerville Department's vehicles. Sidney sent Granger and Darnell to bring their vehicles to the cabin. The two men sprinted into the woods in the direction of the creek.

"All clear," Slade shouted out the door to Sidney. She and Amanda entered and assessed the scene. It was crowded in the cabin. Two of the deputies stepped outside to give them room.

The tactical entry was designed to scare the holy hell out of criminals, and it worked. The suspects were secured and controlled, lying face down and nude on the floor. Thomas lay frozen, stoic. Tammy was sobbing and visibly shaking.

"You'll want to confiscate these," Slade said, nodding at a Glock pistol sitting on a kitchen countertop. Next to it, a half dozen throwing knives were lined up; five sheathed, one unsheathed. "These look like they could slice and dice you in seconds."

"What's a monk doing with weapons like this?" Jenkowski asked, shaking his head.

"We'll find out soon enough," Sidney said. "When we get her back to the station. She has a hell of a lot of questions to answer." Sidney turned to the woman whimpering on the floor, a fugitive from the law for sixteen years. Tammy looked harmless with her hands cuffed, but Sidney knew better. Her gut tightened for a moment as she flashed on Max Stevens bleeding out in the forest, dying alone. At least now his family would get some closure.

"Let's get her dressed," Sidney said. She and Amanda covered the quaking woman with a blanket and helped her to her feet. Tammy's face was tear streaked. She was still trembling, still in shock. The dazzle from a flashbang lasted about 10 seconds, so her eyesight was restored, but she probably felt like she'd been punched in the face. For the next hour or so, her ears would be ringing like a son-of-a-bitch, and dizziness would affect her balance. They got her dressed in sweats. Slade and Jenkowski did the same with Thomas, who was unsteady on his feet. The two suspects were separated and stuffed into the cages of the two department vehicles, their motors running to keep them warm.

It was over in minutes. The mission went down without a hitch. Sidney felt weak with relief. The two elusive fugitives were in custody. Her relief was mirrored on the exhausted faces of her junior officers. They'd all been on the job for twenty hours straight, and still had a few hours in front of them.

With everything under control, the SWAT team left.

Forty-five minutes later, the cabin, garage, and vehicles had been searched and Sidney and her team were on the road back to Garnerville.

CHAPTER THIRTY-FIVE

THEY ARRIVED at the station at 6:00 a.m. After the two suspects were booked into the system and locked in separate cells, Sidney conferred with her officers in the bullpen. Everyone looked overwhelmed by the exhaustion of the long shift, now hitting twenty-four hours. Shoulders sagged and eyes looked glazed.

"Do you need help getting Tammy ready for the interview?" Granger asked.

"Hell no. We're not doing any interviews this morning," Sidney said, hearing the weariness in her voice. "Exhausted cops make mistakes, and we can't afford to make mistakes. We're all going home. I'll grab a few hours of sleep, then question Tammy around noon. I'll need one of you to assist me."

All three volunteered to come in.

"I'll come in," Granger said emphatically, drowning out the voices of Amanda and Darnell.

"You heard him. You two, go home. Catch up on sleep. See your kids. I'll have reserve officers pick up your shifts," Sidney said, feeling appreciation for the loyalty of her team, and for Granger's generosity. As they were single with no kids, she and Granger often took on extra hours so the other two could have family time.

Shooting Granger appreciative smiles, Amanda and Darnell grabbed their gear and left the station.

Since the dispatcher normally went home by midnight, they turned over dispatch duties to the sheriff's office. That meant a reserve officer would have to come in and oversee the prisoners and make sure they had breakfast. "Call Officer Dan Upton, Granger. Then go home. Be back here at noon." Sidney beamed him a smile. "You did a great job tonight."

He gave her a tired smile in return.

Sidney stopped by the conference room, grabbed a bottle of water and a pack of doughnuts, and headed back to the holding cells. To keep the two suspects separated, Thomas had to be put in the drunk tank, an enclosed room, so he could not shout out at Tammy, who was in an open cell at the opposite end of the hall. No way was he going to have an opportunity to drum up some false narrative with her. The cells had no amenities. No creature comforts. Just a toilet and a cot within cinder block walls. In the dim light cast into the dark cell from the hallway, she saw that Tammy was curled into a fetal position, a blanket thrown over her body, facing the bars.

"How're you doing, Tammy?" Sidney asked gently.

Tammy opened her eyes without moving, stared at Sidney, didn't answer.

"You feeling okay? You had a pretty rough night." Understatement. She had been shocked awake by an ear-splitting explosion, dragged to the floor naked, and cuffed; with uniformed men pointing guns at her.

"I'm a little dizzy," Tammy said quietly. "And I have a headache."

"I'm sorry. Those effects will wear off soon." Sidney spoke in a soothing tone, showing concern, communicating that she wasn't the bad guy. "Look, I know you're pregnant. Do you want a doctor to come in and see how you're doing?"

"No," she said drowsily. "Not now. I just want to sleep."

"Sure. Get some rest. In case you get hungry or thirsty, here's a bottle of water and some doughnuts." Sidney set them down on the cement floor inside the bars and left.

Reserve Officer Dan Upton, a young cop fresh out of the academy, arrived a half hour later, a little bleary eyed, with a night's worth of stubble on his face. He was asleep when Granger called. He must have jumped out of bed, showered and dressed in his uniform in minutes flat, and put the pedal to the metal to get here this quickly.

With her suspects in the hands of a competent cop, Sidney finally left for home.

***

"Hey, Granger," Sidney said in greeting, walking into the bull pen at noon. He was already busily at work over his computer. They both wore crisp uniforms and looked somewhat refreshed, having gotten around four hours of sleep. "You check on the prisoners?"

"Yeah. Both deadheads." Aside from red-rimmed eyes, Granger looked alert. "Winnie said they were grumpy as hell when she woke them up for lunch at 11:00. She got them drinks and sandwiches at Pickle's Deli. When I looked in on them ten minutes ago, they had eaten and were dead asleep."

"Not much else to do when you're locked in a small cell. Let's talk to

Tammy. Escort her into the interview room. Get the video and audio set up. I'm going to make a pot of java. Want a cup?"

"Yeah. Jumbo size. Black. Strong."

"I'll make sure a spoon stands up in it."

"Sounds about right."

With Tammy's police file under her arm and holding two cups of strong coffee, Sidney joined Granger in the observation room. Granger thumbed some buttons and an image of the suspect in the interview room appeared on the video screen. "Audio and video are good to go."

Sidney handed him a coffee and they both sipped while studying Tammy Schaffer through the one-way glass. The woman had escaped prosecution for sixteen-years by posing as a man, she had killed Max by throwing a knife like a Ninja, and she made a daring escape from the monastery on a motorcycle dressed in black leather. At this point, Sidney thought nothing could surprise her about Tammy. Yet, she was surprised. The suspect looked anything but tough as nails. She sat stiffly with her shoulders squared, horribly uncomfortable, with an appalling strain on her pale face. Back at the cabin, they had hastily dressed her in a pair of Thomas's gray sweats, and even with the cuffs and sleeves rolled back, her slender frame looked lost in all the fabric. With her cropped hair and face free of makeup, there was something waiflike about her, something immensely vulnerable.

"Not what I was expecting," Sidney said. "She certainly doesn't come across as a hardened criminal."

"No, she doesn't."

"Last night, she whimpered in the cage of the Yukon all the way back from the lake."

"She's pregnant. Her hormones are out of whack."

Granger was a bachelor who grew up with one sibling. A brother. "Didn't know you were an expert on women's hormones."

"My sister-in-law. She's had two kids. My brother needed someone to talk to when she got ... you know ...." Granger circled his temple with his index finger.

"Hmmm." Sidney gave him her penetrating stare. "You do realize you're perpetuating a stereotype about women, right?"

He blushed and cleared his throat. "Sorry."

"Let's go in and peel the onion." She was feeling a caffeine rush from the coffee, and her brain had sharpened. "See what lurks inside Tammy's mind. Take notes."

"Copy that." Granger pulled a notepad and pen from his breast pocket and followed her into the windowless room. They pulled out metal chairs and seated themselves. Sidney sat across from the suspect under the glare of fluorescent lights. She opened Tammy's file, and asked gently, "How are you holding up?"

The suspect sat straighter in her chair, her cuffed hands clasped tightly on the table, her expression wary. "I'm still a little dizzy."

Sidney gave her a sympathetic look. "Can we get you anything? Water? Tea?"

Tammy's eyes filled with tears. "I just want to see Thomas!"

"I'll see if I can make that happen," Sidney said sweetly, knowing it wouldn't happen until both had been questioned and their full statements were locked in on tape. The suspects would be given no opportunity to coordinate their stories. Sidney had a reputation for being tough as nails out in the field when the occasion called for it, but this was different. She needed to dissuade Tammy from asking for a lawyer, which would shut down the interview immediately. Sugar got more cooperation from suspects than bullying. "Tammy, I need you to answer a few questions for me. Do you feel well enough to do that?"

The suspect sniffed and shrugged.

Sidney moved a box of tissue over to her. Tammy grabbed a few. Moving with a kind of nervous tension, she wiped her eyes and blew her nose. Then she stared listlessly at the wadded tissue in her cuffed hand, hiding her expression.

"You know how this works," Sidney said. "You have the right to remain silent. Anything you say can and will be used against you in a court of law. You have the right to speak to an attorney, and to have an attorney present during any questioning."

Tammy didn't move. Not a twitch. She sat as still as a photograph.

"Before we start, I want you to know that I'm not going to bullshit you. I'm not going to lie. I'm not going to make promises I can't keep. And I'll do what I can to help you."

Tammy nodded, her expression wary.

"Let's see what we have here." Sidney opened the file and read. "You grew up here in Garnerville."

Tammy met her gaze, and said tentatively, "Born and raised."

"You come from a farming family."

"Three generations."

"Really? Three generations?"

"My great grandfather bought the property back in the forties."

"I've been out to your farm. It's beautiful. Stunning view of the Cascades."

"Farming's hard work. But I'm glad I was raised that way."

Good, Tammy was putting sentences together. Sidney returned to her file. "You went to Garnerville High, of course."

"Yes."

"So did I. You were a year behind me. I remember you were one of the editors for the newspaper." Sidney smiled, keeping her voice light and friendly. "Remember hard-assed Mrs. Jasper, the gym coach? She made us do extra pushups if we looked at her the wrong way."

"Yeah, I remember her." Tammy's shoulders relaxed a fraction of an inch.

"I see you were a popular student. Good grades."

"That was me. Back then. Another lifetime."

"I hear you." Sidney cleared her throat. "Look, I just need to get some routine stuff out of the way. Just so we're clear, for your protection, and mine, this conversation is being taped."

Tammy's hazel gray eyes darted across the ceiling and located the video camera.

Sidney kept her eyes lowered to her file for a long pause. She needed this woman, who was a proven liar, a felon, a fugitive from justice, and possibly guilty of second-degree murder, to talk to her. She needed to tread lightly, focus on the positive, and avoid any hint of judgement. She looked up and continued to speak in a soft tone. "The monastery is a very tranquil place. You've led a peaceful life up there as a monk for the last sixteen years. Worked with kids. It appears you were greatly loved and respected."

Tammy's face softened. "I loved my fellow monks. And working with the boys."

"I know you did." Sidney closed the file. "We need to talk about a few things, Tammy, like what happened up there in the woods. I'd like to give you the chance to tell your side of the story."

Tammy's expression returned to wary.

"I won't be able to help you unless you talk to me."

Silence. She looked away.

"We've already put most of the pieces together. I just need you to fill in a few blanks."

Silence.

"If you want to help yourself, and Thomas, work with me."

Tammy's demeanor changed minutely, a tightening of her jawline, then it relaxed. But Sidney caught it. She'd hit a nerve. Tammy was certainly anxious for herself, but clearly, she was also deeply frightened for her boyfriend. "Thomas is not going to walk away from this. You know that, right? He's up to his eyeballs in legal trouble. For starters, he's guilty of aiding and abetting in the commission of a crime, and obstruction of an investigation. No question, he's looking at jail time."

Tammy's hands tightened in her lap.

"This could go two ways, Tammy. Talk to me and make it easier on yourself and Thomas. I'll let the judge know you cooperated."

Tammy blew out a ragged breath, stared at her hands.

"We'll take it slow. Okay?"

Finally, Tammy nodded.

Sidney sensed that beneath her fear and nervous tension a light of hope flickered. "Do you know why you were arrested last night?"

"Yes. The man … in the woods." Her face contorted. "But it's all a huge, horrible mistake."

"Tell me what happened that morning," Sidney said gently.

Tammy's mouth pinched with pain. "I didn't mean to kill him. As you said, I'm a Buddhist. I live a life of peace. But he attacked Karune. He viciously punched that sweet boy in the face and knocked him down. Then he raised a huge piece of wood over his head and was about to bash him with it. I didn't think. I just acted. I needed to save the boy." Her face crumpled, as if a dam holding back raw emotion suddenly gave way. Tears filled her eyes and spilled down her cheeks. She continued in a choking voice that was difficult to understand. "But I killed that man in the process. That tortures me every waking second." Tammy bowed her head, covered her face with her cuffed hands and wept, her shoulders shuddering.

Sidney slowly exhaled. She had just gotten the confession she needed, that Tammy killed Max. She glanced at Granger, who had been scribbling notes. He arched his brows and momentarily widened his eyes, not sure what to make of Tammy's display. "Granger, could you get her some water, please?"

"Sure thing." He left the room and returned minutes later with a pitcher and three paper cups. Tammy's sobs had subsided, and she was staring at her cuffed hands, now tightly clasped in her lap.

Sidney filled all three cups, moved one over to Tammy, and said softly, "Here, Tammy. Drink this."

Tammy picked up the cup with both hands and drank a few sips.

"I understand why you threw the knife. You were defending Karune. But then you pulled the knife out of the victim's back, and ran. You left him and the boy there, injured. Why didn't you get help?"

She lifted her head and swallowed. "I was in shock. It all happened so fast. I reacted without thinking. I don't remember what happened after I threw the knife and the man went down."

If Tammy used that line in court, there was a good chance she'd be toast, Sidney thought. In a word, it was bullshit.

Tammy continued, "One moment I was walking in the forest. Happy with my life. Looking forward to a bright future. In a split second, everything changed." Unconsciously, she placed her hands over her belly in a protective manner.

What bright future? Sidney wondered. Was she suddenly going to turn herself in? Admit to the monks that she'd been a woman all along? Run away with Thomas under an assumed name?

"My life spiraled into a nightmare," Tammy said. Again, her eyes filled with tears, but she kept talking in a tremulous voice. "I guess on some level, I went into survival mode. My instinct was to protect myself. Later, Thomas told me what I did. I was so ashamed …."

Sidney listened attentively, not forgetting that this peaceful monk apparently carried a throwing knife with her wherever she went. What peace-loving monk carried a lethal weapon used principally to kill things? "When you got back up to the monastery, what did Thomas say?"

Silence. Tammy sat thinking for almost a full minute. "I take full responsibility for everything I did that morning. I made the decision to go to morning meditation, as usual. I was hoping not to draw attention to myself. But seeing you with the dogs and those big guns scared me. I saw my life disintegrating. My instincts told me to run. I went to the barn, changed my clothes, and escaped on the motorcycle. End of story."

Sidney knew she was lying to protect Thomas. He could have encouraged her to turn herself in, but instead he aided her escape. "Tammy, just a few more questions. The man you killed was a private investigator. His name was Max Stevens. Thomas said you both had seen him the night before. Is that true?"

"Yes. We saw him spying on us. Taking pictures. He ran off into the woods."

"Thomas ran after him, yes?"

Tammy looked steadily into Sidney's eyes and her voice strengthened. "I will not talk about Thomas. At all. Everything that happened to us was my fault, not his. He did nothing wrong. He's a wonderful man. A doctor. He's the father of my baby."

Clearly, Tammy wasn't going to incriminate her boyfriend. She was determined to take all the blame, thinking that would exonerate Thomas. He was in enough trouble as it was, without her testimony. "Tammy, we know the story you told Thomas about your past trouble with the law isn't true. There was no cartel, no Fed involvement, no safe house, no prostitution arrest, no wiretap. Why did you make up that story?"

Tammy flushed, a wave of color rising up into her cheeks. She took a long breath and shook her head a little. "I fed him a little bit of that story over time. It expanded and grew, as though it had a life of its own. I guess I built it up for my own amusement, adding a little more drama each time."

But Tammy knew it was a lie, not a fantasy, and she was lying to the man she supposedly loved. That didn't help her credibility with Sidney, and it certainly wouldn't help her in court.

"It was far better than reliving the horror of what actually happened to me," Tammy added.

"We know what really happened," Sidney said. "We contacted Detective Dan Bunker who worked your case in Crestview." Sidney scanned the notes in Tammy's file, then looked up and met her gaze. "You got into the drug scene as a teenager. Your mom sent you to Crestview to live with your dad. At eighteen, you had another drug bust. You graduated to heroin. Afterwards, you stayed clean for three months. Then you nearly OD'd. Fortunately for you, your apartment manager found you, a hair away from dead. Your roommate wasn't so lucky. He didn't make it. Your prints were found on the drug paraphernalia. His weren't. You got busted for manslaughter. Instead of facing your charges, you ran."

"Biggest mistake of my life."

"Is that why you think Max was spying on you? You thought he was going to bring you in?"

"Yes."

"And the next morning he ended up dead. At your hands. Tammy, you can see why the timing looks suspicious."

Her face tightened and the skin around her lips turned pale, but her gaze was unflinching. "I told you the truth. I'm not a murderer!"

Sidney silently read through the rest of Tammy's file, mentally adding the information Granger had gathered from interviewing Alice at the farm. She started pushing puzzle pieces together, trying to make sense of it all. She lifted her head and met Tammy's gaze. "You said lying to Thomas was better than reliving the horror of what actually happened to you. Your mother said you got pregnant here in Garnerville at sixteen. You went into a deep depression. Started doing drugs. She sent you to Crestview to live with your dad. You had twin babies at age seventeen. Then you started doing drugs again." Sidney hesitated, then dropped the bomb. "We know James Abbott is the father of your twins."

Tammy went pale. She clenched her hands until her knuckles shone white.

"Your mother said he gave you a lump sum of money to keep you quiet." Sidney watched Tammy carefully. Her pregnancy, her sudden deep depression, her drug use, pointed to some kind of extreme traumatic event. Sidney needed to pick at the scab to see what hid underneath. "Can you tell me about your relationship with James Abbott?"

Tammy sat very still, eyes large, perspiration appearing on her upper lip.

"How did you meet?"

Tammy cleared her throat and spoke slowly and hesitantly, as though conjuring up long buried memories. "When I was sixteen, I worked on weekends as a waitress at Jake's Coffee Shop. He came in both mornings for breakfast and always sat in my section."

"He singled you out."

She nodded and stared off into the corner as though staring into her past. "I thought he was charming. He left large tips, and funny notes with happy faces on his napkins. I started looking forward to the weekends, just to see him. I had a schoolgirl's crush. I used to blush and grin foolishly when I took his order. Then the unimaginable happened. He asked me to meet him after work for dinner. I didn't know he was married. He didn't wear a ring."

"So you accepted …."

"Yes." Her voice grew more distant. "It seemed like a fairytale. I'd never really been on a date before, and here a sophisticated, highly-successful man wanted to take me out—a teenager who's divorced mother was struggling to make ends meet."

"Did your mom know?"

"No." She glanced at Sidney. "Mom's very religious. She thought I should only meet boys at church. That night, I told her I was going out with a girlfriend."

"What happened next?"

Tammy sucked in a breath and resumed speaking, her voice tight and brittle. "He took me to Cote d'Azur in Jackson. I'd never been in a fancy restaurant before. I have to admit, it was scary. So much silverware. Crystal glasses. Candlelight. He ordered for us. Steak and lobster, and a bottle of red wine. I never drank before. I didn't like it, but I drank a glass anyway, to show him I was mature. He did most of the talking, and he kept touching me. My hand, my knee under the table." She paused, cleared her throat. "By the time he paid the bill, I was feeling weird. I thought it was the wine. When we left, I was disoriented. He helped me get into the back seat of his Mercedes. Everything was hazy, and I think I passed out for a while."

Sidney caught Granger's eye. It sounded like Abbott might have slipped some kind of drug into Tammy's wine.

"Next thing I knew," Tammy continued. "I was on a bed in a motel room. That terrified me. I told him I wanted to go home." Tammy's anxiety became visible. She closed her eyes, put up her hands to cover her face, and mumbled through her fingers, "Sorry. This is so hard. I've tried not to think about it. But it's still so real, after all these years. Like it just happened yesterday. I've never told this to anyone before."

"You never told your parents?"

She put her hands down on the table and shook her head. "I was too ashamed. I felt so stupid, trusting him like that." Her fingers trembled as she reached for the cup of water and took a sip. "But now, I need to talk about it. I want to get this nightmare out of my head."

"Take your time," Sidney said. "Breathe."

Tammy inhaled deeply, then exhaled slowly. "He handcuffed my wrists to the headboard. I started screaming. Then he turned into a monster. He hit me, hard enough to make my nose bleed. Somewhere along the line, I passed out." Misery and horror were dark in her eyes. "When I came to, I was naked, and he was raping me. The pain was unbearable, but I couldn't scream. He'd put a gag in my mouth. I moved in and out of consciousness. Sometimes, he fell asleep, then he'd be at it again. Hurting me, grunting like a rabid beast." Tammy's jaw clenched so tightly, it looked like it might crack.

Sidney drew in a deep breath and with effort, controlled her heated emotions. Abbott had drugged, abducted, and brutally raped Tammy when she was sixteen years old—and gotten away with it. She glanced at Granger. There was a tension along his jaw that she recognized. It appeared when he was suppressing anger. Sidney pushed on, her tone soft and gentle. "Can you continue?"

"At dawn, the rain stopped," Tammy said, but she could not control her voice. The words choked in her throat and came out choppy and hoarse. "Mercifully, he released my hands and untied the gag. He got up and tossed the sheet over me, as though I disgusted him. He got dressed, taking his time, leering at me. Then he pulled a bunch of one-hundred-dollar bills from his wallet, wadded them into balls, and threw them at me. He told me that was my payment, and that I was a filthy slut. His next words echoed in my mind for years, like the aftershocks of a bomb blast. He said if I ever mentioned what he did, to anyone, my mother and I were as good as dead." Tammy gripped the edge of the table so hard it must have hurt her hands. The movement was some kind of release of tension, even though her muscles were locked tight. Sidney had seen it before in victims recalling nightmarish events.

"I was barely able to walk," Tammy continued. "But I managed to take a shower. I scrubbed myself raw, trying to get his smell off of me. By the time I got dressed, there was a knock on the door. It was a cab driver, waiting to take me home." Tammy stared into space like she was seeing all the nameless horrors all over again. She met Sidney's eyes. "He's a monster. I can still feel his touch. My skin still crawls, remembering."

Sidney's anger at Abbott was a slow burn in her gut. With difficulty, she kept it from boiling to the surface, and said gently, "I'm so sorry you experienced something so terrifying, Tammy. Sexual assault is a heinous crime. I'm sorry you had to live with this painful secret all these years."

"That's why I started doing drugs. Opioids, at first. It eased the pain. But then I found out I was pregnant. I had to tell my Mom. I had to tell her who the father was, but I didn't mention rape. He said he would kill us both. I believed him. Mom was horrified that I allowed a man to touch me. That I wasn't a virgin anymore."

Tammy looked away for a moment and Sidney recognized what she was feeling. Shame. Remorse. Self-hatred. Too often, the victims of rape shouldered the blame, as if they were responsible for the perpetrator's twisted mind, and propensity for violence.

"I managed to stay clean during the pregnancy," Tammy continued. "Even though it felt like monsters were growing inside me. God forgive me, but I didn't want the babies. I never even looked at them. As soon as they were born I started doing drugs again. My mom met with the monster. He told her he wanted to help, but we would have to keep it quiet. He offered a huge sum of money, which helped us keep the farm. At least something good came out of all of this."

Sidney fumed. Tammy's mother did exactly the wrong thing. She should have gone to the police, had Abbott arrested for the sexual assault of a minor. Put the full force of the law behind her. "Did any other people know Abbott was coming into Jake's and flirting with you? Any girlfriends? Coworkers?"

She shook her head. "No."

"Anyone know he was taking you out to dinner?"

"No. My best friend went to our church. Super religious. She would have told me not to go."

"Did you ever tell anyone that he raped you?"

She bit her lip and shook her head.

After her attack, it was clear to Sidney that Tammy was near emotional collapse and in desperate need of therapy. But she suffered alone, self-medicating with drugs. Her rapist walked free while she tortured herself for years—punishment on top of punishment. During the interview, Tammy had not been able to mention Abbott by name but referred to him as the monster. Sidney understood. To some rape victims, speaking the name of their assailant was opening a wound, and giving them dignity they didn't deserve.

Tammy was quiet for a moment, then the corners of her lips curved into a warm, sad smile. "Mom took Riley, thank God. What a sweet, beautiful girl she is." Just as suddenly, her voice became strained, almost a whisper. "Somewhere I have a son. I pray he got a good home."

It had been gut-wrenching for Sidney and Granger to take Tammy's testimony, to coax her demons out of hiding, to witness her extreme distress. And now another emotional assault was waiting to strike this woman. Tammy would soon find out that the son she gave up at birth was a serial killer who would very likely spend his life in jail. It was tragically ironic that both she and Luca had been victims of vicious sexual predators. What would their lives have been like if they had not been assaulted?

"I have just one last question for you, Tammy. How is it that you've become an ace at throwing knives?"

Tammy sniffed, wiped her nose with a tissue. "When I went to rehab, what helped the most was empowering myself through the art of self-defense. I was never going to let a man hurt me again," she said emphatically. "I only took classes for a couple of months, but I was drawn to knife throwing, one of the martial disciplines of Japan. That also led me to Buddhism, which eventually led me to the monastery. A knife was easy to conceal under my robes, and it made me feel safe. It was good discipline to practice regularly in the woods, aiming at inanimate targets. Mostly fallen trees." She glanced down at her hands and said softly, "I never dreamt one day I'd be forced to use it on a man."

Sidney thanked Tammy for being so cooperative and brought the interview to a close. "I meant it when I said I wanted to help you," she said with conviction before Granger escorted her out of the room. Sidney didn't leave, but sat at the table, drumming her fingers, deep in thought.

A few minutes later, Granger joined her and took his seat, his face still tense. "Man, that was an ordeal," he said angrily. "I'd like to find Abbott and take his head off. Anyway we could arrest him, throw his ass in jail?"

Sidney exhaled sharply. "I've been sitting here running all the possibilities through my mind. But after all this time, we don't have a leg to stand on legally. If I went to a prosecuting attorney with what we have, a case based on "he said, she said", he'd say it's not enough. He'd want witnesses. But Tammy told no one. No witnesses. There's not enough to file charges, so no arrest."

"Many rapists are serial rapists," Granger said doggedly. "There could be other victims. The way he raped Tammy was planned, orchestrated—the handcuffs, the drugs. Abbott's a rich man. He could have plenty of lovers if that's what he wanted, but he likes the violence, the domination. He likes to emotionally destroy his victim."

"You're right, Granger. He's a vicious brute. It's been seventeen years since he raped Tammy, and he had plenty of time to rack up new victims. But how do we get them to come forward? Can't put an ad in the paper. Even if this case went to court, the hard part would be convincing a jury that Tammy had been raped. She'd be a horrific witness. She's a proven liar. She has no credibility whatsoever. Abbott's defense attorneys would make mincemeat of her. They'd say the sex was consensual. Yes, she was underage, so it was statutory rape of a minor, but the charges needed to be filed within six-years of the crime. The statute of limitations is long gone."

"What about Tammy's mother?"

Sidney shook her head. "She's in a weak legal position because she accepted money from Abbott."

Granger sighed. "Sometimes bad guys just get away with shit."

Sidney narrowed her eyes, thinking hard. "Not entirely. Abbott and I are going to have a conversation."

CHAPTER THIRTY-SIX

ABBOTT'S SECRETARY informed Sidney that her boss was not in the office. He was playing eighteen holes of golf, then having a business dinner at Bear Canyon Country Club, the oldest private club in the three-town area.

Sidney drove to the outskirts of Jackson, arriving at the club at 6:30. Smooth green fairways meandered beneath huge ponderosa pine trees along the rim of a dramatic canyon. She parked and entered the spacious clubhouse, which was grand in a western lodge architectural style. The interior featured exposed timber trestles, rough-hewn rock, a massive word-burning fireplace, and spectacular views of the Cascades. In the relaxed atmosphere, people milled around in the lobby, the golf shop, and the bar, talking in soft murmurs. The restaurant was more formal, featuring award-winning cuisine, linen covered tables, and an attentive staff.

She spotted Abbott sitting with two men at a window table, which had a view of the fairways and the snow-capped mountains. Mallard ducks and Canadian geese drifted lazily on the surface of a large pond. Sidney watched Abbott from a distance. The servers all but genuflected when they attended his table, but not a single one joked with him or acted like they knew him personally.

Sidney was wearing her uniform, which attracted a number of open stares and she felt eyes following her as she crossed the room. Good. She wanted to put him on guard, make him uncomfortable. She saw that the men had finished their meals and the check had been placed on the table. Her timing was perfect.

Abbott was facing the window, but he followed the stares of his buddies, glancing up with curiosity, then with stark surprise when he recognized her. There was a moment of silence where they just looked at one another. He regained his composure and introduced her to his friends, then asked with a slight frown, "Are you here for dinner?"

"No. Actually, I drove out from Garnerville to talk to you."

"To talk to me?" He smiled, but it didn't touch his eyes.

She didn't miss the questioning glances he got from his pals; one husky and bald, one thin with sharp cheek bones and a protruding Adam's apple. Both wore an attitude of entitlement that was unique to the rich and privileged.

"Maybe you would like to speak in private," she said, friendly, but professional.

"We need to shove off, anyway," his husky pal said, taking his cue. "Long drive back to Portland." He reached toward his back pocket, but Abbott put up a hand. "Don't even think about it. I'll take care of it."

Both men smiled their thanks, made a bit of small talk, then gave their polite goodbyes and left.

"Sit down, for God's sake," Abbott said. "People are staring."

As soon as Sidney took a seat, a server swooped in and hovered at her elbow with a menu.

Sidney smiled politely. "Just coffee, thanks. I'm not staying long."

"Another whiskey, Mr. Abbott?" the young man asked.

"Please."

The server left, and Abbott's gaze sharpened on her face. "What the hell do you think you're doing, barging in here and disrupting my business meeting?" He glanced around at the discreet glances being directed at them. "What's so goddamned important that it couldn't wait?"

Sidney had rehearsed what she was going to say. What she was about to undertake fell into the gray area of her lawful authority, even blurring the lines a little. If she wasn't careful, it could come back to bite her. "I'm sure you heard about the three recent murders we've been investigating, and that we have a suspect in custody."

"Yeah, I heard," he said, eyes alert. "Some crazy kid off his meds."

"His name is Luca Ashe. Last night we brought in another suspect, for the murder of Max Stevens."

"You're doing a great job as police chief," he said with a begrudging note of respect. "I'll give you that. But what does any of that have to do with me?"

"Some information has come out of the investigations that could be of concern to you. You're a prominent citizen, frequently in the public eye. I didn't want you to be blind-sided by bad publicity."

Abbott stared at her, his eyes shrewd and calculating, trying to assess her motives. No doubt, he harbored deep resentment for the way she handled his father's extravagant jewelry purchase. The fact that her mother ended up with twelve thousand dollars-worth of diamond jewelry didn't exactly elicit his trust. He looked more curious than worried. His public relations firm and top-notch legal team routinely quashed any bad press that was thrown his way.

The server returned and set a tumbler in front of Abbott, and a cup of coffee in front of Sidney. While he jiggled the ice cubes in his whiskey, Sidney took her time stirring cream and sugar into her cup, feeling the weight of his stare on her face.

"So what is this concerning news?" he asked impatiently.

She met his gaze. "The name of the woman who killed Max is Tammy Schaffer."

Abbott was an ace at controlling his emotions, but Sidney saw a hint of surprise appear in his gray eyes.

With no judgment in her tone or expression, she smoothly dropped the bomb. "What's surfaced in the investigation is that Tammy Schaffer is the mother of Luca Ashe."

Abbott sat absolutely still, but the muscles of his face tightened, and she saw a tensing of his shoulder muscles. She gave him credit for absorbing the blast with utmost control while his brain added two and two together. He turned away and peered out of the window, hiding his expression. She imagined what he was thinking. Two suspects had just been arrested for separate murders, and by some extraordinary coincidence, they were related. He knew Tammy had twins as a result of his brutal assault on her, and he just realized that not only was his rape victim a murder suspect, but his illegitimate son was a savage serial killer. This wasn't just bad press. This information, if released to the public, could destroy his reputation, and his marriage. How in hell would he do damage control on this?

Abbott leveled his gaze on her. His eyes had darkened, shifting to a predatory slant, and the skin had tightened across his cheekbones. But he said nothing, waiting to see how much she knew.

Sidney summed it up for him. "It appears Luca was conceived during an encounter between you and Tammy when she was sixteen. She was working at a diner you frequented on weekends. Luca Ashe, the killer who committed three horrific murders, made similar allegations. He claims that Tammy Schaffer is his mother, and that you're his father." There, she said it. It was out in the open. Sidney informed him that she knew exactly what he had done. She sipped her coffee, watching him closely, letting a strained silence stretch between them.

The spark she ignited suddenly burst into flame. "That's slanderous garbage," he hissed. "You drove all the way out here to lay this trumped up crap on me? The ramblings of some lunatic serial killer? And some drugged out loser who was a slut as a teenager?"

Sidney kept a straight face, though inside she gloated. Abbott had just lost his cool. And he just admitted he knew Tammy as a teenager, even though his evaluation of her was distorted by his general perception of women. The types of crimes Abbott committed demonstrated his hatred for women, and his need to punish them. The fact that he had just been bested by Sidney had to be rocking him to the core.

A little light flared in his eyes as he realized his slip. His visage turned frightening, and would have warned off most people, but Sidney had stared down men much more violent and depraved than Abbott.

"If you're threatening me," Abbott said. "I'll have your head in a vise so fast you won't know what hit you."

"Threaten you?" Sidney said evenly. From a legal standpoint, she was totally justified in meeting with him. "I came as a favor to you. To inform you that a murder suspect who is going to trial is claiming to be your child, and that another murder suspect is claiming to be the mother of your child. Like I said, I'm only telling you this so that you aren't caught off guard."

Sidney had just put him on notice. Without threatening or extorting him, she had tightened the thumbscrews. Though she didn't have enough evidence to arrest him, now that he knew she was on to him, his compulsion to brutally rape another woman might be curtailed. And perhaps he would think twice before threatening anyone in Sidney's family again.

Gripping his tumbler, Abbott downed his drink in one gulp and raised his hand to let the server know he wanted another. His gut was most likely twisting into knots right about now. Alcohol, and lots of it, might be useful in easing his ricocheting emotions.

"Thank you for your time," Sidney said pleasantly, rising to her feet. She pulled a couple of bills from her pocket, laid them on the table, and left without ceremony. She had just struck one small victory for all the women Abbott had victimized.

CHAPTER THIRTY-SEVEN

ONE WEEK LATER

"CLOSE YOUR EYES. Take a long, deep breath. Hold it. Slowly release. Repeat." Selena's gentle voice drifted through the yoga studio.

Feeling thoroughly relaxed, Sidney heard Selena's bare feet walk quietly from the back of the room to the front, weaving a path between her mat and David's. All twenty students lay prone on their backs. Music quieted their minds, and the fragrance of Selena's lavender candles scented the room. The class had been challenging for Sidney. She was accustomed to heaving heavy weights at the gym until her muscles quivered—not putting her body into an unnatural position and holding it for as long as a minute. Fortunately, she found she had the agility to accomplish the postures, and the strength to hold them. The slow, meditative movements and focus on deep breathing had emptied her mind of thought. Her body felt weightless.

"Hey, sleepyhead. Time to come back to the real world," David's soft voice murmured.

Sidney opened her eyes to see him sitting back on his heels gazing down at her, an amused smile on his face. The other students had gotten to their feet and were rolling up their mats and heading out the door. She had really been out of it, floating in a deep, tranquil space.

David held out a hand and helped her to her feet, then his eyes did a quick appraisal of her body. "I'll come to yoga every day of the week if it means watching you move around in those yoga clothes."

Admittedly, her spandex shorts and cropped top didn't cover a lot of skin. "So you had an ulterior motive for getting me to yoga. It wasn't just to reduce my stress level."

"The way you were snoring, I'd say we accomplished both."

"I was snoring?" she asked, a little horrified.

"Nah. Just kidding." He grinned. "You were lying there as serene as Sleeping Beauty. I was tempted to kiss you but, you know, there were people around."

Grinning back, she punched him lightly on the arm.

"You did great. You're as limber as a gymnast," he added softly. "But I already knew that."

"You are, too."

"Guess our workouts at home are paying off."

"Guess so." She moved close enough to lightly kiss him. He smelled good. A hint of sandalwood.

Sidney heard her sister clear her throat. They turned to see Selena waiting at the door, her hand on the knob. "Anytime you two lovebirds are ready …. I need to start brunch. Granger is coming over, and I'm starving."

"Ditto that," Sidney said. She and David crossed the studio, slipped their feet into their flip-flops parked by the door, and followed Selena out into the warm sunny day. The driveway that swept past the yoga studio led to the front of the tree shrouded house they grew up in. Selena's flower beds were sprouting hundreds of daffodils and tulips, and there were signs of flourishing life in her vegetable garden.

"Great class," David said as they walked.

Selena beamed. "How'd you like it, Sid?"

"A workout," she said. "Emphasis on work."

"Yoga isn't work," Selena said. "It's pleasure."

"Really? That plank pose is a killer."

"You held it without a problem."

"You didn't see my grimace," Sidney said, teasing.

"I took it for a smile," Selena said. "Come on, I know you enjoyed it. By the end, you were in blissville."

"Passed out from exhaustion is more like it."

"So you're coming again?" Selena said.

"Yes," David said emphatically. "We're coming."

"You heard him," Sidney said, smiling at David. "He's taking charge of my mental health."

"You accomplished something I never could, David. She's always laughed when I invited her to a class. She said people shouldn't do some of those poses without a chiropractor present."

"Still true," Sidney said.

They reached the house and bypassed the front porch which was decorated with Selena's flowerpots and tinkling wind chimes. As was their lifetime habit, they entered through the side door into the laundry room that also served as a mudroom. Coats hung on pegs and shoes and boots lined the wall. As they walked into the dining room a posse of four trotting cats greeted them, meowing for treats and attention.

Selena made a detour into the kitchen and started pulling items out of the fridge.

"Can I help?" David asked, careful not to step on Chile and Curry, who were twining between his legs. He was a man who knew his way around a kitchen.

"Sure. You can make a pot of coffee."

"I'm going upstairs to change," Sidney said, feeling a little naked in her tiny spandex outfit. "Then I'll come down and set the table."

Fifteen minutes later, the kitchen had warmed from something heating in the oven and David was helping Selena cut up fresh fruit for the salad. Sidney started arranging glasses and silverware on the table.

In response to the doorbell, Sidney crossed the living room. Only one person came into the house through the front door. Granger.

Selena came up behind her as Sidney opened the door.

Looking handsome and fit in jeans and a blue T-shirt, Granger paused in the doorway, his eyes taking in Selena. Still dressed in yoga clothes, her lissome figure was shown to its best advantage. His grin said everything. He planted a kiss on her mouth and followed them back to the kitchen. Everyone stood around the island, pouring strong coffee into mugs.

"Man, what smells so good?" Granger asked.

"Remember when you rescued that dairy cow during the storm?" Selena asked, donning two potholder mittens.

"Yep. Sixteen hundred pounds of cow stuck in mud."

"All that cream and butter the farmer gave you just got put to good use. I made six quiches. Four are frozen, and two are ready to eat." Selena pulled the quiches out of the oven and placed them on a wooden cutting board. They were browned to perfection and smelled delicious. She quickly quartered each pie. "This one is fresh crab, asparagus, and Swiss. This one is mushroom, spinach, bacon, and cheddar."

With murmurs of appreciation, everyone filled their plates with quiche and fruit salad, then took their seats around the table.

"This is by far better than my quiche," David said. "How did you get the crust so flaky?"

"And how did you get the egg custard to melt in your mouth?" Granger asked.

"Old family secret," Selena said, eyes sparkling. "Learned everything from Mom. She was a wizard in the kitchen."

While they ate in comfortable companionship, they talked about small town trivia. After clearing the table, they all nursed another mug of coffee, and inevitably, the conversation turned to homicide. By now, everyone in town knew about the four murders. The reporters had finally packed up and left town after eking out every gory detail about Luca's crime spree. The brutality of his murders eclipsed the secondary murder involving Tammy and Thomas, and, fortunately for them, they got only a fraction of the coverage. No one probed into any family connection that may have existed between the Schaffers and Luca.

"It feels good to be back on regular patrol duty," Granger said. "I'm almost back to normal. Those two cases were a grind."

"I hear you," Sidney said. "I felt like I was back in Oakland, investigating multiple murders all at once."

"Not to mention you almost got killed a few times," Selena said in a mildly accusing tone. "A little more caution wouldn't hurt." She and David shared a fleeting glance of understanding. Being in relationships with cops was nail-biting at times.

"But here she has the A-team," Granger said with a grin. "We got the job done."

"It's true," Sidney said. "My team really stepped up."

"But you're not bulletproof." The concern in Selena's eyes when she looked at Granger wiped the smile off his face. He placed his hand on top of hers in a gesture of comfort.

"It'd be nice if the town officials recognized the great work you do, and rewarded it," Selena said. "Another full-time cop at the very least."

"A larger building and new vehicles would be nice," Granger added.

"If you keep doing such a great job with what you have," David said. "They'll continue to think you don't need anything else."

"Well, it's time to get real with Mayor Burke," Sidney said with conviction.

"Glad those killers are off the street," Selena said. "It feels safe to be outside again. So what's to become of the three perpetrators?"

"Well, not surprisingly, none of them made bail," Sidney said. "They'll sit in jail until they either go to trial or cut a deal. In my opinion, the smart thing would be for all three of them to cut a deal. None of them will fare well in court."

"Luca has serious mental issues," David said.

"Yeah, he does," Sidney said. "He was brutalized in his foster home."

"Won't that help him avoid prison?"

"Being crazy isn't a get out of jail free card. His lawyers will probably shoot for a life sentence with the possibility of parole. I wish we took better care of the mentally ill, but we end up just warehousing them in prisons. The insanity defense is really tough to win." Sidney noticed strong emotions suddenly surfaced and her words came out etched in anger. "Luca's careful planning of each murder shows he knew exactly what he was doing. He brutally murdered his victims. He held Becky Turner captive for three weeks in a crawl space. And he tried to kill cops on two occasions, including me and every one of my junior officers."

There was a long moment of silence while everyone digested the gravity of her words. Anyone of her officers could be dead. Luca had managed to get two rounds into Kyle's vest. Six inches higher, he would have taken it in the throat.

"Thankfully, no one knows Luca is related to the Schaffer family," Selena said. "His last name is Ashe."

"They don't know, yet," Sidney said. "But it's very likely all the family connections will come out soon. Very few secrets stay hidden for long in Garnerville."

"That's unfortunate," David said. "Alice and Riley have to live here. They don't need the stigma of being related to a serial killer."

"Not to mention Tammy is a Schaffer. Her secrets will come out first. She goes to court first. She already had a psych evaluation. Her lawyer will use it to cut a more lenient deal."

"What was in the evaluation?" David asked.

"The doctor said Tammy's behavior was not unusual for a survivor of violent rape. A victim sometimes suffers sexual identity confusion. Tammy chose to live as a celibate male monk because being female was too damn unsafe in her world. It's not unusual to lie and create alternate realities to cover the unbearableness of the truth. And killing to protect a child? A maternal instinct."

"None of this is good news for James Abbott," Granger said without a hint of sympathy. "He'll be crucified in the press. His world is going to blow apart."

"Yeah, well, he dug his own grave," Sidney said heatedly. "Now he can be buried in it."

"I wonder if any of the Schaffers will ever go see Luca," Selena said. "All he ever wanted was to feel loved. And to have a real family."

"Yeah, I wonder that, too," Sidney said.

"Time will tell with that one," David said, draining his cup. He looked at his watch. "Uh-oh. I have to scoot. I need to drop Dillon off at school.

They're having a game today, then he's staying overnight with a friend. Let me help you clean the kitchen." He stood and started stacking dishes.

"David, go," Granger said. "I'll help Selena."

"I don't mind helping."

Selena and Sidney locked eyes and smiled. It was great to see men fighting over who was going to clean up.

"Go," Granger repeated with a note of urgency.

Sidney suspected that he and Selena wanted them out of the house ASAP so they could have some privacy. It'd been a week since they'd been alone. Sidney understood. She was looking forward to her alone time with David.

"Okay, you win." David put up his hands in surrender. He turned to Sidney and smiled. "Want to ride over to the school with Dillon and me? Then you and I can head over to my place. Take out the sailboat."

She grinned. She loved being on the water. "Sure. Sounds great. Give me a second." Sidney ran upstairs and stuffed a bag with necessities, including sunscreen, a swimsuit, and boat shoes, and then she went outdoors with David to his SUV. This was their third afternoon together, and they were getting their groove back. It was a perfect day to take out his West Wight Potter—clear skies, smooth water. The nineteen-foot long sailboat had berths for four and a workable galley with a sink and a stove; perfect for a light dinner later. Today they'd sail straight out to the middle of the lake and drop anchor, then do a little swimming, relax on deck in the sun, and whatever else teased the minds of two healthy adults. Their only objective was to put distance between themselves and the shore—that meant people, demands, and responsibilities—and just float into the evening on clean blue water.

Also by Linda Berry:

THE KILLING WOODS

Book One of the Sidney Becker Mysteries

CHAPTER ONE

BAILEY'S LOW, INSISTENT GROWLS woke Ann from a dreamless sleep. She found herself sprawled on the overstuffed easy chair in the living room, feet propped on the ottoman, drool trickling down her chin. Half opening one eye, she peered at the antique clock on the mantle: 11:00 p.m.

She heard Bailey sniffing at the front door, and then the clicks of his claws traveled to the open window in the living room. She opened her other eye. The sable hound stood sifting the breeze through his muzzle with a sense of urgency. Ann knew what was coming next. Sure enough, Bailey trotted back to the front door and whimpered, gazing expectantly over one shoulder. Damn those big brown eyes.

Normally Ann would be in bed by now, but she passed out after dinner, exhausted from carting her boxes of organic products to town at sunrise and standing for hours in her stall at the farmers market. By the time she loaded her truck and headed home, the pain in her calves had spread up her legs to her back and shoulders, and she felt every one of her forty-five years.

Bailey whined without let up. He knew how to play her. Ann looked longingly toward her bedroom before returning to the hound's pleading eyes. This was more urgent than a potty break.

No doubt, he had caught the scent of a deer or rabbit and wanted desperately to assail it with ferocious barking to assert his dominance over her small farm. Then he'd settle in for the night.

Since an unsolved murder rocked her town three years ago, Ann resisted going out late after dark. Still, she felt a pang of guilt. She and Bailey had missed their usual after dinner walk. If the spirited hound didn't exhaust his combustible energy, he'd be circling her bed at dawn, demanding that she rise.

"Okay, Bailey, you win." Ann heard the weariness in her voice as she heaved herself from the chair. Fatigue had settled into every part of her body and her limbs felt as heavy as flour sacks. "Only a half-mile up the highway and back."

Bailey sat at attention, tail vigorously thumping the floor.

Still dressed in jeans, a turtleneck sweater, and sturdy hiking shoes, Ann grabbed her Gore-Tex jacket from the coat rack, wrestled her arms through the sleeves, pulled Bailey's leash from a pocket, and snapped it onto his collar. The boards creaked softly as they stepped onto the covered front porch into the damp autumn chill. The moist air held the promise of the season's first frost. Her flashlight beam found the stone walkway, then the gravel driveway leading to the highway. A good rain had barreled through while she slept, and a strong wind unleashed the pungent fragrance of lavender and rosemary from her garden. Silvered in the moonlight, furrowed fields of tomatoes, herbs, and flowers sloped down to the shoreline of Lake Kalapuya, where her Tri-hull motorboat dipped and bobbed by the dock. A half-mile across the lurching waves, the lights of Garnerville shimmered through a tattered mist on the opposite shore.

Following the hound's tug on the leash, Ann picked up her pace, breathing deeply, her mind sharpening, muscles loosening. Steam rose off the asphalt. Scattered puddles reflected moonlight like pieces of glass. The thick forest of Douglas fir, red cedar, and big leaf maple engulfed both sides of the highway, surrendering to the occasional farm or ranch. Treetops swayed, branches dipped and waved, whispered and creaked. The night was alive with the sounds of frogs croaking and water dripping. The smell of apples perfumed the air as she trekked past her nearest neighbor's orchards. Miko's two-story clapboard farmhouse floated on a shallow sea of mist, windows black, yellow porch light fingering the darkness.

Ann didn't mingle with her neighbors, few as they were, and she took special pains to avoid Miko, whose wife had been the victim of the brutal murder in the woods adjacent to his property. The killer was never found, but an air of suspicion hovered over Miko ever since. Ann detested gossip and ignored it. She had her own reasons for avoiding Miko—and all other men, for that matter.

When they reached the narrow dirt road where they habitually turned to hike into the woods, Bailey froze, nose twitching, locked on a scent. He tugged hard at the leash, wanting her to follow.

"No," she said firmly, peering into the black mouth of the forest—a light-spangled paradise by day—black, damp, and ominous by night. "Let's go home."

Bailey trembled in his stance, growled with unusual intensity, and tugged harder. The hound had latched onto a rivulet of odor he wanted desperately to explore.

Ann jerked the leash. "Bailey, home!"

Normally obedient, Bailey ignored her. Using his seventy pounds of muscle as leverage, he yanked two, three times until the leash ripped from her fingers. Off he bounded, swallowed instantly by the darkness crouching beyond her feeble cone of light.

"Bailey! Come!"

No sound, just the incessant drip of water. Ann's beam probed the woods, jerking to the left, then the right. "Bailey!" She heard a steady, muffled, distant bark.

He's found what he's looking for. Bailey's barking abruptly ceased. Good. He's on his way back. She waited. No movement. No appearance of Bailey's big sable head emerging through the pitch.

Ann trembled as fear took possession of her senses. She bolted recklessly into the woods, her light beam bouncing along a trail that looked utterly foreign in the dark. Her feet crushed wet leaves and sloshed through puddles. Her left arm protected her face from the errant branch crossing her path. A second too late she saw the gnarled tree-root which seemed to jump out and snag her foot. She fell headlong, left hand breaking the fall, flashlight skidding beneath a carpet of leaves and pine needles. Blackness enveloped her. Shakily, she pulled herself to her feet, left wrist throbbing, trying to delineate shapes in the darkness, the moist scent of decay suffocating.

The forest was deathly still, seeming to hold its breath.

Soft rustling.

Silence.

Rustling again.

Something moved quietly and steadily through the underbrush.

Adrenaline shot up her arms like electric shocks. Ann swept her hands beneath mounds of wet leaves, grasping roots and cones until her fingers closed around the shaft of her flashlight. She thumbed the switch and cut a slow swath from left to right, her light splintering between trees. Her beam froze on a hooded figure moving backward through the brush dragging a woman, her bare feet bumping through the tangled debris.

The man kept his face completely motionless, eyes fixed on hers in a chilling stare. The world became soaked in a hideous and wondrous slowness. He lowered the woman to the ground and hung his long arms at his side. He was quiet; so was Ann. He radiated stillness. The stillness of a tree. It was hypnotic.

Ann felt paralyzed. Tongue dry. Thoughts sluggish. Then threads of white-hot terror ripped through her chest and propelled her like a fired missile into motion. Switching off the beam, she turned and sprinted like a frightened doe back along the trail.

His footfalls crushed the earth behind her, breaking through brush, snapping branches, his breathing thunderous. Any moment, he would yank her by the hair and pull her down.

Ann's world narrowed to a pinpoint. Everything except survival ceased to exist. She darted off the trail, skidded down a steep ravine, hobbled and splashed across Deer Creek, heard the man bulldoze through thickets, plummet down the slope, stumble, fall, curse, regain his balance, resume crashing after her like a bear through a woodpile, heaving, staggering, steps slowing down as he splashed through the creek.

Ann ran light-footed and sure, shoes springing off the deep mulch of the forest floor. She understood the features of the marsh that lay ahead. The smell of peat moss and a current of frigid air guided her steps. Her footsteps sank deeper into wet earth and soon she was wading into the black shallows through dense clumps of reeds. When she reached a monstrous fir that lay like a great beast across the wetland, Ann crawled beneath the carcass of rotting wood. She backed into the hollow where Bailey once hid and refused to come out. Jagged wood scratched her skin and cold water swelled through her clothes and hair, shocking her flesh.

Imprisoned, she listened, trembling. No sound. Then the heavy weight of a man splashed into the marsh and sloshed along the full length of the fallen tree, circled back, and stopped.

Ann's body went rigid. Threads of nausea reached up around her throat and she tasted bile on her tongue.

With a short guttural sound, the man hoisted himself onto the trunk of the tree and it compressed a few inches into the bog. The ceiling of Ann's hiding place pressed down upon her. Water crept higher, and with effort she kept her nose in the desperately thin space above the water line. The weight of her prison shifted as the man marched up and down the length of the tree. Agitated. Did he know she lay within? Was he taunting her? Or was he using the tree as a lookout to scan the surrounding wetland and woods?

A ghastly creeping terror rose from a place beyond thought. Her heart knocked so furiously against the cage of her chest she felt certain the man would hear. She heard him jump off into the shallows with a big splashy crescendo and the tree bounced up higher above the water line. For a breathtaking moment she didn't hear him move, and then he waded away and the tree settled firmly into the oozing earth. Silence sealed itself back over the forest.

Buy The Killing Woods at:
https://amzn.to/32px75b